Song of Quebec

Dan Close

The Tamarac Press
Vermont

Lines from the anthem 'Gens du pays', by Gilles Vigneault, courtesy of Gilles Vigneault, © Les Editions Le Vent qui Vire, Montreal, Quebec, Canada, represented by David Murphy et cie.

Lines from 'L'Hymne au Printemps', words and music by Felix Leclerc, courtesy of ©Editions Raoul Breton, Paris, France.

Lines from 'File la Laine', words and music by Robert Marcy, © 1957 Editions Musicales du Carrousel (Sacem), used by permission of Alfred Music.

Front cover photo: Cleremont Poliquin, Chateau Frontenac – Ville de Quebec © by permission of Pixoto.com

Cover design: Jonathan Draudt Digitial Arts, Warren, VT

ISBN-13 – 978-0-9907792-2-3

Published by The Tamarac Press, South Burlington, VT

DEDICATED
to the people of the Province of Quebec,
the Quebecois, who found themselves at
sea, and steered themselves to
solid ground.

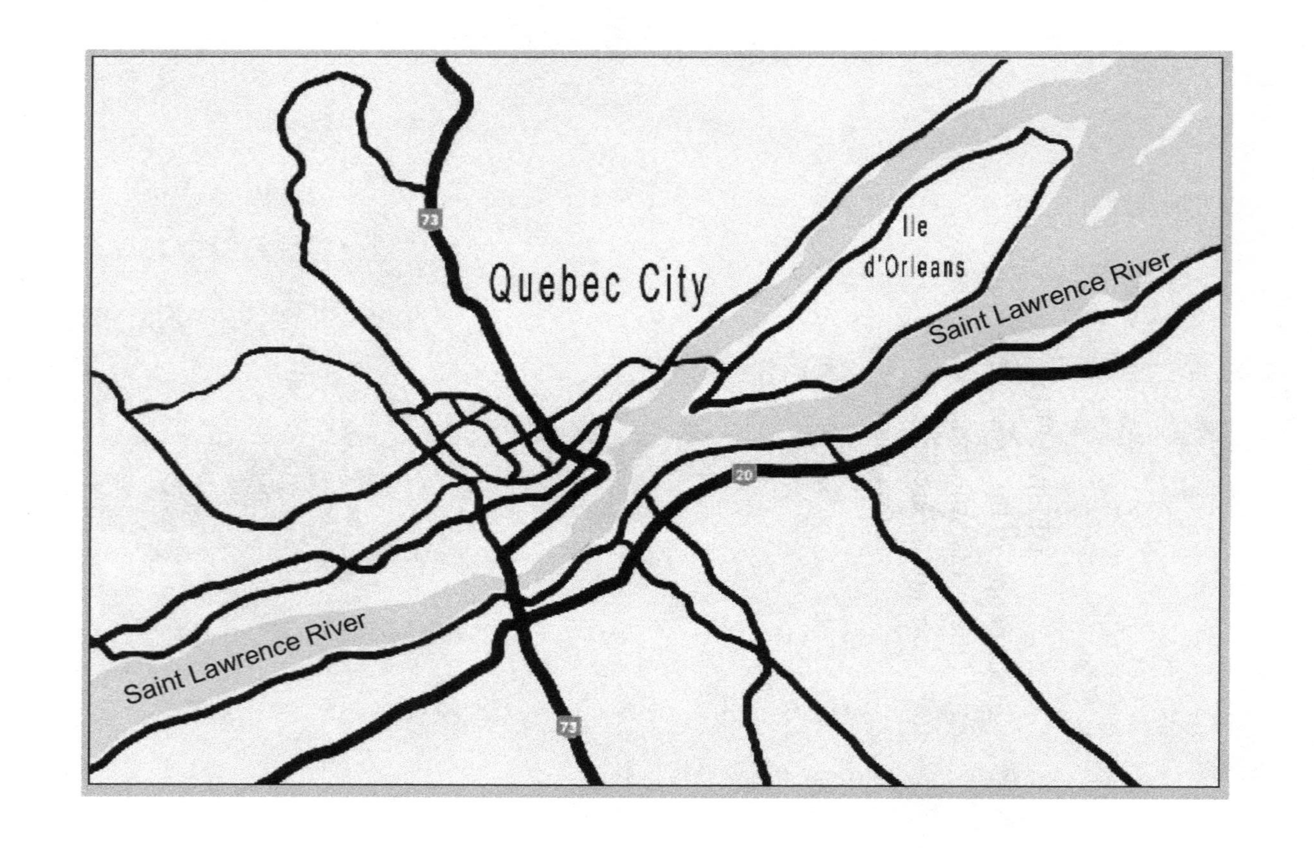
73
Quebec City
Ile
d'Orleans
Saint Lawrence River
20
Saint Lawrence River
73

Le temps de s'aimer, le jour de le dire
Fond comme la neige aux doigts du printemps
Fêtons de nous joies, fêtons de nos rires
Ces yeux ou nos regards se mirent
C'est demain que j'avais vingt ans…

The time to love one another, the day to say it,
Melts like the snow in the fingers of spring.
Let us celebrate our joys, let us feast on our laughter –
Let us live in those spaces where our mirrored gazes meet;
It's tomorrow that I was twenty years old…

Gens du Pays (People of the Country)
Gilles Vigneault

Chapter 1
The Diplomat

It was a brilliant morning. The cold front had come in from the northwest sometime during the night and snapped the air, turning it brisk with the scent of the northlands in it. Blades of grass in the parks of Upper Town, still wet with last night's misty rain, glistened in the sun. The high copper rooftops of Quebec City's old buildings shone with new, dark green streaks. Mica chips in the grey granite stones of this city built upon the rock glittered as they caught the new day's light. Flowing placidly far below, the St. Lawrence River was etched sharply in a bright blue more usual to autumn than early summer.

At the American consulate on Avenue St. Genevieve on the western side of the park called Le Jardin du Gouverneurs, the heavy wooden front door opened and a young man stepped out. His eye caught the figure he was looking for: an older man, halfway across the park, striding purposefully toward the bulk of the Chateau Frontenac Hotel on the opposite side of the square. The young man pulled the door shut behind him and checked his watch, then set off hurriedly in pursuit across the park.

On Rue Laporte, skirting the north side of the park, a car moved slowly along and stopped at one of the small tourist homes that lined the street. A woman came down the steps of the pension carrying a suitcase and went to the car. Muffled sounds of scraping baggage and quiet conversation floated across the air.

In the park itself were just a few people, dressed in their Sunday outfits, going about their business. The bells of the city's churches chimed distantly, softly, calling the few early-rising faithful to seven o'clock Mass.

The young man, his heels clicking against the damp asphalt path, shadowed his quarry at a distance of about a hundred yards. He followed the figure along a road that cut directly through the Chateau Frontenac and emerged on the Place d'Armes. Then, going downhill, he quickened his pace across the plaza toward the narrow Rue du Trésor. At the bottom of the street, he turned left onto Rue Buade and again quickly right, passing the entrance to Notre Dame Basilica.

He noted the ushers at the main door of the cathedral, dressed like 18th century nobles in white powdered wigs, long woolen coats, breeches, white stockings, and black-buckled shoes. They carried six-foot-high ceremonial walking sticks and gazed out over the street to the trees beyond, ignoring him. The young man smiled, amused by the idea that two such different worlds—his own and theirs—could exist in the same place and time. But his smile was quick, as if there were no time for the thought that caused it, and he never slowed his pace.

Just beyond the cathedral, the Cote de la Fabrique sheared off on a downhill diagonal to the left. The young man gave a cursory glance down its length, then stopped and looked directly before him down the long, narrow Rue St. Famille. The old road separated the French Quarter from the fortress-like walls of the ancient Jesuit seminary.

Even in the bright light of morning, those old walls cast strangely dark, almost sinister shadows onto the street. And far down the deserted roadway, too far, the older man was moving rapidly away.

Stepping up his pace, the young man moved after him. Too late. The distant figure turned to the left and disappeared down a far-off street.

"Damn!"

The young man began to run. When he had gotten half-way down the hill, there were two muffled explosions, and he stumbled and fell, clawing at the slippery cobblestones of the road. A figure leapt out of a doorway and stood over him. The figure bent quickly, held a small-calibre pistol equipped with a silencer to the head of the fallen man and fired, then turned and ran down an alley, shoving the pistol into his jacket and pulling a cap down over his eyes.

The body lay in Rue St. Famille, covered with bright blood that oozed and dripped from deep wounds. The blood splashed onto the smooth cobblestones, where it glared in the sunlight. The damp cold of the early morning crept into the body and stiffened it. A little girl, tripping around the corner, found it and stood shrieking. Her cries alerted older citizens who came hurrying to her assistance and stopped short at the sight.

Within the hour, a duty officer at the State Department in Washington had received word over the telex than one of the newer members of the department, a bright young fellow assigned to the innocuous Cultural Affairs desk of the Quebec Consulate office, had been assassinated. Assailant unknown. Motive unknown. Most of official Washington was more puzzled than upset, if it cared at all. But in certain quarters, there was care, and apprehension.

MONDAY, JUNE 21ST

Hange the Federalists to the lamp post!
Yes, we shall win, we shall win, we shall win!
For too long the obscene English
Have smothered us with their Queen and their taxes!

French-Canadian Separatist song

Chapter 2
La Chaudière

The cobalt-blue Ford Mustang slammed on into the vastness of Quebec Province.

The day before, Jack Kearney had crossed into Canada at a small customs station somewhere in the middle of Vermont's northern border. He kept away from well-travelled highways and spent the night in a small B & B in a town he never knew the name of. Now he confined his travels to the back lanes that skirted the edges of endless farm fields.

This afternoon, he had struck Canada's Route 173 at the little town of La Vallee, and now, beside the rushing Chaudière River, his '68 Mustang shot north toward Quebec City. That town lay some thirty miles away under black storm clouds that had come up during the night and stretched themselves over the wide northern sky, dealing mist and darkness on the provincial countryside and bringing strong gusty winds and torrential rain the closer he came to the city.

As he drove along through the gloom, Kearney was assaulted by sound. Surface water slapped against the car's hissing tires. Rain pounded the roof and rolled down the windshield, and the wipers on high speed beat and grunted the water away. Wind slashed against the roadside trees, bending back their branches and tearing off leaves that went hurtling through the air and pelted the car, sticking to the windshield like the wings of gigantic splattered moths. And the rain, threatening to become hail at the slightest drop in air temperature, jack-hammered the roof.

Kearney chanced a glimpse of the swollen river on his left through the fogged-up window. The stream and the woods appeared through a patch of watery glass he had just cleared. The Chaudière ripped, crashed, rampaged its way north through the storm, carrying small spruce trees and smashing spray high into the air off granite rocks, where it met the downpour of rain in a frenzy of crazed nature.

Once, two hundred years ago, that river had taken Benedict Arnold's rabble of backwoods fighters along in little chips of bateaux and canoes toward their siege of Quebec. Every mile of the river rang to their cries. Boats overturned. More were flung high in the foam and air, smashed to pieces on the rocks. Scores of men drowned. But the survivors did not stop until they were at the walls of Quebec City. Neither would Kearney.

He was beginning to feel cramped, and squirmed around to relieve his stiffness. He stretched out his right arm, moving it in circles, then patted the dashboard.

"Okay, tiger," he said aloud, talking to the machine. "Almost there. Just keep purring along. I love you, man, even if your seats could be better." His Mustang was a great vehicle, and he loved its style and power. The sleek lines of its body, the insane rumble of its dual exhausts on acceleration, the five-on-the-floor gearshift, the Lucas running lights that pierced through the night, the magnum wheels, the competition suspension, the 428 Cobra V-8. Oh, man, the sheer muscle of the vehicle! Wasn't anything this baby couldn't do. And he knew every inch of that car: had been over it; under it; crawled all over it.

"But what the hell," he said, feeling pinched. "What can you expect after seven hours of driving?" Kearney was young, and alive, and twenty-five, in peak condition, just like his car, and it was his most important possession, and so he talked to it.

"Hell," he said. "Actually you are almost my *only* possession. What else do I have? A few changes of clothes, a few books stashed away, a tape recorder that I…well, got on loan from the office, I guess you could say. Liberated it. The DC apartment, but the lease is almost up on that baby. Wonder what I should do about that?

"So where do we go from here?" he asked the machine. "And what the hell am I doing here in the first place? Taking an unauthorized leave, that's what. That's what I call it, anyway. Sure, boss, I figured you'd just give me a vacation if I took it first and asked later."

He snickered. "Nice Mustang," he muttered. "Sorry you had to come all the way up here, middle of this friggin' deluge, just because I wanted to. Just because I had to…." His voice trailed off into a pre-cigarette sigh.

He leaned forward and punched a cigarette from the pack where it lay on the console and lit it. The cigarette dangling from his lip, he flipped the radio dial. Out of the garble of unfamiliar stations, he chose one that he thought might be broadcasting from Quebec City. The voice of a woman singing in a throaty, spirited French had more of a cosmopolitan air than a countryside lilt to it.

The recording was replaced by the voice of a DJ, which sprinted eerily up and down the scale from deep bass to an almost falsetto soprano. Kearney found himself grinning without understanding any of it except the word "Gillette". Then there came another recording, this time of a band composed mainly of drums and trumpets and a large, heroic male chorus singing something that somehow was not quite military but not civilian, either. It was a call to arms, to action of some kind, and it was definitely French. It was a haunting sound, compelling. It sounded to him like a national anthem.

By now the Chaudière was out of sight, banking away to the northwest, and the roadsides were lined with inexpensive homes and garish shopping centers—the usual ring of plastic found around any North American city. Kearney was disappointed. No fur trappers, no Indians, no unspoiled primeval woods stretching away forever. No difference from the States at all, except that the signs were all in French.

The road forked and the right-hand prong aimed north, straight as an arrow until, fourteen miles beyond, it entered the city limits of Levis, a town on the southern banks of the St. Lawrence River opposite Quebec City. Levis didn't believe in signs. It took Route 173, tied it in knots, coiled it into a series of rights and lefts, turned it on a series of curves, and sent it shooting down over a precipice toward the ferry station.

Kearney drove down a crumbling road that snaked its way along and finally arrived on the level flat of the river road. He drove along past junked buildings and struggling businesses to the ferry slip. A ferry was already loading. Kearney maneuvered the wet Mustang over the boarding plate, followed the attendant's wild signaling, and came to a stop behind a low-slung yellow Pontiac. Even that bright color was dulled in the cavernous grey hold of the ship.

Kearney turned off the ignition. He yawned, stretched, rubbed his face with his palms, picked up a map of Quebec, reached over and snapped down the lock on the right-hand door, grabbed the keys, and got out of the car. "Stay here. Don't move," he said to the car, and locked it tight. The vibrations of the ferry's engines hummed through him. There was a smell of diesel fuel, and the ferry swayed gently against the river's current.

Kearney took the stairs to an upper deck, the stiffness of a long drive going quickly out of him. He found a combination snack bar and souvenir stand and stopped for a Coke. Waiting for his change, he spied a small flag for sale. He had seen this new flag flying from many passing cars this morning. The design was new to him. A white cross was superimposed on a field of blue, and each of the four blue squares formed by the cross held the white symbol of France—the fleur-de-lys. It was the flag of the Province of Quebec, and it was being flown everywhere in place of the red-and-white maple leaf of Canada.

Gesturing and pointing, Kearney tried to buy a flag. Finally, the counterman understood. "Ah! Drapeau!" he said. "Un dollar. Merci, Monsieur."

Kearney downed his Coke and looked bemusedly at the little rectangle of blue-and-white nylon. Shoving it into the back pocket of his blue jeans, he unfolded his map and walked toward the front of the boat. The rain was down to a drizzle, and the mist over the river began to lift. He walked onto the outer deck and joined a scattered band of travelers standing along the rail. Across the river, looming out of the rain, were the grey battlements of the fortress city, Quebec, the City on the Rock.

The ferry's engines churned the water and the weed-covered pilings of the slip swayed back and forth as the boat chugged into the channel. Kearney stood with his map spread open, trying to tie it in with what he could see across the river.

Quebec City was divided into two sections: the Lower Town squeezed in between the cliffs and the river; and the Upper Town, perched on top of those cliffs and rapidly growing inland. From the river, the most prominent features were the great ramparts and towers of the Chateau Frontenac, the classic old Canadian Pacific hotel high on the cliffs directly in front of the crossing ferry. The Chateau was a massive pile of brick soaring to steep turrets faced in green copper sheathing, and looking like nothing so much as a fairytale castle.

To the west stretched the walls and battlements of the Citadel, built in the 1830s to discourage American invaders. To the east was the Port of Quebec, lined with enormous banks of grain elevators along the industrialized reaches of the Louise Basin. Behind the Chateau were the towers of the Parliament Building and the Hall of Justice.

Beyond that, hidden in the mist except for their hulking outlines, were three massive rectangular blocks that loomed over everything. These were the new Commodore and Caravelle Hotels and the tall, sterile shaft of a new government office building. To Kearney, these last three looked for all the world like powerful, malevolent strangers peering over the fence of an old estate. The sight of them had Kearney muttering to himself. Apparently, he figured, the only place the city would seem like its old self would be from a high window in one of those ransacking giants, where an observer could pretend that the building he was in did not exist. Kearney could not imagine living in a city dominated by such monstrosities. He could see why the Quebecois might be angered by these transgressors.

In fact, they were more than angered. They were in a simmering state of quiet revolt, which was rapidly coming to a boil. Many of them felt that the only recourse they had was to violence.

An occasional bomb had exploded during the building of the modern high-rise structures. The government office tower had set the record, an average of one bomb exploding for every two stories the building rose. The bombing was done by fringe groups, so it was said, and was applauded by nearly every person with no power in the political scheme, which included almost every French Canadian. Those who did not applaud smiled silently and chuckled to themselves behind closed doors. And the visible symbols of an ongoing confrontation were etched like scar tissue across the Quebec sky.

Kearney turned his attention to the smaller, friendlier buildings of the Lower Town. They were of a dark stone that had been used like brick, from the older architecture of a past century. He noticed a small church and checked his map—Notre Dame des Victoires, where the settlers of New France had gathered to celebrate their occasional good fortune in war along the far-flung borders of their empire.

When Kearney looked up again, the boat was closing with the land, nearing the slip, and he was treated to a powerful view of the cliffs. They went straight up, nearly perpendicular, for over two hundred feet. Topping the cliffs, muzzles of great black cannon peered over the river. Higher than everything else from this vantage point, the Chateau soared into the low clouds. The clouds were moving off to the southeast, and high above the ground mist, the edge of the storm was moving off. A great, cool Canadian high, straight out of the Arctic tundra, swept down from the northwest and barreled the clouds along before it. It was almost like a giant cleaver had cut the overcast with one swift stroke and bisected the sky, blue to the northwest, white to the southeast.

Kearney caught a whiff of the new air—fresh and at least ten degrees cooler. The stones of the town glittered in the sunlight, and it was as if the mist and rain had been swept away by a whole new day. Suddenly, he felt brighter, more alert, ready for whatever happened.

The ferry came close to the landing now. Toy-size cars and trucks grew larger by the second, and even tinier scuttling figures took on personalities, became individuals. Kearney hesitated, glanced around once more, trying to choose a road to take once he was off the boat. Then he turned away from the city and went belowdecks to his car. He flipped his new flag onto the passenger seat and got ready to move out.

The ferry bumped into pilings and the hold exploded with the sound of engines turning over and revving. Great clouds of blue exhaust sailed through the air. Kearney blipped the Mustang over the gangplank and made a quick right with tires squealing. He found himself in the right lane of a broad avenue that skirted the cliffs and headed northeast. It was impossible to get into the left lane to turn. The road he had chosen to take him up the cliff whisked by. No chance. Some of the vehicles in the left lane took that road, though, cutting off the oncoming traffic and roaring across lanes of traffic. Giving up any pretense of driving courtesy, Kearney cut off a car with Maryland plates and swerved into the left lane.

He took the next available left, the Cote de la Canoterie, and as luck would have it, it was jammed with traffic. Some old country car had given out just before reaching the top. Drivers stood in the street or leaned out of their cars, yelling curses and advice.

Chuckling, Kearney lit a cigarette. He pulled on the emergency brake, put the car into park, and studied his map. He enjoyed this, the final break in his long journey. From where he sat, there were cliffs falling away to his left. To his right, jutting up over him, were the walls of the Hotel–Dieu de Quebec, the great hospital founded centuries before by the Sisters of Charity. On the horizon, the most impressive buildings seemed to be churches.

The feel of the place was so strange that, sitting there in the middle of a 20th-Century traffic jam, Kearney suddenly felt he was rising, slowly and bumper-to-bumper, into a whole other world set in some different century, in some other place, where itinerant priests in wide brimmed black hats and sisters in great flapping Flying Nun-style headdresses went easily about their charitable works; where the pace of the day was set by the Angelus bell; where there was a solid rock of certainty, green fields to be tended, and sweet raspberry-scented summer air to breathe.

The feeling didn't last long. Traffic moved forward again, up into Rue des Remparts. Reaching there, Kearney made an immediate right onto a small street that led into the heart of the old French Quarter of the city. He was at once swallowed up by narrow streets faced with ancient buildings. Directions meant nothing now. He simply pointed the Mustang's nose uphill, searching out roads to climb, looking for a way out of the grey, depressing stonepiles that surrounded him. He aimed for the top, and after some fifteen long minutes, he rounded a last corner and came unexpectedly upon the Place d'Armes. It was a wide expanse of trees and flowers dominated by a baroque statue of Samuel de Champlain conquering North America for France, scattering Iroquois, Dutch, English, and Sioux in the process.

Here, the center of the city was calm, serene. Lined up around the gardens of the park were horse-drawn carriages decorated with flowers. Even the horses wore flowers. Their drivers slouched about looking bored and important, after the manner of waiting drivers the world over.

Traffic was light here, and Kearney let out his breath and relaxed. He circled the plaza once, getting his bearings, and then drove onto the road that served the Chateau Frontenac as a driveway. It cut through the press of immense brick buildings and emerged onto the rolling green hill of the Jardin du Gouverneurs, a quiet little square fronted by three- and four-story townhouses.

After the humdrum of driving and the uncertainty of direction, this agreeable little park in the very heart of the city was an unexpected pleasure. All the townhouses on the northern side of the square had been converted into guesthouses, and Kearney resolved to stay in one of them. He parked in front of a house called the Chateau Brittany and ambled slowly up the stairs.

Chapter 3

The Palace of Justice

At the same time that Kearney was climbing the steps to the Chateau Brittany a few blocks away, Claude Le Claire stared at a poster that hung on the wall on the far side of his desk and thought of fish. Le Claire was the Eastern Regional Director of the Internal Security Division of the Ministry of Justice of Quebec Province. One of his major duties was to act as liaison between the area's municipal police forces and the Quebec Ministry of Justice information bank, the QMJIB. But right now, when he had the time to think of it, he wondered if he shouldn't establish an office of liaison between himself and the Justice Ministry itself.

The Ministry had moved most of its personnel out to the new offices on Boulevard Laurier, leaving him stranded down here in the old court house with a stack of promises about how soon he would join them. Whenever he thought too much about the whole situation, his mind automatically snapped shut on that particular compartment and moved to the one that opened on salmon in the northwest branch of the Miramichi River.

Le Claire was a veteran of the Justice Department. His first assignment had been to help protect Winston Churchill and Franklin Roosevelt at their Quebec Conference in 1943. He had been part of the guard assigned to the security checkpoints in the Citadel where the great men had their headquarters. He had been very young then, fresh out of police training school, and eager to serve. The army had rejected him because of a damaged eardrum, but the police took him gladly. They had a use for him. He was French and well-educated, the son of a well-known and respected businessman. While during the war, the traditional animosity and prejudice exchanged by English and French Canadians had mostly dissolved in the great effort to free France and destroy the Fascists, still a wild fringe organization of French Canadian nationalists remained, bent on destroying English power in Quebec.

As soon as the Quebec Conference ended, Le Claire was sent underground, assigned the task of infiltrating this group. That he did, with great success. By the beginning of 1945, the group was almost defunct, ripped by dissention and mistrust. Plan after plan had been sabotaged and aborted, and the leaders were at each other's throats. Ninety-five percent of the group's energy was spent in internecine squabbling.

Curiously, coming out from the squalor of the whole affair, the primary fact impressed upon Le Claire was the importance of trust in any organization. He knew how fragile trust was, how handily it could be put aside in the name of ideology, how easily it could be broken by low opportunism. He also learned to respect the goodness he found in certain members of the fringe group. For the most part, he considered the activists criminals, mad idiots with warped views of reality, or opportunists of the most degraded type. But some of the strongest truly believed they were right. Le Claire saw early on that if these people had been able to exercise complete authority, they would have been able to exclude madmen and opportunists and infiltrators such as himself, and run the organization efficiently, accomplishing a great deal of progress, or destruction, depending on your point of view.

The tragic flaw of the majority of these true believers was that their essentially democratic personalities operated in a foreign milieu, outside the law and underground, where democracy always found murky going. Le Claire prized these democrats who were kin to his own mind but were trying to operate on the wrong side of the fence. Listening to them, he could understand their desperation, although he did not share it. They were intelligent, and for a variety of reasons, had decided that Quebec should be a free and autonomous state, divorced from the patronage of English Canada and England. The individual reasoning that had brought each of them to this conclusion showed different highlights and incidents, but always followed the same pattern of mistrust of authority—often with excellent reasons—and an extension of personal rage that expanded to include solidarity with whatever members of society the underground philosophers regarded as their downtrodden sisters and brothers. They fascinated Le Claire.

So Le Claire became an expert in extralegal organization and psychology. After the war, he studied at Laval University and was granted a master's degree in psychology with emphasis on the criminal mind. But this did not satisfy him. He was not so much interested in criminal minds as in those that perceived not themselves, but others posing as legal leadership, to be criminal; minds that perceived themselves as liberators who had the right to take any steps necessary to achieve their goals. So he continued to study, taking courses leading to a doctorate; undertaking research that helped to create his own field. It was the era of the Cold War, and soon Le Claire found himself being consulted by governments and national police organizations that grappled with the formation of communist organizations and fronts all over the world. For a long time, he was assigned to NATO as a theorist, using his early experience as a model for infiltration and counter-subversion.

An outstanding facet of Le Claire's mind was the ability to logically build up infinitesimal bits of knowledge into useful patterns. So it was natural that he knew his home territory extremely well. He understood the strengths and weaknesses of an industrial society. He knew the chinks in the armor of industrial plants where sabotage could be effective. He knew the rusty spots in labor organizations where rot could easily set in. He knew the devilishness of opportunists' minds and how easily unprincipled individuals could use the state to accumulate wealth and power through corruption. And there had been a great deal of that, too, in Quebec Province. Some of it had been uncovered. Much of his knowledge was ripening in his files, waiting for the appropriate time for maximum usefulness.

But too much of his knowledge would never be used. There were simply too may corrupt people in too many high places, forming networks of back-slapping friendships under social umbrellas unassailable even by the law. He could see a problem from many sides, and sometimes, lately, he wondered if those raging underground subversives were not more right than wrong. At times like these, he would break off his logical meanderings to still the whispering ghosts of his doubts and would concentrate on immediate problems.

Right now, tapping the stem of his pipe against his teeth, he leaned back in his swivel chair and reviewed these problems. There were the separatists, always; and always, now, growing in strength. They were both legal and illegal, and while he was concerned with the illegal groups and their destructive capabilities, he was also troubled by the tendency, stronger of late, for legal and illegal activities and organizations to overlap in their methods. That was unsettling. Traditions were being broken, new boundaries of political activity being set, demands for action from both conservative and liberal political factions pouring in on him. This was his major ongoing concern. This week he would lead a raid against the student activists who had been pushing their luck, breaking windows in English-owned buildings, painting slogans—"Vive Quebec Libre!" was their favorite—on walls all over town. Even, for God's sake, stealing English furniture from the Chateau Frontenac and English cannon balls from the museum, leaving behind, of course, French cannon balls.

Le Claire considered these pranks innocuous manifestations of frustrated youth. He had enough operatives among the students to know their thoughts. He sympathized with them to an extent, and he himself knew the frustrations of intelligent young people confronted with social and economic prejudice. Still, their tricks were visible and destructive, and society demanded that they be reprimanded. He would give them another slap on the wrist, both to indicate to them that there were still boundaries to be observed and to placate the nervous conservatives who held power still too tightly in their clenched fists.

The raid, the arrests, would mean nothing but lost man-hours for his department. The kids would wear their lumps and bruises with pride. They would flaunt their arrests like battle ribbons. Still, it must be done, if for no other reason than to show something tangible to the idiots in Ottawa.

There were other less obvious and more troublesome problems that demanded his attention, he knew. A conference of Canadian economists, for instance, stupidly scheduled to convene in Quebec City the same week as the celebration of St. Jean-Baptiste Day, Quebec's provincial—or what some would contend was actually Quebec's national—holiday. The day was always an excuse for disruption. Le Claire was sure that, if given the chance, some fringe group would try to disrupt the conference. There would have to be a measure of security for the economists. Watchfulness, if nothing else.

There was also the murder of two weeks ago. That was particularly disturbing, because the victim had been an American diplomat, an assistant cultural attaché at the American consulate. The young man, fresh from the U.S. State Department's training school, had been given a harmless, absurd first assignment. He hadn't even been in town long enough to make any serious personal enemies. Still, he was shot down in cold blood early on a bright Sunday morning. No leads, and both Canadian and American governments clamoring for an explanation and a perpetrator. Likely political overtones, considering the man's position. But still, in spite of all efforts, no leads of any kind.

Then there were the usual number of nebulous threats and possibilities that led Le Claire's logical police mind to crazed wanderings. A rumor that a radical offshoot band of the FLQ had made contact with the international terrorist underground fascinated him. If true, whom had they contacted? The Cubans? The Palestinians? Libyans? The upstart Baader-Meinhof gang? The IRA, perhaps? And what would their plan be? What outrages could they be constructing?

Le Claire smirked. He would certainly have to get on that, he thought. The idea of international terrorism coming home to Quebec intrigued him. Quebec already had enough homegrown bombings, bank holdups, kidnappings, and the like. No need for more. But the past few years had shown patterns—no, more like faint indications—of strengthening ties between local terrorists and foreign organizations. Nothing as simple as contacts with American Black Panthers and the SDS, the way it used to be. Now, there was a definite international terrorist system at work, with bands of madmen in communication with each other all over the globe.

Ah, the escalation, the escalation, Le Claire thought. Nip it in the bud, warn them against playing with Canada, eh? Damage them severely. Ah, well. A possibility. He would not let himself be excited by it yet. There was enough excitement in his life already without having to conjure up more of it.

His eyes strayed to the wall poster again. It was an artist's idealization of the Miramichi River in New Brunswick, the premier Atlantic Salmon river of the world. In the foreground was a very excited fisherman, his fly rod bent into a bamboo-straining C. Beyond him, in midstream, a great salmon leapt six feet into the air. Le Claire sighed. He would try to get there again this year, but primarily for the solitude and peace. He would not be able to get away until late in the season, when you needed the luck of the gods to get as much as a nibble out of the damned green-backed monsters.

Le Claire stood up and shoved miscellaneous legal papers into his battered old briefcase. He took his grey trench coat, an affectation that amused him, from the clothes tree in the corner and put it on over his blue suit. He slapped his old fedora onto his head and looked into the small mirror on the wall. He smiled at himself. His face was still ruddy, with no trace of the sallowness he feared with the coming of age. His hair was white now, but his stocky body was still in good trim.

Glancing around the room, he noticed that the white cream walls were beginning to look green. They weren't, really. It was just the slight tinted reflection from the salmon poster, but whenever Le Claire realized that he could see the green tint to the office, he told himself he had been there too long. He felt good tonight: the greening of the walls coincided with his departure, so he considered he was leaving just on time.

He walked through the outer office. Sandy, his secretary, had already gone. He had hopes she would still be there. They worked well together. There was a note for him on her desk, propped against the stem of a spot lamp.

"Don't forget! Tonight's your chess night!" it read.

Le Claire had not forgotten and he was glad she had not, either. These little touches she gave him of a more normal life made him happy. He had few enough of things like that.

He closed the door behind him and walked down the marble corridors of the Palais de Justice, out into the cool northern evening.

Chapter 4

Rue du Tresor

At about the same time that Monday evening, having left his new-found room at the Chateau Brittany, Jack Kearney walked quickly downhill, past the Chateau Frontenac and across the Place d'Armes, his ears filled with the quiet sounds of late evening—clicking heels, quiet laugher, the snort of a carriage horse in the shadows. On the far side of the plaza, he crossed Rue St. Anne and walked nonchalantly along, peering at menus in restaurant windows. He chose a quiet-looking place that promised dark, rough-hewn beams, candles at small tables, and an air of leisure. A smiling waitress in 17th Century peasant dress brought him a succulent filet mignon and a half-bottle of the 'house red,' an undistinguished-enough red, but Kearney was more familiar with undistinguished beer, so that made no difference to him.

Anyone looking at Jack Kearney would have observed a well-built man in his mid-twenties with the potential about him to be powerful if he wished, seeming to be lost in his own thoughts and plans. And Kearney did have plans, tentative as they were.

At length full and satisfied, he stood up and walked out of the restaurant. He was just a bit high on the memory of the wine followed by brandy and a good cigar. He walked along the edge of the wide plaza, randomly puffing on the remnants of his cigar, and meandered along with the crowd toward the Dufferin Terrace. But before reaching it, his attention was drawn to a narrow, well-lit street, hardly a street, more an alley, called Rue du Trésor. It was filled with people, both tourists and Quebecois. The walls of the buildings on either side were festooned with paintings and drawings. Beneath the displays, artists spoke with tight knots of people who, for one reason or another—admiration, curiosity, patronage— were interested in one or another of the offerings.

And there was music in that street. It was faint, but it was there. Kearney smiled slightly and walked slowly and silently toward the sound of guitars. He pushed his way through a good-sized group of tourists and looked down at a trio of singers—two men and a young, dark-haired woman. One of the men and the woman played guitars, and the woman and the other man sang. They did not look at the crowd that had gathered, but at each other. They sang in French, a lilting song, and smiled as they sang.

When they finished the song, the man without the guitar turned toward the applause and, producing a tin cup, began to harangue the crowd. He spoke French and the effect of his begging was ludicrous, because although his clothing was not new, he wore it well—a smart cap, a ¾-cut grey casual coat, a scarf turned just casually correct around his neck.

"Pour les troubadours!" he cried, and then he laughed through his prominent Gallic nose, which jutted out from his thin face like a cliff from a mountain. His two companions feigned embarrassment, pulled at him and tried to get him to sit down. But it was too late. The hawk-nosed minstrel was creating something and enjoying his creation.

"Voila!" he cried, as a quarter tinkled into his cup. "Half a glass of beer! Who will buy the other half? Thank you! Merci!" as another quarter ringed the cup and dropped. "And beer for my friend, eh? Ha, ha, ha! Voila!"

The girl's dark eyes flashed with amusement. "Idiot!" she laughed. "Rene, sit down!"

But now Rene was standing his full height, standing tall and straight and nothing could stop him. He held the tin cup in his left hand, while in his right his pipe described circles in the air as he declaimed in French. He launched into a full speech, carrying on like a politician running for office. He cajoled and pleaded, demanded and beseeched, ordered and decreed.

And the crowd loved it. There was no need for a translation here. The tourist crowd, mostly knowing no French at all, cheered and applauded, and Rene, bowing deeply from the waist and laughing with them, sank to the sidewalk. He grabbed the girl's guitar away from her and began to sing. The crowd hushed and listened as she joined him, and their duet was a wonderful song that spoke of love and longing and happiness.

« ...quand mon amie viendra par la rivière, » they sang,
« Au mois de mai, après le dur hiver
Je sortirai, bras nus, dans la lumière
Et lui dirai le salut de la terre
Vois, les fleurs ont recommence
Dans l'étable crient les nouveau-nés
Viens voir la vielle barrière rouillée
Endimanchée de toiles d'araignée
Les bourgeons sortent de la mort
Papillons ont des manteaux d'or
Près du ruisseau sont alignées les fées
Et les crapauds chantent la liberté
Et les crapauds chantent la liberté... »

Kearney didn't understand a word of it, except maybe the last: liberté. All he knew was that it was beautiful. The song sounded lonely and strong there in the night, and then it sank into the walls and was gone. Liberté...

At the end of it, while the troubadours laughed at each other, the crowd, quietly pleased and happy, began to break up and wander away.

Kearney strolled up the street a bit to where a young man sat sketching.

"Excuse me," he said, leaning over the artist. "Do you speak English?"

"Perhaps," said the sketcher, not looking up.

Kearney hunched down next to him, sitting on the sidewalk with his back against the stone wall. "I was wondering if you could tell me...well, I'm interested in folk songs ..."

There was an awkward pause, and then the young artist said, "I watched you watching the singers."

"Yes…well," said Kearney. He paused. "I try to collect folk songs wherever I go. I would like to record those singers. Do you think I could ask them to sing for me? Perhaps I could record them?"

"Are you from a recording company?"

"No. Just for myself."

"Why don't you ask them?"

"Some people don't like to be asked."

The artist stopped sketching. "They are not professionals. Why do you want their music? Why don't you buy a record?"

"Because I want to hear music that is being played right now. I can buy records anytime. I want people's music."

"So, you think if I know them, I could introduce you, eh?"

"Well," said Kearney, "if you would …"

"I can't. If you look up, you'll notice that they have gone."

Kearney looked up and grinned. "Well, that's that. Will they be back?"

"They'll probably be back tomorrow night. So will I. I do know them, and I will introduce you to them. What's your name?"

"Jack," Kearney said.

"Jack," the artist mused. "A harsh American name. I am Marc. A harsh French name. But both easy to understand. You like my work?"

Kearney glanced at the sketch. It showed a small alley in Quebec, with washing strung out to dry between the buildings. It was a pen and ink drawing, made of an incredible number of straight lines.

"It is excellent," Kearney said. "It has good perspective. I would never have the patience."

Marc grinned sardonically at him. "We French Canadians have a lot of patience," he said. "But you may have noticed it is growing thin."

They were suddenly both aware of a figure looming over them, and they looked up to see a tall, thin man in a business suit.

"Marc," said the figure harshly, and once again the rest was, to Kearney, the unintelligible babble of the French language. Marc answered, off-handedly. The lips of the tall man pressed together in distaste, and he went quickly down the street.

"Who was that?" asked Kearney.

"That? That was Genevieve's brother. Genevieve—the singer you were watching. He doesn't approve of her hanging around with us gutter rats." Marc bit the end of his pen. "He is a menace to her," he said thoughtfully.

"He acts like a cop," said Kearney.

"Who, him?" laughed Marc. "Furthest thing from his mind, that one. He wants to be rich. He wants to own Quebec. And what is he? A bank branch manager, for an English bank!" Marc gave a horselaugh.

Kearney chuckled. "It's a good start."

"They will eat him alive," said Marc, collecting his pen and paper. "They will chew him up and spit him out when they are finished with him." He stood up. "Well, good night, Monsieur Jack," he said. "Sleep well. Enjoy our fair, suppressed city, eh? See you here tomorrow, if you wish."

"I'll buy you a beer."

"Save your money for one of my sketches, Monsieur. Or for the girl. She is attractive, no?"

Kearney laughed. "Many of them are attractive," he said. "But that one—Genevieve—seems attracted to her partner, so I guess I'll look elsewhere."

"Genevieve and Rene!" said Marc in mock alarm. "Mon Dieu! What a scandal you project, Monsieur. No, no, no. Rene, you see, is with Angelique, the portrait artist, and Angelique and Genevieve are best friends, and Rene would never think of, even if he is a poet, as he is…no, no, no, he would never think of…well, you see, it is too complicated, but you see, Genevieve is as free as a little Canadian lark right now, and …" Marc shrugged. Kearney betrayed something just then, through his eyes or movements, and Marc continued. "Ah, Monsieur," he said. "You forget. I am an artist. I can read eyes. You are in France, Monsieur. Do as we French do. Enjoy!"

Laughing, Marc sauntered off into the night.

He left Kearney standing in the Rue du Trésor. The American strolled up the street, smiling to himself and thinking about Genevieve. Yes, he would be here tomorrow night. He hoped the girl named Genevieve would be, also. Without her brother. There was something about him that Kearney didn't like. Didn't like at all.

Chapter 5

A Game of Chess

At about the same time that Jack Kearney was smiling to himself in the middle of Rue Trésor, Claude Le Claire was seated in a deep leather chair in a secluded corner at the Officer's Lounge of the Royal 22nd Regiment, situated in a narrow street just outside the walls of the Citadel. He was speaking to his friend, Henry Sparrow, who nominally belonged to the intelligence arm of the Mounted Police, but whom Le Claire had long suspected of being a CID operative out of London.

The two men had just completed a distinguished dinner and were at odds over a game of chess, the board being placed on a low table between their easy chairs. They were also at odds, on a larger scale, over which direction Canada should take in both the near and long-range future. In fact, some of Le Claire's ideological adversaries would have been taken aback by his brusque statements to Sparrow concerning what he thought of some of the activities and methods of the Mounties. Le Claire sneered at the recent public statement of a high Mountie official in which the official declared he was protecting the "public's right not to know" by maintaining silence and refusing to answer questions put to him by a parliamentary fact-finding subcommittee concerning Mountie anti-subversive activities. Le Claire called the remark "both fascist and damned foolish," which caused Sparrow to turn red with anger. But there was nothing Sparrow could say in rebuttal. The remark had been fascist and stupid. Le Claire had hit it right on the head. Still, Sparrow felt that Le Claire should have had the courtesy to refrain from bringing it up, and he thought it especially ill-bred of the French-Canadian to sit there snickering while he, Sparrow, had to stew and take it.

And that piece of nonsense was just the tip of the iceberg. It was merely the symbolic coating over the bulky problem of Quebecois nationalism that had swarmed up into the light over the course of the past two decades. That problem, the eventual hypothetical resolution of it, and the response of the Canadian federal government to it, had divided the two friends as nothing else ever had. And the problem for Sparrow was that he had a sticky feeling that Le Claire was closer to the truth than any of Sparrow's colleagues or superiors, whether they were wise, foolish, or the usual mixture of the two extremes.

Sparrow had to defend Mountie practices, of course, if for no other reason than to maintain his professional pride, but he didn't like having to fall back on a soft argument over something this important. All of this Sparrow considered as he listened to Le Claire now, and he wondered how much of tonight's good feeling toward his friend came from genuine liking for him and how much was actually pleasure over Le Claire's expected reaction to the information Sparrow was about to pass on to him. Would it really be that much of a pleasure to watch Le Claire squirm? Sparrow kept his civility and listened to Le Claire ramble on.

"Then I said to him, 'So you see, Monsieur, while it is not an absolute imperative, still it is important that I receive a copy of the revised plans of the hotel.' A simple request, surely, I thought. Still, he could not bring himself to give them to me."

"He had seen your credentials?"

"Oui."

"And still he would not give you the plans?"

"Non."

"It baffles me how so many people these days refuse to do anything to commit themselves, even in their own defense," said Sparrow.

"He was one of those unsure people, part officious bastard and part craven whiner who, when caught in an unexpected situation, can think only of what is going to happen to his position," Le Claire said, crushing an imaginary pipsqueak in his fist.

"Craven whiner?" said Sparrow, seeming suddenly bemused, and smiling softly. "Craven whiner…Your English has become more remarkable by the day, Monsieur Le Claire."

"Of course, my friend. The elegance of the French tongue translates even into the most savage patois." Le Claire lifted his glass and watched the swirling brandy.

"Oh, yes, yes. Of course," said Sparrow sardonically. He watched as Le Claire, smiling, drew the plans out of his briefcase. He snickered and asked, "How did you get them?"

Le Claire looked at the Mountie over his glass. "I shot him," he said simply.

"In your usual impeccable professional manner, I suppose," Sparrow said. "Now, Claude, how did you convince him?"

"I threatened to extradite him."

Sparrow's eyebrows went up. He cocked his head a bit to one side.

"Well, I damned well felt like it!" said Le Claire. He shocked himself with the strength of his voice, caught himself, and continued speaking in a lower, but still voluble tone. "The idiot! Wasting my time. I pointed out to him that I was responsible for the security of the place, and if I should have to post guards in the lobby, run a bomb check every hour, and search the luggage of all arriving and departing guests, I would do so. I then pointed out that I would be returning tomorrow to speak with the manager and tour the building with him, and that I would be sure to tell the manager the great help or hindrance his assistant manager had been the night before. That salvo finished him off nicely. I think, really, it was the only one that hit."

"So, he handed you the floor plans. Nice of him."

"Assistant managers are a strange breed. Especially Americans. They don't know quite who or what they are." Le Claire moved a rook to Sparrow's Knight 2.

Sparrow watched the move and said absently, "What's your interest in the Commodore, anyway? Hasn't been bombed recently. Concentrating on the Tower, aren't they?"

"The Economic Conference."

Sparrow looked up, his face showing his surprise.

"For two reasons," Le Claire continued. "First, the damned fools scheduled it to end on St. Jean-Baptiste Day, which is always a good excuse for deviltry; a fine excuse for anything from a personal assault to a demonstration to a bomb scare. A national meeting of economists represents the unity of Canada. Anything that can be done to them is done symbolically to Canada itself. It's a natural for them."

Sparrow said, "Ummmm," and slid one of his protecting rooks across to his Knight 1, blocking Le Claire's rook and simultaneously putting it into jeopardy.

"Second," said Le Claire, his eyes dancing. "There is to be a celebrity speaker—Harold Holsworthy, the science fiction writer—and I don't want any…any problems."

"Problems?" asked Sparrow. "What kind of …Oh, come now, Claude, surely you aren't thinking of kidnappings."

Le Claire was silent.

"Don't you think the FLQ learned its lesson in the Laporte-Cross affair?" asked Sparrow. "And why on earth would they want a science fiction writer, anyway? What good would he be to them?"

"What good was James Cross to them?" Le Claire shot back. "What was a British Trade Minister and a Labor Minister to them? Symbols, Henry. Symbols. They are interested in symbols, and Holsworthy is a symbol of British technological progress. Now, I grant you that there is a slight, a very slight chance of anything happening, but I intend to be prepared for it."

"Well, I don't know," said Sparrow. "I can't see it."

"Henry," Le Claire said, "Once again, there are rising expectations. Whenever there are rising expectations, people break loose and do strange and unexpected things. Most of those you arrested are once again free, don't forget, and some of them are dangerous men, desperate men. They see Lévesque taking their revolution away from them." He paused and moved a bishop to cover his rook.

"Anyway, I am not so much concerned with the FLQ. The Front has been shattering, and there are tiny pieces of it, like slivers of glass, breaking and moving further and further left."

"And a sliver of glass in the wrong place can do a lot of damage. That's your thesis?"

"Exactly. You never know where they will turn up, what they will try next. It is becoming very difficult to keep track of them. And they will try something. They have to, before the Parti Quebecois steals their whole basic line, their constituency, and their program. Their raison d'être. If the Parti Quebecois succeeds, then they are outlaws, anarchists. They must be very fearful. They will act to retain their constituency. I am sure of it. But I haven't any clues! I must cover everything."

"I might have something for you," said Sparrow quietly.

Le Claire sighed deeply. He put his hand to his head and massaged his forehead. "Henry," he said, "I don't know why I come here. Perhaps it is because I always wanted to belong to the Regiment. I don't know. But, I certainly don't come here to see you. Every time I see you, you give me more work to do, a new wild-goose chase."

Le Claire moved his remaining knight into a precarious fork position to give Sparrow something to think about. Sparrow moved his threatened pawn and revealed his queen which protected the jeopardized bishop and at the same time made things very hot, by virtue of a diagonal sweep, for Le Claire's knight. Le Claire pursed his lips and stared at the board.

"An American wants to see you," said Sparrow.

"Official or otherwise?" asked Le Claire, distracted.

"Official and otherwise."

"About what?"

"About the murder."

Le Claire grunted. There it was again—another thing with no clues. "The young diplomat's murder, I presume."

"Of course," Sparrow said, "What else?"

"Who is it?"

"Harvey Bannerman. The cultural attaché at the consulate. The young man's former boss."

"Is he CIA?" asked Le Claire.

Sparrow shrugged. "Who knows? At any rate, he would like to meet with you. Unofficially. I believe he might have some information for you."

"Oh, you believe that, do you?" countered Le Claire. "Henry, you know he has information for me. You know what that information is. He told you. Why don't you just tell me?"

"He would like to impart his information to you personally. The

Americans these days are trying to be—or trying to appear, at any rate—completely above board. And Bannerman has some special insights. "

"CIA, definitely," Le Claire said.

Sparrow did not deny the observation. "He would like your cooperation," he said.

"Of course. So direct confrontation is best. Otherwise," Le Claire snarled, "I might feel I was being pressured by Ottawa!"

Sparrow ignored the outburst and pressed on. "His information might be of value to you. You say yourself you have no clues. Perhaps there are clues and you are just too close to the situation to see them."

Le Claire was furious. "Oh, really? So you are all worried about my professionalism, eh? You think perhaps I have lost my touch? You think I need some help, some guidance, is that it? Henry, if you weren't my friend, I ..." He paused. "Of course. That's it, isn't it? Quite nice. Your job is to soften me up."

"Two reasons," snapped Sparrow. "First, because I know you, yes. They asked me to speak to you ..."

"Knowing the volatility of the French temper and pride, of course they would do that," interrupted Le Claire, sardonically.

"Second, perhaps something is happening that is of a different proportion than you might expect."

"Third reason," growled Le Claire. He leaned forward in his chair. "Because, even if one is caught up in a tangled web of a hostile situation, and is perhaps attempting to cut the wrong strands of that web, still, that one knows the territory, eh?"

"They would value your cooperation," Sparrow said, quietly, with steel in his voice.

Le Claire gazed at him hard. "Henry, when did the 'we' become the 'they'?" he asked.

"Claude," said Sparrow, and now he was almost whispering. "This has a possibility of being very, very big."

"Henry," whispered Le Claire. "If I have read your position correctly over the years, if you are what I think you are, in other words, you are perfectly correct in talking to me like this. But if I do what you ask of me now, I am compromised. Compromised! A possible double agent. Do you understand my position?"

In a small, anguished voice, Sparrow said, "Claude, I would not ask this of you except in extreme circumstances. You have no idea of the importance of this thing!"

Le Claire smiled. "You arouse my interest," he said, and sipped his brandy. "When does Bannerman wish to meet with me?"

"Tomorrow morning, at 9:30. On the Plains of Abraham, below the high bluffs, there is a bench which gives a nice close view of Wolfe's Cove."

"I know the place. Near a grove of trees, isn't it? 9:30 a.m. Good. After working hours have begun and before the tourist buses have arrived."

"Bannerman will be sitting on the bench reading the New York Times."

"The cultural section, I presume." Le Claire paused for a second. "Really, Henry," he said. "Isn't this spy-counter spy apparatchik rather ridiculous?"

Sparrow laughed. "Rather! Perhaps you should bring something to read yourself, in case you find you don't like each other."

"Something large enough to cover my face, just in case some nefarious agents of the Liberation Front are lurking in the bushes, eh?"

Le Claire moved his queen to Sparrow's Knight 1, taking Sparrow's protecting rook delicately off the board. "Check," he said. "Check and mate."

Sparrow looked at the board in disbelief, looked at the foreign queen standing next to his defenseless king, and the hostile rook blocking his king's escape route.

"Your queen came out of nowhere!" he exclaimed.

"No," said Le Claire. "Your king came out of nowhere, two hundred years ago."

"Oh, now, Claude," said Sparrow, with a twinkle in his eyes. "Don't be cross." He paused, laughing at himself. "I had almost forgotten the game!" he said.

"I hadn't," said Le Claire. He was deadly serious. "I *never* forget the game."

Chapter 6

Jean-Paul – Genevieve

Genevieve saw her brother as he moved with quick, quirky strides toward her down the incline of the narrow Rue du Trésor. Against the background of a casual crowd, his clothing distinguished, his manner purposeful, he exuded an air of vanity. At that moment, Genevieve despised him and wished him far away from her. But her wishes were fruitless. Her brother was like a dreaded day that came swiftly closer, with no way to stop it. Her only defense was to ignore him. This she did, clinging to Rene's arm, and the two became part of the crowd that surrounded Rene's girlfriend, Angelique, as she completed a charcoal portrait of another tourist looking for diversion in the dark northern night.

Angelique was the kind of woman who radiated romance. She was beautiful and talented, and she worked her art with the sure hand of a professional, capturing the spirits of her delighted subjects. Genevieve admired her friend's sophistication and the chic way she had of tossing her hair and gazing up into the faces of the surrounding crowd, so that, far from her being there for them to gawk at, she seemed to have gathered them all there for her own pleasure. The light from the street lamps shone off her hair and face as she sketched, and the crowd watched her movements, delighted at the deftness that skill and self-assurance bring to an exhibition.

But for Genevieve, the pleasurable aura that surrounded the happy scene had been shattered. She felt the strong, malicious gaze of her brother at her back, knew he was there, and showed no surprise when he grasped her by the arm and spun her around. He moved her so forcefully that she almost lost her balance and let go of Rene, who turned also, puzzled.

The two young men stared at each other. Jean-Paul's look of cold contempt met with Rene's cool disdain. Breaking off the combative glance of Rene, Jean-Paul's glare fell on Genevieve.

"Come," he commanded. "It's time to go home."

Genevieve hissed at him. "You fool!" she spat out. "Let go of my arm! What am I, your slave? Let go of me or I'll scream."

Jean-Paul was not a fool and realized very well his sister's capacity for creating a scene. He let go.

"You are a disgrace," he said. "You know damn well that Father will call tonight. What do I tell him? That his daughter is in the gutter with a pack of hippies?"

Rene spoke quietly. "You have an amazing knack, Jean-Paul, of making the worst of a good situation." He paused, watching St. Andre's face. Still quietly, he said, "Genevieve, do us a favor and take your mad dog of a brother out of here. Dip him in the river and cool him off. Ciao, Genevieve."

Rene returned to watching Angelique, intentionally presenting his back to Jean-Paul.

In a rage, St. Andre pulled roughly at his sister's arm, expecting her to follow him. Inexplicably, she did. They moved quickly along Rue Buade, beneath the darkened showcase windows of the Holt-Renfrew Department Store, then crossed over to walk beside the walls of the Notre Dame Basilica. Genevieve hauled her bulky guitar case along with her. The atmosphere around them crackled with anger. Jean-Paul moved quickly, turning to hurry his sister along.

"Father would be proud of you, little hippie," he said. "Tell me, how does it feel to beg for quarters? Or do you beg? Maybe you give something in return. For dollars, maybe."

He reached his car and jerked open the passenger-side door. Genevieve stopped short. She said nothing and stood there in the night, her mouth open, her face frozen in disbelief. Thoughts and retorts were streaming through her mind, and suddenly, she laughed.

"Why, Johnny," she said, "I had no idea you thought so highly of me."

"Don't call me that!" he said, and spat, for Genevieve had said "Johnny" in such a way that it mocked him mercilessly. It was a common thought among people he had grown up with that Jean-Paul preferred to appear as English as possible, and he knew it.

Genevieve laughed at him again. He grabbed for her guitar case, wrestled it from her, and tossed it into the back seat of the car.

"Get in," he ordered.

"Don't be so rough!" she snapped. She slumped into the car and he slammed the door behind her. He circled around the car and got in, turning the engine on with a roar. Genevieve jumped at his brusqueness.

"You're so rough with everything," she exclaimed. "The guitar, the car, me. What do you want to do, destroy everything? Hurt everything?"

"*You* are the one who wants to destroy," he shot back. "Sitting up there like a goddam whore. What are you trying to do, disgrace the family?" He pulled the car out of the parking space with a lurch.

"Stop it!" she screamed. "Stop talking to me like that! At least I know who I am. You don't care about your family. What family? You care about *you*, and how English you can manage to be. Look at you. Look at your clothes, your job. Your ridiculous snobbish attitude. And Father! What does he care? Mother dead not even a year and he's off on a honeymoon with his English bitch! The two of you are alike. You don't know who you are, and you don't care, either. At least I know who I am, where I come from."

"You don't come from the gutter!" he yelled. "Why do you insist on going into it? Why do you do such a stupid thing?"

"It is not stupid! I am searching for my heritage. Our French-Canadian heritage has been beaten into the gutter. If I have to go there to find it, then that is where I shall go!"

Jean-Paul sneered. "At least I am doing something productive," he said, "instead of sitting around like an idiot mooning over something that never was."

"Is it idiocy to find out who you are?" Genevieve was indignant. "I am Quebecoise, not some kind of white slave."

Jean-Paul continued to drive swiftly. They had left the Upper Town and careened down the steep Ramparts, and now they were on the Boulevard des Capucins, heading along the north shore of the St. Lawrence, driving toward Montmorency Falls. Crossing the Sampson Bridge over the St. Charles River where it came down to meet the St. Lawrence, they passed the area known as the Louise Basin, the economic heart of Quebec's Lower Town with its miles of Canadian National and Canadian Pacific railroad tracks, its warehouses and gigantic grain elevators, its docks and wharves designed for the great ocean-going grain-carriers and tankers.

As they passed the Basin, the brother and sister were silent, looking around at the scene. Freight cars and trucks rumbled along. Clouds of steam and smoke swirled into the air illuminated by hundreds of naked bulbs that stretched in stark rows along the buildings and streets. It was a part of Quebec that tourists never saw, except from a distance, and then only as a massive jumble of industrial rubble marring the quaintness of the old city. It looked like a scene of disorderly, hissing hell that might be portrayed by a 19th Century romantic painter.

But Genevieve and Jean-Paul St. Andre knew its importance, and they knew who owned it and who controlled it. It had a strange kind of beauty for them. As they looked around them, the same thoughts were in both their minds. They wanted what they saw. They wanted it for their people, for the French-Canadian nation of Quebec. In this, they were agreed.

Past the Basin area, they turned onto Route 138, the Boulevard St. Anne that would carry them to the bridge where they'd leave the mainland at Montmorency Falls for the Ile d'Orleans. The traffic thinned, and the tension between the two lessened noticeably. Jean-Paul chuckled.

"I admire your spirit, but not your method," he said. "Maybe you should be a propagandist for the FLQ. You sound like a new recruit."

Genevieve was silent. Then she looked at Jean-Paul and said quietly, "If I were, you'd certainly know it, wouldn't you?"

Jean-Paul's foot let off the accelerator as his muscles tensed.

"What do you mean?" he asked evenly.

"You are a very poor revolutionary, Jean-Paul, mon frère. You want to be caught, it seems. You can't keep your mouth shut."

The car swerved and came to a halt in the dust and sand on the side of the road. Jean-Paul looked at his sister and was frightened.

"What are you trying to say? Tell me exactly what you mean."

The way he said it scared Genevieve. She had very seldom heard that tone of voice from anyone. She stared straight ahead and said simply, "You talk in your sleep."

Jean-Paul grabbed her sweater.

"You sneak into my room at night? Nonsense! Out with it! Tell me the truth!"

"You leave all sorts of things lying around. Papers. Plans. On the porch, I found them. Mon Dieu! How stupid!"

Jean-Paul was livid.

"What do you know?" he demanded savagely. The sound of his voice was like a slap across the face.

"I know you are the leader of a cell, that's what I know!" Genevieve began to cry. "I know it is very hard for me to keep quiet about how you really think. Everybody thinks my brother is a fool, trying to be English, trying to be against your own people. I know differently, but I can't say anything to them. To anybody. Even when we fight, I try to be angry at you for things I know are not true. I keep trying to tell myself that you are what you seem to be, but I can't anymore. Why do you think I put up with you? With your boorish behavior? Why do you play with me like this? Why don't you trust me? I can be trusted!"

Genevieve began to cry uncontrollably and slumped into the seat, shaking, her hands over her eyes. Jean-Paul eased the car back onto the road. As he drove over the bridge to the island, he listened to Genevieve's sobbing.

He could hardly think. At one point, he tried to pat her head as she scrunched up against the far door, but she shook him off. Morosely, he drove along the main road of the Ile d'Orléans, heading west.

The Ile d'Orléans had changed much in Jean-Paul's twenty-four years there. While it was still famous as a traditional farming center, the twenty-milelong island was now equally well-known as a community where businessmen and government officials had erected beautiful homes, especially on the west end. There, between the villages of Ste-Pétronille and St-Laurent, in the Beaulieu district, few farms could be seen. Instead, substantial year-round homes lined the main road.

The St. Andre home was one of these. Set between the road and the river on a point jutting out toward Quebec City, it sat on almost two acres of land. By day, the view extended past the St. Lawrence River and the ships lying at anchor in the roadstead of the harbor to Quebec itself, low and indistinct, far away across the wide expanse of water. By night, the city appeared brilliant in its lights across the dark harbor. The towers and plazas seemed to shimmer and dance, their radiance broken only by the immense black bulk of the ships strung out along the channel, waiting for the dawn.

Jean-Paul pulled his big car onto the white gravel of the driveway. The familiar crunch of the stones against the tires seemed to revive Genevieve. She sat up to watch the small estate unfold as they approached along the semi-circle of the drive. In the light of the moon the grounds seemed comforting, with soft shadows thrown by rhododendrons and willows. The columns of the portico gleamed white, and the solid white lines of the house's wooden walls spoke of a restfulness and peace built over many more years than it had taken to build a simple structure.

This was home, and until recently it had been a good, solid home. The car glided to a halt near the main door.

Genevieve dropped her hands into her lap in a gesture of resignation. Jean-Paul watched her, then silently got out of the car, came around, and opened her door. She got out, stood and looked up at this tall brother of hers who was not what he seemed.

"I'm sorry," she said. "I just don't know what to think any more. I am afraid for you."

They put their arms around each other and walked, not to the front door, but around the house to the back yard, where, across an expanse of trees and lawn, the waves of the St. Lawrence lapped against a small dock and the great stones of a breakwater. The brother and sister, once so close and now so far from each other, stopped by the door that led onto the back porch and looked at each other.

"So," said Jean-Paul, obviously pleased, "They all think I am a turncoat? All of them? Are you sure?"

"Yes," Genevieve said. "All the ones I know. And with good reason, too, the way you've been acting."

"What an excellent cover I've devised!" he said. "I couldn't ask for anything better. The perfect capitalist tool, intent on his personal position and accumulation of money, and damn the population. Ha!"

"You see what a burden it throws on me," said Genevieve. "Less than before I knew, though, I have to admit."

"But you must be brave, little one. We all have our burdens to carry for the revolution," He held her at arm's length. "And yours is light compared to some."

"I am only happy that the Front is closer to power now than it was before, Jean-Paul. It means more safety for you. Less danger."

But the danger was there. Genevieve could not put it away by talking it away. She could feel it, not just in the small surface nerves that caused her to jump at shadows, but deep within her.

And yet, there was a surging sense of life in this danger that caused her to welcome it; a sense of relief, and a sense of dread, and a small possibility of that life being snuffed out early if it went down this road. All that was there in Genevieve's being, and she didn't know what to make of it. She stood there, breathing it in, realizing it.

Jean-Paul's voice broke in. "You must never tell anyone anything of this. You must not hint of it. You must not imply, even, that you know anyone who may know anyone in the Front. You must promise that."

"I shall never say a word," she said, "until after we have won the revolution. Then everyone will have to know! I will see to that."

"After it is over, that is all right," said Jean-Paul. "But not until then." He paused. "It may never be over, you know."

The telephone rang in the study, deep within the house.

"Answer the phone," commanded Jean-Paul.

"I shall not," she said. "This is quite a different matter. I do not wish to speak to Father. The idiot."

"Do you think I brought you all the way out here so you could refuse to talk to him? Answer the phone!"

"Go to hell," Genevieve said, turning to walk inside. "Answer it yourself, and say hello to the English bitch idiot while you're at it. Vive Quebec Libre!"

Genevieve ran upstairs, leaving Jean-Paul alone in the doorway to the study. "Vive Quebec Libre indeed!" he thought. He could see it now. Every time he tried to do something she didn't like, there she would be with her fingers forming a V and her mouth silently forming the words "Vive Quebec Libre." The little blackmailer.

Damn little sisters, anyway. Well, there was nothing else he could have done about it. He had to tell her something—or let her think something, anyway, and that was closer to the way it had happened, really. And if in the future she became too inquisitive, or too bothersome, well, he knew exactly how to take care of that problem. It was so simple it was almost boring.

Jean-Paul smiled, knowing he had not divulged the truth to her. If she had found that out…but no, she would never have believed it. He turned to the phone, still smiling. As far as he was concerned, the FLQ were a pack of mice who went around screaming foolishness; idiots who blew off their fingers with improvised letter bombs. Jean-Paul was not a member of the FLQ. He was a member of the Organization, and proud of it.

The Trotskyites of the FLQ could hold all the damn-fool demonstrations and rallies they wanted, and gather all the sodden support they wanted, too. When the time came to shove, they would not stand a chance against the disciplined troops of the Organization.

The telephone continued to ring. Just as he picked it up, Jean-Paul had an amusing thought. Wouldn't it be incredible to be there when the old man, sitting over there in London with his new young 'English bitch' wife, as Genevieve had described her, learned what his hard-won money was financing!

Jean-Paul picked up the phone. "Allo? Ah, Papa! Ça va?"

Far on the opposite shore, down the hollow, empty streets within the walls of old Quebec, Claude Le Claire strolled, tapping out problems in his mind as he tapped the stem of his old pipe against his teeth. A frown gathered his brows together as he glanced along the streets that had been swept clean as a whistle. Light streamed from gas lamps and spilled an antique glow over the mica-filled granite walls of the old houses. Windows that were kept scrupulously clean revealed warm, wonderfully-furnished parlors inside impressive townhouses safe behind their wrought-iron gates and window grilles.

"Window dressing," he thought to himself. The city was engaged in a refurbishing effort to make itself even more palatable to tourists. Old houses received facelifts, stripped down to their original bare, beautiful lines. It was a worthwhile project, of course.

Our Lady of the Snows, they called her, and it was certainly true. This Quebec was a beautiful city, ever young, constantly renewing. A capital if ever there was one.

But "window dressing," Le Claire thought again. "These houses are window dressing for the tourists. And the tourists are window dressing for the economists, who are themselves tourists. And the economists are window dressing for…what?"

A conference of economists. They represented the economic power of the Canadian nation and government. Here they were, gathered from all the towns and cities of the provinces that swept in a great confederation from the Atlantic to the Pacific. And the greatest of these in size and potential was Quebec itself, with its millions of citizens who spoke a different language and considered themselves a separate nation. And here was the economic conference set right down in their midst, representing power. Representing what some Quebecois would consider a foreign, occupying power.

But if he were one of those who was enraged, thought Le Claire, and if he were to keep his brain clear, what would he see? What would he differentiate? The economists represented power, but were not power itself. They were the mere trappings, the outward signs of power. To hurt or liquidate a handful of them might be a statement of some sort, and it would throw fear into the rest of Canada and build hatred in the great bulk of the English-speaking provincials.

That would be something. But not very much.

If he were a terrorist, what would he, Le Claire, strike at if he wished to aim at the heart of power itself?

He turned his mind to something Prime Minister Trudeau had said last autumn, during the crisis when the FLQ had kidnapped Pierre Laporte, the Minister of Labour, and James Cross, the British Trade Minister in Montreal. What was it he had said? Ah, yes. The speech about 'alternate bulwarks of political power allowed to grow alongside the sceptered one.'

One must always remember that, thought Le Claire. Those who

would create the deviltry thought of themselves as a new government, a new bulwark of political power. They were sophisticated people, these people whom he called terrorists. Politically sophisticated, intelligent, and tough. Some crazies, yes, but some excellent minds there, too, minds that believed they were at war with the established society. What would they go for? What would their statement be?

Liquidation of a few piddling economists would be ridiculous in their eyes. What would be bigger? More grandiose? What would capture the headlines of the world, proclaim their cause to everyone, cause the capitalists to quake with fear and the People to rejoice and sneer at their bosses and economic overlords?

Where would he himself strike with hatred in his heart and a new order to impose upon the earth? Where would he strike?

At the heart of the power. Or at least, the closest he could come to the heart. And what would that be? With the Quebecois' love for cybernetics and science, tools which had been denied them for generations, tools which defined economic power for them, he would strike at …they would strike at...

But what would they do with him once they had him? Of what use would a science fiction writer be to them? Sparrow was certainly right about that. A man who was—window dressing?—had been invited to close an economic conference with a talk on Space Economics? There would be an initial flurry of publicity, surely, but after that, public opinion would turn quickly against them.

Capturing defenseless people was no great trick. They had done it before, and it had turned against them then. Surely they wouldn't make that same mistake twice.

But why this hunch? There were plenty of other things the terrorists could do. Of what use…yet…

Le Claire let out his breath with a sigh. What nonsense. What blind alleys logical flight could lead to. Yet the hunch remained, so embedded in his mind that it would not let go. Something was going to happen. It was going to be big, and it would involve the Economic Conference. It would probably happen in the thoroughly modern, antiseptic space of the Commodore Hotel, where nothing in the least discomfiting was ever allowed to happen. It would happen where the least protection was available, in a public hall where security was lax.

This was crazy.

They would call him crazy. He had no reasons, no evidence, nothing. There were so many more theories that bore so much more realism within them. But he had this hunch, and he intended to cover it. What the hell, the man would have to have coverage anyway.

Le Claire made a decision. Tomorrow he would ask for the file on Harold Holsworthy: space scientist, space technician, science writer, best known to the general public as a futurologist and science fiction writer. Le Claire wanted to know more about him.

TUESDAY, JUNE 22ND

"I am speaking to you at a moment of grave crisis, when violent and fanatical men are attempting to destroy the unity and freedom of Canada. If a democratic society is to continue to exist, it must be able to root out that cancer of an armed revolutionary movement that is bent on destroying the very basis of our freedom."

Pierre Eliot Trudeau, Prime Minister of Canada

Chapter 7

Wolfe's Cove – Le Claire and Bannerman

Le Claire did not sleep well that night. He tossed and turned and finally he lay fully awake well before the sun rose. The previous evening, as soon as he had disposed of his preoccupation with the Economic Conference, another set of problems had come to the fore. These had centered on himself and the role he might be asked to play in cooperative investigations with the Americans, if indeed there were to be investigations. Or actual cooperation.

The major problem, he knew, was that he was being compromised. Sparrow had implied that he would be consulted as a full partner in any dealings, but he hadn't fallen for it. He knew that the people who would be contacting him in these matters did not usually need to deal with someone in his position and scarcely ever did so.

He did not feel flattered. He knew their ways of operating too well for that.

To be contacted was to be compromised, whether more or less, and consequently to lose future effectiveness. The only alternative to that was to pretend to play their game, and Le Claire wanted none of that. To be involved in that type of thing meant to lose a part of your soul, to become unable to recognize yourself. No, Le Claire would never wish that on himself.

The only thing they could possibly want was to extract useable information from him, and this made him furious.

"Clandestine meetings," he muttered to himself. "Clandestine meetings! As if I were a paid informer!"

He had gone without his usual morning coffee. He had paced the rooms of his house, had gone out early to pace the streets. At nine o'clock he had called Sandy to announce that he would be in late this morning and to ask that she send for the file, or anything the Mounties might happen to have, on Holsworthy. Then he had gone to pacing again, this time away from the city toward the wide parkland of the Plains of Abraham.

Now he was in the park itself, walking fast. He was furious. His fists clenched and unclenched as he strode along the path through the rolling hills that were covered with short, cropped grass and well-manicured, well-placed trees and bushes.

What stuck in his craw now was the idea, newly matured, that he was a pawn, and an insignificant pawn at that. Forces beyond his control were planning to use him and his knowledge. They would use him and go on about their business, and it would be made clear to Le Claire just how circumscribed and insular his power really was. He was expendable.

He did not blame Sparrow for softening him up as well as he possibly could. Sparrow had just done his job, done what had been expected of him. Sparrow, too, was a pawn. Le Claire did not even blame Harvey Bannerman. Suddenly, there on the green and glistening Plains of Abraham, Le Claire had a vision of mighty powers beyond his control, pulling his strings and playing with his destiny always. Descending immediately on that thought came another—the realization that he was reacting in exactly the same way as the Separatists had always reacted to the nebulous power of English Canada.

Once started on this line of thought, it became impossible for the man to shake free of the rage that engulfed him.

He wondered what was wrong with him. He should feel honored, not enraged. He wondered if the Separatists, whom he had always fought, were simply not brighter and better connected to reality than he was. Had he compromised his entire life? Was he, in fact, a collaborator?

He tried in vain to stifle these frightening thoughts. The fact was this: the man who had always prided himself on knowing people, knowing what they were about to do, how they were about to act, and how to control them, was suddenly himself being controlled.

"A pawn," he thought once more. "A stinking, valueless pawn."

He was in a mental bind of his own making, and he could not get out of it.

Suddenly, he stopped walking and stood stock still, gazing over the meadows and rolling hills that stretched out beneath the green copper rooves and stone walls of the 22nd Regimental Headquarters building. He prodded his chin with the edge of his rolled-up newspaper. His racing thoughts conjured up visions of powers to the right and left of him, arrayed upon the field of battle. The old armies were at work, banners flying and trumpets sounding. To his left strode the blue-clad legions of Montcalm. To his right, the thin red line of Wolfe's Grenadiers and Highlanders formed and held ready. Indians skulked in the bushes. Rag-tag American mountaineers, their clothes in tatters, hallowed and whooped around the flanks of ever-growing armies.

Now came, superimposed on the older fantasies, partisan mobs of Separatists and English-Canadian police meeting each other with slogans, clubs, tear gas, and hidden bombs. Centuries came together in Le Claire's mind, all in a hodge-podge of conflicts and hatreds. The chessboard of his logical mind heaped high with kings and pawns, castles and queens and knights in all varieties of dress and color. But always, there were too many kings on the board—kings of France and England, of America, of the Press, of Public Opinion, of Subversion.

And there were self-multiplying Economic Barons let loose on the field of war by the kings whose pawns they were, and Princes of Illogic were scattered all about. There were so many you could scarcely count them all. And all of these damned incubilia zipped around with such speed that Le Claire could not keep track of them.

But always, there were the two sides. Always, the hatred. He could not deal with it. It would ruin the chess game for him forever. He gave up any pretext of understanding a world driven mad by its own conflicting drives, its ignorant armies clashing by night. He put the clamoring armies out of his mind and set himself to walking methodically along the macadam path.

"Is Trudeau a collaborator?" he asked himself to still his mind. And his logical mind answered, "Of course not! And who are the

Separatists to claim that they alone are patriots?" And his rage was redirected against all those who claimed that their way, and their way alone, was the right way.

After his fitful night, Le Claire was in a foul, foul mood. He walked quickly, his adrenalin pushing him along, his mind considering retirement.

On the far side of the park, the land sloped abruptly down toward the cliffs fronting the river. Off there, beneath the steep slope, and just above the cliffside road, Le Claire saw a lone figure seated on a bench. As he drew closer, he saw the figure to be a tall, spare man in a gray business suit. The man was balding, and he scrutinized the New York Times through a pair of rimless glasses.

Le Claire sat down on the bench and opened his own paper. Behind it, he looked to his right, directly at the other reader.

"Good morning," said the other, without looking up. Le Claire said nothing, continuing to stare.

The other turned, and with the wisp of a smile said, "I'm Harvey Bannerman." Le Claire snorted and went to reading his paper. Bannerman frowned.

"Le Claire, what's the trouble?" he asked.

"How do you know my name?" said Le Claire. "How do you know I'm Le Claire?"

"Le Claire," said Bannerman, with a puzzled frown. "I know you. I've met you a number of times. It's me. Harvey. You know me."

Le Claire put down his paper. "I know a Harvey Bannerman who is the cultural attaché at the American consulate," he said. "I do not know a Harvey Bannerman who is a member of the CIA. You are most unprofessional, Monsieur. What is the password?"

Bannerman's face turned to stone. His eyes went hard.

"I know what you're thinking, Monsieur," Le Claire said. "Do not be concerned. I have not gone crazy. I am quite reliable. I am also quite angry, sir!"

Bannerman relaxed.

"I am being used for somebody else's purposes," Le Claire continued. "I am not used to this, although my people are. Perhaps you can sympathize with my point of view?"

"A natural reaction," said Bannerman. "But let me put you at ease. I did not ask you to meet with me to seek your cooperation. To the contrary. I have some information for you."

"Why me, Monsieur? Why not through channels? Why this cloak and dagger business?"

Bannerman countered, "Why risk more people than necessary having access to our information? Why not contact you directly? You, Le Claire, are in a position to act on this, and it might require extremely quick action."

Le Claire sighed. He folded his paper and half-turned toward Bannerman. With the trace of a smile he said, "Very well. You have me interested. I take the bait."

"Good," said Bannerman, looking relieved. "You know the situation better than I. I recognize that. I do not intend to lecture you on the......troubles, of your own nation. I...we...naturally appreciate the delicacy of approaching you. Approaching anyone here, actually."

"Out with it, Monsieur," Le Claire said quietly.

A slight breeze blew in from the west. So slight it did not even rustle the leaves. Everything was still.

"I said we had information for you," said Bannerman. "We feel it to be extremely important information." Bannerman paused. "The Boar is in Canada."

Le Claire was unmoved.

"That's fine, Harvey," he said. "Now, if you will do me the honor of explaining to me just which boor you are talking about, I might be impressed."

It was Bannerman' s turn to smile. "You might know him by another name," he said. "Pablito Cortez."

Now Le Claire's eyebrows rose. He whistled slightly. "Pablito Cortez. The wild Cuban Boar," he said. He turned the information over in his mind. "Yes, Harvey. I do know him. Or of him, I should say. A Fidelista. One of the more dangerous of them. Turned up in the Sierra Madre early on. An expert in torture, in mind-bending, in munitions. With a pipeline, it seems, to a lot of very interesting contacts. Do I have it right?"

"Partially," said Bannerman. "Not entirely. There are some in my department who feel he was one of the prime movers influencing Fidel toward the Soviets. With good cause, by the way. He has been in Cuba ever since the Revolution. Never left the island, as far as we know. We think he's the head of international espionage operations for Fidel, at any rate since Che Guevara caught it. To tell the truth, we've always felt he was Guevara' s boss."

"And suddenly he's in Canada?"

"Not just in Canada, Claude. In Quebec. We traced him. He transferred from a Russian fishing trawler to a Canadian one on the Banks of Newfoundland. The Canadian trawler put in at Rimouski three days ago."

"First," said Le Claire, "I want the name of that trawler from you."

Bannerman drew a manila envelope from the folds of his newspaper.

"That information is here," he said, "along with a lot of other interesting little bits. Including several photographs of the Boar. Everything we have on him, as a matter of fact."

"His entire file? I am honored, Monsieur."

"We felt you should have all the information we could possibly give you," said Bannerman. "He worries us. We have been trying to find out why he is taking this chance. He must have something very big planned. You don't throw away an operation the size of his for a lark."

"Something big," Le Claire muttered. "Possibly, yes."

"And something more, Le Claire," said Bannerman. "He's not a Cuban. His real name, as far as we know—we can't trace him back all the way, but most of it—is Vladimir Borovik. That's how he came by the nickname we gave him."

"A Russian!" said Le Claire, startled. He opened his mouth to speak again, but no words came.

"He came west at the end of the war, claiming to be a White Russian refugee. He went to Portugal to live, and then disappeared into South America. The next we knew of him, he showed up in Cuba with Che and Fidel. He didn't just turn up in the Sierra Madre, he was one of the original dozen that came ashore with them. Now he's here. We don't know why."

Bannerman paused.

"Monsieur," said Le Claire, "You know I am not a fool. Neither am I ignorant. And I am up on these things, eh? So why didn't I know he was a Russian? "

"Very few people knew, until recently. You'd never guess it from his accent. Or his suntan. He looks like a pirate, like a Caribbean buccaneer. A quite obvious scar along his forehead, by the way. Evil looking eyes and teeth. A mouth that looks like it eats capitalist pigs for breakfast. Well, you'll see all that. You can form your own impression. I'm prejudiced."

Le Claire sat there looking at the envelope, his eyes trying to burn through it to the material inside.

"I have a proposition for you," said Bannerman, and there was no trace of a smile on his face or in his eyes.

The tone of the voice snapped Le Claire's reverie. "Ah," he thought, "That was the catch, the trigger. Now comes the rockslide." Intent, he nodded imperceptibly at the fastidious American.

"You will find it no surprise," said Bannerman, "that I can approximate the strength of your department quite accurately."

Le Claire heated up. "I doubt, Monsieur, that your use of the word *approximate* is quite accurate," he said, barely holding his temper. "Why not just tell me the number of my people, their names, ages, sex, race, places of business, and home addresses. And strengths and weaknesses. And show me their photographs."

Le Claire looked into space and said wearily, "And tell me how many of them are *your* people, also."

Bannerman ignored the outburst.

"We thought," he said quietly, "you might like, besides the information, some help also, if you feel the need of it."

"So you think it necessary to activate your agents-in-place, eh?" scoffed Le Claire. "You must place a great deal of importance on the movements of Comrade Vladimir Borovik, if you are willing to expose your whole apparatus in my Province! Hands off, is that it? No one else allowed to touch?"

"Yes, you're right," said Bannerman seriously. "We do want him, if we can get him. We'd be willing to share him with you. But, Le Claire, do not overestimate us. That might be a fatal mistake. What I..."

Le Claire interrupted him. "In that case, Monsieur, perhaps I might consider sharing him with *you*."

"What I am proposing," continued Bannerman, "is that we have a number of people who are available…"

"Already here, I suppose?"

"No, they are not. My God, you are an exasperating fellow! They can be here within the hour if…," and he said it again, "…if you feel the need of them."

Le Claire looked into the American's eyes. They were forceful and did not waver.

"Ummmm," said the Frenchman, considering. He knew he should be angry at all of this, this encroachment on his territory, this forcing of so many issues all at once, but he was not. He was too much of a realist to play bureaucratic power games at a critical time such as now. He would somehow bring himself to find a niche for himself in this structure that promised so much activity in the near future.

"Ummm," he said again. Then, "Very good," he said mostly to himself, almost growling.

"Concerning agents-in-place, Le Claire," said Bannerman, "I am going to break a rule. I am going to ask if you have received any information regarding the death of our late assistant cultural attaché."

Le Claire smiled wryly. "I had guessed as much," he said. "You have been much too interested in the problem. All of you—Ottawa, Washington, Montreal. I knew from the pressure, if nothing else, that he was one of your own."

"Do you have anything?"

"Nothing as yet. None of the usual sources have anything. But how could they, when it doesn't concern them, eh? Since we have become such grand confidants, Bannerman, may I ask you what he was doing here?"

Bannerman looked suddenly startled.

"Read your paper, Monsieur," he said in a tone that belied his anxious eyes, "There are some very interesting articles in it." Bannerman retreated behind his New York Times, covering himself with it. Curious, Le Claire looked up, and quickly did likewise with his own paper.

Now he was furious.

"Is this one of your tricks, Bannerman?" he hissed.

"Not mine, Monsieur. One of yours, perhaps? "

"Don't be an ass."

"Then be quiet! That may be a directional recorder he's using."

"Damn!" said Le Claire, glancing from behind his paper. "Photographs, now! Who is he, Bannerman? I don't need this kind of crap."

"Shhh," said Bannerman. "The recorder!"

Kearney had awakened early to the peals of the Quebec church bells. After breakfast at the coffee shop in the Old Homestead Hotel and some browsing about the Upper Town, he had decided to see the Citadel, only to find the fort not ready to receive visitors until 10:00 A.M.

He had a thought that he was probably too early for any kind of business in this town and so, shouldering his camera and tape recorder, he hiked briskly out through the St. Louis gate and over the Plains of Abraham to the top of Wolfe's Cove.

This morning the cove set an idyllic scene. Birds chirped in the trees. The sun was warm. The air was fresh. Beyond the cove, between it and the museum, two older men sat placidly on a bench and read their newspapers. Kearney smiled and began to photograph everything in sight. When he turned toward the two men, he zeroed in on them with his telescopic lens. He smiled again, thinking of what a great picture they made sitting there, immersed in world news that would probably never touch them in any way, shape, or form. An interesting photograph. He reset the focus a bit and shot again, to be sure he got them. Then he put away his camera and picked up the microphone of his recorder.

"It could be," said Le Claire, "that he is simply one of your idiot tourists."

"Shhh!" said Bannerman, with just a trace of a squirm.

"Don't be silly, Bannerman. Come out of hiding. He's not looking at us. He's talking into his recorder. Reading from a tourist pamphlet."

Bannerman looked out from behind his paper. Probably not a directional at all, he thought. Even if it were, the subject would be covering their conversation with his own interference. But then again, perhaps a newer model...well, take a chance.

"Looks normal," he said.

"Ha! As normal as your tourists manage to get, anyway," said Le Claire. He looked at the young man, who was now making his way slowly down the long wooden stairway into the cliffside trees, still talking into his microphone.

"Quite steep," Kearney was saying to the recorder. "Must have been a scramble coming up in the dark. Oh. Pictures 7, 8, 9, 10, 11, and 12, roll 2, at Wolfe's Cove. From here, the Plains are beautiful. The regimental headquarters building sort of frames them on the far side. That damned Caravelle tower is grotesque. Looms over everything. They ought to tear it down."

"He seems to be interested in Wolfe," said Le Claire.

"It's nice to see someone interested in history nowadays," said Bannerman. "If more people were interested, we'd probably be better off."

"Ah, well, Bannerman. So we definitely agree on something, eh? I suppose an interest in history led you into your present work." Le Claire paused. "Cultural affairs, I mean."

Bannerman didn't answer. He stood up and looked at the departing figure, then turned to Le Claire and said, "It would not be good for us to be seen together, Monsieur. I have no official business with you. In the wrong hands …"

"I agree. He must be identified, at least." Le Claire paused and sighed, then said, "Use your walkie-talkie, Harvey. I accept the fact that your people are already in place. Best to make use of them." Le Claire's thoughts turned inward. " Already in place," he muttered to himself.

"Thank you, Claude," said Bannerman. "With your permission." He looked relieved, and spoke at length into a small, thin transmitter that looked rather like a pocket calculator. In spite of himself, Le Claire was impressed.

After he had completed the transmission, Bannerman turned to the Frenchman.

"You will have pictures of him by tonight. We can tackle this from both sides at the same time. I hope for our sakes he is one of our tourists. Things might be complicated, if he isn't."

"Who is taking the pictures, Harvey?"

"Two technicians. Excellent men. They arrived last night. Sackman and Hefelfinger."

" Experienced?"

"Very."

"What do they look like?"

"Anybody."

Le Claire laughed. "It will be difficult to work with chameleons," he said.

"I will arrange a meeting for you." Bannerman smiled a satisfied smile. "Photographs would do you no good."

"You are proud of them," said the Frenchman.

Bannerman's smile grew wider. "Those two," he said, "went into Lebanon and came out with two bishops, a knight, a rook, and a very important pawn. They're very good."

"Ah-ha. And you expect them to go into French Canada and come out with a mad Russian."

"Very good," Bannerman repeated to himself. He was thinking of something far in the past, and only half heard Le Claire's comment. He turned alert, and said, "I said we'd be willing to share him with you."

"And I reiterate, I with you. I don't like his style. Not at all. Where is he, by the way? Still at Rimouski?"

Bannerman reddened. "We lost him," he said.

Le Claire couldn't help but laugh. "You lost him? But how? You tracked him from Cuba to Canada and you lost him at Rimouski? Why don't you just turn on one of your surveillance satellites? And look closely!" he chortled, wagging his finger in admonishment. "Honestly, Harvey, however could you lose him?"

"It is embarrassing," admitted the American. "He had made arrangements. We had expected him to, of course, but nothing quite as intricate as he came up with. There are quite a few of them on his side, Claude. Good ones, too."

"Ah, yes. They would be. We Frenchmen were always masters of intrigue."

"Not only French, Claude. There are at least two Arabs with him. PLO, Black Decembrists. Those two we are sure of. There are others, but we don't know exactly…"

"Do you mean an entire team?" Le Claire was startled.

"We think so."

"Buy why? Do you have any ideas?"

"No," said Bannerman, exasperated. "Theories, yes. Suppositions, yes. But nothing hard. Nothing. What could it be? Anything!"

Le Claire let out his breath. "It gets bigger and bigger, doesn't it, Harvey? All those wild beasts loose in the French-Canadian wilderness. Let's see. Supposing a team, an A team, let's say, eight to a dozen of them, perhaps, at the outside. Then, contacts here. One cell, at least. That's four to five more. Two cells—eight to ten. Perhaps some back-up. We seem to be talking of a force of as many as twenty-five, at least half of them professionals. My God, for what?"

"Assassination?" asked Bannerman. "Sabotage? Kidnapping? We have been reviewing the entire Canadian situation. All kinds of possibilities. We need help. And security."

"You shall have it," said Le Claire. "At least so far as I am able to provide it. This has ceased to be a game. Too close to home," he grumbled. "Who would have thought it?"

"What do you think?"

"I think nothing. I act. Beginning with a review of everything. Strange happenings. Traffic. Incidents unexplained. Speeches. Hints. Apprehensions. Hard facts. Everything. Should I contact Ottawa, do you think?"

"Only as you would normally do, I would suggest," Bannerman said. "Act on your own. Maybe you'll come up with something nobody else is familiar with. That's the first thing we need: as much information as possible. We must find out their thrust."

"You know, a pattern forms." Le Claire spoke slowly as he mused letting his mind cast back over recent events. "The support for the FLQ and the other radicals—from where? The Laporte murder, the flight of the kidnappers to Cuba. The attempt of the Russian diplomats to subvert the Mounties. That absurd Berster border affair. They have been working hard at us for a long time. Now this. And, by the way, what was your cultural affairs protégé doing here? I must know."

"Information gathering..." said Bannerman, and hesitated. Le Claire looked at him and waited.

"Alright. Penetration, too. Financial. Contact."

"Pay-offs," said Le Claire. "Counter-subversion. Ah, Harvey, I doubt that will work here. With the Separatists. They are all too committed."

"There is always a way," said Bannerman. "Always a crack in the structure. It is a natural law."

"Here we have a sieve instead of a crack, I fear," said Le Claire. "And the flow is going opposite from the way you and I would like to see it." He snorted. "Well, I have work to do, I can see," he said. "Finally it comes home. Keep in touch?"

Bannerman smiled his thin smile. "One way or another," he said, and walked off toward the museum.

Le Claire watched him go, then set off in the opposite direction, his hand sweaty against the manila envelope. Suddenly, he was glad Bannerman was in Quebec. Bannerman was professional. It would be a good relationship there. Regardless of whom the Americans had tried to subvert in the past, he wanted their help and cooperation now. What a fight this would be!

Bannerman, walking away on the other side of the museum, was not quite as happy to be working with Le Claire.

Chapter 8
The Tourist

Kearney had an interesting morning, including all sorts of encounters with Quebecers and other tourists. He left the Plains of Abraham and rambled down the long wooden steps that dropped hundreds of feet over the loose shale and rock that was Wolfe's Cove. He took his time and enjoyed the trees and silence and woods that pressed close around the steps.

When he finally reached the base of the cliff, he found himself on a local road leading to the wide Champlain Boulevard. To his right on the river bank, across the road and the boulevard, was the bulk of the Immigration Building and Customs House. Beside it sat a freight yard with rows of freight cars spread over it. Adjacent to the yard was a docking area for the largest of ocean-going ships. The whole complex taken together wasn't appetizing.

Directly in front of him, the small street was quiet in the midmorning lull except for a single car that was stopped on the far side. Its hood was up and two guys were bent over the engine. From where Kearney stood, they looked puzzled.

He turned to his left and continued on the road that squeezed itself between the boulevard and the cliffs of Cape Diamond. The road, lined with older houses and shops, had the feeling of a main thoroughfare in a very small town. It was like being out in the countryside, dozens of miles from any city.

But shortly, the town road ended as it curved to the right and entered the wide boulevard. Thereafter, the route back to the city was all four-lane cement, bounded by rocky cliffs and the river.

Far beneath the walls of the Citadel, after a walk of about one kilometer, Kearney paused to look at a plaque marking the spot where the American General Montgomery was shot to death at the beginning of his and Arnold's attack on Quebec on New Year's Eve in 1775. He stood for a while, wondering what kind of men it took to travel hundreds of miles through a bitter winter to attack a near-impregnable fortress defended by a well-rested and warm garrison.

After a short stop, he marched on toward the ancient Place Royale, the old heart of Quebec's Lower Town. He visited the small church, Notre-Dame-des-Victoires, looked at the ship model hanging from the ceiling, and lit a candle. He didn't know why; he wasn't religious.

Afterwards, outside, as he sat resting on a stone bench in the square beneath a bronze bust of Louis XIV, he was accosted by a strange Frenchman. The man appeared to be in his thirties, had a three-day-old stubble of beard, and watery, leaky eyes. He seemed to be drunk or crazy, and he wobbled up to Kearney carrying a stack of black plastic trays holding pictures of Quebec buildings embossed in gold and silver. He proceeded to try to sell one or more of these garish monstrosities to Kearney, remonstrating in a loud French diatribe. Kearney couldn't understand a word of it.

The more Kearney replied in the negative, the louder and more persistent the drunken fool became. He even, at one point, tried to shove his whole stock of plastic platters in Kearney's face. Soon Kearney's plight itself became the attraction as a crowd gathered. Cameras clicked and people chuckled in the tourist-crowded square until suddenly, giving up on his mark, the drunk turned on the crowd and looked for a new victim.

The tourists scattered, still laughing, as the derelict badgered an entire family. They ran en masse around a corner, the seller of plastic platters in hot pursuit.

Kearney, the calm of his morning stroll wrecked, left the

Place Royale and walked uphill, stopping every now and then for a look at the art galleries on the Cote de la Montagne. Then he crossed again through the center of town. He was almost back to his hotel and looking forward to stretching out for a few minutes when he was stopped by an English tourist. This was not what Kearney was in the mood for, but the Englishman caught him completely off guard when he asked, "I say, do you speak English?"

Forgetting he had a camera and tape recorder looped all over him, and momentarily flattered that he didn't look like a tourist himself, Kearney stopped and smiled. The Englishman, a nervous type, was trying to get to the Citadel and asked Kearney to orient him. Kearney pointed to their place on the man's map and gratuitously threw in some information he had picked up during his morning excursion.

The Englishman thereupon asked Kearney to hold the map. He fished in his pockets, drew out a pad and pen and, mumbling to himself, wrote everything down. Then, seemingly satisfied, he said good-bye. Still mumbling directions to himself, he went off down the hill.

Kearney continued walking slowly up the hill to his hotel. He didn't notice the fellow reading a book in the park across the street. The reader, after making sure Kearney had actually entered the Chateau Brittany, moved to the center of the park where he sat on a rock that commanded a view all around, opened his book, and drew a long, thin wallet out of it. He opened the wallet and pushed a button. Bannerman's voice sounded immediately:

"Section One, here. Where?"

"Near the office. Want to meet?"

"Yes. I have things for you. Where?"

"Site B. Both of you. Half hour."

"10-4."

Hefelfinger was glad of the half-hour respite. He wanted to shave and change his clothes. He didn't know if he was a drunk or a scholar, or a drunken scholar, or a scholarly drunken madman trying to understand a broken engine. Besides, he was out of sync with Sackman, who now looked like a tweedy, myopic don out of Cambridge or York.

Half an hour later, both Sackman and Hefelfinger, looking like junior executives in conservative suits, were in conference with Bannerman in Suite 632 of the Chateau Frontenac. Their rooms overlooked the river, and Sackman, in a fury, was standing at the window watching the little dots of people on the terrace far below. He was furious because the easy mark that Kearney was supposed to be had not turned out to be as cooperative as he should have been. What was supposed to be an early-morning entertainment had turned out to be a half-baked fiasco.

"I swear he was trained," Hefelfinger was telling Bannerman. "He was just too good. He wouldn't touch *anything!*"

"That shouldn't be difficult to rectify," said Bannerman. "You know where he's staying. I'll give you an hour. Get in there and pick up something. Substitute something. A water glass. Tourist brochures. The john handle. Whatever. We need those prints."

"Hell, we don't need prints," Sackman said. "We know he's not a civilian. We know he's somebody. Jim is right. He probably buttons his shirt with his teeth, for God's sake."

Bannerman paused and pursed his lips. "Let's go over it again," he said. "Jim?"

"When somebody dumps a load of pictures in your lap, you don't not touch them. You grab 'em and throw 'em at whoever dumped 'em on you. Not like he did—just sitting there grinning at me. Oh, by the way, I can't pass here, not for a native, anyway. They don't speak *French* French here. It's something else. A dialect. Lots of words the French don't use much anymore. Archaic, I'd say. Different spacing; different cadence. Anyway, I'd have to practice it, so I can't use that as cover."

"I'm sure you can work around it," said Bannerman. "Alan, what have you got?"

"When somebody gives you a map to hold," Sackman began, "You don't hold it by the edges, with your palms. You don't let the wind play with it. You might drop it, so you grab it and leave your prints all over it. He didn't. He wouldn't."

"So," said Bannerman, "by trying not to tell us something about himself, he told us something about himself. Typical. Well, we have these photos, thank you very much. Quite nice ones, I'm sure. And we have his residence. Now, just get his prints and find his car. Ten to one, he has a car. Might be amusing to find out who it's registered to. Damn! He's taking up too much of our time. Get it done as soon as possible. I've got other things planned for your afternoon. Now that you've had your exercise for the day, you can get down to business."

Bannerman snickered.

"I'm running out of clothes," Sackman complained.

Bannerman ignored him. "I have a small list of known operatives in town," he said. "Provided by the Mounties. This seems to be turning into a big operation, and they've asked us to help. So, here you are. Three men. Pictures. MOs. Habits, biographies, records. Everything. Quite excellent profiles, as a matter of fact, professionally speaking. Any one of them might make an interesting target. I'd like to do all three of them, beginning this afternoon."

"What about El Gordo Boro," Hefelfinger asked.

"You don't really want to meet him again, do you, Jim?" Bannerman asked. "After the way you two got along the last time?"

Hefelfinger remembered the Isle of Pines, the concentration camp, the three long years he had spent there, waiting to be exchanged, trying to think of some way to escape.

"Ten seconds, that's all I need," he said. "Less than that."

"We want him alive, Jim," cautioned Bannerman.

"Easier said than done," Sackman spat.

"Well, gentlemen," said Bannerman. "These fellows might turn out to be primary contacts of his here, so be careful. First, though, clear up this little matter of our mystery man. Then contact me. We'll meet at … we'll meet here. I'll provide lunch and we can go over these papers. And thanks for the pictures. I'll get them off to Langley immediately."

Bannerman cupped the roll of 35mm film in his palm

and smiled. That was the worth of Sackman and Hefelfinger, he thought. They not only knew all the tricks of the trade, but they hadn't forgotten how to be normal, either. They were good tourists. Or natives. Or whatever they happened to want to be at the time. They were good psychologists and good technicians.

And when they wanted to be, they were also very silent. When Bannerman looked up, the two technicians were gone. He hadn't heard them leave.

Chapter 9

The Borovik Synapses

There was a musty feel to the dark old room that was strange considering its size. Its windows had not been opened perhaps for years. Certainly the few larger ones had been boarded over decades ago, and the smaller ones had rough wooden shutters over them. Only a few slivers of natural light penetrated the gloom. The smell there was the pungent scent of generations of insects.

The ancient lighting system had long ago given out, and strings of bare bulbs were roped along the unpainted wooden beams of the ceiling, their extension cords tacked hastily in place just a few minutes earlier. The thin light from the bulbs cast eerie brown shadows that wavered over the large room and revealed a makeshift conference table and ten chairs, all of which were occupied.

Vladimir Borovik glanced with a jaded eye over the figures of the men and women seated at the table. It amused him to think that these people, the central committee of an underground organization, would choose as a meeting place a warehouse floor five stories in the air. Further, it amused him that these people, students and intellectuals for the most part, constituted a central committee. There the amusement ended, for Vladimir Borovik didn't trust students or intellectuals. They were not professionals. They were too prone to spew their paltry little hoard of secrets all over the place. Again, they were easily shocked by their own actions, and tended to disintegrate when the game got rough.

And they were too much concerned with theory and ideology, to the detriment of action.

Perhaps this group would be different, he told himself, and rejected that thought immediately. He looked at the group. Five men and two women. Of the women, the young, thin one would be a student leader, he surmised, and the older one would be an ideologue, a writer, perhaps, for some small, semi-clandestine newsletter circulated among the sympathetic left. Of the men, two were very young, and the youngest had piercing eyes and a nervous, jerking manner that Borovik didn't like at all. The other was heavy-lidded and had the burly build of a stevedore. Perhaps the young thug would come in handy.

Thinking of thugs and usefulness, Borovik looked over the three older men. Of the two in their early thirties, one had the appearance of a natural leader – a large, well-proportioned bulk combined with an intelligent cast and an alert manner of wait-and-see, give-and-take, that showed confidence and fearlessness. The other was even larger, and exuded an air of peasant-worker solidarity and philosophical purity. He had a strong, open face that made Borovik smile to himself. Borovik thought he looked like one of those idealized poster peasants from the old days, one of those who was always pitching hay for the starving proletariat or tractoring along to glory and victory against the running dogs of the fascist pigs. Borovik instantly thought of a use for him.

The fifth man Borovik found most interesting, as well he might. This was the only one of the seven Canadians who had any kind of a reputation as far as Borovik knew; and his reputation, in the right circles, had an international aspect to it.

He was a man of spare build, in his early sixties, with long, graying hair that framed a stern, square face. The face, behind its glasses, attempted a perpetual look of nobility and severity. It was the face of a religious zealot, of a person with a majestic goal. It shone with the intense glare of a puritan who knows he is absolutely right.

The man's name was Albert Cartier, and it was his doing that the Organization had come into being in the first place. He had built it over a span of forty years, always waiting and watching, making his moves at opportune times, recruiting new members slowly and carefully, often using advanced psychological methods that most people had never heard of. He was crafty and seasoned, hardened, stamped in the fiery mill of experience and reality. He was one of that rare breed – a combination of theoretician and administrator who was not afraid to stand for his rights, to put his body on the line beside those of his workers, who recognized personal danger as part of existence and stood ready to meet it head-on. He was an old-line revolutionary, hard as nails for all his small frame, and ready for any game.

Borovik recognized real power when he saw it, and realized that he would have to bend this man's will to his own in order to accomplish anything on this mission. Well, he would do it. He had no choice. When he wanted something, he got it. He would never give up. He used whatever he found at his disposal to gain his goal. That was the way he operated, and anyone who got in his way would have to be very careful. Borovik was ruthless. With him, no holds were barred. That was why he was still alive.

From the pleased way all these French-Canadians sat and looked at him, Borovik knew they expected to be included as equal partners in this venture. Best to let them believe that, up to a point. He could see that they looked brisk and businesslike, er, workerlike, ready for action. But they were ideological revolutionaries, and therefore nowhere near the technical quality he needed to get this job done. He had brought his own men for that. Meanwhile, he would see what he could do with them. They would all be useful for certain things.

For their part, the Canadians looked across the table at their new allies with determination and a bit of apprehension. They saw three strong men. Borovik, the acknowledged leader, barrel-chested and bullet-headed, sat facing them, flanked by the Algerian on his right and the Argentinian, Rafael Santiago, on his left. The Algerian was tri-lingual, being proficient in Spanish and French and a master of his native Arabic. He was clean-shaven except for a thin black moustache. The Algerian would help to clarify questionable items that arose in French and were difficult to translate into English, which was the ironic, yet obvious, choice of communication between these allies. Borovik had never found the time to learn any French, concentrating instead on his Russian, Spanish, Portuguese, and English.

Borovik never forgot the importance of first impressions, of dominance, in initial meetings of this sort. There were so many things that could go wrong in a plan of this magnitude that he felt it imperative to impress his new acquaintances with his leadership. He must leave no doubt as to who was boss, and he would use any tool that was handy.

The Argentinian was one of his tools; he understood that and was bored and amused by the idea. Whatever Borovik did was fine with him. It left him free, behind a smokescreen of iron and bluster, to go about his work with as little interference as possible from well-meaning friends. He was there to advise on technical questions, to glean information from the Canadians, and to impress. He had a long and well-known record in the fight against imperialism. To some, he was a near-mythic hero. He had been with Guevara in Bolivia at the end.

All three of them, Borovik and his lieutenants, had the clean, healthy glow of men who spent most of their days and nights out-of-doors. Their eyes were bright and never rested. Those eyes were fierce, like the eyes of alert, trained watchdogs. And their bodies were loose with muscles that could tighten faster than instinct alone would draw them.

That is what the French-Canadians saw, and 'wolves' is what Cartier thought of as he began to speak, wolves in the dark forest under bright northern winter stars. The thought drained the blood from his hands and feet as he welcomed his guests. He wasn't sure why he was apprehensive, but he thought he knew, and the thought itself made him uneasy. He had not felt this way since childhood. There was a twinge of some old fear that he could not quite pinpoint.

"Comrade Borovik," he said in a thin, whispery voice. "We of the Central Committee of the Organization welcome you to the Peoples' Republic of Quebec. Our Organization has been host to many comrades from across the sea in the past. Some we have helped in various ways, and some have aided us. But none as illustrious as yourselves have come to us, and with such a generous plan for fulfillment of the request we have sent to you. We are honored that you are here personally, and we are honored by the presence of the good comrades you have brought with you. I extend to you my thanks, and the thanks of all of us."

Borovik cleared his throat and answered. "We are all proud and happy to be here to aid your cause, comrades. The struggle of our French-Canadian comrades is the struggle of us all, and, as you know, it has long been of interest to us." Borovik paused and seemed to concentrate. "Let me first say," he beamed, "that I must congratulate you on your Organization. To move a number of people, as many as we, across so vast a territory, using such ingenious methods, and so smoothly…I would say it bodes well for our future combined endeavors. I want to thank you for your support thus far, and I will say now that we shall return that support to your aims tenfold, if we possibly can. I am more than delighted," he continued. "I…we… are impressed. It is an auspicious start. To have come so far with no, er, problems, from people who might not wish us to be here…" He laughed. "I am assuming that those problem people did not notice us swimming like fish through the great French-Canadian sea!" There was general quiet laughter.

"Well," said Borovik. "You are all to be congratulated. Now," his expression changed abruptly. "Let us get down to business. You needed help and we have brought help. But right now we need help. We need supplies. Equipment. Safe places to stay. Money is no problem. We have all of it you will ever need and more. But we need to disperse and keep in communication. This is no good. You have nine of us here in one place – this rats' nest," he said, sniffing the air. "One raid by your renowned Mounties," he turned the word into a sneer, "and we are hurt. For a while. And your plans are finished, too. So security must be the first order of business. You must enable us to move freely about. Three of us, at least, must get to Montreal. Others of us must be up and down your river. We must disperse. After this meeting, we must never be all together again. Where are you going to put us, what facilities will we have at our disposal, how will we communicate? This is what is necessary."

Cartier collected his thoughts and let out his breath. "First, Comrade," he said, "We have safe houses where you need them. In Montreal, in Three Rivers, here in Quebec City, in Rimouski, as you already know, and in Les Escoumins, as you especially requested.

Besides these, we have other vantage points which may be used in an emergency. Maps and addresses have been prepared for you. Also keys. The houses are well stocked. Each of us has part of this information. We have prepared separately. When we hand over the information to you, you will be the only one to know the exact location of all our facilities. You must be prepared to parcel out this information to those of your comrades, and I include us, of course, as your comrades, whom you feel should have access to the information."

"I will want the names and communications numbers of each of the preparers on all pieces of his or her work, to facilitate implementation," Borovik said. "No," he suddenly added, "numbers will be sufficient." In his mind, he was already preparing to change the plans of the Canadians. Borovik always liked to have his own imprint dominant in any plan.

"Of course," said Cartier. "With the assurance that the communications posts will be manned at all times. That is the second of your concerns, isn't it? Each of the safe houses has a legitimate telephone hook-up. None are under surveillance that we are able to detect. All have been recently rented or bought, for legitimate businesses or by safe-looking middle class citizens for living purposes."

"This place?"

"Rented by an English firm with an interest in repairing marine engines. Solid walls, and a ready reason for roughly-dressed men to move in and out. Not so much a rats' nest as you may think."

"True. Very good. Still, not a place for all of us to be. And I do not like the idea of the wireless being here. A private house is much safer."

"This wireless is only a back-up," said Cartier. "The major communications center is in a private house."

"Where?" Borovik asked.

"On the outskirts of this city," said Cartier.

"My house," said the nervous young type. Borovik looked at him with renewed interest. He studied the young man's face, and found pride there, and haughtiness. A volatile combination, which might work for good or ill. Borovik put his left hand to his lips and was silent. Then he looked at Cartier and nodded. The older man continued.

"So you see, Comrade," he said, "we are protecting you as much as possible. Insulating you, if we can. This way, with only you knowing the extent of the set-up, you can be sure of not having any leaks. We think we have done well by you."

"Mmmmm," Borovik said. "Good. Just so that I have what I need. Now, fill me in on the local situation. I want to know your enemies in the Movement, first."

"Petty squabbles," said the nervous kid.

Borovik looked at him. "Facts, not opinions," he said slowly. But he said it in such a way that the young man found himself forced to swallow. There was something about the way Borovik looked at you, he thought, as if he would cut you to ribbons in the next breath. But he summoned up his courage and went on.

"The FLQ..." he began.

"I didn't ask you!" Borovik exploded. "I am speaking to Comrade Cartier here. Now shut up!"

"I will not be spoken to in that manner!" shouted the kid, and he jumped up and slammed his hand down on the table. The French-Canadians jumped, startled by the noise. The door to the room whipped open, and a man stood in the doorway. A submachine was slung over his arm, and his finger was on the trigger.

All the Quebecois stared at him, and then at Borovik and his two lieutenants, who hadn't turned or even tensed when the door opened behind them, and who now sat easily. Borovik even had a slight smile on his face, as if he were enjoying the show.

"He is trained to do that," he said. "Take it easy. He generally doesn't shoot comrades." He looked at the kid. "Sit down, kid," he said. "You look pale."

The kid sat down.

"Now, Comrade Cartier," Borovik said, "if you will continue..."

Cartier was puzzled at first, but soon realized he was being coerced by Borovik. In the interest of solidarity, however, he felt obliged to continue. He did so, at first warily, then as he became carried away by his topic, with more confidence and strength.

"We had been building the Organization for a long time," he began. "Since 1935, as you know. When the time came for a wider radical front for the situation, in the early sixties, our cadres encouraged the growth of Le Front de Liberation du Quebec. It was formed, and prospered. We, of course, moved into positions of responsibility in the

Front. Gradually, we brought it around to our way of thinking. But unfortunately, there were certain elements at work that disregarded good advice and determined upon a premature showdown with the Federal Government in Ottawa."

"Thereupon, the Laporte-Cross kidnapping?"

"Exactly. In a supposed attempt to drive the Federal Government to an excessive use of power, and thereby show it for the fascist reactionary monolith that it is, or, if there happened to be a pleasant surprise, to show the government as weak-kneed and ready to topple, like an old tree riddled with rot."

"But it didn't work," said Borovik. "Why not? Was it premature? Not well thought out? What?"

"A combination of things," said Cartier. "The government operated from a base both of strength and weakness, if you can understand that."

"Please clarify it."

"Some of its actions seemed to portray it as ready to capitulate to the demands of the comrades. Meanwhile, the state police and informers who had been busy infiltrating the ranks for years struck suddenly at every cell they could reach. The War Powers Act was suddenly put into force and the army swept through the land. Over half our cells were destroyed. Over five hundred of our comrades were incarcerated. It was almost as if the government had been waiting for this provocation to destroy us. We tried to paint the government as oppressive, but that was difficult to do when every half-hour brought a new concession to the kidnappers. That was for the media, of course, but it worked on the masses of the population. Some even turned informer, and meanwhile our infrastructure was being ripped to shreds by the secret police."

"What was the strength of the FLQ at the time?" Borovik asked.

"Our plan called for five hundred cells of five members and one cell leader per cell. The cells were to be divided into fifty regions, ten cells per region, each region with a commanding officer. Keeping on top of everything, a central committee of ten comrades. But actually, the infrastructure was never completed, had never matured, when that faction of hotbloods decided on the showdown."

"A pity," mused Borovik.

"Perhaps not," Cartier said. "Perhaps it was a positive event, all things considered. We really had no idea of the amount of infiltration in the general organization by elements of the secret federal apparatus. After everything had died down a bit, and we had a chance to survey the situation, we could see that the Mounties and the Ministry of Justice had knowledge of at least one hundred and fifty of our cells, out of a total of about three hundred which were operative. That is, comrades from one hundred and fifty cells had been picked up by the police. Now whether or not the police knew what they were doing makes no difference; we simply had to dismember those cells. Even those comrades we could trust implicitly had been compromised. Now, they cannot be made privy to decisions or new knowledge. They must act on the outskirts of the structure. They must never contact us, because they may be known, and they may be surveilled and followed. They can never again be in leadership positions, but must be content to be followers. And they must follow at a distance."

"So," Borovik said, "It was quite damaging, wasn't it? What else did you do to protect yourselves, besides disassociating from your old comrades?"

"We withdrew from the Front. Not as a group, but individually, over a period of time. We returned to our old cells in the Organization. This is the cause of the friction. The remaining leadership of the FLQ considers us to be individually traitorous, and consequently we are shunned by the FLQ membership at large. Since they don't know where we've gone, they simply assume we have gotten cold feet, and have been psychologically defeated by the government. I can't blame them. If I did not have the information I do, I might think the same."

"It is not a good situation, but I have to agree with your assessment," said Borovik. "I would have done the same as you. The core must be protected at all cost." He paused. "But what of the FLQ now? What kind of shape is it in? It is your buffer, and it should be kept healthy. At least healthy enough to protect you."

"Yes, and it is not," Cartier said. "It was damaged by our defections, and the loss of support from others who assumed that the leadership was breaking apart. You know the type – the adventurers, the bomb throwers, who are in it for the excitement, with no grounding in dialectics."

Borovik didn't like that, but he had to admit the truth of it. He didn't dislike pure adventurers as much as he disliked pure theoretical revolutionaries, but there was truth in what Cartier had said. There had to be an amalgam. A person fused to both action and thought: that was the ideal.

Borovik pondered this quickly, and let out his breath and frowned. Cartier took this to be a sign of disagreement, but even though he knew he had stepped on Borovik's toes, he shrugged off the friction and went on. His plan was too important to be defeated simply by some strained relationships, so he swallowed his pride and continued to fill Borovik in with the truth beyond the propaganda and the conflict.

"So the FLQ is splitting into factions. There is still a structure, but it is unstable. One thing that is positive, though, is that the programs we introduced and promulgated within the FLQ are now being percolated through the mainstream of Quebec society. The Parti Quebecois has embraced many of our ideals, and it is good to see the beneficial effect it has had on our people. So even while the FLQ disintegrates, its programs are adopted. The reality changes. The entirety of Quebec is closer to the left now than it was before the affair. There has been some forced accommodation on both sides."

"But you are not a part of it," Borovik said. "That must hurt."

Cartier sighed. "It hurts, yes, Comrade Borovik. But not so much for personal reasons. Consider. If the Parti Quebecois leads Quebec towards nationalism, using our ideas, still it is a drive toward nationalism, not toward progressive socialism. Once a fascist, always a fascist. Once a nationalist, always a nationalist. Levesque's moves may employ our ideas, but he will use them for his own gain, not for the growth of the Movement. That hurts." Cartier paused.

Borovik was silent, and then said slowly, "And Comrade Cartier, why should I help you, instead of the FLQ? How will that help the worldwide movement?"

Cartier looked at him and leaned against the table. "The FLQ is in complete disarray. Infiltrated. Incapable of concerted action. Its ideas have been taken over by factions more to the center. It is essentially defunct, but it has done its job.

"So now," Cartier continued, "the FLQ must be abolished. We must gather the forces of the people to us and form another organization, one that will operate for the final push. Because it is time. It is time for the final battle here. We must be ready to infiltrate the government structure and be sure that, when independence comes, the government acts as a peoples' government. It must be governed by our Leninist principles.

"To do this, we must build our strength. To build our strength, we must rely on our former comrades of the FLQ – the ones whose cover has not been broken. We must attract them to us and overcome their dissatisfaction. To do this, we must show them that you are backing us. When they see that, they will come to us. So, when this proposed action disrupts the economic conference in such a spectacular way, and we take credit for it, they will come. Have no fear of that. They will come, and we shall have created a fine structure, ready to take over the government at a moment's notice."

"What is your strength?" Borovik asked.

"We have twenty-two cells," said Cartier, "containing one hundred thirty members."

"And the FLQ still has some one hundred fifty cells," said Borovik doubtfully.

"But the FLQ is a sham!" said Cartier, startled that Borovik might be contemplating switching his support. "We are the core. You have said it yourself."

"Not quite, I didn't," Borovik said. "Don't try to put words into my mouth, Comrade."

The man in his thirties whom Borovik had thought of as a worker-peasant type spoke for the first time. "It is this simple," he said stolidly. "The FLQ is soft. We are hard." Then he sat there simply staring into Borovik's eyes.

Cartier continued his persuasion. "Think of the over-all effect, Comrade General! When independence is declared, and we are in position, what is created is a Peoples' Republic right on the doorstep of America. Physically connected to it, along a border that can be crossed with ease anytime one wishes. Imagine the possibilities!"

Borovik had, in fact, already imagined the possibilities. He planned to return to Cuba through the United States. "Crossed with ease?" he said. "Tell that to that German girl who tried it a while back." He paused, looked at Cartier, and said, "Comrade, I would like to talk to you alone for a minute."

Borovik and Cartier stood, and together they went to the far end of the room, their heads close together, Borovik's arm around the older man's shoulders. The rest of the Canadians sat at the table, watching warily and fidgeting a little.

"Comrade Cartier," Borovik said, in a voice that was almost a whisper. "Comrade, your analysis seems almost *too* progressive. But it is thrilling, and I believe you are correct. It will take only a few more blows, with a sledgehammer, perhaps, but still, only a few more blows, before the whole Canadian Confederation crumbles into dust. I can feel it. I know it. It can be done. So. I will support you. I will help you. It means exposing the Organization, you know, and that can be dangerous. Are you prepared to face that danger?"

"General," said Cartier, "you know I have never shirked personal danger. It is nothing to me."

"I did not mean that," Borovik said. "I meant the danger of watching the organization you have built over forty years crumbling along with the enemy. That is a very real danger, you know. It may be necessary. Can you stand that?"

Cartier was silent for a minute. There was a struggle going on deep within him. He stuttered and said, "The Organization is not my organization. It is the Revolution's organization. I am the custodian of it. If it needs to be destroyed for the good of the Revolution, then let it be destroyed."

"I am glad to hear you say that, Comrade," Borovik said. "Sometimes people lose sight of the Revolution and begin to build things selfishly, for themselves, like any bourgeois. I am glad you have not fallen into that trap. Now, Comrade," he continued. "There are some demands I must make if we are to carry off the operation in good order."

"Comrade General," Cartier said, alarmed. "We have always run this organization democratically. We are great believers in participatory democracy, especially at this level of the structure. Everyone here has something to contribute. They will feel…disregarded…if they are not allowed to contribute to the discussion. I suggest that you ask for their opinions and information. It will make things go more smoothly."

"No, Comrade," Borovik said. "If they are true revolutionaries they will recognize that the time for…for theoretical participation is over. It is time for action, for discipline, for obedience."

Cartier thought for a time. "Very well," he said quietly.

"Good," said Borovik. "You have made many concessions. I ask you to make just a few more. Is that agreeable to you?" Borovik knew how disagreeable it was to be force-fed so many pills all at once, but there was no choice. There was no time.

"That depends on what the concessions are, Comrade General. What did you have in mind?"

"Fine," said Borovik. "First, and this particular information need go no farther than yourself, what I am doing for you is tied to some other projects I hope to accomplish while I am here. So sometimes, I might be taking positions, doing things, in ways that might surprise you. Always keep in mind that I am going to be very busy."

"I had wondered why you had come to us in person," said Cartier. "It was not necessary for what we had proposed."

"So now you see," Borovik said.

Cartier smiled wryly with his thin lips. "Yes," he said. "Everything."

"I guarantee you," Borovik said, raising his hand in a pledge, "that whatever else we do will appear to be a part of your general plan, and the rewards will redound in your favor."

Cartier nodded. "And what else, General?"

Borovik pressed his lips together. "I cannot work with that young man of yours," he said, gesturing with his head toward the table. "Call it a matter of personality, if you will. I don't like him. I don't trust him. As a matter of fact, I hate him, and I am sure he feels the same way about me."

"General," said Cartier. "It would take a fool not to see that the two of you clashed, but I assure you he is trustworthy. He is quick, intelligent, and smart. He has many duties on this central committee."

"Divide his duties among the others of the committee, Comrade. While I am here, he is not to be on it. What he and I have is animal hatred toward each other. It is not rational, but psychologically I am sure you can recognize it as more than a simple difference of opinion. It is pure race hatred. His genes and mine are opposed. This will cause disaffection sooner or later. He will try to interfere with my plans, and

I cannot tolerate that. You can see that, can't you?"

Cartier had to agree. The theory of genetic antagonism arising for no known reason between two individuals was still looked upon with more than a grain of salt by the psychological community, but whether it was true absolute antagonism or a combination of physical, societal, and attitudinal factors bore no relevance here. Borovik held the power and would not yield. The younger man would have to go.

"He will not go quietly," Cartier said. "You see how volatile he is."

"Let me handle that," Borovik said. "One other thing. Immediately at the end of this meeting, I want to look over the supplies you have gathered for us. That will be myself and two of the three comrades who depart for Montreal. They will have to leave quickly, and all must be in order. Bring those who purchased the supplies with you."

Before Cartier could affirm this plan, Borovik turned and shouted, "Ahmed!" The door opened again, and the same soldier who had appeared before was there again, in the same attitude. "Ahmed," Borovik said resolutely. "Call our comrades. We have work to do!"

Ahmed saluted and disappeared. In the same breath, Borovik turned toward the Canadians. "We are agreed that your plan is good. It is time. We will do it."

Borovik's men filed silently into the room. "Meet the comrades you will work with," he said to the Quebecois. "Trust them like brothers. They are all dedicated to your cause, and to the cause of the worldwide success of the people. Now it is your time, my brothers and sisters. Now is the time for Canada to feel the glorious shock of revolutionary progress! Now is the time to do all you can, as quickly as you can, to insure the success of our labors. Vive Le Quebec Libre! Long live the proletarian socialist revolution! On to our work now, quickly!"

Borovik's men approached the table and grasped hands with the French-Canadians, who rose to greet them. Borovik turned to the Argentinian and said, "Rafa, take Comrade Gauthier to the communications room and let him show you the set-up of the equipment." Borovik turned toward the kid. "Comrade," he said, "please excuse my outburst before. It is just that I am a bit nervous. Understandable, right? Would you please leave the plan of your house here before you go with Comrade Rafael? Thank you. I am sorry."

Gauthier acknowledged the apology and strode off with the Argentinian. The others fell to exchanging information and code names, and setting itineraries and schedules. Borovik's voice boomed out above the talking. "Just remember this. We don't leave in a bunch. Dietrich and Vasyli, you will be staying in town. You will leave with this comrade." Borovik put his hand on the shoulder of the one in his thirties who looked the part of the leader. "Comrade Alain, his name is. He'll show you to his house. Stay there until further notice from me."

Borovik went down the list, matching his own men with those central committee members who would be most advantageous. He had received fact sheets on all the committee members the day before, and memorized them. Retention of detail was one of his major distinctions. It served him well.

Within the hour Borovik and Cartier, along with Carmelo and Ahmed, two of the munitions experts of the team, had climbed down the dingy staircase to the third floor. There, they were met by Wilfred Lavigueur, the committee member who had reminded Borovik of the old poster peasants. Lavigueur was impressed by more esoteric machines than tractors, however, and Cartier had placed him in charge of accumulating the hardware for this enterprise.

He had done well. The team members were delighted. They smiled at the variety of blasting caps, mostly #6 and #8, available to them. Beside gelignite, there was C4 and specialized M118. They were very happy about the three old T-33 surplus wing tanks that had been bought in the States at different army surplus stores and imported illegally into Canada by three different routes. The Emerson Mark 6 GE Rebreathers impressed them. But what really took their interest were the three customized Sea Robin underwater scooters. They sat there gleaming in their dull blackness like snowmobiles that had been stripped of their treads. They were the newest and best underwater machines that could be bought. Carmelo and Ahmed wanted to try them right away. They joked about them, and looked at them lovingly. They were beautiful machines.

Beyond them, in the shadows, stacked in piles of boxes up the dingy walls, were all kinds of equipment, stripped and cleaned and ready for use instantly. The third floor was a wonderland of military technology, disguised as a ship engine refitter's storeroom.

Over the next couple of hours, all who were going to leave went by different doors and different routes, using different means of transportation. Only those who were to remain in this location, which would be used as a warehouse and supply depot, had not departed. They were two of Borovik's team and the young female student leader. Borovik had asked her to stay personally, to act as messenger and lookout. He had other reasons, too. Already one of the team members was looking down at her, grinning, and asking what she thought her duties were toward foreign comrades who had not seen a woman for a long time. Borovik liked to keep his boys happy.

Comrade Gauthier was also in the warehouse, locked in a closet, handcuffed, and asleep from a relaxant that had been shot into his arm. He had never reached the communications room. Rafa had quietly taken him out of commission on the way down the hall. Rafa was good at that. That was one of the reasons he was with Borovik. Borovik took no chances, and Rafa was his shield as much as Borovik was Rafa's.

Chapter 10

A View of the River

Claude Le Claire stood at the railing of the Dufferin Terrace, high on the cliff above the river under the long shadows of the afternoon sun. His elbows were propped on the wide top railing, and he gazed northeast, down the river toward the point where the Ile d'Orléans plugged the channel like a cork. He had a similar view from his office window, but it wasn't the same. Inside, he was cut off from the wind, and so his entire perception of the scene was changed. From the office window, the eye concentrated on the cityscape. The interest was on buildings, on the old stonework and venerable copper rooves, and the quaint way the old buildings had of sticking up at odd angles all over town.

But out here, in a crisp breeze, the eye held to the land itself. The scene was larger, under an immense blue sky. You could concentrate on the swell of the land, and before you saw the land there was the river, flowing placidly along beneath the green Laurentian hills; the great river—the St. Lawrence itself, beginning to open and widen on its long journey down to the sea.

Le Claire stood and watched the river. Over three hundred ships passed beneath the walls of Quebec City every month, bringing to the interior of Canada and the United States goods from all the seaports of the world; taking from the interior goods destined for all the nations of the world. The river was the heart of the city, the great vein of commerce for the whole of the Canadian Confederation, and at a time like this, from this vantage point, its importance was palpable. Without it, there would be no Quebec, or Montreal, or Toronto. A dozen great cities on both sides of the border would sink into oblivion with the loss of this grand stream.

Le Claire loved the river right now. His eyes teared not from the wind, and his throat tightened not from the tobacco smoke from his pipe. No, Claude Le Claire simply loved his city. He loved it and he would do his best to protect it. It was that simple. He straightened, took a last look at the river, and turning away from it, walked back to his office refreshed.

Le Claire went, and the river rolled on. It swept straight toward the northeast. At Quebec it picked up the waters of the Chaudière and the St. Charles and the Montmorency. Farther downstream, at Tadoussac, the Saguenay swelled into it. A dozen other great rivers added to its strength. Past Rivière-du-Loup it flowed, and past Les Escoumins, where ships anchored to pick up the river pilots who would guide them as far as Quebec City. A hundred and fifty miles from Quebec, it passed Rimouski, and a hundred miles beyond that, swollen so that it was no longer a river but an estuary, it swirled past the great rounded peninsula of the Gaspe, and mixed its waters with those of the Atlantic in the gigantic Gulf of St. Lawrence, formed and bounded by the Maritime Provinces.

And out beyond the protecting breakwaters of Newfoundland and Nova Scotia, in the wide Atlantic, ships made for the St. Lawrence—ten ships per day, three hundred per month. One of those ships brought oil from Kuwait destined for Cleveland. Another, a small British freighter of 20,000 tons, brought rice from Thailand for the mills and restaurants of Montreal. Far to the south, they steamed toward the mists and fogs of the Newfoundland coast, aiming for the Cabot Strait, past Louisbourg and Cape Breton.

Chapter 11

The Reel of the Hanged One

Kearney arrived in Rue du Trésor a little after eight on Tuesday night. He located Marc easily. Marc got up immediately and led him down the street to where the singers were sitting on the curb, almost in the same place as the night before. Marc plunked himself down next to them and motioned for Kearney to sit, also. They sat while they waited for the singers to end their song.

When they had finished, Marc, still sketching, said to them in a thick accent, "Hey, my friends. This American wants to record your songs. He thinks you are good singers. He wants to send you to Hollywood and make you famous. You want to be famous? Then sing for us."

The singers stared at Marc, then looked at each other, bewildered. Then there was a lot of rapid French, and the girl turned to Marc, felt his forehead, and said something else, at which everybody laughed.

"Ah, Monsieur Jack," said Marc, "They are wondering if I have lost my memory, or my tongue, and they want to know what is the strange language I am speaking. So if you will excuse me…"

Then there was a tremendous amount of French tumbling through the air, and individual words that Kearney caught. Rene said, "Hollywood producteur, aha!" and "Voila! Une mimic!" And the girl Genevieve seemed quite pleased, if you could tell by the way her statements, full of surprise, went up the keyboard and turned into questions.

It was Genevieve who eventually turned to Kearney. While Rene and the other singer looked on with interest, she said, "Monsieur, why do you wish to record us?"

She had difficulty using English, Kearney realized. She had paused to translate silently before she spoke, and although the English was correct, it was heavily accented.

Kearney looked beyond the girl's words to her dark eyes. The air was cold this night, and in her costume of jeans and a dark maroon sweater, with her long dark hair outlining her face, she looked as alive as a young wildcat. Her cheeks were flushed with health and life, and her eyes flashed.

Kearney spoke to her eyes. "I record songs wherever I go," he said. "I want to record them before they disappear. I don't know if your songs are really old, or new, but they are beautiful songs, and I would like to keep them. As a memory of Quebec, if for no other reason."

Genevieve translated for Rene, who had been sitting and looking vacantly about during the entire exchange. Now he roused himself and considered the situation. After stroking his chin and humming to himself for a moment, Rene decided for it with a smile and a laugh of assent.

It would be a new lark for them, something they had never done before. "Of course you realize, Monsieur," Rene went on, half-mumbling, shrugging, considering as he went…"that we are not professional singers and that we do this with the understanding that we can hear what we have done later, if we want to, and have you recorded any other songs here in Quebec?" All this was translated through Genevieve and Marc.

In answer to the last question Kearney said, "I recorded the band at the Citadel, at the Changing of the Guard ceremony this afternoon."

At which the third singer, who was named Michel, screamed a death rattle and collapsed against the wall. Rene and Genevieve looked at Kearney with faces turned to stone.

Marc said, "Aha! Les fascistes!"

Kearney knew he had made a mistake. Perhaps not a bad one; more of an interesting one, if anything.

"They are on this tape, Monsieur?" said Rene, speaking for the first time in English, for in fact he knew English very well.

"No, on this one," said Kearney, holding up another tape. "Why? Would you like to listen?"

"No, no, no, no, no!" said Rene, with some alarm. "Why would I want to listen to them?"

"Well, they're pretty good, if you like marches," said Kearney.

"Rumph, rumph, rumph, rumph!" Michel growled a tempo from deep in his throat, meanwhile pounding out a march beat on his guitar.

"Monsieur," said Genevieve. "Do you not realize that they are our enemy?"

"What? No! I'm sorry!" stammered Kearney. "Your enemy? But they speak French. All the commands are in French. They play French songs. Haven't you ever been there?"

"No!" said Genevieve indignantly. "I have no wish to go there. Why should I go there?"

"They are in the pay of the British, do you not understand?" said Rene. "They are as much a part of the British overlords as the big hotels or that damned tower they've just built. They are what we are fighting against. They sit on top of this city and hold it in chains. Do you not know what is going on here, Monsieur? The French is for the tourists. Their weapons are British."

Rene got control of himself. "Pardon, Monsieur, it is obvious you do not realize the extent of the politics in Quebec. Let us give you some real Quebec music, so you have something to listen to besides that rumph-rumph-rumph-rumph, eh? But not on the same tape. Ah! Throw the other away!"

They tuned the guitars and began to sing. At first it was awkward. The singers were nervous and forgot the words to songs, or sang the wrong verses, and stopped often to talk to each other and laugh. And Kearney had constantly to adjust the portable microphone and be sure it wasn't kicked over, for as soon as the singing began, the crowd gathered to listen, which doubly complicated things.

But soon the singers caught the spirit of the songs. They took them and made them work the way they were supposed to, and Kearney got a solid half-hour of music he had never heard before, and he was very pleased. There was one in particular that he liked best of all of them. The one from the previous night, the one where he could only understand the last word, 'Liberté!'

"That one's a beauty," he said. "I don't understand the words, but the music is beautiful."

"Would you like to know the meaning of it?" Genevieve asked him.

"Do you know the meaning of liberté?" Rene cut in.

"As in liberté, fraternité, égalité? The saying of the French revolutionaries?" Kearney answered. "Yes, I think I know that, at least," he smiled. "But as for the rest, excuse my ignorance, but I never studied French."

"Hmmmph," Rene said, ruminating.

"Would you like me to translate it for you?" asked Genevieve.

"I would love that," Kearney said, looking directly at her.

"Well," she said quietly, "It is a song of the spring. I will translate the last few lines anyway, no?" Geneviève translated it for him as well as she was able. She blushed when she spoke, not so much from any feeling of unease, but rather with happiness and the pleasure of what she was doing. She was meeting the song in one language and setting it free in another, giving it to someone who hadn't understood it before and might now. She liked the idea of that. Kearney watched her hands moving in the delicate way she had, and was amused and pleased by her happiness.

'Vois les fleurs ont recommence,' she said. That is, 'See, the flowers have begun again.' The next, 'Dans l'étable crient les nouveau-nés,' that is 'Newborns are crying in the barn.' 'Les bourgeons sortent de la mort' which is 'The buds seem to…to come out of death,' 'Papillons' you know papillons? No? 'Papillons ont des manteaux d'or'. Papillons are butterflies, Monsieur. 'Butterflies have coats of gold.' The next, 'Pres du ruisseau sont alignées les fées' is 'Fairies are aligned by the streams,' and the last, Monsieur, is 'Et les crapauds chantent la liberté!' Do you know crapauds, sir?"

"No," said Kearney, fascinated.

Genevieve hesitated, took a deep breath, looked into his eyes with a special sadness, and said, "The crapauds are toads, Monsieur. 'And even the toads sing of la liberté. And even the toads sing of la liberté!'"

Rene was looking at Kearney with his right eyebrow cocked. "And you understand the meaning of the word 'toad', Monsieur?" he asked. "Who the toads are? Why they are chanting of Liberté? Perhaps, in your country, you may call them frogs."

Genevieve's eyes seemed to bore into Kearney's own.

Kearney considered, and said "I think I am beginning to understand. But not fully…not yet." He paused, smiled, and said, "But I believe I have found some excellent teachers. Thank you."

"You would do well to continue your studies, Monsieur Jack," Rene said, gripping his pipe tightly between his teeth. "If you wish to befriend us, to study our songs, it would be well to understand our culture, eh? And our history."

"Rene," Kearney said, "I think that is excellent advice."

"Ah! Tres bien!," said Rene, relaxing. "Let's go have a beer, and we will tell you of ourselves."

Rene invited Michel and Marie, a girl who had happened by and stayed to listen to them sing, and Marc and Genevieve to a small restaurant, La Nouvelle-France, which had an outdoor garden that could be entered directly from Rue du Trésor. They all sat around one of the large outdoor tables while the waiter brought beer. They listened to the tape as it played back, and laughed at their singing. Rene proposed that they all go to a little place on Rue St. Flavien in the French Quarter, so that Kearney could hear some more good music, if he chose.

"So you can hear something besides your ka-thump ka-thump ka-thump American music, Jack. That is why you like miserable band music. Aha! Ka-thump!" said Rene, draining his stein of beer.

"What place are you thinking of?" asked Marc.

"The Two Guitars. Richard Bézier is playing there," said Rene, making circles in the air with his pipe. "And we can pick up Angelique on the way, if she will let go of her easel and pencils."

"Oh!" said Genevieve, "Monsieur Jack, you must come! It is worth it. Bezier is…is…extremely…how you say… magnifique!"

So they all went out to the street again, and down the route by now familiar to Kearney, down Rue Buade between Holt-Renfrew and the Cathedral of Notre Dame, picking up Angelique on the way. And then they all swept around the corner of the cathedral and down the hill of Rue St. Famille, Marc complaining the whole time about how much Bezier was charging and how he should give free concerts for the people.

But Rue St. Famille was eerie in the dark shadows of the night. The Quebecois looked like panthers in those shadows, and went prancing along, almost running, calling and laughing to each other, and Kearney was hard pressed to keep up with them and watch the unfamiliar outlines of the buildings and streets at the same time.

All he knew was that the avenue constantly descended until suddenly the group halted and formed a ragged circle in the center of the empty street. Rene turned and looked at Kearney.

"This is where the American was killed maybe two weeks ago, Jack," he said. "Perhaps you have heard of it? The diplomat?"

" Here?" said Kearney. "Right here?"

"Right where we are standing. See any blood? Careful! Don't slip!" said Rene. "Someone came right out of that house there," he said, pointing. "And Boom! Boom! Twice in the head. The guy never had a chance. Too bad for him. Maybe. I didn't know him." Rene shrugged. "Maybe he was a bad guy. In that case, good."

"I read about it," said Kearney, looking around. His shoulders gave an involuntary shiver as he thought of Rene's hard words: 'Right here. See any blood?'

"I read about it, but nobody says anything definite. What do you think?" he asked Rene.

Rene lowered his voice to a conspiratorial whisper.

"Some say he was CIA," he said mockingly, and raised his voice. "But probably it was something more usual, like a woman, or drugs. There are some rough people in this town, and they aren't all political. Just most of them!" And Rene gave his wild horselaugh, breaking the dark spell that had woven itself around the little group.

"Enough of this!" said Angelique, and started off, turning the corner into Rue Couillard. They all followed her quickly. The ghost in the street was still too fresh to provoke the way Rene had done.

Kearney stole a quick glance back at the dark street, seeing it curve away into the night; seeing the dark, looming buildings on either side. Then he went on, keeping up with the others.

A yellow light cast by the sparsely spaced street lamps in Rue

Couillard threw dirty shadows on the old stone walls. Kearney and his new Quebecois friends walked slowly along between the walls that rose to meet the red-tiled rooves somewhere above in the murky night sky. They went on like this for some two blocks, until they arrived at a place that had no name.

On the window next to the entrance door there was the silhouette of two guitars with their necks crossed. There was nothing else—no sign, no notice, no menu, no advertisement of any sort.

"Look," said Kearney. "If I am going to record, I will want the permission of the singer and of the management."

"No trouble, no trouble," said Rene, his pipe sticking out of his mouth at a precarious angle. "I will get the manager for you. Come in after you have spoken with him."

Rene and the others disappeared inside, and presently the door opened and a man peered out. Kearney had been looking down the street, puzzling things out, and the figure in the doorway startled him with its sudden "Oui?"

"Good evening," said Kearney. "I am recording singers, for my own use, my own listening, and I would like to record the man who is singing here tonight. I understand he is very good. May I have your permission?"

"Oh, of course, of course," said the figure. "But speak to him before you begin. Do you speak French? No? I will speak to him for you. Yes, he is very good, for a Canadian."

The voice went on rapidly, as if its owner had not spoken to anyone for a long time. "But tell me," it said. "Why do you want to record these people? They are not that good. They do nothing but imitate France, my country. They think they are French. Bah!"

The figure moved closer to Kearney.

"When they come to France," the voice said, taking on the traces of a sneer, "they try to speak French. They speak whatever it is they speak here, and they call it French. Bah! We cannot understand them, and they become insulted. But they don't know French! Can you believe that, Monsieur?"

"But you are here," said Kearney. "You came here. Why did you come, if you despise the country so much?"

"Bah!" said the Frenchman. "It was an adventure. I did not believe the bad things I heard. I believed only the good. It was a good deal," he said conspiratorially. "From the Quebec government, no less. My friends told me, but I would not listen. They are wild Indians, these people. This is what we call them when they come to France, and we are right. Do you like these people, Monsieur? Do you like this place? I will sell it to you. The next time I come over here, I will go to New York, where it is civilized!"

Kearney just stood there and smiled.

"Now I will waste no more of your time with my problems, Monsieur," said the cafe owner. "Come in, come in. Just remember that what you are recording is not true French."

The proprietor led Kearney into a dark vestibule, and then opened an inner door into a whole other world. Outside was the black northern night, full of shadows and deserted streets. In here was this large, stone-walled room divided by great rough wooden beams, where the light came from candles placed not only on the tables but in sconces hung on the walls. The candlelight flickered and picked out of the shadows a room full of people who murmured and laughed, and their shadows danced through the room. There was a general happy mood here of people who were sharing a good time. The setting spoke of a different time and place, and surely, thought Kearney, of a whole different society.

Outside, a visitor could be entranced by the quaint buildings and interesting shops, the various special events and the exotic setting of a city never seen before. But in here, in this space that seemed to float through and somehow to abridge time, one could seem to understand the people and the spirit behind those buildings. Here was the heart of this young culture, listening to itself, learning from itself, building itself, its own attitudes, its own future. Here was the leaven that gave rise to the future of French Canada, and anyone who had ever seen it could never say that the Quebecois were not a distinct race, with a distinct dream.

While Kearney located his new friends, who were motioning to him from a large table set in a corner of the room against the wall, the proprietor approached the singer, who sat by himself in a chair propped against the small window. He bent and conferred with the singer, who nodded affirmatively and got ready to begin, tuning and retuning the strings of his guitar. The cafe owner straightened, and spotting Kearney, made a circle with his thumb and index finger in that timeless sign of Gallic well-being.

Kearney set up his recorder, adjusted the noise level, and waited. The room hushed, and Bezier began his introduction in a low voice that invited the audience's attention. Then he began to sing:

File la laine, file les jours,
Garde ma peine et mon amour,
Livre d'images des rêves lourds,
Ouvre la page à l'éternel retour.

Genevieve translated the chorus for the American, whispering it to him:

Spin the wool, spin the days,
Keep my sorrow and my love,
My picture book of sultry dreams –
Open the page to the eternal return.

Bezier was a burly, big-boned man with broad shoulders. An observer might expect him to put those shoulders into his songs with a mighty shove, but he did not. He respected the songs, respected both the lyrics and the melodies, and he treated his songs with a wonderful gentleness.

Kearney watched this man with the wide forehead and large nose, with the wide face and body that seemed to stretch to encompass everyone within the room, and he realized that here was not a simple performer sending out sounds that rhymed and chimed and jingled and clattered in the night. Here was a man who was a source of this culture. His songs reflected the birth cries of the culture. They were a blended mixture of old and new French songs, of old songs of New France and new songs of Quebec, and they took the audience and invited it to come closer, to come into the song and understand it, take of its power, and be comforted by its immense age and depth. These were songs that started from the soul— the soul of the singer and the soul of his world.

And after the songs were over and the applause had ended, the audience broke into excited commentary. It was obvious that the singer had unleashed all kinds of ideas, but Kearney had no notion of what they were. His new friends were too excited to do much more translating for him. He sat there sipping his cider and watching his tape rewind.

Suddenly, a big metal sphere came rumbling down the table toward him. It was coming slowly, so he had plenty of time to throw his arm between it and his machine. He grabbed the sphere with his free hand and brought it to a stop to examine it. At first he thought it was a bowling ball, but it was a bit too small for that, and it didn't have any holes for fingers, either. Everyone at the table was convulsed with laughter.

"What the hell is that?" asked Kearney.

"An English ball," laughed Rene. "See what we do to our enemies?"

"A cannon ball," explained Genevieve. "Liberated from the museum."

"An English cannon ball?" exclaimed Kearney.

"Of course," said Marc. "Soon there will be only the French cannon balls left, and history will be straightened out a bit."

"Pass it on," said Genevieve.

With a crash that brought on more laughter, Kearney delivered the metal ball to the next table. Soon the entire room was laughing over the progress of the cannon ball from table to table, patron to patron, while the French proprietor, in consternation, tried to capture it and get it out of circulation. Kearney smiled at the man's anxiety and understood a little better his lack of esteem for the Quebecois. If things like this went on in his place every night, life was being made very interesting for the Frenchman. He could see the fellow constantly wondering when the police would drop by and find cannon balls—stolen cannon balls—rumbling across the table tops. Scratch one untaxed business and a lot of profit.

When the little group left that night, Kearney had a deeper awareness of a culture he had known nothing about three days before. He also realized, from the look that he and Genevieve exchanged when they agreed to meet again the following night, that his relationship with the Canadienne could slip out of the casual category very easily.

This troubled him somewhat. He was just slightly, and happily, bewildered. He knew what was happening, but he didn't know why.

It wasn't supposed to happen. He didn't want it to, and he thought he had guarded against it.

Genevieve didn't fully understand it either. As Rene and Angelique drove her home, she sat very quietly in the back seat and scarcely listened to their bantering conversation. Her silence was out of character for her. She had a lot of things on her mind, but beyond her thoughts there was a happy glow somewhere deep within her. It was something that brought a shy smile to her lips and a lightness to her heart. The crazy foreigner had touched her in some way. She was nineteen and it was summer in Quebec, and suddenly it didn't matter much what happened tomorrow, politically or otherwise. For the first time in a long time, Genevieve felt free.

WEDNESDAY, JUNE 23RD,

"We are especially desperate men. Our backs are to the wall. We shall defend our culture and our faith. If one wishes not to be hurt, one must get out of the way."

Marc Bellemare, Separatist (FLQ-RIM)

Chapter 12

Hit and Miss

Late Wednesday morning, Comrade Alain and his two charges, the saboteurs Vasyli and Dietrich, were at the bottom of the hill of Cote de la Fabrique where it emptied into Rue St. Jean. The street formed the tip of a triangle with the narrow Rue Garneau, so anyone who came down the hill and wanted to turn into Garneau would have to execute an almost 180-degree turnabout to get where he wanted to go. At the same time, he would have no idea what was waiting for him around the bend.

This situation caused the terrorists no apprehension whatsoever. They had been concerned that someone could follow them on the drive into town, so they had taken precautions there. Alain had modified his route and destination. Instead of going directly to the vicinity of the warehouse in the Lower Town, he had driven into the Upper Town and parked in an underground garage near the City Hall.

This was simple caution on his part. Neither he nor his comrades had noticed anything amiss when they left his house in St. Foy, and nothing out of the ordinary had happened on the way into town. It was just a vague sense of being observed, which they dismissed as a case of collective nerves. The saboteurs were veterans who knew there was no such thing as a man of steel. They accepted a few twinges and jumpy nerves as an integral part of any operation. But precautions were good.

Precautions were not as effective as usual this time, though of this they were unaware. Alain acted without access to all the facts. He did not know that his cover had been blown some time ago. He did not know that he was now extremely interesting to a lot of people he had never met.

Just as Alain, Dietrich, and Vasyli reached the corner of de la Fabrique and Garneau, two joggers in green warm-up suits came out of Rue Garneau and crashed into them. First they stumbled into Alain, forcing him back against his companions, and then they managed to entwine themselves with all three of the conspirators so that, for a few seconds, all five men were turning around every which way. After hasty apologies, the joggers ran up Cote de la Fabrique and out of sight.

From his vantage point in the park high on the hill across the street, Bannerman had photographed the whole melee. Now, as he put away his high-speed, high-powered camera, he could hardly keep from laughing. The conspirators, after initially gawking at Sackman and Hefelfinger as they jogged away, were now looking sharply in all directions for enemies and finding none. They wouldn't find any, either, Bannerman knew. He was the only one that they had to fear at the moment, and he was obscured among crowds of mid-morning shoppers. Sparrow was down in the garage, out of sight, bugging Alain's car with a small radio transmitter, and no other operatives were in on this little part of the caper. Bannerman was quite certain that none of the conspirators knew him, and in any case, he was too far away for his features to be recognized.

And so he enjoyed the scene. It was one of the lighter moments he had experienced in the Service. The only one recently, he realized. It was a classic hit, and he had set it up. He had positioned Sackman and Hefelfinger, had signaled them when to start running, and had timed the whole thing perfectly. He was proud of himself.

"Tastefully done, sir, tastefully done," he murmured to no one but himself. He had thirty portraits of those two unknowns with Alain now. Within an hour the best of those portraits would be distributed to police forces across Quebec Province.

As the Organization men moved around the corner, Bannerman contacted Sparrow, who was to surveil the three until lower-level officers could be contacted and placed in blocking positions.

"Time," said Bannerman into his transmitter.

"Ten-four," came back Sparrow's reply, and immediately the Mountie sped out of the underground garage, ran across the street, and double-timed it around the corner.

Alain led his comrades at a rapid pace through the French Quarter, moving fast toward Rue des Ramparts, where they would descend to the Lower Town and finally arrive at the warehouse.

"I didn't like that," Dietrich said. "I didn't like that at all."

"Don't be so jumpy," said Vasyli. "Joggers are everywhere, and they don't watch where they're going. They're crazy."

"Oh, you think so? You think so? I say, Comrade, that it was just too much of a coincidence. There was something funny about the way those guys looked. There was something not right."

"Ah, your nerves are getting to you, that's all," said Vasyli. "You …"

Suddenly, Alain stopped short. He took a deep breath. Dietrich and Vasyli stopped and stared at him. He had turned white, and was having trouble breathing.

"What's wrong, Alain?" asked Vasyli, alarmed at the sight of the man weaving slightly. "Are you alright?"

At the same time, Dietrich took hold of Alain's arm to steady him.

"Ahhhh," Alain said, uttering a high-pitched whine that had no beginning and no end. It just hung there in the cold morning air. "Ahhhh," he whined again, then he spoke.

"Perhaps … should call Borovik. Perhaps … now... not go to meet ..."

"What is wrong?" said Vasyli. "Tell me right now! We will help you."

Alain could not describe the terror that had suddenly gripped him. In one crashing moment of understanding, he knew what had happened. Reality in its entirety, with all its ramifications, became apparent to him, and there was no way he could express this fear. Hot adrenalin surged into his gut and his head. He couldn't move, and he knew he couldn't run.

"I... I was looking ... dime ...," he said, his stare going to a hand in his pocket. "... call Borovik ... wallet ... my wallet ..."

"Yes," said Vasyli. "Yes, what about your wallet?"

Alain's hands and feet were freezing. His jaw muscles were so tense his teeth chattered.

"My wallet is missing!" he blurted out.

Then he doubled over and vomited into the gutter.

Vasyli and Dietrich looked at each other, and Vasyli scowled. They grabbed the still-puking Alain by the arms and hauled him into a nearby alley.

Dietrich blazed with anger.

"A coincidence was it!" he shot at Vasyli, and then directed his questions to Alain. "You didn't leave it at home? In the car? In the glove compartment, perhaps?"

"I am not used to carrying it," Alain said, holding his head in his hands. "I had it when we left the car. I could feel it. I adjusted it. They got it."

He looked up, from one to the other of the men. "They got it! My God. No other answer. No question." He dropped his head into his hands.

Dietrich shook the Canadian. "Alain," he said, "Alain, look at me. Stand up straight and look at me. What was in the wallet?"

"Everything!" Alain wailed.

"What?!" Vasyli's voice choked with rage. "What is everything?"

He pinned Alain to the wall.

"Not the plans, not the plans," chattered Alain. "Telephone numbers. An address or two. Enough. Enough to tie me to a lot of people. They must have known. … they must be watching us right now."

That realization dawned simultaneously on all three men but its effect was less extreme on Vasyli and Dietrich than it had been on the Canadian.

"Wonderful," said Dietrich. "Here it is, middle of the morning, a bright summer day, lost in a city we have never seen before. And we're being watched by who knows how many capitalist agents. What would you like to do? Anything special you'd like to see?"

"Some*one* special I'd like to see," replied Vasyli. "I'd like to see Borovik. Alain has a good idea. We should call him and set up a place to meet."

"Of course!" said Dietrich, "And bring all our unseen friends with us to the meeting."

"Well, that is a point," said Vasyli. "We should get rid of them before we meet. How about a movie? I saw a movie house on that wide street before we turned the corner."

"This early in the day?" asked Dietrich.

"My friend," said Vasyli. "This is the decadent West. It was a 24-hour movie house. You know, foreign films, significant short films, you know…"

"Ah?" said Dietrich, brightening. "That sounds wonderful. Now, how shall we go? Straight there? Straight back? And after the movie, where shall we go then?"

"After we leave the movie, how about left, right, left, right, left, right, cab? Assuming no dead ends, of course, and not too much interference. As to how we should go to the movies, now, I would say that jogging appears to be a popular form of exercise this morning. I would suggest a quick jog."

"An excellent suggestion, Comrade Vasyli," said Dietrich, smiling. "Comrade Alain, do you understand what is happening? Can you run?"

Alain had calmed down a bit, and his stomach felt empty, although he was still breathing hard. He nodded his head.

"Can you run fast?" asked Dietrich.

Alain nodded again.

"Then run, damn it, run!" screamed Dietrich.

He grabbed Alain by an arm and almost ripped it out of its socket as he flung the Canadian toward the far end of the brick-strewn alley.

The three broke into a rapid sprint that took Sparrow, waiting half-concealed on the adjacent street, completely by surprise.

"All agents! All agents!" Sparrow shouted into his transmitter. "Coming out the east end of the alley. Cut off. Pursue. Do something, dammit!"

For an instant, Sparrow stood at one end of the alley watching the three figures disappear around the corner at the other end. No! He shook off the split-second of indecision. He was suddenly filled with the spirit of the chase. He damned well would not lose this bunch.

"Shoot to wound. Capture!" he yelled, and he was off like a shot.

But his quarry were already well on their way past him and off and running.

Sparrow neared the end of the long alley and saw his sergeant take a crouching position and open fire on the fugitives.

"In the legs!" he yelled. Then, rounding the corner himself, almost in the line of fire, "Careful! Come on!"

His two plainclothesmen, stationed closer to the Ramparts in order to intercept the terrorists on their way to the Lower Town, were now absolutely out of position. They came pelting up the street, running for all they were worth, but very late to the action.

Up ahead of Sparrow and his sergeant, Alain and his friends ripped around a corner into Rue St. Jean. The three of them thundered down the crowded sidewalk like a football team, leaving a score of bruised civilians in their wake. Busy traffic slowed them up a bit, but not enough for Sparrow and his men to narrow the distance appreciably. The Mounties were still far behind when the three conspirators burst into the vestibule of the theatre past a startled ticket collector and headed for the darkened seats.

Sparrow saw them duck into the theatre and motioned his sergeant to circle around to the side of the building where the emergency exit was located. Then he raced into the small theatre yelling "Police! Police! Get those lights up! Turn those lights on!"

But Sparrow had miscalculated the speed of his quarry. Just as he entered the darkened theatre, the exit door crashed open and light spilled in. Sparrow saw the fugitives racing out and he tried to follow, but the press of theatre patrons blocked his way. Hearing his shout, they thought it was some kind of a police raid, and they were in a panic to escape.

Sparrow fought his way to the exit door, but he was too late. By the time he reached the alley, the conspirators were gone. He heard several rounds of gunfire from the street and, coming around the corner, he saw his sergeant down like a bundle of old clothes on the sidewalk. Vasyli was just disappearing around a far corner.

Sparrow pegged a shot at him, but it was hasty and well off the mark. He ran to the corner, and just as he cleared it, he heard gunfire. His body was whipped back and thrown onto the ground. He looked up to see Dietrich dodge down the street and around another corner, his Luger loose in his hand.

People were running, screaming. Sparrow tried to raise his hand to shoot, but his whole body trembled, and a sensation of warmth trickled down his right arm. It just lay there, weak and useless. He breathed deeply and stared straight up at the empty sky.

Chapter 13
Jamboree

Hefelfinger was whooping when he came into the safe house in Sillery.

"Haven't had so much fun since my last vacation," said Sackman, laughing. "Bannerman, that was beautiful. Where did you get these suits?"

"Oh, a little store out by Place ... oh, you mean the inside pockets? Did them myself, actually. Do they work?"

"Do they work, he asks," Hefelfinger said to Sackman. "Do they work!" He put his hand down inside the warmup pants and extracted his transmitter.

There was no change in the appearance of the pant leg it had come out of, and even though the transmitter was less than a quarter of an inch wide, it still had bulk. It should have made a noticeable difference in the way the fabric draped. There was nothing.

"You could always be a tailor if they come through with more budget cuts," said Sackman, taking a wallet out of his own pants and waving it. "Although I don't know where they'd find someone to replace your sense of timing."

"Ah, gentlemen," said Bannerman, delighted. "Bless your souls. You found a little trinket for us. My, my."

He took the wallet from Sackman and opened it.

"Alain Barbeau is his name today. Comrade Alain Barbeau,

I think we can assume. An upstanding citizen. Driver's license, no tickets. Visa charge card of Alain Du Bois. That's yesterday's Alain, I suppose. A Renfrew's charge card, belonging to Marcel Du Bois. So, Alain was Marcel at some time in the past."

Bannerman whistled. "Look here," he said, fascinated. "A whole bunch of things to go through. Our Alain was a packrat. And ... Aha!"

Bannerman's voice grew excited. "Can you believe this? One of those stupid little secret compartments. Paydirt. Telephone numbers. Partial addresses!"

Bannerman squinted. "They must be addresses. Why, hell, gentlemen, it's not the mother lode by any means, but all kinds of leads here. Damned sloppy work by Monsieur Barbeau, or whatever his name is. I just hope he didn't tell his new-found friends he lost this. Could get pretty sticky for him."

"Oh, about those friends," said Sackman.

"Yes?" asked Bannerman, his eyes bright with anticipation.

"Strange," Sackman continued. "When we hit them, I could have sworn one of them said 'Vas?' "

"What?" said Bannerman.

"Right, 'vas.' Sort of grunted it out, before he remembered he was supposed to be French-Canadian. But there's nothing in the world like a surprised German saying 'vas?' with a shocked look on his face. Can't hide that, really."

"By God. German?" said Bannerman. "German, Cuban, Arab, what the hell else did Borovik collect, do you think? What is this, practice for the final assault on the Pentagon? What is he after here? Why is he exposing himself like this? Wrack your brains, will you? Be here on call. I'm off to see some of our allies."

He was out the door in a flash, stowing film and wallet as he went.

The door slammed.

"We done good, Al? Huh? We done good?"

Sackman turned and looked at Hefelfinger, who was hunched over and beginning to drool. He had crammed a woolen skullcap over his head and beads of sweat were breaking out over his forehead.

"It's good to see you getting back to your old self, Igor. Now just put that corpse's arm down," Sackman said evenly.

"Aaarrggghh!" said Hefelfinger, his index finger exploring a crack between two teeth. "Master not be nice to Igor, Igor change to werewolf." Then he belched.

"God, Hefelfinger, sometimes you are absolutely disgusting."

"Not Hefelfinger," said Hefelfinger. "Werewolf change to mummy. To vampire mummy. To zombie. Hefelfinger brave and fierce. Shapeshifter, too. Heh, heh, heh…"

"Right," said Sackman. "Now be a good little spy, and eat your gruel. I mean lunch. God, you're intolerable sometimes!"

"I love my work," Hefelfinger said.

"When it works, it works," Sackman declared. "But when it doesn't, it…"

"It all works out in the end. You'll see. This will work out. I know it will."

"We'll see, buddy. We'll see…"

"I can't wait to get my hands on that bastard," Hefelfinger said, smiling.

Chapter 14

Fire and Ice

Bannerman swirled past Sandy's desk in such a rush that she had to drop her phone and grab at papers before they were strewn across the floor.

"Hey!" she yelped. "You can't …"

"Okay, Sandy," came Le Claire's voice from the inner office, before the door slammed.

Both men started to speak at once.

"They are here in the city!" Then, startled, both stopped and waited for the other to continue.

Le Claire recovered first. "Sparrow is in the hospital. Lucky for ..."

"What!" exclaimed Bannerman, interrupting again. "I was with him just over an hour ago. What happened?"

"Shot. His sergeant is dead. Lucky for Sparrow the hospital was close by. He'll recover. His arm. What do you have?"

Bannerman held up the film capsule.

"The guys who got Sparrow. Thirty pictures, at least. I got 'em for you, but we're going to need lots of copies. From what I just found out, probably copies to Ottawa, Washington F.B.I., my place, Scotland Yard, Interpol…every service we can think of."

He dropped the capsule on Le Claire's desk. "But first, to your people," he said. "If you get them out fast, those bastards won't even have time to change their clothes."

Bannerman threw the wallet onto the desk. "Now, their contact here was this fellow. Phone numbers, addresses. Incredible break, I think."

"Correct, Monsieur!" Le Claire looked through the wallet, beaming. "Any more positive identifications? You bit off his fingertips, perhaps?" He laughed. "Seriously, now, did you get prints?"

"Not on the wallet, I'm afraid," said Bannerman. "Not any more. Maybe on some of the IDs? But his car is parked five minutes' walk from here. And if it isn't, it's easy to find. Sparrow bugged it within a minute after Monsieur Le Contact got out of it."

"Incredible," said Le Claire. "I have to thank you. Such quick work."

"Who can process this film for us?" Bannerman asked.

"My own department," replied Le Claire. "They can have it for you within the hour. I'll take it up to them personally."

"Oh, no." Bannerman raised his hands in protest. "This film is mine. I go with it. It's not that I don't trust your people, Le Claire. I just want to make sure I'm there to run with it as soon as it's ready."

"That important to you, eh?" asked Le Claire, assenting.

"That important," Bannerman affirmed.

The intercom buzzer rang. Le Claire picked up his phone and listened while Sandy relayed a message. He jotted down something in pencil on his office pad.

"Thank you, Sandy. Any more calls, I'll be out at Headquarters on St. Louis, okay?"

He turned to Bannerman. "A cabdriver, shot. Body dumped on the street. Three men. Our friends, no doubt of it from the descriptions."

Le Claire went to a large-scale map of Quebec City and the surrounding area that hung on the wall. It held four red pins in a haphazard arrangement, each with a number printed on it. The pins were connected by strands of red wool. Le Claire gestured toward the array.

"So far, only Sparrow's information."

He pointed at the individual pins. "Here, the house in St. Foy. This one, where surveillance began."

"Where I left him off," Bannerman added. "Certainly screwed up there. Never expected them to go for their guns. Yet."

"Through the French Quarter, you see." Le Claire traced the red line. "Here, where the sergeant was killed. Here, where Sparrow caught it. And here," Le Claire put another pin into the map, "where the cab was seized. Perhaps it does not mean much yet. The movie theatre the fugitives ran into, for instance. A random choice of darkness for them, perhaps. But all things mean something in a pattern. There is no random choice, really. Finally, the whole thing comes together. It will be interesting to see where the cab is abandoned."

Le Claire and Bannerman stared at the nearly empty map, their imagination and logic trying to fill it up.

"Why not a pin for my murdered colleague?" said Bannerman.

"We do not know that he was connected to this problem," said Le Claire.

"Of course he was!" exclaimed Bannerman. "You know he was."

"No," said Le Claire. "You know he was, Bannerman. I don't. Give me evidence, if you can."

Bannerman sighed. "He was on to something big, he said. Something to do with sabotage. I didn't know his contact; never heard of him. It was ridiculous. He hadn't been in Canada two months, if that. It wasn't logical. He couldn't have made ... "

"What was the name of his contact, Monsieur?" asked Le Claire quietly.

"I don't know," said Bannerman. "Only a code name, Le Claire, or I certainly would have told you before this. It was 'de-la-something.' Damn it! It's in the files. De la Montagne, I think."

Le Claire stopped short. He felt cold fear as certainty crept into him. He tried to shake it off. Intuition had no place in police work, but there it was again. The same feeling he had about the Commodore, he had about this name. But what was intuition anyway? Simply a drawing on old, unused information, perhaps. Connections somewhere deep in the uncharted part of the brain.

"Any other information about this contact, Harvey?" he asked. "In your files? Anywhere?"

"I know he had access to information about the waterfront," Bannerman said. "But it was an initial contact. Eddie was trying to develop it. That's what he was doing when they got him. He was on his way to a follow-up meeting. That's all I have. A code name with access to the waterfront."

"I wish you had told me before," said Le Claire. "I wish I had known before."

"I wanted to see what you might come up with on your own," said Bannerman.

Le Claire nodded.

"Do you have something?" Bannerman asked.

"I am not sure," said Le Claire. "I am not certain. I will have to think." He paused and looked up. "But of one thing I am certain, Harvey. I am going to need to requisition a lot of detectives. Good ones. Let's go to headquarters."

"By the way," Le Claire said, putting on his jacket. "Have you any information about your mystery man from yesterday?"

"No. Nothing yet. Perhaps this afternoon. How about you?"

"It's in the works, but nothing yet. Visual identification takes a little longer. But your photographs are in circulation."

He pointed to Bannerman's pocket. "I hope these are as good as the ones you got yesterday. Excellent quality. No need to be fuzzy about identification. Zip! Just like that."

"How do you like my phantoms?" asked Bannerman, a quiet smile crossing his thin lips.

"Very impressive," Le Claire said. "Send them around anytime. Come. To Boulevard Laurier."

Chapter 15

The Mind of Comrade Alain

"Are you positive you weren't followed?"

Borovik stared at Dietrich with intense interest. Cartier, standing next to Borovik in the dim light of the warehouse hallway, looked on, shocked and wary.

The Russian's face was calm, almost as if he had expected this development.

"That is the important thing, of course," said Dietrich. "We took extreme precautions. If they followed us here after the chase we led them on, then there is no hope for it. What I mean to say is that if they are here, they got here before us. There is no way they could have followed us."

"Who was it? Who gave chase?" Borovik demanded. He continued to stare at Dietrich.

"Americans, I am quite sure," said the German. "There was one that had a distinctive run…"

"Everyone has a distinctive run," Borovik interrupted. "As well as a distinctive walk. It is the same as fingerprints. What was distinctive about this one's run?"

"It was gangly, like a spider. Arms and legs every which way."

"Like a spider," mused Borovik. "File that away, Dietrich. Tell the others first." He turned toward Cartier. "You see what strange little bits of information we collect, Comrade. It is small things like this that we must be aware of. They keep us alive."

He paused, then continued talking to the Canadian. "I will have to interrogate your comrade Alain. Let me see…" Borovik paced the hallway and rubbed his chin, then came to a decision.

"1 will use hypnosis. I would like to use the serum, but it takes too long, both to act and for the effects to wear off. No, we will use that if we cannot get the information without it, or if we suspect the information we acquire is not accurate. But time is most important here."

He turned back to Cartier. "I wish you to be present, Comrade, in case he speaks only his native tongue. And you also, Comrade Dietrich, to verify what he says about today's activities. We will do this …" He paused and made a silent decision. "We will do this in the small room on the fourth floor. Bring Comrade Alain there now, Dietrich. Comrade Cartier and I will be there presently."

Borovik drew Cartier aside.

"A word with you, Comrade," he said. "It may be necessary to suspend Comrade Alain's activities, depending on how much information he has acquired. This may affect you emotionally. I want you to be prepared for this. Once again, I ask you where your allegiance lies—with the Revolution, or with your individual emotional state?"

Cartier looked up at the bullet-headed Russian.

"Alain is my friend," he said. "We have been friends for twenty years. But he knows, as well as I do, that the Revolution comes first. There is no problem here."

"That is good," said Borovik. "Because when I say 'suspend,' I do not mean temporarily. You understand?"

"Of course I understand!" snapped Cartier. "What do you suppose I am, a fool? Come, let's get this over with."

Cartier grabbed Borovik's arm and propelled him down the hall. Surprised by the strength of the old man's grip, Borovik let the veteran lead where he pleased. Cartier certainly acted like a professional, he thought. You had to give him credit for that.

When the two leaders walked into the small room, they saw Alain seated on a straight-backed oak chair.

Vasyli and Dietrich lounged on either side of him, lazily guarding the man, who needed very little guarding. When he saw the two enter, Alain involuntarily sucked in his breath. Once more he had a resurgence of the fear he had first known when he realized that his wallet was missing.

Borovik walked up to him.

"Please do not be alarmed, Comrade," he said. "I must interrogate you to find out what the pigs may have learned from you. But I certainly do not mean to frighten you. The interrogation will be painless, you may be assured of that. Once we have found out what they have learned, then it will be time to decide whether or not you should continue with us. Agreed? If not, then you will simply be dropped from active participation in this matter. But do not be afraid; just answer the questions. We will judge the importance of the information you provide, eh?"

Alain broke out in a cold sweat. Borovik went on.

"Surely, after your experience, you do not feel that you are the best judge of the circumstances, eh?" The Russian's voice became low, soothing, friendly. "Let us judge that for you, Comrade."

Alain sat there staring at Borovik's open, friendly face. Suddenly, he wanted to trust this man. He gave his mind over, his fear left him, and he relaxed.

"Alain," said Cartier, "we are going to…"

An abrupt gesture from Borovik silenced him. The Russian Boar was staring intently into Alain's eyes.

"We want you to rest, Comrade. We want you to go to sleep. So when I say 'three,' you will go to sleep, and you will not wake again until I say … until you hear the word 'Champlain.' Then you will wake, and you will feel refreshed. Is it agreed?"

There was an almost imperceptible nod from Alain.

"Good," said Borovik. "Three."

Cartier looked at Borovik. He was incredulous. His mouth hung wide.

"Now he is open," said Borovik. "Now we will find out everything."

"But ... but ...," stammered Cartier.

"We have perfected many things," said Borovik, smiling at him. "Hypnosis is one of them. It is all in the method."

"No preparation ... no exposition ... "

"No hocus-pocus at all," Borovik said. "Right to the heart of the matter. It saves time. Now, Comrade Cartier, let us see what we can find."

Borovik turned back to Alain.

"But ..." Cartier said, wondering how Alain liked being discussed openly as if he were some specimen under a microscope.

Borovik had already anticipated his question.

"Any discussion not directed to him seems like a faraway buzzing somewhere in his mind. You needn't worry what he thinks about us, or our reaction to his information. It is as if we don't exist. It is like a vacuum, you see, and I am a voice that cuts through the haze and communicates with him. He may see my face, far, far off. My voice may echo through his mind, that is all, and only when I speak directly to him. As now. Watch his face change, when I address him."

"Alain," said Borovik softly, "Alain, it is your friend, Borovik. How are you?"

"Fine," said the hypnotized revolutionary, his face showing the shallow lines of a semi-intent interest in the proceedings. He spoke in French, as Borovik had predicted. Cartier translated.

"I need some information," said Borovik. He sounded almost apologetic. "Only you, Alain, have that information. Will you give it to me? It is very important."

"Oui," said Alain.

"What is your name, Alain?"

"Marcel Du Bois."

Cartier started, and Borovik's mouth creased into a thin smile.

"That is your real name?"

"Oui. My given name."

"What other names do you have?"

"Alain Du Bois. Alain Barbeau."

Borovik looked at Cartier, who appeared shocked.

Borovik scratched his chin and went on.

"Do you have identifications for all those people?"

"Oui."

"Were those identifications in the wallet that was stolen?"

"Oui."

"Have you ever been in jail?"

"Oui."

"Under what name?"

"Alain Barbeau."

"That is the name he always used in the Organization," said Cartier. "That means ..."

"Wait," interrupted Borovik. "Alain, have you been in jail under any other names?"

"Oui."

"What names?"

"One other, Marcel Du Bois."

"Thank you, Alain. Do you fear me?"

"Oui."

"Why?"

"You have power. "

"What kind of power?"

"Power to kill me."

"Why should I kill you?"

"I am guilty. A bad mistake."

"Mistakes do not make you guilty."

"Oui."

"Why?"

"Against orders."

"What is against orders?"

"Names. Addresses. Telephone numbers. Should have been memorized and destroyed."

"And they were not?"

"I had no time."

"Where were they?"

"In the stolen wallet."

"Alain," said Borovik. "Give us the names, the addresses, the telephone numbers."

"Charles Pepin, 156 Rue St. Louis, 565-4382. Marcel Lefebvre, 29 LeSage, Trois Rivieres, 923-9234. Jean Sauvé, 1521 Boulevard Henri-Bourassa, 886-4823."

"See, you did memorize them."

"I see."

"There was no need to keep the record of them."

"A mistake."

"You do not remember them now. You cannot remember them. Is that clear?"

"I cannot remember them."

"You will never remember them. You have never heard of them. No matter who asks you. Is that clear?"

"I will never remember them."

"Comrade Cartier never gave you those names, addresses, or telephone numbers."

"He never gave them to me."

Borovik turned to Cartier. "Who are they?"

"Cell leaders," said Cartier. "I added them to his section especially for this operation." Cartier's face had turned ashen.

"He knows other cell leaders?"

"With these, there are eight in his section."

Borovik rubbed his eyes.

"Cartier," he said, "I can erase the memory of these. These are only slips of paper to him. But the others are real people, with strings of incidents and emotions tied to them. It would take a lifetime to erase the memories of them out of his mind. And even if I did, of what use would he be? He would be like a zombie. Wait a minute."

Borovik gazed again at Alain.

"Alain," he said. "Did you ever kill anyone?"

"No."

"Did you ever want to?"

"Oui."

"Were you ever humiliated?"

"Oui."

"Tell me."

"My teacher in second grade. She said I smelled. She told the whole class."

"Did you smell?"

Alain began to cry.

"I was sick," he said. "I shit in my pants. I couldn't help it!"

"Alright, alright," said Borovik. His voice was soothing, like a kind father's.

"Forget that now. Alain, what are you proud of?"

"My work for the Organization." Alain's back straightened, and he seemed to grow larger. "And once I saved a child from drowning. From the river. On a ferry boat."

"When did you last have sex with someone?" asked Borovik.

"Two weeks ago."

"Did you like it?"

"It was really good."

"What did you do?"

"I stuck it…." Alain laughed savagely. "I had her squirming all over the floor. God damn! You should have heard her scream when I …"

"Your girlfriend lets you do that?"

"No girlfriend. Some cunt. Some whore."

"Why are you angry?"

"Gave me the clap, the scurvy cunt!"

"Where is your girlfriend?"

"She ... left me."

"Do you believe in God, Alain?"

Alain made his right hand into a fist and raised his arm halfway up.

"I rage against Him!" he muttered.

"Why?"

"Why does He let this happen?"

"What?"

"This mess. The people. The poor, the sick, the living dead, the hopeless. Why has He done this to us? Why does He laugh at us? Damn Him. Damn Him to the miserable hell he created and called Earth. Damn Him."

Alain began to drool.

"Be calm," said Borovik. "Be quiet and wait for me. "

"Where?" Alain asked.

"Right here," said Borovik. He turned to Cartier.

"I do not know this man," said the Frenchman. "I have known him all my life, and yet I do not know him."

"It is your friend, alright, but hidden parts of him that you would never look for unless you were in my position. I had to know, to defend myself. But you don't need to look so shocked, Comrade Cartier. I am sure that if we asked him, Comrade Alain could tell us many more sordid tales than he has already let out. And he is not so different from most men. Did you notice, by the way, how easily he spoke?"

Cartier nodded his head and left it drooping against his chest, mourning for the man he thought he had known so well.

"That is why I am afraid of him," said Borovik.

Cartier's head shot up.

"You afraid of him!" he spat sarcastically. "Of course! Of course!"

"Listen to me," said Borovik. "He has too much guilt. It will come out. He hates, but his hatred will turn any which way. It is unpredictable. And he is violent, and fearful. He has been hurt much in his lifetime, and he seeks revenge. Right now he is not too much different from the average person. But that incident with the wallet was not a problem; it was a symptom. The man is disintegrating. He does not belong in a revolutionary organization. There is too much stress on him here. If they catch him, he will spill everything. And 'everything,' in his case, is quite a lot."

Borovik paused, and looked at Cartier, who seemed to have withdrawn behind some kind of shockproof shield.

"Cartier, come," said the Russian. "Come outside with me."

Cartier got slowly to his feet. Borovik turned to Alain again.

"Wait," he said. "Wait for me here. It will be only a short time, Alain."

"You will hurt me," said Alain. Then, again, in a shrill, drugged-sounding voice, "You will hurt me!"

"I will not hurt you," said Borovik, calmly. "Just wait here. Wait."

"Wait," said Alain. "Wait."

"Come," said Borovik to Cartier, and led him out of the room.

When they were in the hall, Borovik said, "He is very, very close to the surface now. He will wake up soon. When he wakes up, he will have even more guilt. 'Did I tell them anything I shouldn't have?' he will ask himself. And of course he has, and somehow he will sense that. He will be even more unstable. Did you realize that he retained the vestiges of a God concept?"

"I did not," said Cartier. "For twenty years, I did not. In the social animation sessions, and the group psychology sessions, not an inkling of his true thoughts appeared. I do not understand it. I do not understand that, nor do I understand how you could hypnotize him so readily."

Borovik said nothing about how simple it was to hypnotize a deeply neurotic subject under the right conditions. Instead he said, "There are new methods, Comrade, ever-developing methods."

It was then that the two men heard the quiet popping of a small-calibre pistol and the sound of Alain's body hitting the floor.

Back in the interrogation room, Vasyli put away his gun. He looked at Dietrich with a rueful smile. He had caught the signal for the liquidation from Borovik as the leader left the room, and he acted immediately.

But as he drew his pistol from its holster, he felt sorry for the prisoner who still believed in God. Perhaps his reaction was so sharp because Vasyli remembered when he, too, had believed. So, feeling a strange conflict rising in him, he determined to free Alain's soul and send it on its way unhypnotized.

"Champlain!" he whispered.

Alain's eyes sprung open and he glanced wildly around. His muscles tensed and he jumped from the chair. But the three small, deadly slugs entered the back of his head even as he rose.

Vasyli smiled now because he wondered if Dietrich had guessed his reasoning. But how could he? It was so primitive, he told himself. It was the kind of reasoning that smacked of werewolves in the Carpathian moonlight, of wolfbane, of salt over the shoulder, and black cats, and prayers, and the sign of the cross, and ... Vasyli snapped shut that train of thought just as he snapped the pistol back into its holster.

So he smiled. He smiled because he was afraid. Afraid for more than one reason, and he had a right to be afraid.

"You didn't have to do that!" Cartier screaned. "You didn't have to! There was no reason to it. We could have kept him here. He wouldn't have interfered. You're a butcher, Comrade! A plain butcher!"

"Get hold of yourself, old Comrade," Borovik snarled between clenched teeth. "How many times do I have to tell you that I will do anything to insure the success of the Revolution?"

"To insure your own success, you mean!" Cartier had turned livid with rage.

"It would seem," said Borovik, "that you, too, Comrade, are caught up in the disease of neurotic emotionalism. We cannot allow this, you know." He grabbed the old man's arm and dragged him down the hall to a small room. He flipped the wiry old communist into the bare cell, and with the trace of a smile said, "I will give you twenty minutes, Comrade. At the end of that time, I will be back. I will want two things from you. One, you will have calmed down and become your old rational, valuable self. Two, you will have expunged from this operation all the comrades who have had contact with Comrade Alain. You will have replaced them with comrades from different cells. You will let me know who they are and everything about them. When I come back, we will set up this program again, revised. Be ready when I return."

Borovik slammed the door. Cartier stood in the middle of the room, looking around at the white-washed walls. There was no way out of this damned little cell, and no way out of this situation, either. Not for the present. He was trapped in an operation with a madman. Borovik was insane, he was sure of that. Perhaps he had not always been, but he was now, and he would bull through with his crazy plans, whatever they might be, until he achieved his ends. What to do about all this, Cartier did not know. But he knew he would have to formulate some mode of action. He would have to do it quickly, and it would have to be good.

Chapter 16

Watchers of the Sea

Far downstream from Quebec City, where the St. Lawrence became more a sea than a river, there was situated on its northern bank the small town of Les Escoumins. Along the low stone quay of the town stood the watchers. They were the old men who watched their portion of the sea; the old men who had once been seamen and dreamers, who had gone out on that sea on the long and short voyages that had become the central happenings of their lives. Now the old men watched through the haze for the ships to come in or go out through the gates of land again, to go out, go down, to the sea.

And there were pairs of young lovers there, too, strolling, talking low and soft, building new dreams to go with new days, breathing the air of new freedom and promises. Each year, as is the course of things, the old men grew older, and they thought the lovers younger.

Mixed with the old dreamers and young lovers were the solitary wanderers of the earth— sea sailors and land sailors between ships and ports, all riders of the wind who had somehow been blown to this sleepy little town.

They came and went, all of them, and all of them watched the sea, and the ships of the sea, and the little coastal speedboats that carried the river pilots back and forth from ship to shore.

The speedboats buzzed like summer flies, and that was the only startling movement on the river. All else was slow and stately. So unobtrusive were the watchers on the quay that they were scarcely noticeable. To a cursory eye, the cool stones beneath the poplar trees were practically deserted except for that old fellow over there in the black captain's cap, sucking at his pipe; and that couple who seemed to blend into the shadows of the trees like classic Grecian lovers blended into a romantic painting.

Beyond the town, up and down the river, were hay and weed-filled hills that sloped gently up for just the right height. The hills were cut diagonally by ageless red-brown slashes that were cow tracks, and the tracks were dotted with white and black spotted grazing cows. From a distance, these hills turned two-dimensional and hazy, almost as if they were painted by some century-old French impressionist.

The cows and the river pilots were the major industries of the town, if you didn't count the pulp mill far up the little river somewhere back of the hills.

The town looked toward the big river that here was a sea. The windows of the houses opened to it, and in the mornings the sun entered the upper rooms beyond the wide windows and filled them with a summer freshness.

Les Escoumins was not the place for savagery to bloom, but in this world of short spaces and faster-than-light politics, savagery was everywhere, and struck like lightning, anywhere, without a warning.

That was the way of the new revolutionaries. And so savagery was here, in sleepy summertime Les Escoumins. It was behind the windows of a house that overlooked the river. It was out of sight of the innocent watchers on the quay. It was hidden, lurking, as all terror is when it is waiting for its prey. Its eyes were the lenses of a pair of binoculars, held in the hands of Charles Morin.

Morin was in the main room on the top floor of his grandmother's house on the Rue St. Thomas, two houses down from the corner where the street was crossed by the Boulevard Montcalm. The house was fortunately situated, being one of those in the row that looked out across the twenty-mile width of the river.

Morin sat in a straight-backed chair that faced the window, his legs propped on a cold radiator that stood against the wall. He swept the river with the black binoculars, concentrating his attention on the incoming ships that waited in a long, dark line to pick up their river pilots. He knew what ships they were, what their cargoes were, what their destinations were. He knew their respective speeds and the times they were due to arrive at ports up and down the river. He had all that information from a river pilot, an old schoolmate of his who would rather not have certain information concerning his adolescent past made public. Morin had cordially agreed to withhold that information provided that the pilot kept him well-supplied with the latest daily knowledge on ship movements.

Morin felt smug. He was getting the information he needed, easily. His grandmother was away in Montreal, visiting his parents. All of them, every member of his family, thought he was camping with his friends at a cabin in the north country, enjoying a well-deserved vacation after a year of grueling graduate studies. They were all so proud of the brilliant boy.

Morin snickered at the myopia of his dull relatives who could not see the truth of any matter, and who always trailed light years behind the political reality of the times. He would show them who was a nice little student, making progress toward social stupidity and a little niche in the state bureaucracy each and every day. Morin was going to surprise them in a way that would make them sit up and take notice.

His grandmother's neighbors were not surprised to see him. He had spent his summers growing up here, and visited often. The neighbors might have been taken aback by his companions, had they ever seen them. One was named Abdul Rashad, and the other, Mahmoud al-Bakkar.

Abdul was a native of South Yemen. He had spent his childhood sitting on the hot white stones of the docks of Aden harbor, gazing out over the oily, flat soup that was the Red Sea, gazing toward Africa. Years later, he had gone across that sea, as an advisor to an Ethiopian Revolutionary Army unit that had attempted to lift the Eritrean secessionists' siege of Asmara. While there with them, Abdul had come into contact with Cuban comrades who were also acting as advisors. His acumen in military matters was quickly recognized, and his progress across Africa was facilitated by both the Cuban and South Yemeni governments. His specialty was urban warfare tactics. He was dangerous.

Mahmoud's upbringing was different from Abdul's. Far from being a wharf urchin, he had grown up in a wealthy family of Lebanese

Arabs. His family had relatives all over the Levant, some of the family extending even into Palestine and Gaza. Two of Mahmoud's uncles were fierce supporters of Yasir Arafat. They had, on occasion, lent the Palestinian leader both financial and political aid. Mahmoud grew up in the political atmosphere charged with the smell of gunpowder that finally disintegrated into the disaster of the Lebanese civil war.

During his years of study at the American University at Beirut, Mahmoud had at first concentrated his courses in the pre-legal field. But he soon found himself attracted more and more to political science courses, especially those taught by Karen Schiller of West Germany.

Shiller emphasized the Leninist dialectic, and seemed able to show that it really worked. Her examples of revolutionary behavior, culled from as many nations of the world as she was able to review, suggested that the proletarian revolution was gaining strength by the day, as well it should. In her worldview, no quarter was to be given to the capitalist dogs of American imperialism, as none was deserved. These oppressors of the working class were to have their necks wrung. Any means that would contribute to the downfall of the American oppressors was to be considered valid.

The American oppressors appeared to be delighted with her course. They paid her well to teach it. One of her best students was Mahmoud al-Bakkar. When he ran for the Student Senate on an avowed Marxist revolutionary platform, the American advisors smiled at him and congratulated themselves on their liberality.

That was their problem. The Americans were playing a game. Mahmoud was not. Mahmoud was playing for keeps. And after a few years of this, with one side playing games and the other side playing for keeps, the American University in Beirut was a burned-out shell, and Mahmoud was a trusted liaison officer of the Palestine Liberation Organization. He had decided to take the road of open warfare against the western imperialists.

He eventually came to the attention of Vladimir Borovik, who invited him to Cuba for specialized training. And now, here he was in Les Escoumins, using his ever-sharpening skills to deadly effect. He was enjoying himself. This was an easy assignment, and the scent of summer on the river reminded him of his home.

Abdul, Mahmoud, and Morin were all very much in a relaxed

mood this beautiful Wednesday afternoon. They had time to take things easy. Their real work would not begin until Friday. For now, it would be enough to become ever more knowledgeable about the ships, and their passage on the river.

The three men relaxed in the sunlit room. Morin lazily watched the ships. Mahmoud sat in an easy chair, his leg thrown over one of its arms. He smoked an American cigarette, one of the first he had had in some time. Cigarettes were one of the few things he would give the Americans credit for; American cigarettes were the best in the world. They killed you with true mildness and flavor.

Abdul lay on the couch, his eyes closed. He was chewing gum, and wishing that it was instead chat. He dreamed of the narcotic green leaf of the Horn of Africa. He wished for a new, fresh, supply of the tongue-numbing, mind-opening stuff that the men of Yemen chewed, allowed by Allah for their satisfaction. And seventy-two virgins. He would like that gift promised by Allah, also. When, of course, the time was at hand. Other than that, he was content.

Chapter 17

This Matter of Alain

When Borovik returned, he found Cartier standing quietly in a corner of his cell. The past twenty minutes had been critical for the Quebec revolutionary leader. While one part of his mind had been racing to complete the arrangements and requirements that Borovik demanded, another part wondered how to thwart the Russian. For Jacques Cartier no longer trusted Borovik. He viewed his actions with alarm and found them detrimental to the Revolution. No good, he felt, could come of wanton slaughter, and that, he could see, was exactly what was on the Russian's mind.

This was a crisis for Cartier. He had always been able before to rationalize the slaughter of bourgeoisie, of reactionaries, even of Party members and functionaries who had gone astray. Sometimes there was no other way to carry out the goals of the Revolution. But in this matter of Alain, there had been no need. Alain had blown his cover, that was all. He could have been hidden, been given a new identity, been sent away perhaps. Even as far away as France. It would only have been for a short time.

There was no need to kill the man. Borovik had acted like an animal—like a wounded animal that strikes with death and vengeance in its heart, in its eyes.

Cartier was convinced now that Borovik had plans other than to help the Organization turn Quebec more to the left. Whatever those motives were Cartier did not know, but he was certain that Borovik's hidden objectives were so deep and important to him that he would strike murderously at anything that might stand in his way.

Now the big man's soft steps were sounding in the hall. The door slowly opened, and Borovik's frame filled the doorway. He stood outlined in the shadowy light of the dingy hall. Cartier looked with resolution toward the dark figure.

"I trust," said the shadow quietly, "that you have calmed down by now?"

Cartier nodded almost imperceptibly.

"Good, old Comrade," said Borovik. "It is for the good of the Revolution, eh?"

Cartier thought he detected a mocking quality in Borovik's voice.

The Russian went on.

"Your temper is good, old Comrade. It keeps your spirit fired up. But it is much more valuable when it is kept under control. See, in the future, that it remains so."

Cartier wanted to lash out at the Russian. This was incredible. He was being lectured to. This gruesome, bullet-headed hulk was lecturing him!

But instinctively, Cartier knew that any further display of temper would give this lunatic the excuse he was looking for to dispose of him, just as he had done with Alain. Now this was dangerous ground, for Cartier realized he was not dealing with a normal man who could be reasoned with, cajoled, persuaded, finessed. He faced a man whose only purpose in life was to destroy life.

There was nowhere for Cartier to turn. He could not appeal to Borovik's superiors. Even if he had known who they were, Cartier knew for certain that they had placed Borovik where he was, knowing full well what type of man the spy chieftain had become.

They must have noted his slip off the deep end. Perhaps they even wanted him to self-destruct. At any rate, whatever their reasons —personal or official—they wanted him right where he was. So that door was closed.

And he could expect no help from his own people. The Canadians were outgunned. Borovik was too slippery, too quick. And any facile attempt at explanation, any major revelation of a change in plans, would open up Cartier to accusations of treason to the Revolution. There would never be enough time to explain.

No, only one alternative was open to the French-Canadian. He would have to deal with Borovik from a position of strength. A position he would have to create for himself. That was the way with all bullies.

This was a simple game now, a basic game. With a multitude of refinements, admittedly, but with a simple childhood base—draw the line somewhere. Cartier smiled.

"I need no lessons from you, Comrade General," he said. "I am no fool. You need my help. I can give it or withhold it. You had better treat me with some respect."

Let him think about that, Cartier said to himself.

"Oh, yes, I suppose I'd better," said Borovik. He seemed amused. He moved into the room, close to the old Frenchman. Borovik towered over the old man and glared down at him.

Cartier stood his ground on his own terms. He did not raise his eyes to meet the Russian's, but rather spoke to the front of the spy's shirt. He spoke quietly.

"There is no time for your nonsense, Comrade," Cartier said. "You cannot break me easily. Without me, you are a fish out of water, regardless of what information you may eventually get from me. And what you get will take so long to decipher, it will wreck the scheduling of all your plans."

Borovik grunted and backed off a step. The old man had some unexpected sparks of fire in him yet. Better not to push him too far just now. He was still pretty tough.

"There is enough time for me to turn your brain into a vegetable and send you screaming like an idiot through the streets," Borovik suggested. Then, taking a more conciliatory tone, he said, "Ah, come, Comrade. We are victims of some tension right now, you and I. We are not meant to come to this pass. We are meant to work together. Listen, this problem of your friend, I am sorry. I did not know he was your friend. Perhaps that would have made a difference. But perhaps not. Look at my position. See it from my side. I cannot have anything go wrong. It is as simple as that. I need your help, yes, but I will do without it if I must."

Borovik paused.

"Please help me if you can," he pleaded. "You have no idea of the importance of our actions now." Borovik's conciliatory tone struck

Cartier. He didn't know what to make of this. It was out of character.

"Just what are you planning, Comrade General?" he asked. He was truly puzzled.

"I cannot tell you," said Borovik. "You must trust me when I say that it is for the good of the Revolution."

Cartier did not reply. He simply looked up now into Borovik's eyes and nodded his head. He hoped he had hidden well the disgust he felt toward the Russian, for at this point Cartier despised the man.

Sensing an end to the confrontation, and feeling that he had things under control once again, Borovik let out his breath and relaxed perceptibly.

"Well, then," he said. "Shall we get to the business at hand? Who are the new troops you have for me?"

Cartier paced the room, his hands ticking off the names of new comrades who would be brought into Borovik's battle. He had constructed the new list during his twenty-minute period of incarceration in the white-washed cell.

Borovik stood in the center of the room, holding his jaw in a cupped hand. The muscles in his face worked furiously.

When Cartier had finished, he said, commenting quickly, "It sounds good for the most part, but I have two questions. First, I remember this St. Andre fellow from the list you gave me before. I remember I puzzled over him then. I don't understand it. He seems so...so….ah, I must fish for a word ... so out of place. His father is a capitalist. I don't like it. People like that usually are in a thing for the sport. I don't like it."

"His assets outweigh his liabilities," said Cartier. "Besides, he is trapped. Perhaps he does not realize how deep into our business he is, but if he does not, he will certainly learn quite rapidly. He will not be able to back out, either. He is vulnerable at too many points. If he softens, there is his father, there is his sister to be threatened. If we must, we will let him know that. But look, Borovik, look what comes with him. This is the main thing, that mansion of his out on Ile d'Orleans, looking—looming—right out over the shipping lanes. That is the important thing. It was Alain's man, Jean Sauvé, who had access to the waterfront in the old plan. We certainly can't use him now. This is an ideal replacement. And St. Andre's cell members can keep an eye on him for us. They can let him know they're doing it, too. That will keep him in line. None of them are his type of person. I deliberately assigned them to him when we formed the cell, for the same reasons you have just stated. I did not quite trust him myself. But you shouldn't worry, Borovik. I have him tied up tighter than a fly in a spider's web. There is no way he can get loose."

Cartier smiled.

Borovik grunted, seemingly satisfied. He paced the room, stared out the undersized window at the gray streets of Lower Town, and turned to face Cartier once again.

"This other," he said. "This Charles de la Montagne. Who is this? He is not on your list. I have never heard of him."

"Not every person I know is on that list, Comrade General," said Cartier. "This one—de la Montagne—is an old and valued friend of mine."

"He is not of the Organization?" asked Borovik, perturbed.

Cartier said nothing for a moment, then, "He is valuable to me. He knows, for instance, where I am right now, and at what time I am supposed to leave."

"You're bluffing!" spat Borovik. Cartier simply smiled.

Borovik turned again toward the window and looked out. His glance took in the Louise Basin, with its steam and money and sweat.

"He is right out there," said Cartier. "He knows the waterfront. He knows everything that happens on it. He is my friend. He can be yours, also..."

Or my enemy, Borovik thought. And you have thoughtfully preprogrammed him. Oh, you are cagey, old man...

He cursed silently and turned toward Cartier.

"Good!" he said, swallowing his pride. "Good. Done the way a commissar would do it, my intricate friend. We work together once again!"

But beware, he thought to himself. Beware, old man. You are finished if I can get my hands on you, afterwards.

Borovik opened the door and ushered Cartier out into the hallway.

Chapter 18

The Leopard's Eye

That evening in the Rue du Tresor both Genevieve and Kearney arrived fifteen minutes earlier than they were supposed to. They came onto the street from opposite ends, and when they spotted one another, walked quickly toward each other.

"I don't know what to say," said Kearney, when they were together.

"I do not understand," replied Genevieve, puzzled.

"I just have to learn French," Kearney said, more to himself than to the girl. He shrugged.

"I cannot speak English," Genevieve said. "It is the language of the oppressor," she added sharply, in explanation.

"I said I will learn French," Kearney repeated.

"No," she said. "I will do better with learning more English. You are not an oppressor. So I will learn." There was a lilt of decisiveness in her voice.

They looked at each other and laughed. Kearney took her hand in his.

Rene and Angelique found them like that, silent, happy, staring at pictures pasted on the walls of the buildings that fronted the street.

"Look at this!" said Rene, laughing. "Dumbstruck. Shall I translate for them? Tongue-tied. Does it need translation? No. They are miserable. Look at them. They love it. Ah, poor things! Do you not feel sorry for them? Ah!"

"Quiet, idiot!" said Angelique. She punched Rene's arm and the poet went spinning off, wailing about his broken bones. Angelique smiled at Genevieve and Kearney and said, "Sometimes in his babblings, he comes up with something good. We were wondering if you would like to go to the Leopard's Eye."

"Oh, yes, of course!" said Genevieve, excited. "That is, if... if..."

"Jack," said Kearney.

"....if Jack would like to see it. Would you, Jack?" she asked, looking up at him.

"Sure," said Kearney. "What is it?"

"A bistro," said Genevieve. "A discotheque."

"You are privileged, Monsieur," said Angelique. "Again, where we take you, there are no tourists."

"The arrangements are made?" asked Rene, returning. "We are off?"

"Look at this, will you?" said Angelique. "He is never there—always off writing down notes, mumbling to himself, making trouble. But he always shows up when everything is ready. Let's go!"

Place Royale was the heart of the Lower Town. It was the site of the original French village beneath the black cliffs of Cap Diamant. There, surrounding the small Notre Dame des Victoires church, the rows of stone houses had been lately sandblasted, refloored, and refurbished to a state better than the originals had ever been. During the day it was a place for tourists. By night, eerie shadows played across the old grey stones of the square.

The basement of one of these old houses had been transformed into the bistro known as The Leopard's Eye. It was another headquarters of separatist sentiment. Tourists were discouraged.

When Kearney entered the cellar gateway and the inner door opened, he was assailed by the shouts and loud music of a great crowd. And Rene's appearance at the door did nothing to alleviate the noise. A general clamor went up, several people ran to him, and he was hustled away quickly toward the center of the timbered cellar.

"Does he know everybody in Quebec?" Kearney asked Angelique.

"Almost everybody," she said, and there was a smile playing over her lips. On Genevieve's, too, the American saw.

"Come," said Angelique, drawing Kearney over to the bar. "We can wait for him here. He will be back soon enough."

"What's he doing?" asked Kearney. He watched as Rene was ushered onto the stage.

"He's reciting his poetry," said Genevieve proudly.

"Really!" Kearney was impressed. So Rene really was a poet, one with a large audience, by all appearances.

Kearney stood and listened. The crowd quieted.

Rene waited for total silence, then said a few sentences quietly. Then he took a deep breath. He seemed to become larger, and he began to recite in a strong, harsh voice that Kearney had never heard him use before.

Kearney realized at the same time that Angelique was close beside him, the scent of her hair around him, her lips next to his ear, whispering to him, translating Rene's poem.

Rene had the flair of a natural actor, and his voice boomed out over the cellar room. His intensity communicated itself to the poem and the people listening.

People were standing and stamping and roaring their approval and support. Their will was to revenge Quebec. They were in a frenzy. Rene stood on the stage and shook his fist at the rafters. His eyes seared across the room, and fell upon Genevieve. Through the din, his voice cut across the room.

"Genevieve! Genevieve! Come! Come, join me!"

Genevieve made her way up to the stage, twisting and writhing like a sinewy mink through the crowd. Kearney became aware of Angelique's laughter, as the artist held his arm tightly and pulled at him.

"He has always promised her, and now he keeps his promise. Look how excited she is, Jack!" And Angelique laughed again out of pure pleasure.

Rene and Genevieve were alone on the dark stage, spotlighted by the deep red and orange lights. They stood before the microphones and began to sing an anthem of the FLQ, one of the songs that had set Quebec marching on the road to the future. Immediately, the place became bedlam, as the crowd roared its approval and quieted once again for the words.

"Come from your farms and your factories
You peasants of New France!
Come from your mines and forests green,
You cheap laborers soaked by the rich;

You sons of Brittany and Beauce,
Of Languedoc and La Rochelle,
You sweepings of the streets of Paris –
Rise up! It is time to take back our heritage!

This is our land! Let's take it back.
It's been too long that we have waited.
Two hundred years of servitude
Under the boots of the bloody Brits.

Two hundred years! Two hundred years!
The cries of our women and starving children
Echo through the winter streets.
Do you not hear them? Can you not hear
Their pitiful cries? – Avenge us! Avenge!

Come! Let us now throw off the chains
That have held us imprisoned for centuries –
It is up to us – today! – today!
It is time for our nation to rise again!

Come from your farms and your factories,
You peasants of New France!
Come from your mines and forests green –
Rise up! Now is the time of our freedom, our liberté!"

The place exploded with applause. Rene pulled Genevieve off the stage and came staggering over to the bar, moving like he was drunk, which he was, but not on alcohol. He was drunk with the power that leadership in a movement brings, and he needed a beer to cool himself off. For her part, Genevieve was trembling with excitement and collapsed smiling on the bar between Kearney and Angelique.

"How did we do?" she asked Angelique weakly in French. "How were we?"

"Oh, my little sister," answered her friend, throwing an arm around her. "You were fine. You were wonderful. Listen to them. They are still applauding. Now you are a real professional, eh? And you are good, Genevieve! You are *really* good!"

Angelique squeezed Genevieve tightly and said to Kearney, "Hey, Jack, is she not good?"

"She's wonderful," Kearney said, circling the singer with his brawny arm. "I'm going to keep her."

Genevieve hugged him and spontaneously jumped up and kissed his cheek.

"Hurrah!" said Rene, and toasted them with a raised stein.

The four of them basked in the momentary glow of triumph. Around them, there was talk of insurrection.

Much later the two couples left the Leopard's Eye and went strolling along the Dufferin Terrace. Afterwards, they drifted through the little park behind the Frontenac, heading haphazardly toward Kearney's small hotel. Kearney and Genevieve lagged far behind Rene and Angelique. They wanted to be alone, and the other two respected their wishes.

They walked quietly beneath the still trees, murmuring to each other, trying to say things just right for each other. It was the time of night when everything is still. There was no breeze, and no sounds of people or their machines came through the dark night air. Far below, the lights of Levis and lower Quebec lined the dark ribbon of the great river that swept on restlessly, tied to the call of the moon that never slept.

In the darkness in the center of the park, Genevieve and Kearney stopped. They kissed, as naturally as if they had known each other forever, and then embraced and smiled gently. A pact was formed, with no words spoken.

By them.

Even as they embraced, they heard Rene's voice from what seemed far away. Kearney looked up. Rene and Angelique were outside the park, on the sidewalk in front of the American consulate, and Rene was laughing about something. Suddenly, the consulate door was thrown open from inside, and Harvey Bannerman stood there, glaring at Rene with contempt. Angelique gave a little jump, and Rene for once was at a loss for words.

Finally he said something that Kearney could not hear, and the door slammed shut again.

Rene and Angelique moved up the sidewalk, Rene shrugging and muttering to himself.

Kearney's fingers tightened on Genevieve's shoulder. He was strangely alarmed.

"What did he say?" he asked the Canadienne. "Was it in French? I couldn't make it out."

"I do not know," she said. "I could not hear. But was that not strange, Jack? Come. Let's find out."

They hurried out of the park and caught up to their friends.

"What happened back there?" Kearney asked.

"What happened?" spluttered Rene. "I do not know what happened. What do you think happened? You saw as much as I."

"He was fooling around as usual. Talking about the Americans, this time," said Angelique. "About how they work such short hours at their consulate…"

"Their hours are posted on the door," explained Rene.

"He said they should be ashamed to work such short hours," Angelique continued. "Suddenly, the door jerked open and that man was standing there, looking furious at us."

"That man…," said Kearney.

"Do you know him?" Angelique asked.

"Of course," said Rene, exasperated. "He knows all the Americans. What do you think?"

"I don't think I know him," Kearney said. "But I think I've seen him before. I don't know where. I can't remember."

"You will remember," said Rene. "Some night, in a dream. You will jump out of bed remembering where you saw him."

"Possibly," said Kearney, with a grin. "What did he say?"

"Nothing," Rene said, shrugging.

"He just stood there, glaring," Angelique said. "Then Rene said 'Go away!' and he did. He slammed the door. He had gone away. It was strange, no?"

It was strange, Kearney thought. It was spooky.

"Maybe he just wanted to scare you, Rene," he said. "Maybe you insulted him, and he just wanted to show you someone was there."

"Perhaps," said Rene, smiling softly now. "If he heard what I said, perhaps I did insult him. My apologies, my American friend." He paused, then went on. "But his actions do not follow."

"Why not?"

"You forget where you are. In this part of the city, at this time of night, a politically sensitive place like this ... you must be prepared for action when you open a door like that."

"Perhaps a guard ...," offered Genevieve.

"Perhaps," said Rene. "But surely he looked like more. I do not understand his actions! What do you think, Jack?"

"I don't know how our embassies work," Kearney said. "I have no idea. If he simply wished to frighten you, I guess he did what he wanted to do. You look kind of frightened."

"I suppose I must admit to that," said Rene, chuckling.

"Let's stop talking about it," said Angelique, with a small shudder. "Here we are, Monsieur, nearly at your hotel."

The four of them stood still on the dark street corner.

Angelique continued, "I hope we showed you something of Quebec, Jack. Now perhaps you know a little more about us than when you arrived?"

"Thank you," said Kearney. "I learned a lot, especially that you are all very talented, and celebrities, besides. I didn't know that."

"Ah, yes. In certain quarters," said Rene. "But unfortunately, nobody we know has any money. C'est la guerre! Fortunes of war!"

They laughed. "Thank you again," Kearney said. "Goodnight."

"Goodnight, Jack," said Angelique.

Kearney turned to go, and as he did, Genevieve slipped her hand into his and fell into step beside him. Kearney looked down at the young Canadienne and smiled, and she returned his smile.

"Oh!" said Angelique, surprised, watching them go. "Genevieve!" she called out. She had not expected her friend to go with the American.

Genevieve stopped and turned. "Yes, Angelique?"

"Oh. Oh, nothing. Goodnight."

"Goodnight, Angelique. Goodnight, Rene. See you tomorrow."

Genevieve turned and walked into the night with Kearney.

"Oh," said Angelique. She spoke very softly, almost in a whimper.

Rene, lighting his pipe, said out of the side of his mouth, "One would think you were her mother."

"She is not like that."

Rene shrugged.

"She was not like that," he said. "Now she is like that. Tomorrow, she will not be like that. Do not worry so much. You cannot protect her. She will find her own way."

"What if he hurts her!" exclaimed Angelique.

"Don't be foolish! He would not hurt her. Jack is not one to hurt people. You can tell that."

"What if…"

Rene lost his temper as they walked along the dark street.

"What if! What if! Why a stranger, you mean. What of her reputation? Well, I say, better an American stranger than a Quebecois fool, like that Pierre Deschamps she was running around with last fall. Anyway, they will do what is right. You can tell, the way they are together. They care for each other."

"That doesn't stop people from being idiots."

Rene opened his mouth to speak but thought better of it and shut up. He could tell that this conversation was one of those with no ending to it. When Angelique had an idea about something, she would work it around for hours until she was satisfied with it. Nothing would dissuade her, so it was best to remain quiet.

The two of them walked along in silence toward their loft off St. Louis Street. Finally, Angelique said, "Rene, besides recording folk songs, what does Jack do?"

"He ...," Rene stopped short, and took a puff of his pipe.

"He …," he repeated, puzzled. "I don't know what he does. We should ask him. Tomorrow, we will ask him, eh?"

He paused for a moment. "That's a good question," he admitted. "Never thought to ask him."

Angelique pressed her lips tightly together. Suddenly, she felt a strange sense of foreboding, of danger, almost, surrounding her friend Genevieve. And concerning Jack.

"Perhaps I am just jumpy," she said. "Perhaps I was more frightened than I realized by that man in the doorway. Maybe that is it?"

"Perhaps," said Rene, putting his arm around her waist and drawing her to him out of the chill of the night. "Perhaps, but I have seen with you, Angelique, that your feelings usually are right."

Angelique sighed and put her hand to her head. She was tired, and her thoughts would not let her rest. They would exhaust her, as they had done before.

Chapter 19
Night

From the gloom of the upper hallway, lit by an old yellow lamp, came deep-night noises that sounded like people were watching. But no one watched, and no one came, and Kearney unlocked the door to his room.

Genevieve walked through the door and stopped.

He had left the windows open, and the cool night wind of summer blew the flimsy gauze curtains into the room like old white ghosts illuminated by light from the streetlamp. The curtains looked almost phosphorescent.

Genevieve crossed the room and caught one of the curtains gently in her hand to push it aside and look out at the night. The streetlamp showered light on the quiet street, on the silent cars, on the rustling trees in the park across from the hotel. From far away came late-night city sounds—a car bumping over some rough pavement; a far-off siren; a ferry hooting on the dark river.

Genevieve took a deep breath.

Kearney, too, breathed deeply, lit a low lamp on the dresser, went back to the door and locked it.

Genevieve turned and looked at the room: the bed against the far wall dominating the center of the small space; the gabled ceiling that gave the impression of a garret; the solid old furniture, beat-up and sturdy. All these things together gave certain feelings—of quietness, of security, of possible happiness. Of home.

Kearney stood looking at her from across the room, his hands in the pockets of his jeans.

"I like it," Genevieve said.

Kearney started the beginnings of a smile. Didn't move.

Stared at her.

"I like it, Jack," Genevieve said again. "It's nice here," she said very quietly. "It feels good."

She tugged her bulky maroon sweater over her head, folded it, walked to the dresser, placed the sweater there, lifted her eyes to Kearney's.

He watched her slowly lift her hands to her head and push back her long black hair. It fell across her thin white shirt, over her shoulders, half-way down her back.

He went to her, and they held each other, and looked for an instant into each other's eyes. They kissed, and he stroked her hair. She writhed against him like a cat. Together they fumbled open the buttons of her shirt, and he pulled it off her and threw it roughly over a chair. As he turned to crush her against him, Genevieve gasped, put her hands flat against his chest, closed her eyes, and whispered, "Wait!"

She pushed him away from her gently. Kearney watched her, half-naked, the black hair on her white skin; her rounded, firm breasts shadowed in the dim light. She walked lightly over to the bed, pulled down the bedspread and the blanket, straightened the pillows. Then she stood by the head of the bed, smiled shyly, half-looking at him, almost like she was seeking acceptance of her invitation.

And with that act, something changed in Kearney.

Suddenly, there was more than lust in him. He stood at the foot of the bed, his mouth half-open, his eyes understanding. He nodded slightly. Then he went to her, kissed her, picked her up still kissing her, and cradled her in his arms.

Genevieve moaned. He lay her gently on the bed. She breathed deeply and sighed as he unbuttoned her jeans and pulled them down and off, then her panties, she helping with her body movements. And Kearney almost went crazy with lust, and stood over her and looked down, panting, and saw—her. Saw Genevieve. Naked and waiting for him.

Open, vulnerable, wanting, her arms back over her head, her legs opening, opening more, her body beginning to shudder and move, inviting, inviting.

She looked up at him then with faraway eyes.

"Why do you stand there?" she whispered. "Come. Come to me …"

He ripped off his clothes and knelt beside her on the bed, first pulled her up to him, felt her incredible warmth, and kissed her; then dropped softly to her side on the bed. He wanted to touch her all over, hear her secret moans, let his hands know her entire body, do it right, for her, for both of them. But he couldn't wait. He wanted her. He wanted her now. He wanted to get into her now.

And she wanted him.

"Please," she half-moaned, half whispered, "Please ... now...oh, God. Please... now ..."

He went into her, between her beautiful white thighs, went in fast, and deep, and surged into her like waves of wildness, she groaning "Ahhh!" in the half-lit room, and circling him with her arms and legs, her nails digging into his back, he thrusting, thrusting, she meeting him and crying, low at first, then louder and louder, fiercer and fiercer. "Ça m'est égal! Ça m'est égal! Ça m'est égal! Ahhhh!" Until finally she was only animal sounds, and he all animal, and they came together and they cried out.

Afterwards, they smiled at each other as they lay in each other's arms, and they laughed a little, and hugged each other. They lay warm together in the night, drawing the covers up over them. And Kearney wanted to know what it was she cried out, but he didn't dare ask. He didn't dare to want to know. In case. Because he wanted her. He wanted this girl, this girl who said her name was Genevieve. And he didn't know her. He didn't know what she was, or what it was, even, that she wanted.

Kearney dozed for a short while. When he awoke, Genevieve,

still in his arms, was crying. He tried to comfort her, kissed her, hugged her. Quietly, she withdrew from him, slid away from him. Buried her head in the pillow and continued to sob. Finally, exhausted, she fell asleep. Kearney puzzled, looking at her. What was it she had said! What did those words mean?

"Ça m'est égal! Ça m'est égal! ..."

He wanted her. Not just in bed. He wanted to hear her voice, her music, her beautiful laughter. He wanted to be near her quickness, her mind. He wanted to comfort her. He lay his hand gently on her back.

A small sound of contentment came from her. And Kearney slept.

THURSDAY, JUNE 24TH

"There are some young guys behind me who make me *feel nervous."*

René Levesque, Parti Québécois
Premier of Québec Province

Chapter 20

Dawn

Genevieve awoke, took a deep breath, and smiled.

She drew back the warm blanket and sheet and stepped out of bed. Naked and warm, she walked across the floor to the window. Silently, slowly, she raised the shade. It was morning, an hour after daybreak.

Her movement, and the change in the light, woke Kearney. His eyes still closed, he put out his arm to draw Genevieve to him, and she was not there. But the place where she had been was still warm. He opened his eyes.

He watched her standing by the window. In the dim light her skin took on a shadowy olive tint. She was staring through the glass out into the park, past the park, into the grey, overcast dawn.

"Genevieve," he called in a whisper.

She turned and smiled. "Jack," she said, "Come here. Look."

He got out of bed and went to her. As he came near her, she grasped the sash and threw it upwards, the old wood rattling and creaking like the building itself was coming down. She giggled and stood close, pressed her stomach against the sill, and leaned out into the wind.

"What the hell ...," Kearney said, amused. "Genevieve, come in here! Come here. Everybody can see you." He tried half-heartedly to pull her in.

"So what?" she said, feeling the cold free wind blowing across her body. "Do you know them? Do they know me? Ha! Windows full of tourists. Tourists!" she called gently, "Oh tourists! Come see a Quebecoise. She is hanging naked out of a window for your delight, but she isn't doing any wash today. She isn't drawing any water from a well. She isn't waiting tables. She isn't making it for pay and prostituting herself like her government does. Times have changed. She's looking out over her beloved Quebec, and it is beautiful, and the day is beautiful, and she is with a wonderful man, and ...." She whirled, shivering, and hugged him.

He jumped at the touch of her cold skin.

"Oh, Jack!" she said, "I'm freezing. Hold me."

They stood there, holding each other, the gentle breeze blowing the white gauze curtains around them.

Genevieve held tight to Kearney and said, "What a beautiful day it is. Listen to how quiet it is. The park. The river. This house. All is so quiet. Like it was all ours. Like no one else was anywhere near here, Jack. Just you and I."

She paused, then said, "Nobody saw me, Jack. These tourists, they don't get up early enough. Only you have seen me like this."

"Tourists should get up earlier," he said. "They don't know how beautiful the early morning can be. You are beautiful, Genevieve."

She felt him swelling against her. Her own body was warming again, and with a sudden urgency, clutching him more tightly than ever, she said, "Take me, Jack," and then playfully she added, "Take me back to bed," and she giggled.

Their lovemaking this time was long and loving, and playful.

They slept for a short time more and awoke refreshed.

After they showered, Kearney plugged in an instant coffee maker, and they sat in bed sipping coffee and watching the morning news on the TV. The news made Genevieve spit like a cat.

"The MacDonald Commission yesterday continued inquiries into questions regarding the veracity of some Royal Canadian Mounted

Police officials, into the accuracy of reports made to cabinet members, and into whether or not acts undertaken in the name of national security may have been illegal," the newscaster was saying, "And, indeed, the inquiry calls into question whether answers to the commission members' questions themselves were truthful. Yesterday afternoon, for example, John Galsworthy, an RCMP detective operating out of Kingston, Ontario Province, admitted that he had not revealed the entire truth to the commission during his previous testimony, given months ago. At that time, he was asked if Maurice Messier, a prominent Parti Quebecois politician, was under surveillance. Galsworthy stated during that testimony that Messier was not under surveillance. Yesterday, under prodding from commission members, the Mountie revised his testimony, admitting that his interpretation of the question might not have been correct.

" 'The question was,' he said, *'Was Maurice Messier under surveillance by the RCMP?'* I took the question to be an inquiry into the then present state of things. At the time of the question, Monsieur Messier was not under surveillance by the RCMP.'

"When he was asked if Messier had ever been under surveillance by the RCMP, Lieutenant Detective Galsworthy admitted that, for a time he had indeed been surveilled."

'I do not, however, look upon my previous testimony as being false,' he said. 'It was merely an incorrect interpretation.' "

"His explanation was met with stunned silence by commission members. Referring to the original question, whether or not government cabinet members knew in advance of the RCMP's alleged illegal acts, one highly-placed source said, 'We are beginning to doubt whether we shall ever know if cabinet ministers were aware of the situation, much less whether or not they condoned it. Take it for what you will.' "

"Fascists!" said Genevieve. "Fascist bastards! Listen to that, Jack. Do you see what kind of country we have here? Do you see why we want to be a separate people? Bastards!"

"Well, back to the real world," said Kearney. "I knew it couldn't last."

"It will last," said Genevieve. "I want it to. But not now. I have to go home, and then go to school. I'm not free to loaf like some people. Will I see you tonight?"

"Tonight?" asked Kearney. "Do I have to wait 'til tonight? What's wrong with sometime today?"

"Oh, it's impossible," Genevieve said, slipping into her blouse. She was half-dressed, and looking around for the rest of her clothes. "First I must go home, and do you know where that is? Ile d'Orleans. Do you know the island? Then I must shower, and change, and eat, and get all the way out to the University, and do you know where that is? And then I take two courses in chemistry, and then lunch, and then all afternoon I study in the library. Do you see?"

"If I drove you home," said Kearney, "it would save a lot of time."

"Oh," Genevieve said, considering.

"We could stop and have breakfast someplace."

"We could," she said tentatively. And that would give Jean-Paul time to get away to work before we got home, she thought to herself. It wouldn't do for Jean-Paul to meet Jack. Not just yet, anyway.

"Of course we could!" she exclaimed. "That would be delightful. You know, I didn't even think about you having a car."

"Of course I have a car," said Kearney. "I'm a rich American. All Americans have two or three cars hanging around somewhere or other."

"You know, Jack," said Genevieve, smiling, "I never thought of you as an American."

"No?" he asked. "What am I, then?"

"You are just …you," she said.

Chapter 21

Ile D'Orleans

They ate at a small breakfast shop Kearney had discovered on the Place d'Armes. Genevieve was delighted. She laughed as they sat in a booth waiting for their coffee.

"You know," she said, "normally I would never come into this place. I always thought of it as a place for tourists. But it is nice. It is fun."

"If these are tourists," said Kearney, "they are all French tourists. Besides, the prices here are too reasonable for tourists. Besides, your eyes are gleaming."

Genevieve laughed. "You are funny, Jack," she said. "You say such nice things." She lowered her voice. "I have a secret. That is why my eyes gleam."

"You wear contact lenses."

"Oh, you are impossible!" she laughed. "No. Come here."

Kearney leaned across the table. "What?" he asked. Genevieve leaned across the table and kissed him.

"I have not been happy for a long time," she said. "And now I am happy. You have done this, Jack. Je suis content. Merci."

Kearney looked at her. He tried to speak, but instead, he just stared.

Somehow, the sounds of the restaurant—the tinkling of utensils, the murmuring of the patrons, and all else covered by the scents of coffee and bacon and croissants—somehow, it seemed too reasonable, too secure, too good to be true.

When they picked up the Mustang from the garage, Genevieve was as much taken by Kearney's small Quebec flag, which she found on the front seat, as she was by the car itself.

"Oh, Jack!" she said, delighted. "You have adopted our flag!"

"How could I not?" he answered, smiling. "It seems to be flying everywhere. Look at it! All over," he said, pointing out beyond the windshield. "I don't see many Canadian flags at all," he added.

"And you won't!" said Genevieve. "Especially today. Saturday is Quebec's National Holiday—the feast of St. John Baptiste, and we begin to be ready for it. Do not look for many English flags today. Oh, Jack! Saturday will be the parade. You must come with me. Will you? Everyone will be there!"

"Sure," said Kearney. "I'd like that."

"Très bien!" she smiled.

Still early in the morning, the Mustang sped along the causeway that crossed the marshes and marched diagonally up to the bridge to the Ile d'Orléans. The sun was trying to break through a misty overcast.

"I do not believe you," said Genevieve. "You must have been here."

"I've only been in town three days," he said.

"All the tourist books say to come here," she persisted. "Do you not read them?"

"Yes." He smiled. "But there's a whole city."

"I am insulted," said Genevieve, pouting. "You did not come to see my island. Well, I will show it to you, then. We come to the end of the bridge. Turn right here, Jack, at the intersection."

He turned onto the road toward the western end of the island.

"I love your car," Genevieve said. "It hums, or vibrates, or growls, or something."

"It's a good one," he said.

Genevieve rolled down her window.

"The air is so fresh here," she said. "Jack, stop the car a minute. By the field, here."

He pulled off the road.

"Turn it off," she said.

He turned off the ignition and looked at her, puzzled.

"Listen," she whispered. "It is so quiet here. Listen to the birds call—the robins."

Kearney reached out and pulled her to him. They were motionless in each other's arms for a long minute.

"Jack, turn me loose," she finally said. "The neighbors will talk."

"No they won't."

"The shift lever is sticking me."

"Move a bit."

"You are breaking my back. Really."

He let her up. They sat looking at each other, laughing.

"I'd better get you home," he said.

He headed the car back on the quiet road to the west.

Far across the river, Quebec sat like a grand monument perched on its cliff. But after a couple of miles, the road turned away from the view of the city and the harbor and curved back toward the east, this time passing through the small, quaint village of Beaulieu and then running along the southern side of the island. After a mile or so, the houses were spaced farther apart, and they were larger here.

"Here is the driveway, Jack," said Genevieve, pointing. "On the right."

He turned in past the hedges and gates and stopped.

"Where's the house?" he asked.

"There, way over. Beyond the trees. Don't you see?"

He looked across well-manicured acres at the imposing white house with its black trim.

"This isn't your house, is it?" he said. "This is your school. We came to the wrong place."

"No," she said quietly.

Kearney looked over at her. Genevieve shrugged.

"It is too large," she said. "I always tell him that." She paused. "But he won't leave. He likes it here."

"Don't apologize for it," said Kearney. He looked at the house again. “I feel like a fool,” he said. “Here I am, the rich American with his cool car.”

“Do not despise me for it,” said Genevieve, looking at the floor of the Mustang.

“It’s nothing to be ashamed of,” he said. “Besides, it isn’t yours, is it? Did you buy it?”

She cast a sidelong glance at him.

“Sometimes it embarrasses me,” she said. “When I see how little other people have...”

Kearney looked at the house again.

“Will you show it to me?” he asked.

“Surely, if you wish,” she said.

Kearney put the car in gear and started down the long drive. Genevieve, distracted, stared at the lawn and bushes. She didn’t see the three cars parked on the far side of the portico, out of sight of the road.

“Busy place,” said Kearney.

Genevieve looked up. Startled, she recognized her brother’s car, but not the other two. “Something has happened!” she said. Then, “Jack, wait out here, please... my brother …you don’t know…wait here.” She jumped out of the car.

The solid slam of the car door echoed in Kearney’s ears as he watched Genevieve run toward the house and disappear inside. He eased the Mustang past the other cars, parked it on the edge of the driveway, and got out. He lit a cigarette and walked slowly around the grounds. His meandering led him onto a great back lawn that spread out under clusters of ancient oaks and led down to the river. He took in the view as he smoked.

Genevieve pushed open the grand door to the house and walked hurriedly into the main room, calling for Jean-Paul. At once, lithe as a cat, he was there on the stairs, taut with anger.

“Jean-Paul!” she cried. “Whose cars are those? What has happened? Is it Papa?”

“Where have you been all night?” he demanded, bolting down the stairs to grab her by the arm. The look in his eyes terrified her, and suddenly she was afraid of her brother.

"You've been with him?" He jerked his head to indicate Kearney outside. "Where were you?" Jean-Paul asked again, but in a controlled, wispy voice that seemed to burn with a hidden fire.

"I was with Rene and Angelique." Genevieve blurted out the lie. "What are you doing? Why are you acting like this?" Her voice rose louder.

Jean-Paul made a sign for her to be quiet.

"Who is he?" he said. "Tell me. Tell me the truth. I have to know."

"A friend," she said. "He is a friend of Rene's, an American... Why? Let go of my arm, Jean-Paul. You are hurting me."

Jean-Paul relaxed his grip and let her go, but he remained tense, a coiled spring.

"A friend of yours, too," he said.

"He kindly offered to drive me here, and then to school," she said. "He wanted to see the island. He is a tourist. Why? What are all these questions?"

Jean-Paul shot her a look of mistrust, which was immediately replaced by one of decision and dismissal. Whether Kearney was or was not her friend, she could see that Jean-Paul now judged him a distraction, someone of no further concern. Her brother had more important things on his mind.

"You will have to tell him to leave," he said.

"I will what?" Genevieve exploded. "What is going on here, Jean-Paul? Who is here? Who owns those cars? Tell me!"

"Be quiet!" he hissed. "Are you a fool? Can't you guess who is here? Have you completely forgotten our last conversation?"

"Oh!" Genevieve said, understanding. She glanced around. "Jean-Paul," she said quietly, "Is it safe to have these people around here? What if somebody sees ..."

"Dammit!" said her brother. "What the hell have I been talking about? Will you go out there and get rid of him?"

Genevieve's curiosity was aroused. A thought came to her. "Is it for Saturday?" she whispered. "For the parade?"

Jean-Paul glared at her.

"Don't worry about what it is for, little sister. You know I could not tell you even if I wanted to. Now will you please get that American out of here? Please?"

Genevieve was excited by this intrigue. She wanted to have a part in it. She didn't want to throw obstacles in its path.

"What should I tell him?" she whispered.

"Tell him? Tell him? How should I know what to tell him! Tell him there's been an accident. Family matters. Tell him Father's been hurt in an airplane crash. That's it! Tell him you'll have to fly to Alberta in two hours, that you won't be able to see him again, for a few days anyway. Tell him that."

Genevieve hesitated. She couldn't tell Jack that. She couldn't do that.

"That is unbelievable," she said.

"Then invent something!" Jean-Paul cursed. "Invent somebody!"

Genevieve paced the room, hand to her chin, thinking.

"Will you hurry!" said Jean-Paul. "Listen, you little idiot, there are people here who do not like the idea of wasted time. Do you understand?"

Genevieve nodded. She slipped out the door. The sun had broken through the overcast, and she stood beneath the portico for half a minute, gazing out at the garden. Then she walked around the corner of the house, searching for Kearney.

She found him on the back lawn, halfway between the house and the small barn that served as a tool shed.

He walked toward her smiling, and when they met she told him simply, "Jack, I have to ask you to go. There are problems. Family matters."

"Nothing serious, I hope."

"I am afraid so," she said. "My aunt—my mother's sister—oh, you don't know. My mother, you see, died a little over a year ago, and now her sister…an automobile accident, and she is in the hospital. We must go to her. So you see…"

"I'm sorry, really sorry," said Kearney. "I can see that you…" He didn't finish the sentence, but frowned and said, "You're as pale as a ghost."

He paused. They walked toward his car.

"When will I see you again?" he asked.

"I will try to be at the Rue du Trésor tonight. How about eight o'clock? Perhaps she is not hurt as badly as they say. If not, I will come. If I cannot come, I will send word to Angelique, all right?"

They reached the car. Kearney put out his arm to touch her shoulder, to draw her to him, but she stepped back out of his reach.

"Please, Jack," she said, "I must hurry."

"I understand," he said. "If you need me, don't forget where I'm staying."

"How could I forget?" she smiled. "Bonjour, Jack."

He slid into the Mustang, backed up, and drove off. Genevieve waved to him as he went down the drive, then went back into the house. Jean-Paul was waiting for her in the main room. He was nervous.

"Come here," he said. He led her through the hall into the dark-paneled corner room, their father's den. As if from far away, Genevieve heard hurrying footsteps on the stairs, and then the front door slammed.

"What did you tell him?"

"What we agreed upon. I invented an aunt."

"How did he take it?"

"How was he to take it?" she said. "He saw the situation and left." She shrugged.

"What else was he supposed to do? It was not his problem."

"Good. Listen," said Jean-Paul, whispering. "I cannot tell you much. These are not just my people, my section. There are others here. This thing is very big, and you must not breathe a word of it."

Outside, a car started. Genevieve could hear the sound of it receding as it moved down the drive. Jean-Paul continued.

"Some of them," he glanced upward, "wanted me to keep you here, not let you go."

"What!" said Genevieve, as the fearful implications of his words hit her.

"I persuaded them that you were trustworthy," he said. "They agreed to let you leave."

"Oh, Jean-Paul!" she said, "Again, I am frightened for you! What kind of madness is this? What is happening? It is for Saturday, isn't it? I know that. I can guess it."

She paused. "Are you a hostage too? Will they let you go?"

Jean-Paul laughed.

"No, no, no," he said. "I am not a hostage. I will drive you to the university, as a matter of fact. Get your things." He hesitated, and then said, "Perhaps you should pack some extra things. Perhaps—would you do this for me, Genevieve? Would you stay away from here tonight and Friday night? Would you stay with Rene and Angelique?"

Genevieve looked at him, unbelieving, her mouth open.

"It would be better for both of us if you did that," he said.

Genevieve nodded. She stumbled out of the room and up the stairs as if in a daze. She found it difficult to breathe. Slowly, she began to pack her things. She could feel the presence of others—strangers—in her house, and she was frightened.

Instead of driving back the way he had come, Kearney turned right out of the drive and sent the Mustang along the south road of the long island. If the map was correct, this new route would eventually lead back to the bridge anyway, and he might as well see a new part of the place. He lit another cigarette and studied the landscape casually as he went along.

That's a shame, he mused to himself. A damned shame. An image of Genevieve filled his mind's eye. How affected she was. White as a ghost. Probably feels guilty, too. Staying out all night. Being with me. Not being there when she was needed. They're probably furious with her. Tough. Tough luck for you too, Kearney. Just when things were beginning to move right along. Hell, what kind of a way is that to think? Don't be a pig. And …hey, what are you thinking so much about her for? Not supposed to do that, remember? Supposed to keep this on the cool side, right? No involvement. Summertime romance, and all that. What's the matter, you falling for that kid?

Engrossed in his thoughts, Kearney didn't see the big car barreling up the road behind him. The first he realized it was there, it was next to him, in the passing lane. Its driver hit the horn, and Kearney jumped.

"Shit!" he thought, as the Oldsmobile cut in on him, forcing him off to the side of the road. He slammed on his brakes, skewing the car to a stop in the loose sand. The Oldsmobile stopped directly in front of him, blocking his path. Kearney recognized the vehicle at once. It was one of those that had been parked at Genevieve's house.

Before he could throw his Mustang into reverse, three men leapt out of the Olds and ran back toward him. One stopped beside his passenger door, one came up on the driver's side, while a third, who clutched a knife, disappeared under the front of the car. Kearney heard the hiss of air coming from a slashed tire. Then the doors were yanked open, and he was pulled out of his bucket seat by a strong hand.

"Hey!" he yelped. "What the hell are you doin'…!"

The one who had him by the shirt smashed him against the side of the car and stood him up straight. Feeling like a rabbit trapped by dogs, Kearney looked around at his captors. They were all big, mean-looking, and excited, with faces that he couldn't read. Their features, except for their darting, brilliant eyes and their flaring nostrils, looked like stone. Their expressions were angry, but beyond that, Kearney couldn't tell what they might have in mind.

"My wallet is in the glove compartment," he said.

The one in the center, the one who held him, twisted his shirt tighter and glared at him. His voice came thick and slow.

"So, you like Canadian girls, eh, American?"

So that was the way they were going to play it—he was poaching on somebody else's territory. Well, he thought, that was easy enough to take care of.

"What the hell are you talking about?" he said sharply.

"Don't take me for a fool," said the slow-talking one, tightening his grip even more. "You know what I mean. The girl back there. You get laid with her, maybe?"

"Get your goddamned hands off me," Kearney said, and his voice was like ice.

The tall Canadian released him and backed up a step.

The man began to laugh. The other two smiled thin, wicked smiles that showed spaces between stained teeth.

"You stay away from that girl, American, if you know what is good for you," said their leader. "You never see her again."

"It's none of your business any way you look at it," said Kearney, standing his ground.

"You think it is not?" said the big one, grinning.

Suddenly, the Quebecois lashed out with his open hand and gave Kearney a slap that felt like a semi ripping across his face. The big six-footer stood there in fighting position, laughing and whooping like an Indian. The blood lust was up in his friends, too. They began edging forward…

The last thing Kearney thought was, "He's fast as lightning." Then he lunged for the Frenchman. The man side-stepped him. His punch missed its mark, and suddenly he was vulnerable.

They were good, Kearney had to admit that. They were trained. They passed him around from one to the other like he was a sack of wheat, giving him something to remember them by as he went spinning from each to each. The whole process didn't take half a minute. At the end of it, he was propped up against the side of the car again, in the grasp of the tall leader, gasping for air.

"Mebbe you understand now, eh, Yankee? Mebbe you leave that girl of mine alone, eh? Mebbe you go back to the States and leave Canada alone, eh? Mebbe we never see your face again, eh?"

With every question the huge bastard shook Kearney so hard his teeth rattled.

"Is that right, Yankee? Is that right?" The big Frenchman was close up to him now, screaming in his face.

"Right," Kearney said, gasping for breath.

"What?" howled the Frenchman.

Kearney retched. "Right," he said, and gasped again.

"Remember that!" the Frenchman snarled. He hauled Kearney upright, balancing his wavering body, and gave him a wild left to the stomach. The wind knocked out of him, Kearney collapsed, a sack of bones in the dirt and greasy sand on the side of the road.

"Remember that!" whispered the Frenchman, and he was gone, his footsteps receding in the gravel alongside the asphalt highway.

The rear tires of the beat-up Oldsmobile spun and sent sand and stones flying against the Mustang's grille as the Canadians sped away.

Kearney had plenty of time for reflection. It took him a while to get up. He realized that he was drooling blood into the sand. Choking on the dust and heavy dank air of the asphalt, he raised himself against the car and checked himself out. He was bleeding from the lip, but that was okay. It was only a superficial cut.

He had a lump on his forehead that throbbed and blazed, and his nose felt like it was broken. It wasn't bleeding, though. He figured a couple of hours with his head stuck inside an ice-making machine would do the trick on that score. He smiled, shallowly and gingerly.

His whole body was sore and stiffening fast. His knees wobbled and buckled as he staggered to the trunk of the car to get the spare and the jack. Laughing silently to himself, he figured that after he applied some icepacks, a sauna, a whirlpool, and a massage would do the trick. Then an afternoon of sleep. Oh, right, he thought, like any of that is going to happen.

It was incredible that so much damage could be done to a body in so little time. But that was the way life worked. Years and years of placid days were lived only to bring a person to those special moments of love and hate that shook the foundations of the world.

The time was ripe for philosophy. There was plenty of time to think. Changing a flat in soft sand, with the smell of your own blood coursing down your face, took a good long time. At least he wasn't the only one, Kearney reflected with satisfaction. Each one of those guys had a souvenir from him. One had a broken finger; another had a couple of cracked ribs. The bullying leader had a mouthful of loose teeth that wouldn't settle back to normal for a couple of days, at least, and maybe a fractured jaw that might, with luck, give him trouble for months.

Kearney was proud of himself. Each of those injuries had been delivered by what had seemed to be an accident, or just plain luck. That was what he wanted. It was his revenge. Even while he seemed to be beaten to a pulp, each of his opponents would remember him for a while, and think twice about attacking him again. Maybe.

He hoped they wouldn't compare injuries, that they would just suffer in silence, individually. It might not be good for him if they realized that they were *all* hurt.

That would be too much of a coincidence.

Kearney didn't think they'd talk. They were all laughing when they left him. Assholes like that always kept up a front as long as they could.

Questions came piling into Kearney's mind as he drove back to the city. What was this business all about, anyway? He wasn't sure, but he guessed the reality behind it was pretty grim. There were too many loose ends that seemed to want to connect, but they connected wrong.

He was certain of three things: Genevieve didn't know about this attack; Genevieve didn't have a steady boyfriend, unless he himself was it; and Genevieve didn't have an aunt.

There was trouble brewing; he knew that, too. But there was nothing he could do about it until he saw her again. Things had gotten more complicated than he had figured on. He drove into town, his mind buzzing. He had some tracking down to do.

Chapter 22

Falling Among Friends

Sparrow lay back on the stiff white sheets of his hospital bed and contemplated his shattered arm, which was suspended in a sling in front of him, its plaster cast drying and caking as the morning wore along. The Mountie wanted to reach up and pick the dry flakes of plaster off with his fingers, but on the other hand, he didn't know if it would be worth the effort. He had spent the last half hour contemplating this problem.

Just as Dietrich's bullet had stopped him in his tracks, so it seemed that his mind had stopped along with his body and now spun in wide circles, concentrating fiercely upon all sorts of incidentals that didn't mean a damn. So he sat and watched his arm and tried to move his fingers.

He was in the middle of this wild-swinging neurotic fit when Bannerman came breezing into the room carrying fresh air and purpose along with him.

"Unfortunate," said Bannerman, spinning his hat onto the bed in the vicinity of Sparrow's feet. Sparrow said nothing, but watched intently as the American sat down on the uncomfortable chair by the head of the bed.

"I don't know if I can trust Le Claire," Bannerman said. "I have to rely on him, and I would like to work with him, but he's so damned quirky. What do you think?"

"You can trust him," said Sparrow laconically.

"I trust *him,*" said Bannerman. "But I don't trust his mind. He keeps coming up with wild theories. No facts. No, I don't mean that. I mean he has all kinds of facts, but he doesn't seem to connect them with his theories. Or vice versa. I think he's gone…gone…"

"Balmy?" Sparrow grimaced. "I don't think so. He has a large store of information to sort through, that's all."

"He's convinced that Borovik's going to do something at the economic conference. He's fixed on that. No reason to it. What would Borovik want with a bunch of economists? What the hell would that do? What the…"

"Don't get so worked up, Harvey," Sparrow said.

"You know as well as I do that any thrust toward the economists would be for show." Bannerman was more upset by the minute. "What the hell is that son-of-a-bitch here for, anyway?"

"Bannerman," said Sparrow. "Will you please calm down? You're getting my cast all agitated. Look at the way it's swinging."

"Can you move it?"

"A bit."

"Can you get up?"

"No."

"When can you get out of here?"

"When can I…?" Sparrow paused and frowned. "Bannerman, don't be so beastly. The arm was shattered. Splinters. The bloody bastard was using dum-dums. I'm not going anywhere."

"Shit," Bannerman said. He jumped up and began pacing the room. "Can't you try, anyway? I'm working in a vacuum. I need help."

"I tried," said Sparrow, with resignation. "I had to take a leak before and I decided to use the john instead of this pisspot they have here."

"And?"

"Well, I took the cast out of the sling, you see, and that's the last I remember. Apparently, it fell on me, but I don't really know what happened, because I simply screamed and passed out. Shock, they said, from moving the damned thing. I can't even wiggle my fingers now, you see."

Bannerman stared at Sparrow's fingertips.

"Le Claire is convinced that Borovik is going to try to kidnap Harold Holsworthy," he said calmly. "Holsworthy's going to address the economists on Saturday. Is there any conceivable reason Borovik would want an eccentric science fiction writer?"

Sparrow frowned. "I seem to recall..." he began and then stopped. Bannerman waited. Sparrow looked at the CIA man and said, "I'm surprised you don't know, Harvey. Don't you know about Harold Holsworthy?"

"Henry," said Bannerman, "1 am brimming over with all kinds of information. I am receiving hourly bulletins from Washington. But I know less than nothing about this lunatic Holsworthy. Tell me."

"Well, old man," said Sparrow, settling in and forgetting about his arm for a moment. "He's not just a science fiction writer, you know. He's a scientist. The writing is for fun. But he's done quite a bit of work with rockets, satellites, space exploration, things of that nature. Frequent visitor to Canaveral in the early days. Interesting chap. His work might just be of value to ...interested parties, shall we say. I'm sure we have a dossier on him. Like to see it?"

Bannerman was staring out the window, his hands in his pockets. He turned. "I'd appreciate it, Henry," he said. "I'll get ours from Washington, too. Just to be on the safe side. Probably faster, but I'm sure...yes, I'd like to see it."

"Good," said Sparrow. "I'll have it to you sometime today."

"Finding out about Holsworthy may make me feel better about Le Claire, too," Bannerman said. "It makes his theories more plausible, at any rate. I was beginning to wonder about him."

"Oh, don't worry about Claude," said Sparrow. "Say, I've an idea. Why don't you just let him go on with his conference business? If he's right, all well and good, the situation is covered. If he's wrong, what's the difference?"

"As long as he doesn't siphon off too many men on a wild goose chase."

"Oh, I dare say we'll have a sufficient number of bodies," said Sparrow. "How about you? Getting any help from your people?"

Bannerman had a sudden vision of hundreds of World War II bombers and troop transports blackening the skies, roaring north with their groaning loads of supplies and men, crossing the border into Canada while thousands cheered. It was like a movie with John Wayne and the whole bunch of them.

He smiled at the image.

"Washington's beginning to perk up," he said. "I've already received some good help —well, you know that—and a few more are on the way. My reports must be causing some nervousness." Bannerman seemed to relax, as much as any feral cat could relax. He sat down in the chair by the bed once again.

"And, you know, Henry, we've discovered a joker in the deck, and he's about to be turned." Bannerman smiled again. "Turned to good use, I hope. That's something Le Claire is doing for me—bringing him in. Have to see him about it this afternoon."

Sparrow mulled this over. "Unexpected help, hey? Good. I suppose we can use the help. What kind of information is Washington supplying?"

"Oh, interesting stuff, Sparrow," said Bannerman. He got up and began to pace up and down once more. "I'm beginning to get a fleshed-out picture. A lot of business on activities in Cuba. Incredible amount of activity there since Fidel opened up his African connections. Africa's become a gigantic filtering pipeline from the Mideast to Cuba. All kinds of characters moving about."

He stopped pacing.

"Washington's been putting together scenarios on who these fellows here might be," he said. "We've done quite well. We know five of them. Borovik, of course. The two Arabs. Another Russian, a Vasyli Sergeovitch Bukharin, straight from KGB headquarters. And a Hun of a disaffected West German, Dietrich Fischer, who's been around a long time. That's the fellow who got you." Sparrow grunted.

"Well, beginning from that," Bannerman continued, "we're digging into their past records—their proclivities, their skill areas. Trying to see what kind of a team Borovik's put together. What he might try to do with it. And who the others might be—complements to the known factors, so to speak. Also, we're looking for who is where, who has been spotted where, outside his usual stomping grounds, who has moved into and out of Cuba, among the professionals, I mean. What kinds of interesting weapons are moving about…"

Sparrow beamed at Bannerman's recitation. He interrupted with a wistful sigh. "I say! Wouldn't it be fine to capture him?"

"Henry," said Bannerman, gazing intently out the window, "I'd buy you a good Cuban cigar if we did. I'd buy you a dozen of them." He stood there and slowly pounded a fist into his palm. "But I don't have enough information. I need more information. With what we know of his team, he could do anything with it. I've got to know which way he is going to move!"

"Go to it, old man," said Sparrow weakly. He settled back onto his pillow. "Lots of work…good for the morale...all that…"

Sparrow slipped off into a heavy sleep. Bannerman looked at him, picked up his hat, and went out the door. He suddenly wanted a good cigar very much.

Chapter 23
St. Lambert Lock

Thursday afternoon Borovik was in the old warehouse sitting at a wrecked roll-top desk in a room that he had converted into his headquarters. Just off the office was a large walk-in closet that contained the guts of what had become his primary radio station, capable of sending and receiving messages worldwide. The headquarters proper contained his desk and a swivel chair. A bare bulb hung down from a wire that stretched from the high ceiling to the midheight of the dingy room. There was no other furniture. A ripped and patched shade covered a large window. Beneath the window was a squat radiator shedding ancient white paint. Cardboard coffee cups littered the window sill and the corners of the room.

Borovik felt good. He was proud of the team he had put together. They were dangerous men, well-versed in conventional and unconventional warfare. Any one of them could enter a house, open the bathroom medicine chest, and put together enough volatile ingredients from innocuous-sounding products to blow the walls out of the house.

That was what Borovik intended to do to Canada—blow the psychological walls out of it, and create a bit of economic chaos on the side. The initial request for help from Cartier's Organization had given him the idea. It was a thrilling concept. It would be a major revolutionary strike, closer to the mainland United States than any before. It would put the complacent Americans in a state of panic when they realized that the savage striking arm of the revolutionary front had penetrated what had always been their secure northern frontier.

It would also throw the American and Canadian authorities into furious political battle, thus weakening and damaging—perhaps permanently, he thought with a gleam of hope—the American-Canadian-British axis that he hated so violently, that had thwarted his plans so often in the past. Here was a chance for him to strike at its heartland, in the festering sore of Canada that was the separatist cause. And all this would happen almost on top of the vulnerable American border, the border that he intended to cross on the way out of here. For after he was done, and the mission accomplished, Borovik planned to add insult to injury. He intended to return to Cuba by way of the United States. Just for laughs.

Borovik contemplated this added fillip like it was a red cherry on a mound of whipped cream. A chuckle rose from deep within him. Except for a few incidental embarrassments, his plan was nicely under way and going remarkably well.

The Russian's gaze riveted once again on the scrap of paper sitting on the desk in front of him. To an uninitiated observer, the notations on it would appear as nothing more than squiggles, doodles, and dots. But those squiggles meant everything to Borovik, and he was intent on deciphering them. They told him the current disposition of his forces, their locations and their activities, and looking at them was like looking at pieces in a chess game—a game that Borovik could not lose. The possibility that his plan would be discovered in its entirety by his adversaries, that they could react with sufficient force and speed to abort it once they had found it out, that possibility was infinitesimal. Borovik knew the odds. Well thought out plans simply were not interdicted.

So, confident and happy, he sat and stared at his pieces, dredging up out of his mind flashes of possible obstacles; and, in turn, he thought up schemes to counteract those obstacles. And he chuckled. He enjoyed this playful aspect of the terror he was about to unleash.

His innermost circle of defense was the Argentinian, the one man he trusted implicitly. They had been together so long, they knew each other's minds. They were like two halves of a machine, fused straight down the middle, and interlocking at so many different angles that it was impossible to pry them apart. They were more like twin brothers than comrades.

Right now, the Argentinian was on the opposite side of one of these walls, prowling about, checking out the building, learning the defenses of the place, the better to defend it at minimum risk to themselves and maximum loss to any invader.

Later in the afternoon, the Argentinian would go out to the house on the island where so much mayhem would soon be launched, and check it out in a similar manner. Vasyli and Dietrich were there now, studying the grounds and facilities, planning the alterations necessary for the transfer of equipment from the warehouse to the island. That transfer would happen tonight. Borovik was not going to make the same mistake that had been made with the missiles in 1962. This time, nothing would be left lying around in the open.

The Cuban had been given charge of communications, and he divided his time between the radio and the final set-up and testing of the sophisticated electronic equipment.

Abdul and Mahmoud were en route from Charles Morin's house in Les Escoumins, loaded with information. They had wired some inkling of it ahead, and that was a major reason for Borovik's happy frame of mind. Their report concerned certain shipping movements, and those particular movements fitted Borovik's plans to a T. The Lebanese and Yemenite were due to arrive in Quebec City just after sundown. They would proceed by stages to the warehouse, where they would help with the transfer of the strategic material.

The Italian and the Algerian were in Montreal on separate missions. They, too, would report to headquarters in the evening. The Italian would have negative news to relay, but the Algerian's information would allow Borovik's final arrangements to blossom into death-dealing splendor.

The Algerian, calm and satisfied, stood on the tourist observation deck of St. Lambert Lock and looked out over the entrance to the St.

Lawrence Seaway. Beyond it, across the wide expanse of the river, the aluminum-gray towers of Montreal rose beneath the protecting heights of their mountain. The air was clean with the smell of a summer shower just past.

The Algerian watched the oil tanker Kedristan enter the lock. There was the gurgling and hissing of water as it entered from the higher level, and the full, wallowing, black bathtub of a ship rose to the level of the inland waterway. There was a fascination in the sheer size of the thing. The Algerian knew that empty, the black bulk would rise higher than a five-story building; but even now, full, the rising of that monster on the man-made tide was astounding. Ancient memory cells called up thoughts of beached whales and oily dinosaurs; and modern sensory cells, attuned to a technological revolution, still could not believe that what they recorded was really happening, and so, protesting, insisted, "No, that's not right. It's too big to move like that. Just won't go."

But it would, and it did.

And after it did, it moved along in that thin slip of waterway, not ten feet away from where the Algerian stood, and again the eyes said, "No. Impossible." Something was out of kilter and yet in sharp focus, and that was the basis of its fascination.

The Algerian watched the tanker go; watched a string of black hulls of assorted tonnages and silhouettes move slowly to the west along the river's edge, beads drawn on a chain of supply and demand. They were like compartments of civilization, moving about to carry goods wherever necessary, wherever the race of humans wanted to build next.

The Algerian understood history and civilization, and culture, and economics. He had studied them all out of hatred for the foreigners who were in his land when he was a boy. The hated putrefying whiteness of their sun-hidden skins had made him sick, and even now the memory of those boyhood thoughts made him shudder as he relived the old feelings.

In those days of growing up under the hell of European colonialism, he had sustained himself with pride, with the knowledge of the ancient Arabian Moslem culture that had extended from Spain to India and even farther for hundreds of years, while the northern barbarians lost whatever culture they might have once possessed and replaced it with nothing. His mind dwelt on the accomplishments of his ancestors, and he drew his strength from them.

Now he thought about his present situation. He found amusing the knowledge that once he had fought against Frenchmen to the death, and now he was fighting for other Frenchmen to the death. And possibly, right over there in those tall, glass-and-gray steel towers that seemed to float upon the land like a fleet of ships upon the wide waters, there were men who had once fought blindly against him as he had fought blindly against them. And now they were allies. And could they see any better now? Or did they all view their actions with the blindness that was usual in their complicated lives?

"What of it?" thought the Algerian, angrily. He dismissed his mental meanderings. What difference did it make? Better to get back to what was tangible, visible, meaningful. He suddenly longed for meaning, for logic, as a farmer longs for rain and sun and rich soil. He turned back to his immediate problem.

He gazed up and down the river, wondering where he would be able to do the most damage. There were two or three prime locations, but almost anywhere along the lock system was a good enough place for the job he had to do. So many spectacular locations presented themselves, though, that he had to keep reminding himself that this was not a propaganda ploy, but an economic act.

The ship with the bomb attached to its hull would enter the Seaway system, and once it was there, he would simply have to press a button at any opportune moment. The bomb would explode, and in such a confined space it would rip the lock system to shreds.

With luck, the crude oil the ship carried would go up in a fireball, but that was asking a lot. That would be an unexpected dividend. It was harder than generally thought to ignite crude oil. The main thing was to destroy the Seaway.

The Algerian affirmed to his own satisfaction that the plan was a good one. Then he left the observation deck and found a cab waiting in the parking lot. He ordered the driver to take him to the intercity bus terminal on Rue St. Francois. He was going back to Quebec City to report to Borovik, and the bus seemed to him to be the most innocuous method of transportation.

He carried a Pakistani passport, and could pass for a Pakistani, but there was no sense exposing himself more than necessary. Ever since the problem Vasyli and Dietrich had encountered yesterday, with the wild shootout and chase, members of the team played it close to the chest—they were to draw no attention to themselves for any reason whatsoever. The word had gone out. Walk away from sticky situations. Choose the least noticeable means to an end.

So the Algerian wanted nothing to do with a private car. He had abandoned it. He wanted no part of inquisitive police. He would not take an airplane, with its mandatory search and probable seizure. No, he would take the lowly, efficient bus, with its laughing students, its old people, its down-and-outers of Quebec society who left you alone. That would be safest.

O'Rourke spotted him.

O'Rourke was a Mountie from Saskatchewan. He had been called into Montreal in the general beef-up of security forces that had begun on Wednesday morning. Before he was assigned to a post, he had attended a briefing in the cavernous gymnasium of the Quebec regional headquarters building. The voices of the lecturers had rung off the walls and ceiling and demanded attention.

O'Rourke and a hundred other Mounties were shown slides of some seventy-five men, images gathered from Ottawa, Washington, London, Paris, Rome, Bonn, Tel Aviv, Tokyo, Cairo. They were the faces of known terrorists.

The Mounties were given books with the same faces to study, to memorize, to learn as many as possible of them before leaving the briefing. They were not to take the books with them.

That announcement caused some hearty laughter and snickering. They were not told who the men were; they were told only that they were extremely dangerous. The men were not to be apprehended; they were simply to be spotted and trailed. O'Rourke and his mates were to report any suspicious sighting immediately and use their best judgment in trailing a subject. Wait for assistance was the main point of the advice. Do not attempt to apprehend a subject singlehandedly. Do not approach them. Trail them, and report in.

At first there was curiosity among the Mounties. But the eyes and voices of their instructors reinforced the message: "Don't ask questions, fellows. Just do your jobs. This is too big for questions. Believe it." Their instructors did not say the words, but they projected the thoughts, and that was enough. The Mounties were trained, and trained well. They would do their jobs, and do them right, and ask no questions.

There was enough information for them from other sources, after all. They knew Sergeant Griffith was dead in Quebec City. They knew that another highly-placed Mountie officer was injured. They suspected that the officer might be more than a Mountie; the media hadn't gotten anything out of the force's spokesman except a fictitious name. And there was a double guard on his hospital room. He had very few visitors, and they were not the usual visitors one would expect to find visiting an injured cop. There was plenty of room for speculation. Something was up, and it was big.

Sergeant O'Rourke and some of his fellow officers were assigned to cover all transportation access points in the Montreal area. Others were assigned to various points in Quebec Province. O'Rourke drew the bus terminal assignment. He worked the terminal posing as a plainclothes detective assigned to spotting runaway kids.

And that's where he saw the Algerian, late Thursday afternoon.

He was pretty sure he recognized him. Then he was very sure.

O'Rourke wandered casually close to the man. He noticed the Algerian's eyebrows. They were thick and bushy and joined in a mass of hair above his nose. People could change a lot about their characteristics. The Algerian had shaved off his moustache and beard, for instance. But he hadn't done a thing about his eyebrows.

He watched his target climb on board an express bus bound for Quebec City.

The man was overdressed for bus travel. He wore a blue business suit with pinstripes, and carried an obviously new attaché case. But he didn't look like a businessman. There was just something about him that was out of place. His manner, his stature, his whole being cried out to O'Rourke that he just didn't belong.

The Mountie stood behind a pillar and called the sighting in over his transmitter. He could just see the bus door by peeking around the side of the tiled support. The Algerian had gotten on the bus, and he hadn't gotten off. The doors closed, and the bus pulled out of the terminal. Sergeant O'Rourke resumed his search for wanted faces.

When the bus left the terminal, it was followed by an unmarked, beat-up looking undercover police car containing a pair of detectives. The car followed the bus to the Interprovincial Autoroute, where another unmarked car waited to pick up the tail.

Altogether, the bus was escorted to Quebec City by two unmarked cars, a police helicopter, and two more unmarked cars, in succession.

The bus never stopped. When it arrived at Quebec City, the Algerian disembarked. Hefelfinger was waiting to pick up the tail and follow him through town. The CIA operative admired his prey's dogged adherence to the rules for shaking off scouts. After a multitude of twists and turns, the Algerian went into a small hotel, where he stayed for fifteen minutes. The hotel was on the Dufferin Terrace, right around the corner from the U.S. consulate. Hefelfinger waited outside and took the opportunity to call in this information.

The Algerian came back out of the hotel and walked through town to Rue St. Jean. He walked along this main street of shops and restaurants until he came to an alley that opened onto an inner courtyard where artisans displayed their pottery and macramé beside an open-air restaurant that sprawled its tables out into the center of the small plaza. Wooden outdoor staircases clung to the sides of surrounding buildings and led to apartments high above.

The Algerian chose one and scrambled up to the second level.

Hefelfinger stood by the iron grillework gate to the courtyard, fingering some macramé and watching his quarry out of the corner of his eye. He was quite sure he hadn't been spotted. He was equally sure the Algerian wasn't entering a trick apartment with an alternate exit. He had walked up those stairs with the weariness of an alert but tired man looking forward to a good rest. Either the man was the best actor in the world, or he was going to flop face down on a bed and stay there for a while.

It didn't matter anyway. The Algerian was surrounded, or would be in two minutes. Hefelfinger was wired and sending out signals like a computer. His team was converging on the area right now. There were six of them, with four always remaining on duty. They would follow the Algerian to the end.

Hefelfinger took a book out of his back pocket, sat down at one of the restaurant tables, and ordered an espresso. All he had to do now was watch the Algerian's apartment door until he was relieved. Then there would be the matter of apprehending and questioning the building's landlord. But that would be later. For now, he sat and sipped his coffee, and tried to read the building's structure.

In the quiet summer evening, Borovik's plan was beginning to fray around the edges. Borovik didn't know that. He couldn't see it. But there was an invisible rip in his security system.

Chapter 24

The Black Heart of Night

Kearney was half-hidden in a shallow doorway that night when Genevieve came up the Rue du Trésor. He jumped out into the street in front of her, startling her more than he had intended. He had forgotten about his bruises. He stood there grinning down at her like some kind of a Halloween goblin.

"Oh, Jack! What has happened to you!" she said, seeing his face.

"What?" he said. "What do you…oh, you mean this?" He gingerly touched the lump on his forehead. "It's nothing. I fell down a cliff on the Plains of Abraham. Come on."

She allowed him to steer her into the outdoor courtyard of the Nouvelle-France, where they found an empty table and waited for service. Genevieve knew he hadn't told her the truth, and she looked at him with concern.

"Listen," he said, "Why didn't you tell me about your boyfriend?"

"My what!" she exclaimed. "Who told you I have a…Do you think I have a…" She was indignant. "Do you think I go around picking up American tourists, perhaps? Do you take me for a whore!"

She made a move to get up. Kearney gripped her hand tightly. "Let go of me!" she hissed.

Kearney held her fast. "Do you know anyone who might think you are his girlfriend? A man who might become jealous?"

She stared blankly at him. At the next table, a group of university students celebrated a victory of some kind. She darted a glance at them, then returned her gaze to Kearney.

The waiter brought them two steins of beer. Kearney took a sip of his and waited.

"You did not fall," said Genevieve.

"Who were those people with your brother?"

Genevieve remembered the footsteps on the stairs that morning, the door slamming, the car starting up and going fast down the driveway, and the horrible, death-like atmosphere those men left behind them in the house.

Her heart and mind froze as she realized what had happened; what was happening. She stared at Kearney with frightened eyes.

"Jack," she said. "Do not ask me. I cannot tell you."

"Don't you think I should know?" he asked. "They told me to stay away from you. What if they come for me again? What do I do?"

"They will not bother you again. They are too busy," she said. "You were an obstacle, and they think now you are gone. Do not ask anything more of me. Please, Jack."

"I don't know what to do," he said. "People try to kill me and you tell me not to worry. How do I handle this? Do you want to see me dead?"

"No!" Genevieve was trembling. Then she made a decision.

"Later," she whispered. "Later, I will tell you."

Kearney released his grip on her hand. She sat and stared across the table at him. She looked scared to death.

"Later after what?" he asked.

Her voice was barely audible. "After Saturday. Please, Jack."

He looked at her hard. "I trust you," he said. "I know you wouldn't let me be hurt."

She nodded, her lips tight together. Suddenly, she felt very tired. She held her head in her hands.

"Jack," she said, "Let's go for a ride together. I'll show you…"

Genevieve did not finish her sentence. Kearney was looking beyond her, his eyes happy and a smile on his face. Genevieve turned and saw Angelique and Rene coming through the gate to the garden. For the first time she could ever remember, she felt no desire to see them. She was, in fact, annoyed that they had chosen that moment to appear. She closed her eyes, took a deep breath, and tried to compose herself.

Rene sat down at the table, and while Angelique was saying hello, he pulled his coat collar high around his neck, his cap low over his eyes, and glanced furtively around the area. "A conspiracy!" he whispered. "Are you ready for Saturday?"

"What's Saturday?" asked Kearney.

"Aha, American!" Rene said, whispering dramatically. "Saturday is the parade in honor of our national holiday. The government says it is our provincial day, but what does the government know? It is the feast day of St. Jean-Baptiste, and on Saturday all the religious societies, the patriotic societies, the humbled societies, the hangdog societies, the hands-out-for-crumbs societies, all will gather here in this big, magnificent capital city of ours and march down the streets with trumpets and drums—boom, boom, boom. And there among them will be the rabble-rousers, the revolutionaries, the strumpets and scum of humanity, trying to upset the plans of the masters and leading the marchers astray toward some form of sanity rather than their present march of destiny toward a blank, unscalable wall of cream-and-stucco cement frustration."

Rene banged the table and looked around. Angelique and Genevieve were laughing at him, and Kearney smiled.

Rene burrowed his head even farther into his coat and said, "Hey, American, you want to see the revolution in action? Come with us. We go now to make up some revolutionary notices, myself and the artist. For the demonstration, eh? You come, yes?"

Rene paused and looked at Kearney's face. He frowned and said in a normal voice, "Hey, Jack, what happened to your head?"

Genevieve answered for him even now. "He fell in the park, being a tourist." She forced a laugh.

Rene looked from one to the other, and said to Genevieve, "Ah, so he fell on his head. And that is why he is with you, eh, little one?"

He studied Kearney for a second, then said, "So. You want to come?"

Angelique ripped into the poet with anger in her voice. "Rene! Don't you know when to keep your mouth shut? We'll be in trouble!"

"Ahh," said Rene. "Who is listening? You think perhaps they have a bug under this table? Don't be so paranoid, mon cher."

A beer stein crashed to the pavement beside the table next to them. Startled, they jumped and looked up. Four students, moments ago laughing and enjoying a drink, were being attacked by as many men in suits and trench coats. Like so many items on an assembly line, they hauled the youths out of their seats and slammed them against the stone wall.

"Hands on the wall! Spread your legs! Up against the wall!" The harsh commands were hurled in French, but they needed no translation. They would have sounded the same in any language.

The efficient plainclothesmen ran their hands roughly over the students' bodies, checking for concealed weapons, then peeled their hands off the wall to be handcuffed behind their backs. All four students' hands were manacled. The cold rings of steel snapped shut.

Kearney spun around to look at the entrance to the café. Standing behind Genevieve was a short man with a ruddy complexion and white hair, wearing, like the others, a trench coat and fedora. He kept his hands in the pockets of the trench coat, looked directly at Kearney, and said evenly, in English, "You are under arrest. Put your hands on the top of your head."

"What?" shouted Kearney, leaping to his feet. "What the hell… hey!"

He was grabbed from behind by two plainclothesmen and dragged to the wall.

"What do you think of our Canadian justice?" shouted Rene, as he was being dragged out of his chair.

Two more officers took Genevieve and Angelique by their arms and began to haul them up. Angelique, white as thin paper, came quietly enough, but Genevieve suddenly began to scream. It was a blood-curdling scream. The cop who was handling her dropped her, and she curled up in a ball on the ground and kept screaming.

The pinpoint efficiency of the pinch was thrown into turmoil. Three cops jumped on the girl, but they couldn't get her quiet.

Now in handcuffs and held by the two cops, Kearney was still able to turn his head away from the wall. He looked out over the scene and grinned. Everybody in the place—tourists and Canadians alike—were watching the three cops going after Genevieve.

"Shut her up! Shut her up, dammit!" yelled Le Claire.

One plainclothesman got his hand over Genevieve's mouth and yelped in pain. He jumped up, holding one hand in the other. The crowd laughed and applauded. Genevieve's screams grew louder. Another detective, more cautious than the first, and wearing gloves, placed his hand over her nose and mouth. Gradually, her screams subsided, replaced by muffled moans. Her body writhed as it searched for air. The cop relaxed his grip a bit, and she gasped.

The crowd began to boo the police, and curses were hurled at them from bystanders they could not see.

"Quiet!" roared Le Claire. "Quiet, or you will be going with them!"

As if to emphasize his point, a dark green police van roared down narrow Rue du Trésor and came to a halt at the gate to the courtyard. Its rear doors were flung open and the prisoners were herded quickly aboard, single file. They sat silently on benches inside the van, their hands cuffed behind their backs.

Le Claire stood by the open doors of the vehicle.

"You are all under arrest," he announced, "for treasonable acts, and terrorism, and treason against the sovereign nation of Canada."

"You're crazy!" shouted Kearney. "I'm an American."

"Of course you are," laughed Le Claire. "Shall we take you to the American embassy?"

"Yes!" yelled Kearney. "That's exactly what you'll do!"

"Close these doors," Le Claire said to one of his detectives. "Let's get out of here."

The doors, reinforced with wire fencing, slammed shut. The prisoners sat on two benches, facing each other. Rene looked around, and started a chant.

Everyone, including Kearney, picked it up and roared it out.

"Vive Le Québec Libre! Vive Québec Libre!"

It echoed through the hollow metal of the paddy wagon. The prisoners began to stamp their feet in time to the chant.

"Vive Le Québec Libre! Vive Québec Libre!"

Genevieve started to scream again. They could hear the angry roar of the crowd outside and the sound of bottles and rocks hitting the sides of the truck.

"Vive Le Québec Libre! Vive Québec Libre!"

Then they felt the transport sway as it rounded the corner into Rue de Buade. It picked up speed, and the sound of the mob lessened. Soon there was silence outside.

They stopped their chant then, and Genevieve stopped screaming. Quietly, composed, they all sat looking at each other.

"Damn!" said Rene. "Do you know what this means? We'll be up all night printing those flyers—if they let us out tonight."

"They'll let us out," Kearney said. "They have to let us out." He paused, and asked uncertainly, "Don't they?"

"No, they don't," said Angelique. "We are under suspicion."

"Suspicion of what?" said Kearney.

"Suspicion of anything, Jack," Rene answered. "They can say anything. That's the devil of it."

"Well, they can't keep me," said Kearney. "I wasn't kidding. I'll demand to see somebody."

"We had better think of something else," Rene said quietly. "They will only laugh at you."

"We'll see about that," said Kearney indignantly.

"Jack," Angelique cajoled him. "Just do as they say and be quiet. We cannot argue. We have no time. We have to get out of here. We have no time for issues, not now."

"What are these other guys here for?" Kearney asked, looking over the four university students.

Genevieve smiled. "For stealing English cannonballs and chairs from the Chateau," she said with a small smile. "And besides that…"

"Wait!" interrupted one of the students. He jerked his head to indicate Jack. "Who is he?"

"A friend," said Rene. "A friend."

"…besides that," continued Genevieve, "There is a statue missing."

"That's ridiculous!" Kearney exploded. "This treatment for nonsense like that?"

Rene sighed. "It makes no difference, Jack. It is a pretense. It is just something so they can show they are still the boss. Just something to let them be brutal."

"Brutal!" Kearney snorted. "Brutal! I'll show them who's brutal! The bastards." He ground his teeth.

"Poor Jack!" said Genevieve, smiling. "It has not been your day, has it?"

Kearney grinned at her. He was amazed. She was so young, and already a professional agitator.

"Where did you learn to scream like that?" he asked her. "How is your throat? "

Genevieve lifted her head proudly. "It will be ready for the parade Saturday," she said, her voice sounding hoarse now.

"Say, Jack," said Angelique. "Are you a lawyer, by any chance?"

Kearney smiled. "No," he said. "No, I'm not."

"What do you do?" she asked quietly.

Kearney looked at her and grinned sheepishly.

"I'm an accountant." he said. "For a firm in Philadelphia."

One of the students laughed through his nose.

"Ah! Une capitaliste!" he said.

Rene looked across at the boy and chuckled. Genevieve looked down at the floor.

The transport pulled up in the courtyard of the Justice Department headquarters, and the prisoners were ordered out. They were escorted through a side entrance of the building and into a large green room that was the department's intake area. Le Claire whispered directions to a uniformed officer who sat behind a desk, and headed out of the room.

Kearney's voice boomed out, echoing through the room.

"Hey, you sheep-headed goatfucker! I told you I wanted an American representative here. Where the fuck are you going? Turn around, you shithead!"

Le Claire stopped in his tracks, his ears ringing. A detective jumped toward Kearney, and Kearney bent low and put his shoulder into the man's stomach, sending him flying.

"You prick bastards!" Kearney yelled. "Fight fair. Take these cuffs off me and I'll take you all on at once. Come on!"

Le Claire turned on a dime. He walked across the marble floor to Kearney and stood directly in front of him. He looked up at the tall American, who glowered down at him.

"Can you prove you are an American?" asked Le Claire.

"My wallet is in my back pocket," Kearney fumed. "There are ten pieces of identification in it. I also have a passport, but not on me. But I can produce it with no problem, if you want to see it."

"I'll take your word for it," Le Claire said. "Sergeant McElroy," he said to a detective. "Hand me that wallet." The sergeant fished the wallet out of Kearney's pocket and handed it to Le Claire, who inspected its contents casually.

"Humph," he said.

"Satisfied?" Kearney demanded.

"Yes, Monsieur," said Le Claire.

"Good. Now, these people," Kearney indicated Genevieve and Rene and Angelique, "are my friends. We were sitting there minding our own business when you gentlemen …," he made his tone conciliatory, "…well, you made a mistake. Why don't you just let us go?"

Le Claire looked at Kearney. His smile clearly asked if Kearney thought him a fool.

"Monsieur," he said. "Just because you are an American, it does not follow that you are not also a terrorist."

"Oh, for God's sake. Do I look like a terrorist?" Kearney exploded.

"What does a terrorist look like, Monsieur?" asked Le Claire, as though they were in casual conversation.

Kearney had no answer to that. "Damn!" he said.

"The charges stand," said Le Claire to the desk officer. "And add these charges: resisting arrest, assaulting a police officer, and using foul and abusive language to a police officer in a public place."

"Damn!" Kearney cursed. "That does it. I want a representative from the American embassy."

"Surely, Monsieur, "said Le Claire, "you are not that naive. You do not really believe that every American who gets into trouble outside his country is automatically represented by the State Department?"

Le Claire's eyes opened wide.

"Not in cases of civil complaints, he isn't," said Kearney. "But you have accused me of something which makes an international case out of this. In which case," he stated emphatically, "I am entitled to official representation."

"Oh, really?" asked Le Claire caustically.

"Yes, really," Kearney rejoined. "Because of that terrorism charge, and you damned well know it. What do you think you're doing, playing with a baby?"

Le Claire hesitated for just a brief moment, and then he spoke quietly, shrugging his shoulders to indicate he would concede the point. "Very well, Monsieur, you may have your representation."

"What?" Kearney was taken aback.

"You may have your representation," Le Claire repeated. "I shall go now and contact the consulate. I am sorry, you see, Quebec is not a nation—not yet, at any rate—so we do not have an embassy here for you, but we do have an American consulate." He looked Kearney in the eye. "That should do, non? What's the matter?"

Kearney's mouth hung slack. He didn't speak.

"What's wrong?" Le Claire asked with all innocence. "Do you not wish representation?"

"I'm just surprised, that's all." Kearney said, gathering his wits. It was the truth. He was so surprised his mouth was as dry as sandpaper. Le Claire smiled a thin smile at him, and Kearney didn't like that, not at all.

"As you say, Monsieur," said Le Claire. "I am not playing with a baby. You know your rights. But the charges stand. Agreed?"

"Agreed. For now," Kearney said between clenched teeth.

"Sergeant," said Le Claire. "Take the handcuffs off the American here. And his friends, too."

Le Claire's tone was suddenly jovial. "Oh, take them off everybody. They aren't going anyplace." He turned quickly, crossed the room, and disappeared through the door.

Kearney stood looking after him, rubbing his wrists where the handcuffs had chafed them. Angelique came up and stood close to him.

"How did you know that?" she whispered.

"How did I know what?"

Rene and Genevieve joined them. "How did you know you were entitled to American representation in this case?" Angelique watched him with the look of an inquisitor.

"I didn't," he said nervously, scratching his head. "I didn't know. I was bluffing. I just wanted to make so much trouble he'd let us go. I didn't expect this at all."

"You *should* be a lawyer," Angelique said. "You cause more trouble than you're worth." She walked away.

Kearney's thoughts were racing at speeds that blurred past and future into one perilous present. He knew that Le Claire never had to take the abuse Kearney had dished out, that Le Claire didn't even have to listen to him. There was nothing in international law—absolutely nothing—about an American having to be represented by an American Embassy official when accused of any crime – of any nature – with or without international ramifications.

Kearney knew that. Le Claire knew that.

He had to, considering his position. Besides, Le Claire could easily have held him on a simple civil charge. There was no need to insist on retaining the accusation of terrorism if he wanted to keep Kearney in custody. No. When Le Claire capitulated the way he did—running right off find an American official—a cold, tight sweat had enveloped Kearney, body and mind.

There was only one reason the Frenchman would agree to Kearney's demand. That was the reason for the detective's crooked smile. Somehow, Le Claire knew that there was nobody in the world Kearney wanted to see less than a representative of the U. S. Department of State.

Less than half an hour later Le Claire was back in the doorway, crooking his finger in Kearney's direction.

"Monsieur?" he said, and motioned Kearney to follow him.

Before he could stand, Genevieve's fingernails dug into his arm. She looked at him with fear in her eyes. Hiding his own apprehension, Kearney whispered, "You look out for me and I'll look out for you, and they won't be able to touch us."

Genevieve nodded and let go of him.

He crossed to the door and marched with Le Claire down the corridor. The sickening institutional green ceiling and walls were bathed in the wavering light of dirty fluorescent bulbs that hung overhead like rigid deathworms.

"I wanted to get your attention," Kearney said to Le Claire as they walked along. The Frenchman looked at him quizzically. "I didn't mean it personally when I cursed at you."

"It was a rare experience," said Le Claire, smiling again. "I have never heard those words used quite like that before—I mean in that order. But Monsieur, you must be nervous, eh? You must have much more to think about right now than my personal feelings?"

Le Claire stopped in front of a door and opened it. He motioned Kearney in and, when the American went through, Le Claire closed the door behind him. There was a finality about the click of the lock that made Kearney's heart jump.

He found himself in a conference room containing a table, a corner lamp, and a number of conference chairs. A large amber glass ashtray sat at the center of the table. Across the room, another door led to an unknown destination.

For a moment, he thought it was a trick. Perhaps this was a ploy to separate him from his companions. Maybe he'd be kept here indefinitely, incommunicado, sweating. His eyes darted around the room. His mind memorized details.

Then he heard a muffled noise from behind the opposite door and he turned to face it. The knob turned and the door opened admitting a tall, balding man in a blue suit carrying a briefcase. His stride was purposeful but not intimidating. He smiled at Kearney and extended his hand.

"Hi," he said, "I'm Harvey Bannerman. I'm the First Secretary at the consulate. What seems to be the trouble?"

"I was picked up with some Canadian friends in a police raid," said Kearney. "I think I'm being accused of terrorism, but I'm not sure."

"Oh?" said Bannerman. He seemed totally surprised. "Well, we'd better sit down and talk this out. Have a chair."

They sat at opposite ends of the table.

"Anyway," said Kearney, "I want to get out of here. I don't know what kind of rules they're playing by, but I don't like them."

"You could scarcely be expected to," said Bannerman, "considering your present position. Tell me, do you have a police record in the States?"

"No," Kearney said, somewhat surprised.

"Ever been in trouble with the government? Non-payment of taxes or anything like that?"

"No," Kearney said emphatically. He didn't know where these questions were going. "Why?"

"Well, we could probably fly you out. Would that be satisfactory?"

That idea stopped Kearney cold.

Then, "No, it's not satisfactory!" he said heatedly. "What happens to my car? What happens to my things?"

"Oh, a car. Well, that's another matter," said Bannerman thoughtfully. After a pause, he said, "I suppose someone could be found to drive it down, eventually."

"Look, that's ridiculous!" Kearney exploded. "Can't you just get me out of here? I'll take my car and leave. I promise."

"No, no, no, I'm afraid that's not possible," said Bannerman, puttering around with his papers on the table. "You see, the Canadians would not permit it. They have no idea that you're a fine, upstanding U. S. citizen. All they know is that you have been consorting with known terrorists and terrorist sympathizers."

"I have been *what*?"

"Consorting with FLQ members," Bannerman said. "Every FLQ member is considered by the Canadian government to be a potential terrorist. Those people you came in here with are FLQ members. At least the Canadians say so. Don't you listen?"

Kearney frowned, his mind racing again.

"The man—Rene Favre—did he not say, just under an hour ago, that he and the woman—Angelique...," Bannerman consulted his notes, "...were going to run off some notices for a demonstration planned for Saturday? And did he not invite you to witness that?"

Kearney stared silently. Bannerman looked at him, grimly now, and continued.

"Interesting people you're running around with, Mr. Kearney," he said. "How did you happen to meet them?"

Kearney made some feeble gestures with his hands.

"I don't know," he stammered. "I just happened to run into them, I guess."

"Oh," Bannerman deadpanned. "And the young lady you're

sleeping with—I don't suppose you had any idea that her brother was an FLQ cell leader, now did you?"

Kearney leapt to his feet and gripped the sides of the table.

"Now wait a minute!" he said. "What gives you the right to imply that the girl and I are sleeping together? What the hell is this, anyway?"

"Oh, come now," said Bannerman. "When one takes a woman to his hotel room at midnight and emerges with a satisfied grin and the same woman some eight hours later, it's pretty easy to surmise what's been going on."

Kearney stared down at him, speechless. He couldn't believe his ears.

"How did you meet her, Kearney? Just by accident, too? Sit down."

The last was a sharp command, and Kearney obeyed.

"Do you realize the time we've wasted on you?" Bannerman said.

"I don't know what you're talking about," Kearney muttered.

"Sure you do," said Bannerman, his voice seeming bored now. "What the hell are you trying to do, be a one-man army?"

Kearney just sat there, staring at the older man. Then his shoulders slumped.

"You might as well come clean, son," said Bannerman. "I have everything right here." He tapped the pile of papers on the table. "It took some doing, but we finally found you. We ran your prints through every print bank in the free world and came up empty, until someone had the bright idea to check our own files at Langley. And there you were, one of our own. An interesting discovery, don't you think?"

"Well, you got me," Kearney said, his shoulders slumping even more. "So now that you know who I am, why don't you just let me get back to what I'm doing?"

"Not so easy," said Bannerman. "I'm in trouble enough with these Canadians. Very sensitive people, some of them. I do not need the charge of sponsoring a loose agent hung on me. I need the cooperation of these people."

"I can't leave," Kearney said. "I'm too close to it. I can feel it. I know I'm close."

"I have no intention of allowing you to leave," said Bannerman.

"I need all the help I can get. You don't know it, but you've stepped into the middle of a hornets' nest. You're—listen, you're not going to like this, but I have to say it—you're going to have to let your personal vendetta—that's what this is, isn't it?—you're going to have to let it go for a while."

"What do you want me to do?" Kearney said.

"I don't care why you came here," said Bannerman. "Get that straight. You are in my section now, and under my command." Bannerman looked down at his notes. "It says here you were not given an immediate post-graduation assignment because of several unresolved character traits. One overriding negative trait was impetuosity. Well, you've certainly proven the psych department right on that one."

Bannerman looked up and skewered Kearney with his gaze.

"But I'll have none of that here, do you understand? You will report in to me on a scheduled basis. At least three times a day, and also for special reports, if you begin breaking through to anything. Any questions?"

"No," said Kearney. "But will you tell me what you want me to do?"

"Stay where you are. That should be easy enough for you to take, right?" Bannerman said. "Do what you're doing. Just realize you aren't doing it for personal motives any more. You certainly have good instincts, I'll say that for you. How did you happen to hook up with that girl, anyway?" He waited for an answer, genuinely interested.

Kearney looked down and studied his boots.

"It was easier than you think," he said. "I accessed the files." He looked up at Bannerman.

"What!" Bannerman appeared shocked. "So you knew who she was? What her position was, before you came here?" Bannerman smiled.

"I studied the files on about a hundred of them," Kearney said. "I would have been satisfied to make contact with any of them. I just happened to spot her first."

Bannerman snickered. "Kearney, you're a bastard," he said. "Leading a young lady down the primrose path like that. Ruthless. Absolutely nasty. It'll look great on your record, though."

Kearney just stared at him.

"Don't look so down, Jack," said Bannerman. "After all, you've been trained to do this. To achieve the objective, right?"

Kearney didn't answer.

"Don't feel too sorry for her," said Bannerman. "She wasn't a virgin when she hopped into your bed, was she? I'll *bet* she wasn't."

Kearney felt sick. He rubbed his eyes.

"Well, enough of that," said Bannerman impatiently. "Just don't get too involved emotionally with her. Stay with her, though. She's a good lead. Now, who beat you up?"

"Guys from her brother's cell."

"Are you sure of that?"

"No doubt of it."

"Good, good," said Bannerman. "You're right in there. Fine. What location is that cell operating out of, do you know?"

"I'm sure we ran into one of their meetings this morning," Kearney said, his voice droning. "Her father's house—the St. Andre house—on Ile d'Orléans. Big house. Faces south. Fronts the river—the main channel, actually."

"Really," said Bannerman. "Well, well, well. Nice meeting you, Kearney. Glad we could have this chat. I have the impression you're going to be very valuable to this operation. Good instincts, like I said."

"Glad I could help," said Kearney, disgusted.

"Oh, don't take that attitude," said Bannerman. "Listen, I'll fill you in..." And Bannerman outlined the situation for him.

"...so you see what you've got yourself into," Bannerman concluded. "Do you note its importance?"

"Good Jaesus!" Kearney said, his excitement showing now. "Came to the right place, didn't I?"

"You sounded just like your father then, with that phony Irish accent," Bannerman said softly. He paused. "I worked with him for a good many years, you know."

Kearney's eyes narrowed. "What happened to my brother?"

"We don't know, Jack," Bannerman said. "We honestly don't know." Bannerman was almost whispering. "I'd tell you if I knew."

He got up and paced the short width of the room. Kearney watched him. Bannerman was lost in thought, almost talking to himself.

"Infiltration. Suborning. Payoffs. I had him working on the FLQ, trying to drive a wedge in there, as close to its heart as possible, to see who or what was there. He was doing well, too, I think. I know some money disappeared, and he was building quite a thick file..."

"Can I see it?" Kearney asked.

Bannerman ignored him. "He was on his way to a meeting. Guess he got too close for somebody's comfort…" His voice trailed off.

"Can I see the file?"

"Later," said Bannerman crisply. "After this caper. Listen. If you ever meet an operative named de la Montagne, you might be interested in following him up. That was the guy Eddie was on his way to meet when…when they shot him. Have you seen the place they shot him?"

"Yeah," said Kearney. "There's nothing there. Nothing but… nothing."

"Jack, Eddie was a good man," Bannerman said. "It was good working with him. They broke all the rules on this one. I don't blame you a bit. But this other thing is too big, and I need your help, and, who knows, maybe it's connected."

"That's a dangerous assumption to make in this business, isn't it?" Kearney managed a sardonic grin. "That's what they taught us in school."

"Perhaps," said Bannerman. "But perhaps not, in this particular case. I'm not just trying to con you, you know. I don't have to. I can just order you."

"Yeah, I know," said Kearney. "Hey, Bannerman, how long have you known I've been in town? Just out of curiosity."

Bannerman smiled. "Tuesday morning," he said.

"Damn!" said Kearney. "That's incredible. I just got here Monday night."

"You scared the hell out of me and a friend of mine on the Plains of Abraham," said Bannerman. "You took our pictures."

Kearney laughed quietly, remembering the two old men sitting on the bench in the park, reading their newspapers. "Any tourist could have done that," he said.

"No," said Bannerman. "This is a small world, with just so many trails in it. If you're looking for something, you're going to find it. And you're going to meet everyone else who's looking for it, too. That's a law. Didn't they tell you that?"

"No," Kearney said, shaking his head. "But it's good to remember."

"Yes," said Bannerman. "Now, look at these telephone numbers. Memorize them. You'll be needing them. And don't talk in your sleep."

"I won't," said Kearney. "I've been checked out for that."

"Yeah, but do you realize what a screwy mess you're into?" Bannerman said. "That's bound to tell on a person. Watch out."

"Okay," Kearney agreed. He studied the numbers. "Hey, were you kidding when you said they were all in the FLQ?"

"We have nothing solid on any of them." Bannerman said.

"I kind of thought that," said Kearney.

"...but with all the noise they make, with their singing and poetry and posters," Bannerman continued, "they might as well be. Bunch of damned fools. I'd sure give a lot to know who's using them, who the FLQ really is. I'll say this for the Front, they sure have a tight structure."

When Kearney returned to the intake area it was deserted except for the desk officer and Genevieve, who sat on a bench near the entrance. She looked crumpled, somehow very small, like a kid. And very frightened. She looked up when she heard Kearney's footsteps, and she jumped up and ran to him.

"Oh, my God," she said, "I thought you were never coming back. Are you all right?"

"I'm fine," he said, hugging her. "Where are Rene and Angelique?"

"They left," she said in a low voice. "They had things to do, remember? It was strange. The head of the police—the short man?—he came back and told Rene it was all right to leave, said that he recognized him as a singer, and that a mistake had been made. I don't understand this at all."

"Let's get out of here," Kearney said.

They stopped in the darkness at the bottom of the granite steps.

"Maybe we made enough noise," said Kearney. "Maybe we convinced them that we would be too expensive to keep."

"No, I don't think that was it," said Genevieve. "I don't know what the reason was, and that makes me frightened."

"I want you to know," said Kearney, "how much it meant to me to see you sitting there when I came back. It was a wonderful thing for you to do."

"We are friends, are we not?" she said, as they walked down the dark boulevard. "We are more…perhaps…?"

He put his arm around her waist and she sighed and dropped her head on his shoulder. "I cannot stay with you tonight," she said. "I must stay with Rene and Angelique. I promised my brother, if he wants to find me."

"Your brother makes too many demands on you," Kearney said. "So does the rest of your family. How is your aunt?"

They walked through St. Louis Gate, through the wall that defended the old town. Their steps echoed against the vaulted ceiling.

"You know I have no aunt," said Genevieve. "I lied to you."

"I know," Kearney responded. "But with a good reason."

"My brother has strange friends," she said. "Do not ask me to say any more."

"What is this mystery of your brother?" he asked, smiling.

She gave him no answer. She reached up and kissed him.

"Can we meet tomorrow?" she asked. "I cannot go to school. I feel crazy. I cannot concentrate."

"Anytime," he said. "You know that."

"I will leave a message at your hotel," she said, and then she turned and ran up a flight of stairs that led to, Kearney supposed, Rene's loft. He heard her knock at a door. Then she called, softly, "Goodnight, Jack!"

He waved from the street. In the darkness, he could feel her leaning toward him.

"Jack?" she called, in a low voice, "Jack, I love you!"

Then there was the sound of a door opening, some muffled greetings, and the door shut, and she was gone.

Kearney walked home. He knew it was his duty to call Bannerman and suggest he put a tap on Rene's phone, but he knew he wasn't going to do that. There was probably one on there already anyhow, if everybody suspected Rene so much. And Kearney wondered why he wouldn't consider tapping Rene's telephone, and immediately he knew the answer. A strange kind of fear took hold of his body and made it cold. It was a fear that he could not do his duty, that he was for some reason too weak, too swayed by personal relationships to function the way he was supposed to. He was not strong enough to destroy, the way he had been trained to do. Was this some kind of flaw, the basic flaw that Bannerman had alluded to? Maybe it was, he told himself, and self-doubt gnawed at his mind.

FRIDAY, JUNE 25TH

"And it is by force that we too – the men with dirty hands, the hewers of wood, the drawers of water, the bootblacks, the laborers, the anonymous and underpaid pencil-pushers, the waitresses, the miners, and all the 'cheap workers' in the textile mills, shoe factories, clothing factories, and canneries, in the industries, department stores, and railroad companies, in the ports of the St. Lawrence, on the rocky land of Quebec, and in the cooperatives strangled by the trusts – it is by force, and not through resignation, passivity, and fear, that we shall become free."

Pierre Vallieres, Ideologist of the FLQ

Chapter 25

Grains of Truth

Le Claire didn't want to be at his office at eight in the morning. He didn't have any choice. Time was beginning to blur. There were too many things going on, and he had the disquieting sensation that something was building to a crest. It was like he could feel the tension in the earth just before an earthquake. Dogs felt that tension and began to yowl and whine. Chickens felt it and scurried about clucking and beating their feathers.

Le Claire snorted, wondering if he bore a resemblance to a dog or a chicken. He was grateful for the steady clicking of Sandy's typewriter in the outer office. It added some kind of stability and serenity to his morning view of Quebec's rooftops.

He drained the last of his black coffee, trying to clear the fog out of his brain. He couldn't think. Too many things were closing in on him from all sides and zipping past him without converging. It was a dismaying state of affairs.

Outside, the steady clatter of Sandy's typewriter stopped. Le Claire heard the muted tones of a conversation, and then his intercom rang. With some urgency, he felt.

"A Monsieur de la Montagne to see you, sir," Sandy's voice came across in her clipped professional tone.

Le Claire's heart leapt.

So! De la Montagne again. After all these years. And something had driven him even to enter Le Claire's office.

"Send him in," Le Claire said. "Immediately."

The door opened and de la Montagne stood in the entrance, gazing down across the room at the stocky little detective. De la Montagne was tall and grizzled. The bones of his face and hands pressed against his skin, like they were trying to work their way through to the surface. His eyes gleamed from deep, black sockets. He wore old blue jeans, a black turtleneck sweater, and a black woolen skullcap. He looked as if he could slip untouched between streams of machinegun fire, and there were times in the past when he had.

The wiry old stevedore and the tired detective looked at each other with twinkling eyes. Le Claire pressed the buzzer of his intercom, and Sandy's voice answered.

"Sandy," said Le Claire. "If the cart is still in the hall, please go out and get two coffees – one black and," he raised his eyebrows in question, "one with cream, no sugar." De la Montagne nodded and smiled. "And two buttered rolls and…what the hell, two Danish."

"Right," said Sandy. Le Claire clicked off the intercom and chuckled quietly. De la Montagne closed the door and came across the room, and the two men grasped hands, grinning at each other.

Theirs was a strange friendship. It was old, and based on a deep respect. They hardly ever saw each other nowadays – save once last year, it had been twelve years since their last meeting – but they enjoyed each other's company immensely.

They had been comrades once, in the old days, during the war. De la Montagne had been on the fringe of a radical group Le Claire had tried, with some success, to infiltrate and subvert. De la Montagne had never trusted Le Claire; had, with some insight, realized who he was and what he was doing. The stevedore had done his best to prevent it, but the others in his section had overruled him, and Le Claire had been left to penetrate with success and sow disruption and discord throughout the ranks of the radicals' membership.

When Le Claire finally moved in and blew the radical apparatus apart, de la Montagne was nowhere to be found. Under deep cover, he disappeared, gathered up remnants of the chastened subversives, and started building again. Le Claire's penetration had been a lesson well learned by the wary survivors, and now they listened with new respect to the man who called himself Le Montagnard.

As for de la Montagne himself, he had the uncanny ability of keeping aloof from the savage internecine political warfare practiced by the Quebec Left. Time and again he saw the Left fought over and dismembered. Always he counseled common sense and the memory of the common cause that had brought them together in the first place.

Through all this time, respect for the man continued to grow. By 1970, he was high in the ruling council of the FLQ. He had been among the group of Front leaders who met secretly with police in the autumn of 1970 in an attempt to resolve the kidnappings of the British Trade Minister James Cross and Quebec Minister of Labor Pierre Laporte, and to decide the fates of their kidnappers. It was then that de la Montagne and Le Claire met officially for the first time since 1945.

De la Montagne bore no grudge against Le Claire. To the stevedore, the detective was simply one of the multitude of phenomena to be dealt with in the arena of radical politics. He actually admired Le Claire for the job he had been able to do back in the war. Le Claire returned the warm admiration, and accompanied it with great respect. Not trust—never trust—but respect. Both men were imbued with that particularly French trait of mind that is the fascination with logic and philosophical accuracy, and they admired each other for it.

Le Claire had always wanted to play chess with de la Montagne, but there was never any time. And this, the present, was the real chess game anyway.

"Well, old friend," said Le Claire, rising and offering his hand. "What brings you to the lair of the capitalist tiger?"

"Business, as usual," said de la Montagne, shaking hands. "And business not as usual. How have you been, old enemy?"

"Harassed by your idiots, as usual, but otherwise intact."

"Good," said de la Montagne, "I have some…"

The door opened and Sandy appeared. "The cart was right outside," she said, and carried a tray filled with cardboard coffee cups and rolls across to the desk. She left the room and closed the door behind her. The two men converged on the tray and divided the goods.

"You were saying?"

De la Montagne sat down and ripped off a hunk of roll with his teeth.

"I was saying," came the muffled voice, "that something is up." De la Montagne swallowed and looked down at the remainder of his roll, studying it.

"Something specific?"

"Sure," said the stevedore nonchalantly. "Do you think I came here to talk theory?"

"Aha!" Le Claire said, taking up the game. "Would it have to do with politics, then?"

"Quite possibly."

"Some nefarious, scheming act by a depraved madman or group of madmen?"

"Of course."

"Aimed at destroying the state, and building, on the remnants, the revolutionary world order?"

"Something along those lines."

"And you, for once, do not agree. So you have decided to become a turncoat and come over to the other side. And here you are."

"But of course," said the stevedore. "How could I stand the idiocy of my situation any longer? So here I am to turn myself in. I will tell you the entire structure of the FLQ, and its plans, and all about all the splinter groups, and all their plans. Then I will lead the forces of capitalism in the final countercharge, and die storming the barricades of the workers in some slum district of the city. It will be tragic. You will raise a statue to my memory. I will be revered by all concerned parties."

The two men laughed loudly—loudly enough to puzzle Sandy on the other side of the thick wall.

"I am here under truce conditions?" asked de la Montagne, taking out a white handkerchief and coughing into it.

"Of course," said Le Claire.

"Good," said the stevedore. "Then I will tell you something. Something is going to happen with the waterfront. Sometime soon. Very soon."

"So?" Le Claire shrugged. "Don't do it. That is simple enough."

"Ah, not so simple!" said de la Montagne. "I have nothing to do with it." He paused, and then spoke confidentially. "It is a friend of mine. He runs a small splinter faction. One of those where we put our crazies – the ones so mad with hatred and despair that they cannot think straight anymore. Well, this particular group is like that. And there is some trouble. They have something planned. To coincide with the festivities, I suppose."

"Your friend asked you to come to me?" asked Le Claire quietly.

"No. But he wanted me to. I could tell. Something strange is happening. I sense he is losing power, losing control. A factional fight, perhaps? Who knows? But…." De la Montagne's voice trailed off into a questioning silence. The atmosphere in the room was suddenly intense.

"Well, you see," Le Claire said. "I think you are playing games with me. I don't think you are telling me everything you know."

"I am telling you the truth," the stevedore said. "This friend—he is not a man who is easily scared. He doesn't give a damn what happens. Suddenly, now he is frightened. *Very* frightened."

"That is what happens when you deal with a man like Borovik," Le Claire said.

"Who?" said de la Montagne, frowning.

"Oh, come," Le Claire said. "You know as well as I do. Borovik. Pablito Cortez. Do you think to make me believe that you, of all people, do not know Vladimir Borovik, AKA Pablito Cortez? Surely you know that Cortez is here!"

"What!"

"Don't feign surprise, Mountain Man," Le Claire said. "What do you think I am, a complete fool?"

"Wait a minute," said de la Montagne. The two men sat silently, delving into their own minds.

Le Claire at length broke the silence. "You did not know Pablito Cortez was a Russian?" His voice held sympathy for his old comrade.

De la Montagne did not speak; did not betray by the slightest sign that he had almost spoken. So Pablito Cortez was Russian. Well, that was possible, but what of it? All things were possible in the revolutionary struggle. But the idea that Cortez was here in Quebec—

that information threw an entirely new light on the situation. If Cartier was acting in conjunction with Cortez, if Cortez were putting extreme pressure on Cartier, if Cortez's plans had frightened Cartier, who was frightened by nothing…

"I will be in contact with you again, before this is through," said de la Montagne. "I have that feeling. Shall we set up some codes, exchange telephone numbers?"

"Why not do it the same way we did it before?" asked Le Claire.

"Fine with me," said the stevedore. "The number?"

"How about this one?" Le Claire asked. He scratched a number on a pad and handed it over to the stevedore.

De la Montagne took the paper and glanced at it. "WAITAT8?"

"Yes," Le Claire said. Just dial WAIT AT 8. In English, remember. It would make no sense in our tongue." He paused while de la Montagne, smiling slightly, looked over the number.

"It is so complicated," the stevedore said. "I will never be able to remember this. I will get the time wrong, I am sure of it. Don't you have something simpler, less complicated?"

"You must just remember it," Le Claire said, in a pedantic manner. "Memorize it now, then you must destroy the evidence. Eat the paper," he suggested.

"I might as well," said de la Montagne. "It would taste better than this bread you offer. Since when do you patronize English bakeries?"

"It was a compromise," said Le Claire. "If I eat this for breakfast, they allow me frankfurters for lunch. Good proletarian food."

De la Montagne twisted his face into an attitude of disgust.

Le Claire smiled. "You do not agree?" he asked.

"Do not try to trap me like that," the stevedore said. "The revolution says nothing about eating habits. Yet." He rose, and seemed about to leave.

"What did you come to tell me?" Le Claire asked.

"I do not know," said de la Montagne. "Your information throws new light on everything. If it is true," he added. He took a deep breath and coughed again into his handkerchief. "I will be in touch with you. I am sure I will have some information for you. But first, I must dig."

"Can't you tell me anything right now?"

De la Montagne came over and leaned across the desk. "Only

this," he said. "Something is going to happen on the waterfront. It is going to be physical and political both."

"Tell me what it is."

"I cannot tell you!" de la Montagne said vehemently. "I do not know for sure. All I can say is, you'd better get your surveillance apparatus going all over the harbor. And I don't mean simple foot patrols. *You* know what I mean, and you'd better get to it fast. I will admit something to you. When I came, I thought I was bringing something solid to you. But now I am not sure. I don't know what the truth is. My position—it is like hanging in air. I am used to being like this, but every time it happens, it always leaves the stomach a bit queasy."

"And perhaps, this time, the lungs? Have you seen a doctor, old friend?"

"Bah! Doctors! What do they know? I have work to do," the stevedore said, and he strode across the room. Grasping the door handle, he turned back. "Au revoir, Claude. See you soon. Expect a call at any time."

De la Montagne opened the door and was gone, leaving behind in the heavy air of the room the impression that he was going to get to the bottom of everything, starting with Borovik and why the Russian was dealing with Cartier's crazy band instead of working with the Front. The Montagnard was visibly seething about that as he left, and burning with energy.

Le Claire wished he had some of that same energy. He sat behind his desk and thought. He felt he had committed a tactical error, feeding the stevedore all that information about Borovik. He should have let him ramble on for a while, gleaned all the information he could from the man. Well, that wouldn't have been fair, though, thought Le Claire, and it would have been against the rules of exchange, too. And it all might still come out right. Too late now to worry about it.

De la Montagne—what a joke, calling him that, as if he didn't know his real name. At any rate, de la Montagne seemed cooperative enough. Things might work out this way.

But why had the stevedore shown up just now? It must be big. Still, you couldn't trust him. The whole thing might be a wild goose chase, a trap, set up especially to move Le Claire's forces into the wrong positions. What else might be up?

The whole waterfront scenario countered Le Claire's pet theories about a revolutionary strike against the economic conference. Or perhaps, these two things were connected in some way? Always a possibility. He chewed on his pen for a second, then, leaving his coffee half-finished, he got up and left the room.

Coming into the outer office, he stopped by Sandy's desk. His sergeant looked up at him.

"Sandy," he said. "I'll be out until noon. While I'm gone, I want you to look over the files on this terrorist situation. Drop everything else for the time being. Set everything up for me—our people, their locations, their covers, their contacts—everything. I'll want to note the entire situation at a glance."

Sandy nodded, and made notes. Le Claire stood by her desk, staring into space.

"Boss?" Sandy said, her voice just above a whisper.

He looked at her.

"Was that *the* de la Montagne?"

Le Claire smiled at her.

"Yes, Sandy," he said. "That was *the* de la Montagne. You were sufficiently impressed?"

"It was like seeing a ghost." She smiled. "It was like a legend walking into the room."

"Yes," Le Claire said. "A legend. An unknown legend. One that will never be known to the general public. I wonder how that feels to him? Do you realize the power that man has?"

"Only what you've told me," said Sandy. "And that's enough. It's scary. Do you remember what you said about him?"

"What?" said Le Claire.

"You said that if I ever saw de la Montagne, I would know that the situation was as bad as it could get."

"I said that?"

"Yes, you said it. Were you right?"

Le Claire thought for a moment.

"Yes, I suppose I was," he said. "Hard to tell, but I suppose I was." He was quiet for a moment.

"You know, Sergeant," he said. "Someday soon I will retire. And when I do, I'm going to blackmail that son-of-a-bitch. I'll threaten him with opening his file to the FLQ. I'll make him out to be a traitor. I'll make things so hot for him, he'll have to quit. That's the only way he'll ever do it. Then," Le Claire said, "I'll have somebody to go fishing with. He deserves a vacation. He's never had one, y'know. He deserves something, don't you think?"

Sandy smiled at him.

"Boss," she said. "You're the one who needs a vacation."

"Ah, well," said Le Claire. "I suppose I do." He took a deep breath. "Later," he said in a strong voice. "Right now, we have work to do. Both of us. Sandy, I'm afraid you can't go out to lunch. There must be someone here all the time, from now until after the weekend."

"Hey, that's not fair!" she said.

"De la Montagne might call," he whispered. "Wouldn't you like to talk to him?"

"Not at the expense of my lunch hour," she said, disgruntled. "Say, boss, did you ask him who shot Sergeant Griffith and Henry Sparrow?"

Le Claire put up his hand as if to fend off something unthinkable.

"No, no, no!" he said, with some agitation. "That is against the rules. No. In a parley like this, you take what is offered. It is not an inquisition, eh? He came of his own free will."

"Anyway," he continued, "if I'm not back in time, I'll have lunch sent up to you. Condition red. Read your contract. It's right there."

Le Claire grinned. Then he was out the door and away.

Sandy sat for a moment, then got up and cleared off the large conference table along the wall. She took Le Claire's large city map from his inner office and propped it up on the table. She took down the portrait of Sir Stanley Rogers in Le Claire's office and opened the wall safe behind it. She locked the door to the hall, returned to the safe, and removed the coded files of agents and informers that Le Claire had built up over the years. She would start with them and go on to more official sources later. She had a day's work cut out for her, and she had only half a day to get it done. But she was fast, accurate, and perceptive. She wasn't a cop for nothing.

Chapter 26
Fields of Flowers

By eleven o'clock on Friday morning the gray cloud cover had broken, and the day turned sunny and bright. Genevieve sat on a bench in the flower garden that bordered the expanse of the Plains of Abraham. Her eyes were closed and her head was thrown back to catch the sun.

Kearney saw her like that as he approached. She had called his hotel to tell him where she would be. Before he came up to her, he stopped to look at a nearby statue. He smiled when he saw it was of Joan of Arc, and continued on his way to where Genevieve basked in the sun.

Leaning over her, he said, "How appropriate."

Genevieve opened her eyes and smiled at him. He pointed to the statue.

"My little warrior with her big voice," he said, "protected by the Maid of Orleans."

Genevieve laughed. "She stands here with her sword," she said, "barring the English from advancing any farther. But she was crazy. She heard voices."

"Sometimes voices help," Kearney said.

"It depends on the voice," said Genevieve. "I hear your voice and it helps." She hesitated. "I hear other voices, and they frighten me," she said in a hollow tone.

"Last night," Kearney said, "When I heard your voice, when you said goodnight, I never heard a more beautiful voice." He sat down next to her and put his arm around her. "Thank you," he said.

They sat there in the sun and watched the breeze toss the flowers and beat against the Maid's granite pedestal. For a long time they were silent. Kearney detected a disquietude about the girl, but he said nothing, and in a while she spoke.

"I must talk to someone," she said. "I must talk to you. Everyone I know is…is too involved in things. I do not know who knows what. I cannot say anything to them. Can you keep secrets?"

"There's an old proverb," said Kearney. "It says, 'The only way a secret is safe among three people is if two of them are dead.'" He looked at her. "But it says nothing about two people who love each other."

Genevieve looked away, across the field of flowers. Suddenly, her words came pouring out. "I am afraid," she said. "My brother is mixed up in something dangerous. Nobody knows. They all think he is sympathetic to the British. But he isn't. He is really FLQ. He is a cell leader. Something dangerous is happening at our house. The men who beat you up, they are members of his cell. But there are others, too. Jean-Paul has told me to stay away from the house. I am frightened by what I see, so I do not go there. Jean-Paul puts on a big front, but I think he is frightened, too. I think something big is happening, something he never counted on. I think they will kill him if he doesn't obey." She stopped, and covered her eyes with her hands.

"You say there are others?" Kearney asked quietly.

"I am sure of it. There are many. More than just one cell. Yesterday, when they left to catch you, still there were others there. Things do not operate that way, I have heard."

"Are you sure it's the Front?" Kearney asked. "Are you sure your brother is in the Front? Maybe he just told you that. Maybe these are just friends of his…"

"My God!" Genevieve cried. "You have no idea what I have been through. Do you think I see things? Imagine things? Do you think I am an hysteric? Jack, Jack, do you think I am crazy?"

"I think you are very frightened," said Kearney. "I'm sorry I asked you that. I should know better. I believe you. Come on. Tell me."

"You don't know. How could you know? You don't know what is happening here. Rene and Angelique, they are my dearest friends. They love me; they take care of me. I cannot talk even to them. I do not know if they are in the Front, or in some other thing, or with the police…no, my God, they are not with the police...I don't know…a week ago I knew everything…I thought I knew everything…I was certain. But now I am certain of nothing. Everywhere I turn, what is real turns unreal. What I see, I do not see. I do not know what I know anymore. Oh, Jack, you will not disappear from me, will you?"

She looked at him with tears streaming down her face. He looked at her, looked at the dissolution of this girl who should be happy and carefree, and was caught instead in a web of intrigue that bound her to nothing, that murdered reality.

"Your mother is dead?" he asked quietly.

"Oui."

"Your father is away? With his new wife? His English wife?"

"Oui."

"…and now your brother."

He held her by the shoulders and looked into her eyes. "Do you realize how young you are?" he smiled. "Do you realize that all of a sudden your world has gone crazy, and you are trying to hold it together all by yourself? Do you know how hard that is to do?"

"I am old enough," she said. Pride was coming back into her voice. "I could have been in the army for three years now. In some places, people are never young. Vietnam. Palestine. Ireland. I am old enough."

"I won't disappoint you," he said. "I promise."

"Thank you," she said.

He hugged her, and she wrapped her arms gently around his neck. "I'm so tired," she said. "I have to go back to Rene's. There are things to do. To get ready."

"You can't go like this," Kearney said. "The minute they see you they'll know something is wrong. Come on. Let's walk a bit."

They got up and walked slowly along the path that led out to the broad plains. In the sun, Genevieve's eyes dried, and her breathing became less labored. Her body slowly stopped shuddering.

"A little while, and you'll feel better," Kearney said. "You've given yourself a shock."

Genevieve's only response was to breathe deeply, like she was fighting for breath. "My God," she said, "I should not have behaved like that. Maybe I am crazy."

"No," Kearney said, "No one should have to put up with what you have. No one can stand that."

They walked along in silence for a while.

"When did you notice all this Front business at the house?" Kearney asked. "Has it been going on for a while?"

"No," Genevieve said. Her manner was quieter now, her mind working, trying to make some sense out of things, to sort them out logically. "I knew about my brother some time ago. It has been a strain."

"One would never have known that," said Kearney.

Genevieve smiled and gently pressed his arm. She continued. "Oh, no, I am good at hiding things, you see. Well, all this business, as you say, began only yesterday, as far as I know. So you saw some of the same that I did. But I saw more, and I became frightened. And my brother – my brother! Told me to stay away, to stay away from my own house! I couldn't believe it. Until after the weekend, he said, at least. I don't know what is happening. But I am very sure it is to do with tomorrow. Something big for tomorrow. That is very sure."

"I agree with your brother," Kearney said. "Stay away from that house. Promise me that. I love you too much to see you in danger like that. Promise me you'll stay away from that house."

"I promise," she said, "but I am afraid for my brother."

"Have you thought about going to the police?" he asked.

"Never!" she cried. It was more a spontaneous reaction than a reasoned answer. "What then would happen to us? Are you naïve?"

"I guess you're right, for your brother's safety, anyway. But if what you've guessed is true, he's gotten himself in one hell of a jam. I'm just glad I'm not in the middle of it. But you're right about the police. Best not to go near them."

Genevieve looked at him with frightened eyes.

"Listen," Kearney said, "I can't do anything for your brother. But I can help to protect you. That's something I can do. And that's what I *will* do. Do you feel better now? Let's go to Rene's. I have a plan."

"What are you going to do?" Genevieve asked. Her heart leapt with fright.

Kearney started walking to town, his arm around Genevieve's waist, half guiding her, half pulling her. "You can't say anything to them, right?" he said. "But I can. I'm an ignorant foreigner. I don't know the implications of what I say. I can say anything. Foolish, dangerous, it doesn't matter a damned bit. And I'm angry. You're in trouble and I want to do something. So just let me do the talking. Wait. Maybe, if you want to, you can try to stop me. Just try. See how far you get. Ha!"

"What on earth will that do?" Genevieve said. "It will just make things worse."

"Look," Kearney said. "It's politics. This way, they get the information. I'll tell them just what you told me. And don't worry. I won't say anything they shouldn't know. You want them to know, right? Then if they take it the wrong way, you can always deny it. You can say I didn't understand it. That you didn't say that at all. Then you can tell them something else. That way, you're covered, your brother is safe, and you've got the information to your friends. Politics, right?"

Genevieve considered his proposition. She nodded her head. "I see what you mean. My English is not that good, right? You misunderstood me."

"Right," Kearney agreed, "If you think they're taking it the wrong way."

"I do want them to know," said Genevieve. "And I'm sure they'll be sympathetic. But isn't it horrible, Jack, to be like this, not even trusting your own friends? Okay, let's do it. What else can I do?"

"They'd know something was wrong, anyway. You look like a sick sheep," he said.

"How dare you!" Genevieve said. She stuck her nose up in the air, sniffed, and laughed. "Do I?" she asked.

They left the park hand in hand. They were going very fast, almost running.

"Rene! Rene!" Kearney started yelling as soon as they started up the stone stairway to the loft.

"Quiet, Jack!" said Genevieve. "You'll get all the neighbors!"

And then Rene was at the top of the stairs, looking startled.

"I've got to talk to you," Kearney said, dragging Genevieve along behind him. "This girl's in trouble, and she needs your help."

"Jack, for God's sake, stop it!" said Genevieve.

"Stop announcing it to the world and come inside," said Rene. "What's wrong with you?"

They went inside to a large room with stone walls and an immense skylight. Angelique sat at an easel, a paintbrush poised in mid-air. She looked at them with a perturbed expression.

"Genevieve is in trouble," Kearney said to Rene and Angelique. "She says you are her friends, and yet she can't tell you. But I can, and I will."

"Will you keep quiet!" Genevieve shouted, making Rene jump. Angelique got up and came over to where they were all standing by the doorway. Rene closed the door.

Kearney talked along, ticking off the points on his fingers. "First of all," he said, "I didn't fall in the park. I got these lumps from her brother's friends, when they warned me to stay away from her. Jean-Paul is a cell leader in the FLQ. He and his friends are planning something for Saturday, they're using the house on the island to plan it, and that's why Genevieve is staying with you, regardless of whatever excuse she gave you."

Genevieve walked across the sparsely-furnished room and collapsed on the couch, burying her head in its pillows. Rene and Angelique looked at Kearney, speechless. Kearney continued.

"She has to stay here because this is where she told her brother she would be. She's petrified that something will happen to him." He lowered his voice to a whisper. "She's in really bad shape. You've got to help her."

Angelique turned and ran to Genevieve. Rene said, "Jack, come with me a moment, will you? In here."

He led Kearney into another, smaller room. The view out a large window was of a courtyard filled with trees. It was a peaceful scene. There was a small desk in one corner of the room, and a large bed in the other.

Rene closed the door, turned, and accosted Kearney. "How do you know all of this?" he demanded.

"She told me," said Kearney, bluntly. "She told me, just now. She couldn't hold it in any longer."

Rene paced the room, tapping his teeth with the stem of his pipe. "Why would she tell you?" he asked. "She hardly knows you."

"We've gotten rather close in the past couple of days," said Kearney, reddening. "Look. It's because I'm not mixed up in things here. She didn't think she could tell anybody. She had to tell somebody or bust. There I was."

"So now you know she's in trouble, eh? The fun is all over, so you're going to drop her fast and run. Right, Yankee?"

"No!" said Kearney. "She's afraid for her brother. She told him he could find her here, like I said. She has to stay here. Hell, I'll stay here, too, with her, if you let me. But you've got to help her."

"We would have helped her, of course," said Rene, "and asked no questions. Why is it so important to you to tell us all this? Why do you think we should know this?"

"Listen," Kearney said. "I don't know the situation around here, but I've got an idea things could get pretty wild once they get started. I thought you should know that because it might give you a better chance to stay out of the way of things. Genevieve wouldn't tell you this because she thought it might interfere with your politics somehow. But I don't give a damn about your precious fucking politics, so I told you. And I'm not trying to dump Genevieve. I'll stay here with her."

"That would be impossible," said Rene. "What if Jean-Paul's friends show up? They would kill you this time, and leave your body for me to explain. Besides," he added, "Angelique thinks you're a spy."

"What?" Kearney tried to laugh, but it didn't come out right. He stared hard at Rene. "What do *you* think?" he said.

"I don't know," said the poet. "I'll wager you are not what you say you are, but I'll not go beyond that. Yet."

"Well, I'll be damned," Kearney said. He leaned against the wall and stared out the window. He lit a cigarette.

"When are you leaving town?" Rene asked.

Kearney frowned. "Why?" he asked.

"Because of Genevieve, strange as that may seem to you," Rene said. He nodded toward the outer room. "Do you know how dependent she has become on you? Do you know she thinks she loves you?"

"Yes," said Kearney, quietly.

"Do you know anything about her background?" Rene asked.

"A lot of it," he said, and took a drag on his cigarette. Exhaling, he continued. "She told me."

"Do you love her?" Rene asked.

Kearney was silent.

"If you don't," Rene said, "it would be best for you to leave now. It will hurt her, but she will get over it, and be wise and bitter like the rest of us. If you stay too much longer, and then leave, you will break her heart. She has heartaches enough, don't you agree?"

"You listen to me," Kearney said. "When I leave this town, she's coming with me." He crossed to the door and opened it. "I'm leaving for now," he said. "I've got things to do. But I'll be back later. I'm taking her to dinner, if she's able to eat anything."

He walked through to the outer room. He almost ran over Angelique, who was standing there with her finger to her lips.

"Where is she?" Kearney demanded.

"Shhhh! She is resting." Angelique turned and pointed. "See?"

Genevieve was lying on the couch, covered with a quilt. She looked at Kearney with eyes that were drained of all emotion. He went to her.

"I'll be back in a few hours," he whispered. "We can go for a walk, if you like. Or dinner. Anything you want."

She nodded slightly. He kissed her. "Now, get some rest. Sleep. Go to sleep."

Genevieve closed her eyes. Kearney crossed the room as quietly as he could and joined Rene and Angelique at the door. They went outside with him and closed the door behind them.

"Jack," said Angelique. "Be good to her. Be kind. Do not hurt her."

"I can't hurt her," Kearney said.

"She screamed in her sleep last night," said Angelique. "She screamed and then called out for you."

Kearney nodded. "I'll be back in a little while," he said.

Angelique and Rene watched him go down the stairs. When he

had disappeared into the street, Rene said, "So. Your attitude seems to have changed. You do not think now that he is a spy?"

Angelique shrugged. "I do not know," she said. "But my little sister needs him right now, and he seems kind, and that is important, is it not? What do you think?"

"I don't know either," said Rene.

"Perhaps just a clumsy American," Angelique said. "A bull in a china shop, eh? Crashing around where he should not be?"

"Perhaps," said Rene, "but…no. What he has found out from Genevieve. What he knows of her brother. Interesting. Inaccurate, but interesting. He asks all the right questions. Or the wrong ones, depending on how you see it."

"Yes," said Angelique. "What about Jean-Paul? It certainly surprised me."

Rene shook his head. "And me. I don't see it. He's just not right. None of the cells in my section, anyway. I wouldn't want him. But who knows? I'll have to ask around. Starting with your 'little sister'."

As soon as Kearney left Rene's apartment he looked for a safe telephone. If Angelique and Rene suspected him, he reasoned, who else might? It was time to be cautious.

He finally found what he thought was a safe location, a public telephone booth half hidden in the back of a small variety store, and he tried to contact Bannerman. The first number he called was the consulate, but Bannerman hadn't been seen for hours. The second number brought no results; it was a dud. On the third try, the telephone rang twice and Bannerman himself answered.

"Jack here," Kearney said. "You're a hard man to keep track of."

"No time for small talk, son," Bannerman said. "What do you have?"

"Remember that house on the island I talked about last night?"

"Yes."

"You seemed interested."

"What do you have?" Bannerman asked again. The voice sounded like hard steel.

"Confirmation. The house is being used by a large radical group. Activity yesterday, possibly last night, today, tonight, at least. Possibly all weekend. Informant warned to stay away from the area. Sounds live to me. I would recommend surveillance."

Bannerman held the receiver away from his ear and looked at it. 'Would you?' he thought. 'Cheeky little bastard.' Then he asked sarcastically, "Would you have any suggestions on the surveillance? Do you think you might be able to tell me which house it is, for instance?"

"Yes, sir," said Kearney. "It's just west of a large religious retreat house. Lots of grounds. Sign near the road says 'St. Andre'."

"Jack," Bannerman said, "Do you expect me to tell someone to drive down the road inspecting signs? If you were a terrorist watching the road, would you think someone exhibiting those particular behavior patterns just might be looking for something? Like yourself, for instance?"

"Uh, yes, sir," said Kearney.

"Okay. Get over here. I'm in room 632 of the Chateau Frontenac. Get here on the double."

"Right, sir," said Kearney. "Sir? Are you there now?"

"Did I say I was here?" Bannerman asked.

"Well, I didn't hear the call go through a switchboard."

Bannerman laughed. "Get over here, son, and I'll let you in on a little secret."

The line went dead.

Chapter 27
The Conference

When Bannerman opened the door for Kearney a few minutes later, the CIA station chief was carrying a telephone on a long extension line. He turned his back on Kearney while he muttered an ending to a call, then turned to face the younger man.

"That was from the gentleman who brought you in last night," he said. "I think your information may be even more pertinent now. There seems to be quite a bit of information, in fact, that points to an attempt to do some damage to the harbor. What use would that island property have, say, as a sabotage base?"

"It goes right down to the river," Kearney said. "Surrounded by trees and bushes. There's a little dock. You could launch a boat there."

"How about mortars?" Bannerman asked.

"You could probably spot from the roof of the house."

"Missiles?"

"Missiles?" echoed Kearney.

"Why the hell not?" Bannerman said. "How do we know what they're planning?"

"It's secluded enough," Kearney said. He walked over to the window. The river and harbor were spread out beneath him like a giant map. Far off on the rim of the harbor, the green bulk of the Ile d'Orléans sat like a wedge in the river, just past a half-dozen ships anchored in the roadstead.

"If I had binoculars, I could probably see it from here," Kearney said.

Bannerman took a pair of binoculars from a chest of drawers and handed them to Kearney. "Show it to me," he said.

Kearney scanned the far island, concentrating on buildings he remembered having seen while he was over there.

"No," he said after a while, "It's no use. You can't see it from here. If the roof is there, it blends in with the trees at this distance."

"Okay," said Bannerman, "Draw me a map. Large scale. As detailed as possible. The house. The grounds. Surrounding properties. Possible cover. Don't forget anything."

Bannerman pointed to a table in the far corner of the room. Paper and a map of the island were laid out on it. Kearney went to work.

Bannerman picked up the binoculars and played them back and forth over the distant island. All the while Kearney worked, Bannerman searched for something in the harbor.

Suddenly he stopped short. He took the binoculars away and looked with his naked eye. Then he took up the binoculars again and swung them in a short arc back and forth across the far end of the harbor.

"Jesus," he said. He kept the binoculars to his eyes. Kearney turned to look at him and saw his lips move. Then Bannerman said quietly, like he was almost afraid to say it, "They're going to hit the ships."

He turned to Kearney and laughed. "Jack!" he said. "They're going to hit the ships! Come here and look. Come here!"

Kearney jumped up and went to the window. Bannerman shoved the binoculars into his hands. "Look," he said. "Look at your island. Look where your house is, approximately. Look at the river, just before you get to the island. What do you see?"

"Ships," said Kearney, softly. He swung the binoculars back and forth. "Six ships. Tankers. Freighters…"

"And nothing closer to them in the world than that damned island of yours!" Bannerman shook his head. "Jesus! Right in front of our eyes." He stopped, and glanced around wildly. "Jack, let's see that map of yours. Finish it?"

"Just about," Kearney said.

"Let's look at it." They went over to the table. "Nice work," Bannerman said. "Where would you suggest an approach?"

"From here, and here," said Kearney, pointing at his drawing. "From the east, through the retreat house property, right here. From the west, through these woods. Woods all around, bordering the lawns. Lots of cover. Hey, how about from across the river, there? Telescope could do it."

"Nice," said Bannerman. "Nice. Jack, if you wanted to hit those ships, what would you hit them with? Torpedoes? Rockets?"

"No," said Kearney.

"Of course not," Bannerman said.

"Mines," Kearney said.

"Right," Bannerman said. "Mines. And when would you mine them?"

Kearney looked out the window at the ships. "Tonight," he said. "Before dark. While I still had enough light. And I still had the ships."

"Nice," Bannerman said. "But not good enough. Tonight is too late. The ships are there. Might as well get them right now, before somebody gets onto the plan, right? They're mining them right now. I'd swear to that!"

Bannerman took a deep breath. "Of course, this is all conjecture. Theory. But there's some strong evidence. We've got to get those ships out of there. I'm *going* to get those ships out of there. Jack, thanks for dropping by. I think you hit something right on the head, like a good Irishman. And thanks for your maps. They'll help a lot." Bannerman headed for the telephone.

"Should I go out there?" asked Kearney. "What should I do?"

"Hell, no," said Bannerman. "You'd get in the way. Go back to your radicals. This may be only part of the problem. You may be sitting on some other part just as big."

Bannerman dialed a number. "Oh, I promised you a secret, didn't I?" he said smiling, while waiting for an answer from the other end if the line. "This room was used by President Roosevelt's party during the conference with Churchill in 1943. They had direct lines installed, for security. They're still intact. I found them. Easy to find if you know what to look for."

Bannerman winked and motioned Kearney to leave. “Hello, Sandy?” he said into the phone. “Claude there? Damn! Get him to call me, will you? Yes, he knows where…Something big, I think…”

Kearney opened the door and came face to face with a man who was about to knock. Startled, both men jumped back and looked at each other. Kearney thought the other man looked familiar, but he couldn’t place him.

“I say,” said the man at the door, “could you possibly show me the way to the Citadel?” Sackman brushed past Kearney, pushed him out of the room, and slammed the door behind him. Kearney swore he heard laughter coming from the room.

Chapter 28
Transit in Zenith

About the time Jack Kearney was leaving Room 632, Claude Le Claire also was walking down the plush carpeted halls of the Chateau Frontenac. He arrived finally before the door to the fifth floor suite newly occupied by Harold Holsworthy, OBE, Knight of the British Empire, science fiction writer and space scientist. He nodded to the plainclothesman stationed beside the door and received a smart salute in return. He tapped hesitantly, almost furtively, on the door, and was rewarded immediately as it opened to reveal a tall, thin, balding man in his late fifties who wore spectacles and a blue business suit. The man had a grim, dissatisfied look about his lips.

"I say, are you the head of this operation?" he asked impatiently. "What the devil's going on? I feel I'm in a jail of some sort. Well?"

And this was Harold Holsworthy, a man not used to being told what to do and when to do it. Looking at him, Le Claire smiled and said, "It is beautiful to watch eternal stars from the seven planets of triumphant light."

"Oh, really?" said Holsworthy, brightening noticeably. "Well, that does change things a bit, doesn't it? Come in, Mister…?

"Le Claire. Thank you very much, Sir Harold." Le Claire walked into the suite and Holsworthy closed the door behind him, leaving a very confused plainclothesman standing in the hallway. The plainclothesman was sure he had heard a code of some kind, and in fact he had.

"Well, well, a fan," Holsworthy said, smiling. "It took me aback, I'll tell you. I must have written that line thirty years ago. One of my favorites, though."

"I have enjoyed that book again and again," said Le Claire. "To me, it is closer to philosophy than science. I have always wanted to tell you how much I've enjoyed your work, and now, look, I have the opportunity!"

"Well, thank you, Mr. Le Claire," Holsworthy said. "Although I probably would appreciate your interest to a much greater degree if you would tell me what's going on here. You are the head of a department that's protecting me from something, I take it."

"Exactly," said Le Claire.

"Well, what is it?" asked Holsworthy. "What are you protecting me from, if I might ask? It might help, you know, if I knew what I was getting myself into." Holsworthy stood in the center of the room, his attitude demanding an answer.

"Of course," said Le Claire. He strode across the room to the windows, looked out onto the balcony, and turned toward Holsworthy. "It is unfortunate," he said. "The planners of the economic conference did, in one respect, a poor job of planning."

"Economists sometimes do," Holsworthy said, grinning a boyish grin.

"In this case," Le Claire continued, "they scheduled their conference to end this Saturday, on St. Jean-Baptiste Day, which is the day chosen for the celebration of Quebec's provincial holiday, which was actually yesterday, if you can follow that. The day has always been an excuse for demonstrations and such by radicals, and it is quite possible, as the economists represent what the radicals consider the power of Canada and the western alliance over Quebec," Le Claire paused for breath, "that an attempt of some kind will be made to disrupt the conference."

"Aha!" Holsworthy said. "And as I am the main speaker tomorrow, that would place me in some danger. But not much. No more, in fact, than anyone else there. What else, sir? Or are you guarding every conference participant in this overprotective manner?"

"There are some prejudicial factors in your particular case," Le Claire said.

"What are they? Stop playing with me, Mr. Le Claire, or fan or no, I warn you that you will receive no cooperation from me."

Le Claire was beginning to feel some unaccustomed embarrassment. It was some time before he spoke.

"My associates do not feel this is necessary," he said, making a sweeping gesture with his hand. "I am putting my reputation on the line. A lot of them think I am crazy. Perhaps I am, but I feel that you need the protection."

Le Claire paused and took a deep breath and said, "Now, I have seen your file, and I know a little of what you are doing. Not much, but enough to assume that your work is reaching far into sensitive areas. What I am talking about is all classified information, of course, and I am not supposed to have access to it. But there are ways. I take a great risk here. I would appreciate it if you could say we never held this conversation."

"Of course," said Holsworthy quietly. "I don't know whether to feel flattered or miffed to find out that Canada has a file on my activities. A bit frightening, actually, but go on."

"You are a natural resource," Le Claire said. "It is only logical."

"Hmmm," said Holsworthy. The man had great presence, and Le Claire was beginning to sweat.

"A group of terrorists, led by a man quite highly placed in the ranks of the Russian KGB, entered Canada some days ago. We know some of them are here in Quebec City. We feel they are all here, and that they intend to strike in some manner. Tomorrow."

"Really!" Holsworthy said, his eyes widening and gleaming. A smile broke across his face again. "This is exhilarating!" he exclaimed. "Please go on. No, wait. You feel that these terrorists present some danger to me personally. Why? Why should they be interested in me?"

"If they know as much about you as I do," Le Claire said, "and I am sure they know more, they want your knowledge of certain technical systems."

"Technical systems," mused Holsworthy. "Technical systems.

Mr. Le Claire, come here a moment, will you? I want to show you something."

Sir Harold led Le Claire to a desk in the corner of the room. He opened a briefcase and pulled out an 8 X 10 black-and-white photo of a house, surrounded by bougainvillea and tropical plants, that sported a deep dish antenna on its roof. The roof had been modified into a platform to receive the antenna.

"This is my house outside of Nairobi," Holsworthy said. "I am the only individual in the world – as opposed to a government – who has a satellite tracking station all his own. Isn't it splendid?" Holsworthy stood there looking down at the photo with a combination of pride and excitement in his bearing. "I am engaged in beaming educational programs into schools in six African countries. I have a fixed satellite which hovers just overhead of Kilimanjaro. We bounce the programs off the satellite into schools way out in the bush. In English and six major African tongues. Financed by the World Bank. That is my work. It is good work, but hardly anything for the Russians or any terrorist group to try to get. They would have no use for it. So the question is, again, why?"

Le Claire looked at the picture with some interest. "Perhaps your educational work does not fill all your time," he said.

Holsworthy studied Le Claire for a moment. "You *do* read between the lines, don't you?" he stated. "So your theory is at least partially based on fact. Extremely pleasing to my ego, too. I suppose I've decided to be flattered by your attention, Monsieur Le Claire. What did you say your position was?"

"I did not say," Le Claire said, smiling. "It is 'Eastern Regional Director, Internal Security Division, Department of Justice, Province of Quebec, Canada.'"

"Oh my God!" exclaimed Holsworthy. "I do hope that is the entirety of it. There isn't any more, is there?"

"You asked," Le Claire said. The two men broke into laughter.

"Well," said Holsworthy, "We'd better get on with it. What are the other theories?"

Le Claire suddenly felt a profound sense of gratitude toward the scientist. Now that the results of his intuitional theory had been confirmed by the eminent scientist, he felt less alone than he had for the past week. He had received a partial acceptance of his ideas, and that pleased him.

"Some expect a disruption of tomorrow's festivities in some spectacular way," he said. "Either something big on the waterfront, or somewhere else in town. But I don't buy that. This group has entirely too much potential for something like that. A group like the one we are dealing with has the potential to smash violently at the entire root structure of a society. It isn't interested in absurd demonstrations or any other such nonsense."

"So, in your mind, that leaves me," said Holsworthy, mulling over Le Claire's information.

"Yes, that leaves you," Le Claire said. "You say I read between the lines. So do they."

"Fascinating," said Holsworthy, deep in thought. "So tell me, Monsieur Le Claire," he said at length. "What do you intend to do with me in the meantime? I have a dinner appointment with a friend of mine, for instance. He's due here at five tonight for a bit of an informal conference, then we were planning to go out. Will you let him in to see me?"

"I will inform the guard…the plainclothesman…at the door. His credentials will have to be checked, of course, and there will have to be visual identification from you, but there should be no problem after that. Where did you intend to dine, by the way?"

"I have no idea," said Sir Harold. "Charlie…that's Charles Broughton, by the way – he's a mathematician of yours – well, Charlie said there were any number of fine places about the town."

"This could present some complications," Le Claire said. "You know, these terrorists, their activities are not confined to tomorrow. We will have to take measures to protect you. And a man of your stature – suppose someone recognizes you on the street, in a restaurant, comes over for an autograph or to shake hands? My boys might decide to jump first and ask questions later. It wouldn't be good."

Holsworthy puzzled over the problem. "And I do always seem to be recognized, although it beats hell out of me how they do it. Do you know, I was once in a taxicab in New York City with Walter Cronkite, and the cabbie recognized me, and he didn't recognize Cronkite. My God, was Walter ever put out! But you know, I don't understand it."

"Well, you see, we are fanatics," Le Claire smiled.

Holsworthy returned the smile. "I say, Le Claire," he said, "Why don't you join us for dinner? Can you suggest a good place?"

"Why, that would be an honor!" said Le Claire. "And I could be doing my job and having a fine time at it too. That would be a change for the better."

"Good!" said Holsworthy. "Then it's arranged. How about say, eight this evening? I'm afraid I've just had a late lunch."

"Fine," said Le Claire. "May I suggest the restaurant here in the Chateau? The food is excellent, there is a fine wine list, and the area is easy to secure. Just down in the elevator and back up again…"

"Elevator?" Holsworthy asked.

"Yes," said Le Claire, puzzled. "Why?"

Holsworthy seemed troubled by something. "I don't especially like elevators," he said. "Could we possibly use the stairs?"

"Well, security would be better in…but, of course, taking the stairs would throw them off… The stairs, then, if you'd like. Did you walk up here?"

"No," Holsworthy said, "Your 'boys', as you call them, hustled me right onto the thing. They also took the liberty of moving my room reservation from the second to this floor. But you see, I don't like elevators. Not at all."

"I'm afraid I must take the blame for switching your room," said Le Claire. "Se…"

"Security," chorused Holsworthy. "Oh, yes. I see. Makes perfect sense."

"My apologies," said Le Claire. "Are you a claustrophobic?" he asked.

"Oh, no, nothing like that," said the scientist. "I just don't like elevators. Do you know – Kubrick, Asimov, Bradbury – they won't fly. Clarke will fly, and scuba dive, but he steadfastly refuses to learn how to drive a car. We're a strange bunch, aren't we? We devise concepts and rockets to the moon, and talk constantly about zipping through the galaxy beyond the speed of light and the curve of time, but damned if you'll ever get *me* on one of those things."

"Elevators or rockets?" asked Le Claire, laughing at the revelations of such common human fears in these great heroes of his.

"Either!" Holsworthy exclaimed, his eyes popping in mock terror. "Listen, Monsieur, may I stop calling you Le Claire? My name is Hal."

"And mine, Claude," said Le Claire. "You do me another honor," he added respectfully.

"Oh, piffle!" said Holsworthy. "8:00 tonight, then?"

"8:00 tonight," said Le Claire. He shook hands with Harold Holsworthy, Knight of the British Empire, and walked out of the room.

Le Claire had turned off his beeper while he interviewed Holsworthy, not wishing to be distracted, but once in the hallway, he switched it on. It instantly came to life. He hurried down to the main floor of the Chateau and found a fairly secluded telephone where he dialed his office.

"Sandy?"

"Boss? Two calls. Important. De la Montagne called and…"

"So soon!" said Le Claire. "What did he say?"

Sandy sounded definitely disturbed. "His contact is dead, boss. Killed by the Russian. The body is at their old headquarters, in a warehouse in Lower Town. De la Montagne checked it out. It's been abandoned. Also one other body, possibly more. Want the address?"

There was no answer.

"Boss?"

"No, no, Sandy, that's all right. Hold on to it for now. Damn, what bad timing! I should have been there. What else did he say?"

"He said he would have to go underground after this one. Deep underground. 'Au Revoir', he said."

"Damn! Why wasn't I there? Sandy, you have no idea what I could have gotten out of him. Do you remember exactly what he said?"

"No, boss, but…"

"Ah, that's a shame, Sandy," said Le Claire. "A shame." He fell silent.

"Boss?" said Sandy.

"Yes?"

"I taped him."

"You did what?"

"I taped him. The whole thing. I figured it was important. Guessed right, huh?"

"Well, bless you, my girl!" Le Claire said. He was beside himself with joy. "Good work, Sandy! You have no idea. It is Springtime! And you're the Easter Bunny!"

"Referring to my weight?" asked Sandy.

"No, no, no, Sandy! Never!" Le Claire said, laughing.

"I always figured you two had a code," she said.

"You never know, Sandy. You never know," said Le Claire.

"I thought so," she said.

"Sandy, set up that tape and have it ready to run for me."

"Right, boss."

De la Montagne had been waiting for Cartier for half an hour. He was sitting on the edge of a wharf in Louise Basin, dangling his legs over the side, spitting into the water. One of his men slouched in a loading doorway behind him, generally looking over the scene.

De la Montagne was a patient man, but his patience was beginning to reach its limits. His butt was getting sore. He shifted his weight, resting his palms on the wood and pushing down. Blood circulated through his rear end.

Half an hour. Normally, reflected de la Montagne, a delay of this length in the life schedule of Albert Cartier would mean that he was dead. But perhaps not. These were strange times for Cartier. Perhaps he was simply busy. The stevedore waited, smelling the scent of tar, and watching an oily scum on the dirty water by the dock. A condom floated by, and de la Montagne gave it the finger.

A figure appeared far down by the root end of the dock. De la Montagne glared at it. It wasn't Cartier. It was a younger man, who seemed to amble along with no special place to go.

The figure came up the dock almost to de la Montagne, then stopped just short of him. It was Villemaire, a young lieutenant of Cartier's. He hitched up his pants and sat down near de la Montagne. He remained at a respectful distance, and looked morose, and tough, and somehow dulled.

"Cartier is dead," he said in a matter-of-fact manner.

"I knew that as soon as I saw you," the stevedore said. "How did it happen?"

"I don't know. Does it matter?"

De la Montagne shot the man a look he reserved for fools.

"Circumstances," he said harshly. Villemaire looked puzzled. "What were the circumstances?" he demanded. There was a savage, wolf-like quality to his voice. It frightened Villemaire, and he began to stutter.

"I was waiting for him at our appointed place," he said, "where I could keep out of sight and observe the HQ, too. Cartier did not come at the appointed time. I waited. I saw them leave. A truck. A car. On foot. Still he did not come. Then I knew he would not come. So I left and came to you."

"Fool!" de la Montagne snarled, jumping up. "Where is your mind? He may be dead, yes. He may be a hostage. He may be injured. You did not check the place?"

"N-no," said Villemaire. "His orders were…"

"Damn his orders! Use your mind, can't you? Get up!" he hauled Villemaire roughly to his feet. "Where is the place?" he demanded, the spittle sticking to his lips. "Show it to me!"

Villemaire stiffened. "I…I…" he stammered.

"Come on!" the stevedore shouted. "There is no time to waste."

"I'm not going back there," said Villemaire. His tongue was dry.

"You are going where I tell you to go," de la Montagne said, seething.

"The hell I am!" Villemaire shouted, tearing himself out of the stevedore's grasp. De la Montagne's man moved quickly to cut Villemaire off from any avenue of escape.

"The hell you are," de la Montagne said quietly. "You're going to do just as I say. You listen to me. I know who killed the American diplomat." He paused to let that sink in. Villemaire was bug-eyed, petrified. "I saw you do it. Now, you do what I say or the wrong people will find that out. And you're finished. Now, you follow my orders, eh? Come on, Georges!" he called to his man, took Villemaire by the arm, and started down the wharf at a trot.

When they arrived at the warehouse, de la Montagne led the terrified Villemaire straight through the front door. The place was deserted, as he had suspected. All the supplies were gone. What was left of the radio was wrecked.

They went through the place carefully. They found Alain Barbeau's body first, then Cartier's, in the small white room Borovik had chosen for his cell. Cartier's throat was cut. The blood was still shining and wet, slowly adding to the spreading pool on the rough plywood floorboards.

They never found the kid's body. It was stuffed inside a trunk inside a closet, and the stink hadn't penetrated the metal trunk yet.

De la Montagne hit Villemaire over the head with a length of wood. Villemaire crashed to the floor, and Georges and de la Montagne dragged him over to a steam pipe and tied him to it. "Requiescat in pace," said the stevedore. Georges smiled.

There was nothing else to be done with him. Villemaire had lost his judgment. He was useless.

And, thought de la Montagne, Borovik was a pretty good tactician. He saw a problem and took care of it. Too bad he was so vicious. And too bad the Russian hadn't seen fit to contact him. Bad politics. Well, too bad for Borovik. The Revolution didn't really need his sort right now. To hell with him; and to hell with any support for him either.

De la Montagne sent Georges on a little errand. He himself went to call Le Claire.

"And what was the other call, Sandy?" Le Claire asked.

"Harvey Bannerman," said Sandy. "He said you'd know where to find him. 'Immediately,' he said. 'Very important.'"

"Okay, Sandy, I'll take care of that right away," Le Claire said, "Now here's what I want you to do. Get hold of Richard Moreau and his investigation team. Tell them to get into that building and search it thoroughly. Tell them to be careful, there might be booby-traps, eh? And get the special fire team under Lockwood to accompany them. The whole thing might be a trap, although I doubt it very much. Then set up the tape. I'll be there as fast as I can."

Le Claire found an extremely agitated Harvey Bannerman following his elevator ride to the sixth floor. Bannerman had the door open for him before he was half-way down the corridor. "Come in, come in," Bannerman kept saying, motioning with his arm.

"This is Sackman," he said when Le Claire entered the room. "We've got to coordinate. Sackman will lead a team, but you should be in on it too. It's a house on the Ile d'Orleans. It's getting hotter and hotter by the minute. Come here, take a look. See those ships? That's what they're after." And Bannerman outlined his theory.

Le Claire looked glumly out the window while Bannerman talked. When the CIA man was through, he continued to look across the harbor.

"Well?" said Bannerman.

"An excellent theory," said Le Claire, swallowing his pride. It was the waterfront after all. "I believe you're right."

"Then we've got to move those ships," said Bannerman. "Who do we contact in the Port Authority?"

"I think we're too late," said Le Claire. "They are already in operation. Their headquarters has been abandoned for at least an hour. If so, they are far ahead of us. But we will give it a try anyway, no?"

"Are you giving me confirmation?" Bannerman asked, his glittering eyes narrowing.

"Their headquarters is abandoned,' said Le Claire, dispirited. "That is a fact. Where they have gone I cannot say."

"I think *I* can," Bannerman said. "Who do we contact?"

"His name is Roger Cadieux, but I must warn you, he is no friend of mine. Jurisdictional disputes, that type of problem, you know?"

"Will he cooperate?" asked Bannerman.

Le Claire shrugged.

"*I* think he will cooperate," Bannerman said, heading for the phone. "Where's his office?"

Chapter 29

The Lawn Party

Borovik took long, energetic strides across the lawn, breathing the fresh air of the countryside. He felt exhilarated. It was his first time in the open air in more than three days. All that time he had been cooped up in the foul-smelling, pest-ridden dust of the warehouse. Now, finally, he was at the point of putting his plan into operation. The time was right, the conditions were right, and he had all the information he needed.

He was some three hours ahead of schedule, but that was no problem. It was his policy to be ahead of schedule when there was no dovetailing to be considered. The only information he had lacked was scheduling for the ships coming up-river, and Abdul and Mahmoud had returned from Les Escoumins with that information late last night, courtesy of a less than scrupulous pilot or two. So everything was ready to go, and it looked good.

There had been some trouble. Borovik had not anticipated the problems created by Cartier's flamboyant ego. Cartier had refused to be intimidated, and had refused to subordinate himself to the goals of the Revolution. So, Borovik had had no choice. When they found Cartier with his throat cut, these dilettantes and pissants of the so-called Movement would understand what the demands of the real Revolution were like.

Not all his contacts with Movement people had been negative, however. This cell he was working with now, for instance. These comrades were hardy and brutal men – good peasant stock, egalitarian offspring of the downtrodden masses, the kind of workers that Borovik appreciated. The cell leader wasn't bad, either. This fellow – St. Andre – was the very one Borovik had once expressed doubt about, but he was turning out very nicely. The wild anger in his eyes and his attempts to secure the success of the mission were traits that Borovik found difficult to disparage. He didn't fully trust the lad, but still he had plans for him. He intended to make full use of him, his position, and his abilities.

For the first time since leaving the trawler, nearly all of Borovik's men were gathered together in one location. Only the Algerian was missing. He was on his way to Montreal once again, in preparation for the next morning's activities. All the others were here, gathered on the long, sloping lawn behind the grotesque bourgeois mansion. Abdul and Mahmoud had just arrived with the truck, and the others were helping them to unload it. They got a lot of help from St. Andre's people, too. Borovik liked that.

The truck had been backed up as close as possible to the embankment that led down to the river, and out of it came all the equipment necessary for this phase of the mission: the Sea Robin semi-subs, the surplus U. S. Air Force T-33 wing tanks, equipment as bulky and unwieldy as two creosote-soaked telephone poles, as delicate as the General Electric Emerson Re-breathers, as small as the tiny coils of steel wool, and as snaky as the detonating caps with their spider-like appendages.

Borovik reached the embankment and squatted with the men of his diving team in a circle around a large map of Quebec's waterfront. On the map were marked six black, oblong strokes strung out along the western side of the Ile d'Orléans. Borovik pointed to them.

"Now this one," he said, pointing to the first ship in line, the one closest to the northern shore. "This is the tanker *Ras Zabol,* out of Kuwait, bound for Cleveland. Which it will never reach, of course." Borovik chuckled. "Dietrich, you will take that, along with Vasyli, here. The ship is due to depart upriver three hours from now, so you are forewarned. After you have finished your work, you will continue to the northern shore of the river, just here, before the Montmorency comes into the north channel. You will notice the change in the color of the water, and follow that line to shore."

"So there is a change in plans?" said Vasyli with some surprise. "We do not return here?"

"I always keep ahead of them, Vasyli," Borovik said. "Remember that. It is your lesson for the day. No, I want to leave this place alone, for a little while, anyway. Too much activity, too much chance someone will get curious."

"And what happens at Montmorency?" Dietrich asked.

"It is a deserted place," Borovik said, "cut off by highway systems. Sink the Sea Robin, come ashore. There will be someone to meet you. Do not worry about that."

Dietrich nodded his head.

"Good," said Borovik. "Now, Paolo and Jaime." He looked at the Italian and the Cuban, "Jaime, your communications activities – the radios and radio-transmitters are all finished? Set on the correct frequencies?"

Jaime nodded.

"Good. Then you are ready. And you also, Paolo?"

"All things, ready," said the Italian.

"Fine," Borovik said. "You two do not have so long a swim, at first. But a bit more work to do. You will take this last ship in line, this *Dunvegan Castle.* She's an old ship. British. 20,000 tons. Freighter. She's right for our purposes, and so is her schedule. Place two charges – one on her shaft. She's a singleblade, with bolt-on hubs. The second, beneath her keel-plate. Be careful of that second charge. Be sure it's correctly placed. I want that ship split in two, do you understand? Crack it wide open. Like a Carpathian walnut!"

The divers nodded their heads.

"Good. For your escape, then. You will return down this side of the island. Get to the south shore of the river. Over there. You see that point? It's two miles downstream. Fix it. It's a park. There will be someone to meet you there. It's a long swim. Just hold on to your Sea Robin and let it do the work for you. Then sink the Sea Robin and swim ashore."

Borovik addressed all the divers: "There will be all the air tanks you need. The Sea Robins will have them all over, like barnacles. You will have all the air you need. Under no conditions will you surface, until you are ready to land. And watch out for air surveillance! Understood?"

More nods from the silent divers. Two of them were smoking cigarettes, and seemed to be lost in worlds of their own. They all followed Borovik down to the dock.

The Argentinian was efficient. That was one of the things that made him so dangerous. He was directing the dispersal of the equipment on the dock.

The Sea Robins were already in the water, festooned with extra air tanks and other paraphernalia. Bags full of tools hung off them. Long aluminum struts were attached to them lengthwise. The water slid off their rounded muzzles as though they were made not of metal, but rather of the skins of black and vicious sharks.

Now large screweyes were forced into the telephone poles, and the surplus wing tanks were clamped and hung to them. The U.S Air Force wing tanks, designed for holding jet fuel, now held ballast and enough gelignite to blow a ship clear out of the water. The tanks had been bought in the United States, in separate army surplus stores, by two Canadians who explained that they wanted to use them as pontoons for a diving float at their cabin on a far northern lake.

The wing tanks were painted a dirty gray. They looked like stiff, dead porpoises.

The telephone poles, with the wing tanks hung beneath them, were lowered gently into the water. The divers checked their personal equipment and slipped into the muddy river beside the poles. They draped their arms over the logs and the Sea Robins as the Argentinian ticked off the equipment list. They checked each piece, not simply for its presence, but also, as much as possible, for its condition. It was a long list. Finally satisfied, the divers gave their thumbs-up signs.

The men on the dock dropped netting over the poles, and the divers secured it. Then the Argentinian gave them their compass headings. They would swim straight out into the river for three hundred yards, then turn and head diagonally across the current at a reading of 285 degrees. The Argentinian had calculated the current of the river, as well as its direction of flow, and had taken these factors into account. If they followed his directions, they should be right on target.

The divers slipped their face masks on and placed their breathing tubes in their mouths. They waved and dipped beneath the surface.

Slowly, each of the machines crawled out of the space beside the dock and, guided by the frogmen, pointed out to sea. Dietrich and Paolo steered the machines; Jaime and Vasyli shepherded the deadly cargo.

Borovik could scarcely hear the whirring electric engines of the Sea Robins. He and the rest of the team stood on the dock and watched until all traces of the expedition were lost beneath the choppy river waves. Then they clambered up the embankment and started briskly across the lawn.

"Abdul. Mahmoud," Borovik called, and the two Arabs slid silently over to him. He took small plastic and metal bits out of a bag and distributed about a hundred to each of them.

"Take these," he said, "and scatter them though the forest on each side of the house. Do your best to hide them. But do it quickly. Start at the dock, go around each side of the house. Surround the house. Meet in the front and come back to where the cars are parked. Meet us there."

He gave more bits to the Argentinian. "The whole house," he said. "Every room." The Argentinian loped toward the building and silently disappeared inside.

"You three," Borovik said to Jean-Paul's cell members, "Guard this house tonight. Show yourselves outside of it at times. Tomorrow, leave at 9:00 A.M. and go into the city. Join the parade. You will receive further instructions there. If anyone tries to enter the house tonight, try to stay out of sight. If you can't, kill them. But do not go looking for trouble. Understand?"

The French-Canadians wanted to be good soldiers. Borovik's orders seemed strange, but they would follow them. They agreed, as silently as the others had done.

"Good," Borovik said. "Get into the house now. All except you." He pointed to one of them. "First, drive the truck up to the driveway. Then join your comrades." The three men moved off.

"Now, Comrade Jean-Paul, I want to talk to you briefly," Borovik said when they were alone. "I have been watching you, and I sense you wish to help our cause even more than you are doing presently. Would you like to accompany us for a time?"

Jean-Paul was stunned. "Of…of course…" he stammered. "You do me a great honor, sir."

"It may be dangerous," said Borovik.

"If it helps the people, I do not care for danger!" Jean-Paul said heatedly.

"You may have to go into hiding afterwards."

Jean-Paul shrugged.

"You may have to leave the country with us," Borovik said.

"The Revolution is a World Revolution," said St. Andre.

"I am convinced," Borovik said, laying his hand on Jean-Paul's shoulder. "You will come with us. Do what I tell you. Follow orders, and this will all turn out for the best. Do you concur?"

They arrived at the portico, and stood by the nearest of the three cars parked there.

"Of course, my Comrade Commander!" Jean-Paul said. "I am proud to assist you in any way I can."

"Good," said Borovik curtly. "Get behind the wheel of this car. You will drive me."

Jean-Paul jumped into the driver's seat without thinking. The Argentinian came out of the house and when he saw St. Andre sitting in the car, peering intently ahead, his eyes glittered. He looked at Borovik and the two men exchanged the slightest of smiles. To Jean-Paul, these were the smiles of comradeship exchanged in battle. He was proud to be associated with these warriors.

Too deep to be noticed on the surface, the two terrorists were exchanging a bellylaugh.

Suddenly, Abdul and Mahmoud appeared. Mahmoud joined the Argentinian in the second car and Abdul climbed into the truck. Borovik looked around, raised his hand, and the engines started.

Jean-Paul's hand was on the key when Borovik got into the car.

"Let's go," Borovik ordered.

"Sir?" said Jean-Paul, nervously.

"Let's go, damn it!" roared Borovik!

"Yes, sir!" said Jean-Paul loudly, and the little caravan started off, with wide intervals between the vehicles. At the first opportunity, they all took separate roads.

Ten minutes after Borovik's vehicles left the driveway, the first of Sackman's men appeared in the trees and shrubbery around the house. They were careful to stay out of view. Borovik's heat sensors picked up their presence, but didn't transmit that fact to anyone. Nobody was listening. Borovik didn't care. He wouldn't care until later. Meanwhile, anyone who showed up might be amused by St. Andre's cell members. Let them spend their energy on that. Borovik didn't give a damn how many agents surveilled the house tonight. As long as most of them were gone by tomorrow – that was the important part.

Chapter 30

Divers

Twenty-five feet below the surface of the turbulent river, the divers knew the day only by the thin beams of sun that stroked through the water and flashed off the small particles of mud and sand carried along by the swift current. To the divers, this was like moving through space, far from the nearest star. There was no natural orientation here. This was no pleasant journey through the emerald seas of the tropics, where the rainbow-hued fish swam through towering orange coral castles. This was quite different. There was no floor to the river that they could see, and no rooftop to the water. There was no sky and no earth, no trees or rocks. There was nothing but this brown emulsion with the pale gold light that flashed in the silent, somber deep. Visibility might be fifteen feet at good times, but usually held to ten or less. There were no fish here, and only an occasional weed or twig, tumbled along by the current, swept slowly across their field of vision. Devoid of the extension of sight, the divers might be blind men groping through a night of no beginning and no end. Only the unnatural compass and watch kept them in touch with their place on earth, and the divers kept their eyes glued to their instruments, watching for some semblance of nature that they could understand.

The swim out to the three hundred foot mark was accomplished not by sight but by time, by the Argentinian's calculations of the river's movement and the knowledge of the possible speed of the Sea Robins. And when that time was finished, Dietrich began a slow arc to the right that brought them down a bit deeper into the murky night and leveled the compass off at a reading of 285 degrees. Then they headed west upriver.

The uncanny whine of the Sea Robins' engines seared gently through their inner ears. Bubbles of spent air broke from their lips and entered the tubes of their rebreather apparatus, where they were diffused into pockets of air so small that no trace of their passing could be seen on the surface of the water. The sound of air bubbles burbled in their ears, and the uninterrupted hiss of new air from the tanks distracted their minds. The only other sound in this underwater world was the cumulative groan of ships' engines that came from miles around and changed the water from a natural living space to a medium for carrying the drumlike sounds of modern industry and commerce. The whole of the sound was an ever-present throbbing in the divers' ears. They felt the pressure of their facemasks on their foreheads and cheeks. They felt the dry clinging scrape of their rubber suits as they kicked and swayed along. They felt the pressure of the fins against their feet. The weights around their waists tried to bring them down and forward into the darker night of the time ahead, and ever they were drawn swiftly forward by the machines named after the strange red-gilled fish, and they went forward in time, for there was no space, just a pressure in their eardrums. And space came up from nowhere in the shape of twigs that tumbled into their sight, and space fell back to nowhere as they watched the debris of several seasons disappear past them into the turgid, tumbling gloom. And so there was no space, and likewise time was not there, and they were in a void where the only hold on sanity was that granted by the dials and needles of watches and compasses.

It took strong wills and minds trained to unnatural behavior to keep them down there, not let them break and cast off the weights and speed to the surface, to rip the tubes out of their mouths and gasp for air and feel the wind and hear the gulls with their wild cries and beating feathers. To see the sky. To touch the earth. And they stayed down, and watched their dials and needles, in that nothingness where nothing ever changed. They did this for an eternity, and, unnoticing, began to breathe deeply, as if looking for something more solid deep down within their own resources. Perhaps they thought of some dry place deep in their minds' primeval memories; or perhaps, if they searched inwardly far enough, they came upon the lightning of their flashing souls. They subsailed on for ages that did not end, out of the twentieth century, out of any century, into the time before there was a continent to dispute, and their thin lines of bubbles became capes over them, and they spread their arms, and some unreal power turned them on a lathe of strength, and they became harbingers of destruction and wild laughter and the death of innocence. And they swam on for how long they did not know, and they knew nothing but the hands of the watches. And those hands, to their puzzled, frowning faces peering out into the cold, dark sea from behind their plastic goggles, those hands seemed stuck in time, seemed liquid, seemed moving quickly or slowly as they wished; and quirky time itself melted before their eyes, and they were overwhelmed in a sea of misgivings.

And then the light of the water gradually changed, and they sensed that and looked up. And there, far in the distance, was the dim shadow of a great ship. They came closer, and the ship's hull was wreathed in a green light from the cilia-like hair it bore. The weeds of temperate and tropic anchorages mingled on the hull, and waved in the tide, and lent a softness to the harsh curve of the metal hull. And it was slimy to the touch.

And the fear of falling, falling in an unending, twisted fall to some unknown depths that never were – that fear diminished, and the men breathed easier and went about their work.

Vasyli and Dietrich waved and went on, toward the far shadow of another ship, and Paolo and Jaime gave themselves to the exploration of the musky hull of the *Donvegan Castle.* While Paolo drove the Sea Robin in small circles beneath the freighter, Jaime scraped away at its hull with a little ball of steel wool. The algae and slimy weed quickly disintegrated. Jamie dove to the Sea Robin and released the magnetic anchor, and soon the machine was clamped to the hull at the end of a fifteen-foot nylon rope, leaving both divers free to go about their business.

First they swam to the stern of the ship, carrying with them a sack containing the C4 that looked like nothing so much as white modeling clay. They packed the mass of C4 on the stern near the rudder pins and attached a #6 blasting cap to it. With luck, when it went off the blast would disable the rudder, twist the screw shaft, and bend the screw blade itself. And it need not be that powerful an explosion. It was meant only to disable the ship's ability to steer. It was a positioning charge, which would allow the current to carry the ship against the will of the crew.

They finished quickly and got out of the area as soon as possible. It was not good business to be around the stern of a ship if its master decided to fire up the engines unexpectedly. Revolving screw blades and maneuvering rudders could do nasty things to divers.

They returned to the underside of the ship, directly beneath the keel plate. There was a spot on the keel where, correctly placed, a charge would rip the hull wide open, bow to stern, and crack open watertight bulkheads as fast as a man could crumble up a piece of paper.

Paolo and Jamie didn't have to look for the spot. They were experts. Jaime pointed it out, tapped on it with his knuckle. Paolo concurred, his head nodding affirmatively through his halo of bubbles.

They went to work. First, four small patches on the hull were cleared with the steel wool. As they scrubbed the weed away, the divers noted the recent history of the ship. Next to the hull itself were the barnacles and fat, deep-green and brown globs of kelp from northern Atlantic waters. The kelp was covered in turn by the long, fine strands of pastel green weed, some two feet in length, that were the result of anchorages in tropical harbors. It was this accretion that gave the hull the hairy appearance of an old sea dog.

The divers scrubbed through all this tangled mass and cleared patches on the hull. Then they took the four long aluminum struts from the Sea Robin and, with acetylene torches, fixed them to the hull, each pair of struts angled toward each other so that they formed a kind of cradle.

They unhitched the wing tank from its creosote log and floated it into position, clamping it to the struts so that it was, in effect, an eight-foot-long barrel of explosives hung some ten feet below the freighter.

Paolo and Jaime floated back and enjoyed the sight of their work. Their objective was not to plant a bomb on a ship. That was simple. Their objective was to create an explosion that would rip a ship in two, and that is what this mass of gelignite, positioned correctly, would do. It was not the initial explosion, but its echo, that would do the job.

When the bomb exploded, much of its force would be directed upwards. The shock waves would hit the hull, caving it in a bit, but most of the force would bounce back and down into the sea. When the force hit the river bottom, the floor of the sea would act as a giant trampoline, hurtling the explosion upwards again. It was this force, double or triple the force of the initial blast, depending on the depth of the water, that would rise like a giant fist and toss the ship entirely out of the water like nothing more than a discarded wood chip.

That was the destructive beauty of their work that Jaime and Paolo floated calmly about, admiring.

When they were satisfied that everything was set just right, they fixed a #8 blasting cap to the gelignite. Paolo gave it an extra tap or two for good measure, and Jaime, as much as he could, grinned at him around the outside rim of his air hose.

It was a sickish kind of grin. But the hearts of the two men were happy. They clouted each other's shoulders, released the Sea Robin, reversed their compass direction to 105 degrees, and took off again into the murk, each holding onto a side handle of the machine.

Beneath the ship, everything was once again calm. The fresh water of the Lakes came down the channel, exploring the green hulls of exotic ships. The wing tank meant nothing to the water, and neither did another floating pole. Neither did a body.

Chapter 31

Port Authority

Roger Cadieux's office was normally a quiet, sunny place with a good-sized window that overlooked the main channel of the river. Cadieux was the head of the recently reconstructed Port Authority Police Department, and as such spent most of his day constructing new personnel plans and discarding previously tried, unworkable ones. And he looked out the window a lot. There was plenty of time for that.

He was a man who liked plans and well-constructed days that could be controlled by scheduling appointments in a rational manner. So he was puzzled when his secretary buzzed him and said that a Monsieur Le Claire was outside waiting to see him.

'At four o'clock on a Friday afternoon?' he asked himself. 'Has the man no decency?'

"Does he have an appointment?" asked Cadieux.

"No, sir," said the secretary. "He says it's important that he see you, though."

'Does he?' thought Cadieux. 'Damn him.'

"Very well," he said off-handedly. "Send him in."

The door burst open, taking Cadieux by surprise. Le Claire marched into the room, with Bannerman close on his heels.

"Monsieur Cadieux," said Le Claire, "I apologize for breaking in on you like this, but something has arisen that calls for drastic action."

Cadieux looked at them blankly. He didn't like Le Claire, and he didn't like the looks of the man with him, either, who was in the act of closing the door tightly.

"I will come right to the point, Monsieur," Le Claire said. "My department has reason to believe that terrorists are planning to mine ships in the harbor. In fact, they may have already done so. It is imperative, Monsieur, that you give us your cooperation in this matter."

Le Claire's choice of words was hasty and ill-advised. He regretted his last sentence as soon as he uttered it. He could see Cadieux stiffen.

"Go on," Cadieux said.

"Well," said Le Claire. He cleared his throat. "That is the situation. The details? There are six ships holding in the roadstead by the Ile d'Orléans. We feel that these ships, and their crews, are in danger. We feel you should move them – away from the island, into the wide part of the harbor where they can do the least damage should they explode. Their crews should be taken off them – all but skeleton crews of volunteers, if any. All other shipping in this sector of the river should be halted. You should contact the Coast Guard, the Navy, for diving teams to inspect the ships. Not only these ships, but all the ships in the harbor."

"Monsieur Le Claire," Cadieux said to the detective, who was beginning to bend across the desk in his anxiety, "would you care to sit down?"

"There is no time!" Le Claire exclaimed. "Every second…"

"Surely there is a minute or two," said Cadieux, who had regained his composure. Le Claire capitulated, and sank into a chair.

"Now, sir," said Cadieux, with a sympathetic smile, "I do not know if you have gone mad, or what. You come breaking into my office with wild stories and even wilder suggestions which, if I acted on them, I would surely be censored for, and you demand of me actions which, if they were proposed to you, even you, Le Claire, would surely consider for a moment or two before roaring out with some mad plot in mind. Now, let us say I know nothing of this.

Could you begin, Monsieur, by telling me just who these terrorists might be? Are they the same ones who blow up our mailboxes, perhaps? Or…"

Cadieux was winding himself up to go on sarcastically for a good long time. Le Claire sat and glared at him, and sighed.

"…or is it the ones who steal the cannonballs, whom you so love to prosecute? Do…"

"If I may be permitted to interrupt, Monsieur?" said Bannerman.

Cadieux was beginning to get furious. "Perhaps you may, Monsieur," he said sternly, "and perhaps you may not! Who the devil are you, anyway?"

"He is an associate of mine," said Le Claire, trying to protect Bannerman's identity.

"Oh?" Cadieux thundered. "And what…?"

"My name is Harvey Bannerman, sir," the American said politely, "and I am not a Canadian. Perhaps that might be sufficient for the time being?" Bannerman's eyebrows rose in a questioning manner.

Cadieux grunted, and stopped short. He regarded the American with a renewed, wily interest. Le Claire could see the Port Authority chief was thinking politics, and groaned inwardly.

"May I continue?" asked Bannerman.

"Go on," Cadieux directed.

"Within this half hour, the governors of the Port Authority will be receiving calls directing them to cooperate with Monsieur Le Claire here. It might be advantageous to your position were you to anticipate those calls, and begin to act immediately on his suggestions."

"Really!" sneered Cadieux, "And who, Mr. Bannerman, will be making these important calls of yours, eh?"

"The Prime Minister," Bannerman said quietly. "Of Canada," he added.

"Eh!" said Cadieux, who actually threw himself against the back of his swivel chair. He sat silently for a long time.

"Cadieux," Le Claire said, "there is no time."

Cadieux shot him a vicious look, and Le Claire cringed inwardly, though he did not show it. He knew Cadieux would be out after his scalp after this was over.

The intercom buzzed, and Cadieux flipped the switch.

"A call for you, sir," said his secretary. "From the Treasurer of the Board of Governors. He says it's urgent, sir."

"Hold him. I'll be on the line right away," said Cadieux. To the detective he said, "By God, Le Claire, you had better be right on this. And you, too!" he shot at Bannerman, "Whoever the hell you are."

Cadieux picked up the phone and listened. "Yes, sir," he said. "Yes, sir. I have been apprised of the situation. I have already begun procedures, sir." He listened again. "Of course, sir. You may come down right away. I must go now, sir."

Cadieux put down the phone. "Well, all right, here we go," he said to Le Claire. "I am going to call the river pilots first. Then what would you suggest?"

"Helicopters," Le Claire said. "As many as we can get."

Chapter 32

Die, Diver, Die

Vasyli and Dietrich had just put the finishing touches on the gelignite beneath the tanker *Ras Zabol.* They hung onto one of the stabilizing fins of the big ship and congratulated each other. Then they unhitched the Sea Robin – they were beginning to think of it as a horse – and began to move out of the area.

They still towed the telephone pole behind them, intending to sever its line somewhere a good deal away from the ship. They were more cautious than Jaime and Paolo, and determined to leave no sign of their presence.

So the pole was tied behind them, and it was giving them more trouble than it was worth as the Sea Robin slowly moved the length of the ship. As bulky and sodden with tar as it was, still it had that damned tendency to rise, and it was trying to bring the Sea Robin up with it.

This tug-of-war had turned into a stalemate of sorts, with the edge going to the Sea Robin, but the twenty-foot-long pole still bobbed too near to the tanker's hull, and angled upward besides.

Vasyli indicated a plan to Dietrich, and went hand over hand up the cable to a point where he could get a hold on the log. He intended to add his weight to its bulk and drag it downwards with him, and his method was actually having some effect when all hell broke loose.

The first danger signal was the rattle of the *Ras Zabol's* anchor chain being drawn up, and immediately after that the big ship's engines turned over. Whoever was running the ship wasn't even waiting for the anchor to come up, for he immediately had the *Ras Zabol* running full speed ahead.

Dietrich saw the black, whale-like bulk of the tanker gliding quickly over his head. He saw in the dim distance the rudder and the giant twin screws drawing inexorably toward him. He aimed the Sea Robin straight down, held on tight with one hand, and with the other tied his clutching hand to the machine. Then he felt the turbulence hit him. It tossed the Sea Robin around with the nonchalance and the fury of a tornado, and Dietrich, realizing he was in the middle of big trouble, turned to look at the log that dragged him back and destroyed his hope of life.

He turned just as Vasyli lost his grip on the log and went spinning away, completely out of control, sucked upward by the wash of the great ship. Dietrich turned back and saw the rudder and screws of the ship, the blades lost in a whirl of white water and bubbles. They came faster now. Dietrich knew only one way to escape this fate. Twisting and turning, held fast to the Sea Robin by the thinnest of parachute cord, he brought his knife out of its thigh holster and cut the thick rope that held the log.

The log shot upward, and as the Sea Robin lurched down into the deep, Dietrich saw the log, driven by unforeseen currents, smash into the tumbling Vasyli and pin him to the tanker's hull. Then, as if it were an angry living thing, it backed off and smashed him again and again.

Dietrich, horrified, pulled down and down, saw Vasyli, limp and out of control, being drawn toward the screw blades of the black tanker. All he could do was stare with widening eyes as his companion was drawn into the maelstrom at the tanker's stern and disappeared there.

Then Dietrich himself was in more turbulence. It was all he could do to keep his facemask and air hose intact. By the time calm returned, he was far down in the stream, deep below the bellowing roar of the fast departing ship.

He steadied the Sea Robin and looked around for signs of Vasyli.

He was nowhere in sight, and Dietrich began a slow spiral ascent in an ever-widening search. He rode the machine up to nearly ten feet below the surface but he dared not go any higher. There might be a search on for him. Whoever had hauled the ship out of the roadstead more than two hours before its scheduled departure time might be part of an enemy defense team. There was no way of knowing.

Lying there dead still in the calming waters, Dietrich saw the thin stain just at the periphery of his vision. He knew it for what it was: he had seen it before. He gunned the Sea Robin downwards. At fifty feet he caught sight of Vasyli. His mask had been torn off and the air hose had ripped out of his mouth. Blood streamed from his nose and ears and marked his slow downward glide. His left leg stuck out at the knee at an impossible angle. No air bubbles came from his mouth.

He might still be alive, but Dietrich could do nothing for him. He grabbed the body by a loose hose and towed it toward the island, toward shallow water. As he left the channel, he saw the shadow of land rising to meet him. He lowered the body to the river's murky bottom and rolled two huge boulders over what used to be his diving partner. That way, there would be less a chance of detection, of incidental discovery, of identification. He no longer thought of the Russian as a person, but as a problem to be dealt with. There was no other way to think of it in this business.

The effort of burying Vasyli had taken considerable energy, and energy used a lot of air. Dietrich switched to a new air tank, checked his compass heading, allowed for the distance he had already traveled out of the way, and headed for the north shore of the river. Back on track, he tried to calculate the total time he had spent at different depths. He thought he was safe on that score, at least. He had to be. There was no allowance for the 'bends' in this operation.

Captain Scott Devers stood on the bridge of the *Dunvegan Castle* looking out on an astounding scene. Ever since the first message had cut through the airwaves just minutes before, he had been readying his ship for the arrival of a river pilot. The other five ships in the roadstead were doing the same. The big tanker on the far end of the line had begun to move almost immediately; it was well out of the line now, heading west into the wide part of the river. A helicopter even now lifted off its deck. Two other Coast Guard helicopters were whirring overhead. One was depositing the pilots on the ships. The other seemed to be patrolling above the action. At one point it took off downriver, hovered over a spot near the Ile d'Orléans , and returned in a hurry, resuming its circular patrol as if it had never left.

The helicopter depositing the river pilots made a pass at the *Dunvegan Castle*, fluttered off starboard, and returned to touch down lightly on the aft cargo hatch cover. A man jumped out and ran toward the bridge. Immediately the 'copter was airborne once again.

"Weigh anchor!" Devers shouted to the crewmen forward. "Quick, lads! Get it up!" The winch turned and groaned. Anchor chain crashed into its compartment. Devers whistled down the pipe to the engine room. "Get the steam up, Mr. Stacey. Get it up now. We need it now!"

"Aye, sir!" echoed through the pipe. The ship shuddered.

Devers turned to see the pilot bounding up the stairs toward the bridge, taking them two at a time. The man jumped through the door, assessed the situation in seconds, grabbed the wheel, and commanded, "Full ahead. Give me full ahead!"

Devers relayed the message to Stacy in the engine room and turned to the pilot.

"What's going on?" he asked. The mates were paying careful attention. "I mean, it's quite a spectacle, ships and planes and such running hither and yon. But what is it all about? Have you any idea?"

The pilot concentrated his attention on the waters ahead. It was quite a spectacle. Six ships were making at full speed toward the open reaches of the wide river. The pilot darted a look at Devers. "I've no idea," he said "We came away too fast to gather rumors. The bosses are certainly sending up a shout, though."

"Come now," said Devers. "You have six ungainly ships looking as if they were in some kind of frantic regatta, and you can't say what it is? Do you expect me to believe that?"

"Enjoy your regatta while you can," said the pilot. "You're to be off this ship when we anchor her again. Believe what you want."

"What?" said Devers. "Leave my ship? On what authority?"

"For Christ's sake!" the pilot spat out. "You don't want to die, do you? They think these ships are mined." He took a deep breath and pounded his fist on the wheel. "Can't you get any more speed out of your engineer?"

Within half an hour all the ships were at anchor once again, far apart, up and down the deepest stretch of the main channel. Boats were carrying their crews off in droves.

Dietrich found the line of the muddy Montmorency current with no trouble at all. He guided his Sea Robin along just to the west of the line and headed in toward shore. At a depth of thirty feet, he found an old wreck, and went down and tied the Sea Robin to it, then swam on his way.

A hundred yards from shore, he poked his head above water. Gratefully propping his facemask high on his head, he submerged his face and let the cold water run over it. Refreshed, he rubbed his creased face with his hands, opened his eyes, and looked around.

There was a small beach ahead of him. A lone figure walked back and forth, peering out into the harbor. It was Borovik himself.

Dietrich went down again, swimming in as far as possible before removing his air tank. He stood up then in the water, emerging like some lagoon monster. He was in two feet of water, only twenty-five feet from shore.

He walked in. Borovik strode quickly over to where he would hit the land. The Russian held a sand-colored duffel bag, and shook it toward Dietrich.

"Get that wetsuit off," Borovik commanded. "What the hell happened?"

Dietrich felt suddenly weak from exhaustion. Leaning on the Russian for support, he turned and looked toward the river, saw the ships steaming away, the activity swirling about them. The helicopters especially disturbed him.

"Shouldn't we be under cover?" he asked.

Borovik began to walk slowly toward a culvert that connected the beach with the Montmorency Falls parking area on the far side of the highway system. "They aren't looking around here yet," he said. "It's too early for a wide search. They'll think of it soon enough, but not in time. Where's Vasyli?"

"Dead," said Dietrich. "Hit by the props, or the rudder. I don't know. He's in a safe place."

"The mission?"

"Our part, complete."

They reached the culvert, and Dietrich stripped off the suit. Borovik had sports clothes for him. He changed quickly. "I assume the other team was also successful," he said. "They had time enough."

"We will have to wait for news of that," Borovik said. "Meanwhile, they are on to us. We will have to go into hiding for a while. And remake our plans. We need a replacement for Vasyli, and I think perhaps I have him. And congratulations to you, Dietrich. I am saddened by Vasyli's death. He was a good man."

Dietrich walked through the long culvert with his head bowed, remembering his partner.

When the two men emerged from the culvert into the Montmorency Falls parking lot, Jean-Paul and Abdul were in the car, waiting for them. They got in and sped away. Their departure went unnoticed by the few tourists in the area.

Chapter 33
Light

Le Claire rushed out of the elevator on the fifth floor of the Chateau Frontenac, hurrying past his plainclothesmen in the corridor. There were three of them there now – two at the door and one a short way down the hall. They acknowledged him with salutes. He nodded to them and knocked on the door.

There was no answer. There was not a sound from behind the door. Le Claire looked at his men with a puzzled frown. Their worried faces gave him no satisfaction.

He dug in his pocket for a passkey. Motioning for his men to remain as they were, he unlocked the door, drew his gun, and stepped into the room.

It was empty.

Le Claire moved swiftly across the expanse and opened the door to the bedroom of the suite. That too was empty. He opened the closets and searched under the bed. Nothing, he thought. Nothing. Returning to the living room, he was about to summon his men when he heard what he thought was laughter coming from outside the window.

He had forgotten the balcony.

He went to the glassed door and looked outside. There was

Holsworthy, and another man bent over the stone railing and laughing. They looked like a couple of overgrown boys.

"Watch this one, now," Holsworthy said to the man Le Claire assumed was Holworthy's friend, Charlie Broughton. "Watch the reaction." There was more laughter.

Le Claire cleared his throat. The two men jumped, and turned to see him standing there. Holsworthy recovered quickly.

"Oh, Le Claire!" he said. "You gave me a turn." This is Charlie. I told you about him?"

"Monsieur?" said Le Claire, acknowledging Broughton with a slight nod.

Broughton smiled and extended his hand. "Oho!" he said. "The reason old Harold here is so nervous tonight. How do you do?"

"Claude," Holsworthy said, "Come over here, will you? I want to show you something." The scientist took Le Claire by the shoulder and guided him over to the stone railing. "Look down there," he directed.

The balcony faced southeast and overlooked the harbor. The sun was going down in the west, behind the towers of the Chateau. It threw long purple shadows across the streets and across parts of the Dufferin Terrace below.

"Now watch," Holsworthy said, "Do you see my pen?" He held up a thin silver pen that looked quite expensive to Le Claire. It was definitely not an everyday pen. It was the type a highly-placed executive might receive as a gift. It had a retractable point.

"Look now," Holsworthy said, leaning over the railing. "Watch that fellow down below there. See him?" He pointed to a solitary figure walking across the shadowed portion of the Terrace.

"Yes," said Le Claire, tentatively.

"Watch," said Sir Harold. He aimed the pen toward the man five stories below. With a steady hand, he pushed the pen's release mechanism and suddenly a thin line of red light hit the boardwalk directly in front of the stroller. The light, a keen line as straight as a razor's edge, hung like red lightning in the air between the pen and the boardwalk. It lasted perhaps a second. Then there was a click as Holsworthy retracted the mechanism. The man on the Terrace jumped slightly, startled, and looked around. Holsworthy and Broughton howled.

"You see," Holsworthy said, "He knows something has happened, but he doesn't know what. His eyes picked up a fact of light – reminded him somewhat of lightning, I suppose, but he's never seen red lightning before – doesn't know what to do with it – memory cells can't find it. Anyway, he knows there's been a bright light near him – his eyes know it, anyway – but he didn't see it. Watch this one."

Holsworthy chose another subject and repeated his performance, garnering the same result. He snickered.

Le Claire looked at him with his mouth open. "What is that thing?" he managed at last.

"A ray gun, just like Flash Gordon's," laughed Broughton.

"Nothing *that* exotic," Holsworthy said pleasantly. "Just a little magic. It's a laser beam, built into a pen casing. Diminutization of parts. Interesting from a technological point of view, but a toy nevertheless. Harmless. A toy for mad scientists." He chuckled. "Would you like to try it? Careful, it's delicate."

Le Claire held the pen tightly in his hand. "You could hit the moon with this," he said.

"Oh, I suppose you could," Holsworthy said, "if you had a reason to. It's been done. I prefer more immediate objects. A better reaction than moon rocks. Try that couple down there."

Le Claire grinned. He was beginning to see a strange sort of humor in this, something akin to what a pagan god might feel as he hurled thunderbolts across the sky. He pointed the laser and fired, placing the beam a yard in front of the unsuspecting couple. Accuracy was remarkably easy with this thing.

The couple stopped short, turned, and looked quickly in different directions. Then they looked at each other. The man rubbed his eyes. Le Claire could imagine the conversation. He laughed.

"It's wonderful," he said. "But you'd better take it back. I don't want to drop it." Even as he spoke he aimed again and released another shot.

"Don't get carried away, now," Holsworthy admonished him, albeit with a broad grin. He took the pen and placed it, like any normal pen, in the inside pocket of his suit coat. "Shall we go to dinner?" he asked.

The three men left the balcony. When they were inside the room, Le Claire turned to the two scientists.

"Gentlemen, I have bad news," he said. "Our situation has changed. There is no sense hiding anything from you. I am sure you are discreet. If you look toward the river, you will see that the ships in the roadstead have changed their positions drastically. They are being searched for mines and bombs even now. The situation is serious, and we have no idea what will happen next.

"So you see," Le Claire continued, "Under these circumstances I feel I would be derelict in my duty if I did not grant you the greatest security I can offer. In short, gentlemen, it will be easier to protect you here rather than downstairs. We would be grateful if you would amend your plans and decide to eat your dinner here."

Holsworthy was silent. Broughton was shaken. "Hal told me of the situation," he said, "but not the extent of it. This is incredible."

"It is merely a precaution," Le Claire said. "Your dinner bill would, of course, be picked up by my Department. We would view it as a business expense."

"Really," said Holsworthy, brightening. "Do you suppose the wine steward has some…" He changed his mind immediately. "No, never mind. It would not do, without a beautiful woman to gaze at across the table." He hit Broughton's arm. "Certainly not a thing to share with this ugly mug."

"I should hope not!" said Broughton, in mock alarm.

"Shall I send a waiter up with the menus?" Le Claire asked as he made for the door.

"But aren't you going to join us?" said Holsworthy.

"More bad news," Le Claire said. "For me, this time. I have much to do. Unforeseeable earlier today. Regrettable. I am disappointed. I had looked forward to meeting with you."

"Another time!" said Holsworthy. "Not 'perhaps,' either. Definitely. Le Claire, I want you to know I really appreciate what you are doing for me. I won't forget this. Dinner, then, when all this is over with. I will want to know all the details."

"A pleasure, Sir Harold," said Le Claire. "A pleasure and an honor." He opened the door.

"And, oh, Claude," Holsworthy said, "*Do* send up that waiter, will you? I'm starved."

Le Claire laughed and shut the door.

Cadieux's office was a focus of activity by the time Le Claire returned there. It had become something of a headquarters, with representatives from the Port Authority, RCMP, local and provincial police forces, Coast Guard, Army, Navy, Air Force, and government agencies coming and going, coordinating, planning and finding time for quick exchanges of classified gossip in corridors and corners.

Le Claire looked around for Bannerman, but the CIA man had left on some undisclosed mission. Le Claire focused on his two major security operations of the next day: identification of radicals at the St. Jean-Baptiste Day parade, and tightening coverage for the Economic Conference. Over everything lay the weight of the continuing search for Borovik and his terrorist cohorts. Le Claire's Department was spread thin, but he still had all his points covered. He telephoned an exhausted Sandy and asked her to remain at her post for just a short time longer, when he would join her at his office and review the operations she had been covering. Sandy granted him a sarcastic affirmative, and he started out, leaving notice at the Port Authority concerning his plans and where he might be reached.

By now, most of the ships had been searched. The *Ras Zabol's* mine was de-activated, costing the Coast Guard diver a number of years off his life through sheer terror. When he broke the surface of the water clutching the blasting cap in his hand, a cheer went up from his crew. He was fished out of the water and was excused from further duty for the day. He graciously accepted the offer, along with a beer, in a temporary state of hope that he would never again see the bottom of a ship. Though well-trained, this had been his first real piece of work, and his guts were a seething mass of jello. But he was now a veteran and, temporarily, at least, a hero, and that was some compensation.

The launch picked up speed and headed downriver toward the last ship in the line of six, the *Dunvegan Castle.*

Chapter 34
The Belt

Louis Chicoine was the most observed man in Quebec. Since the night before, when the Algerian had visited his room in the small hotel, his movements had been recorded with deadly accuracy. A camouflaged camera, set at an angle behind the barred windows of the U. S. Consulate, peered through Chicoine's hotel window. Two of Le Claire's men at the Department of Justice, bored stiff, played cards in a hotel room across the hall and listened for sounds from their quarry's room. When he went out, he was followed, and while he was out, his room was bugged.

They took his fingerprints off his coffee mug. They found them again on a public telephone he used. As soon as he had finished his call and gone off, the telephone cable fell to a pair of wirecutters, and the telephone's handle made its way to a police laboratory, where it was dusted.

They nicknamed him 'The Termite', and a half-dozen agents were ready to jump him as soon as they got the word.

Two facts about Chicoine had brought on such a heightened interest in his every move. First of all, he had received a visit from the Algerian; and secondly, the window in his room looked out onto the small, quaint courtyard that served as the back yard of the U. S. Consulate.

It was too much of a coincidence. Although they laughingly compared the man to a termite, they knew he was more dangerous than a bug. He was more like a cobra, poised to strike. He had penetrated far too close for comfort to the heartbeat of American operations in eastern Quebec Province.

When he leaned out the window of his second-story room, Chicoine could almost touch the fire escape of the consulate building. Almost, but not quite. To accomplish his task, he would have to rely on a grappling hook and some climbing rope.

The rear wall of the American Consulate building was well fortified. A high, outward-curving iron fence cut it off from the common courtyard, and once over the fence, anyone would find himself falling into a moat-like depression as deep as a cellar with no outlet. Above, an aluminum extension ladder was lashed to a fire-escape, it's treads in the 'up' position. Gates of wide-gauge wire mesh covered the windows, locked in place from within. The windows themselves were all wired into an elaborate electronic alarm system. The brick wall of the building showed signs of recent modifications. The roof, which contained an extensive array of radio receiving and transmitting equipment, was cut off from the neighboring rooves by its height and the addition of wire fencing.

The entire back wall of the building was in contrast to the façade facing on the street. From the front, the building looked like an old townhouse. From the back, it looked as formidable as a bunker. A civilized bunker, but a bunker nevertheless.

Chicoine was there to create a diversion. In addition to serving as a contact for the Algerian, he was there to blow the American Consulate to smithereens as part of the St. Jean-Baptiste Day festivities.

He doubted he could do it with the materials he'd been provided, but he would give it a try. At the very least, he would knock out part of a wall. The Americans would be frightened and embarrassed, and everyone would have a good laugh.

When two plainclothes Mounties broke down the door to his room, Chicoine was seated on the bed enjoying a beer and a soccer match on

TV. He was too surprised to react. The Mounties grabbed him and threw him against the wall. As they were searching him, Bannerman, who had entered immediately behind them, located Chicoine's luggage, threw it onto the bed, and ripped it open. He found the grappling hook and rope, but little else of interest. Two of Le Claire's men approached from across the hall, and the hotel's proprietor, attracted by the commotion, came running up the stairs to stand in the doorway, gaping. They all watched Chicoine's predicament with interest.

"Nothing on him, sir," said one of the Mounties.

"Nothing? I don't believe it," Bannerman said. He walked over to Chicoine, who was still spread-eagled against the wall, and studied his back.

"Nothing on him, right?" Bannerman said. "Watch."

He grabbed the back of Chicoine's belt and pulled. With little effort, a six-inch piece of belt split off in his hand.

"Turn him," Bannerman commanded. The Mounties spun Chicoine around, and Bannerman removed the rest of the belt. The buckle was a miniature polished blasting cap.

"Idiot," Bannerman said to Chicoine with contempt in his voice. "You must be an idiot. You must work for idiots. You must all be a pack of idiots."

Chicoine's face muddied with anger, but he said nothing.

"Interesting stuff," Bannerman said, holding up the belt. "It's called M-118. This much, placed correctly – which he probably couldn't do – could bring down this hotel."

The Mounties were sufficiently impressed.

"Don't rent this room," Bannerman said to the proprietor. "And don't leave the building. You are under suspicion. Lock this door." He addressed Le Claire's men. "Guard this place 'til your investigation team gets here. Guard him, too," he said, indicating the startled proprietor.

"Let's go," he said to the Mounties. They grabbed Chicoine, handcuffed him, and dragged him out of the room and down the stairs.

As the group of men emerged from the hotel's front door, there was a roar like thunder, and a flash of light shot up from the purpling shadow that was the river. Startled, they all stared across the Duferrin Terrace and down to where the *Donvegan Castle* rocked and shuddered on the water in the twilit evening.

Chicoine laughed. "Idiots, are we?" he said, and laughed again. "You have trapped a minnow, and let the barracuda go free."

"Take him," Bannerman ordered.

They dragged the laughing Chicoine down to their waiting car. In the distance, the *Donvegan Castle*, its stern anchor chain snapped and its controls demolished, swung slowly around, dragging its bow anchor across the bottom of the channel.

Genevieve and Kearney were in the middle of dinner, two-thirds of the way through a bottle of wine, in a small restaurant halfway up the steep Cote de la Montagne. Genevieve had seemed to revive with the coming on of evening, and she was happy and forgetful, which made Kearney happy.

"Isn't this better than one of your gross, giant restaurants in one of your gross, giant tourist towers?" she said. Her eyes sparkled.

"They aren't *my* tourist towers," Kearney protested.

"Why, then, whose are they? Certainly not mine!" said Genevieve. "We Quebecois hate those damned American hotels. That's why we keep bombing them. We cannot stand tall, narrow buildings. It is against our natures."

"Why, that's not true," said Kearney. "The University – Laval University – has tall buildings, and Laval is Quebecois. You can't deny that."

"Yes, I can," said Genevieve petulantly. "There are two tall buildings at the University," she announced. She took a sip of wine and ran her tongue suggestively across her upper lip. "We call them the erections of the University." She giggled, and threw back her head and laughed out loud.

The sound of an explosion came from somewhere outside. Genevieve frowned. A general hush settled over the patrons of the restaurant.

Holsworthy and Broughton, up in the fifth floor suite at the Chateau, were working on a bottle of after-dinner Drambuie.

"Ah, a taste of the old '45," said Holsworthy, lifting his glass in a toast. "Brings the Scots blood up. Good for the digestion."

"…'s good for the forearms, too," said Broughton, who was

sprawled out in an easy chair, ahead of Holsworthy three to two on large shots. "Makes 'em heavy. Can't feel 'em. Strange. Heavy and yet can't feel 'em. Should've gone into physics. Strange." He lifted his arms to examine them.

The *Donvegan Castle* explosion rattled the windows, sobering the two scientists.

"I say," said Holsworthy. "Let's have a look, shall we?" They headed for the balcony. As they rose, they were joined by a startled plainclothesman from the hallway who, fearing the worst, had let himself into the suite. The three men crossed to the balcony and stepped outside.

The *Donvegan Castle* was midway across the river from the Chateau. It still rocked from the explosion, and was beginning to turn fitfully against the current. A small Coast Guard launch circled it at some distance.

"I say," said Holsworthy, "I say…"

From his vantage point in the safe house high on the cliffs of Levis on the south shore of the river, the Argentinian watched the freighter turn. His pick-up of Jaime and Paolo had gone smoothly, but as they drove back to the city, he noticed the sudden erratic behavior of the ships as they scurried for the deeper water of the central channel. He sent the two divers on with Mahmoud to make contact with Borovik, while he himself left the car to make his way on foot to the safe house. He was dressed quite properly as a businessman and aroused no suspicion as he walked down the street with his attaché case.

Now the Argentinian waited. He'd had no choice. He held off for as long as possible. He had watched the authorities' search the other vessels, and finally he seen the Coast Guard launch approach from up-river. There was no more time. He had pressed the button, and now the ship was twisting and turning in the river. Still the launch came on, more wary now, describing a wide circle around the stricken ship. A solitary figure waved to it from the bridge.

The Argentinian watched, and waited. The ship swung away, now at almost a right angle to the current.

He looked down at the control panel in the interior of his attaché case.

He looked at the ship again. It had swung directly across the current.

He pressed the second button.

Holsworthy and the others felt, rather than heard, the muffled woomph as the gelignite went off under the keel of the Donvegan Castle. They saw the ship rise, then settle again. The waters around the freighter grew calm, then seemed to gather in a rising boil as the magnified shock waves bounced off the river bottom.

Then the *Donvegan Castle* rose up.

It rose and rolled and split like a berserk flower opening to the sun. Pieces of it flew in all directions, and the water roiled into a fury. Something in the ship exploded, and the *Donvegan Castle* seemed to convulse in a kind of metallic agony.

Holsworthy, Broughton and the cop were no fools. They jumped for the door and grabbed for the floor, lobstering their way to any available cover. Then the shock waves hit. Windows crashed in, brick dust flew, and the Chateau itself shook.

Devers, the captain of the freighter, who had chosen to remain on board, died instantly from a massive concussion and a broken back. Blood streamed from the ears of many of the Coast Guard divers on the launch. Every fish within a quarter of a mile of the freighter died from the impact of the gelignite fist. On shore, unlucky spectators were viciously cut by flying glass.

Holsworthy raised himself up on his elbows from his position under the mahogany table. He looked at Broughton, who still clung to the carpet alongside him.

"Charlie," he said, "I think I've gotten myself into the middle of something rather large."

With the second explosion, the patrons of the restaurant poured out into the street, Kearney and Genevieve among them. Genevieve had turned pale, and clung to Kearney as they stood in the middle of a gabble of suppositions, explanations, and theories that spewed forth in cracked and splintered pieces from the panicked crowd.

"My brother," said Genevieve. She looked up at Kearney. "My brother!" she said loudly, and she began to run.

Kearney ran after her. "Wait!" he shouted. "Wait!" He caught her, grabbed her arm, spun her to a stop. "Where are you going?"

"To Rene's," she cried. "To Rene's!"

"My car."

"Where is it?" she said, looking around like a trapped animal.

"Up on top. By the cathedral," he said.

"Faster this way," she breathed. "Come!" she began to run again – through an alley, up sidewalks so steep they turned to stairs, across wide plazas, through darkened streets filled with gesticulating, excited crowds of Quebecois and tourists alike.

By the time they reached Rene's apartment they were gasping for breath, and they felt the blood thumping past their ears. They flew up the steps and through the open door, and stood gasping inside the apartment.

Rene was on the phone.

"Rene…" Genevieve said. She fought for breath. "My brother… is it Jean-Paul?"

Rene shook his head. No. He turned away, and continued to speak into the phone, too low to be heard. Angelique came over to them and said simply, "Jack, you cannot remain here. It's nothing personal, but we can't take any chances. You get my point?"

"I get it," Kearney replied. "I understand it. I just want to make sure that Genevieve will be all right."

"You have our assurance of that," said Rene, who had finished with his telephone conversation, "but of little else." He walked across to them, and Kearney saw that his eyes were hostile. "The sooner you leave, the better. Why not right now?"

Rene turned abruptly, went into the small bedroom, and slammed the door.

"What's wrong with him?" said Kearney.

"Nothing," Angelique said. "Just pressure. He's very busy just now. Jack, will you please leave?"

Genevieve watched all this with a puzzled expression. "Angelique," she said, "I don't quite follow what is happening here. If Jack must leave, he must, I suppose. But you must tell me why."

Angelique stood there with her lips pressed tightly together.

"Come, Jack," said Genevieve. She led him out to the stairs. "I do not know all that is going on here," she said, "but I feel calmer now. Better, in some way. I feel that everything will come clear very soon."

"What about tomorrow?" said Kearney.

"Will you meet me?" she asked.

"Of course," Kearney said. "We were going to the parade, remember?"

"Meet me at…" Genevieve put her finger to her lips and thought. "…at the first cannon at the top of the Cote de la Montagne. It will be good to see the city from there. At ten o'clock. Is that good?"

"Fine," said Kearney. "At ten o'clock, then." He kissed her, and noticed that her body was somehow different. The tension had gone out of it, replaced by a sense of surety and quiet strength. It was strange. She was completely changed.

"Tomorrow," Genevieve whispered. She slipped out of his arms and went inside, closing the door on him.

She turned to face Angelique and said calmly, "What about my brother? I know you know something. I can see it in your eyes. Tell me."

Angelique put her hands in the back pockets of her jeans. "We don't know about him. We feel very strongly that he is not FLQ, at least not in this area. Beyond that, we know nothing, but it is unlikely…"

"You are FLQ," Genevieve said.

Angelique nodded. "We could not tell you before," she said sadly. "It was impossible. Now, listen," she said with a note of alarm, "Jack must never know!"

"Do you think he already knows?" Genevieve asked.

"We think he is a spy," said Angelique. "Does that shock you?"

"No," Genevieve said. "It is strange, this feeling I have. It is like coming to see reality for the first time. When you do that, even the most horrible things can become acceptable. Perhaps Jack is a spy. What difference does it make? You are FLQ, what has that to do with me? Jean-Paul is out in the darkness somewhere, in some kind of nightmare. So? My father is crazy and forgets who he is. Everything is crazy. Everything that surrounds me falls into a pattern of craziness. When life is like that," she spoke very slowly, "then everything in life turns out to be crazy. Life itself is crazy. So, you can take the whole thing and see the whole thing. You can deal with it. You can look at it and see the insanity of it, and accept it. You can do away with it!"

Angelique looked at her in horror.

"You are all crazy!" Genevieve shouted. "What do you want to be involved with this craziness for? What does it mean to you, this nationalism? This revolution? All it means is death! Death! What good does death do?"

She practically screamed out the words. Rene opened the door and looked out, alarmed.

Genevieve's eyes burned through him and she asked, her voice calm again, "Why is everyone I know crazy?"

Angelique came up to her with two pills and a glass of water. "Here" she said. "Take these."

Genevieve took the sedatives without questioning. Her hands trembled as she brought the pills to her mouth. She sat down on the couch and bent over, hiding her face in her hands. "You are all I have," she said to her two friends. "Please. Let me know you are real. That you are not crazy. That you are not FLQ."

"We are not FLQ," said Rene, gently. He sat next to her and put his arm around her. Angelique knelt on the floor in front of her.

"How do you know about Jean-Paul, then?" asked Genevieve.

"We asked around," said Angelique. "We are not FLQ, but we know some people who know. What I told you, that is what we were told."

"And sometimes we boast, eh? We are not perfect," said Rene. "Lie down and be calm."

Genevieve remained sitting, bent over, holding her head in her hands. "I am calm," she said. "That is the trouble. I am calm. There is black emptiness all around, and I sit in the middle of nothing, and I am calm. Don't let go of me. Please. Don't let me go."

"We won't let you go," whispered Angelique. "We will hold you."

"I know," said Genevieve. "Isn't it peaceful here? Thank you for lying to me. You see, you must, right now. There is nothing else."

And then the tears came, and Rene and Angelique were relieved, and looked at each other with sadness.

Away from the heights of Quebec, away from the central city that is the gem of the metropolis, along the low river valley of the St. Charles, stretched the working-class suburbs of the city. There the ambiance was not elegance, and the rows of four-story wood-framed houses appeared held together by tin and neon signs and spider-worked webs of black and orange outside fire escapes. That was the truth of reality for Quebec's proletariat, and it was a poor, scruffy hold on life's bounty for the poor who lived there. Many radicals were born and made in the slums of Charlesbourg and Giffard.

That was where Borovik stood, alone, in the back room of a row house. He stared out of a window into a dark, tangled garden that had seen no gardener for a long time. He was thinking.

He had heard the explosion, realized the probable cause, and had immediately begun reviewing his plans. When Mahmoud, Paolo, and Jamie arrived they confirmed his suspicions.

Decisions made, he left the room and went downstairs to the cellar rooms that served as a kitchen and general bivouac area for his team. Almost all the troops he could rely on now – Mahmoud, Paolo, Jamie, Dietrich, Abdul, and the new one, this French Canadian, Jean-Paul, were gathered round. All but the Algerian and the Argentinian and Jean-Paul's three cell members were there. They sat or stood around a large old kitchen table that served as a focus for activity. They comprised the core of this tiny, vicious band of committed fighters, this little army commanded by Borovik, and they were ready.

The Algerian – would he hear of the escapade in Quebec and return, realizing his ship would not arrive in Montreal? One could not count on that. Even if he did hear, would he arrive on time?

And the Argentinian – when would he arrive, if ever? There was no way of telling.

Borovik stood on the cellar stairs and smiled a grim smile at his men. "It is your time," he told them. Are you ready?" he asked them. They all smiled back in apparent confidence.

"Well, look at the capitalist!" Borovik said. His smile grew wider as he studied the Italian. Paolo peered haughtily at the others as he walked about, showing off his elegant new suit.

"Paolo di Gordini at your service," he said with a sneer. "Representative of Ferrara Leather. You, boy! Carry these bags."

The rest of the crew burst out laughing. Abdul gave him the finger.

"Paolo, good luck!" said Borovik. A horn honked outside. "Ah! Your cab is here. No time to waste. Have a good sleep, and we'll have your people to you in plenty of time tomorrow. Bongiorno."

Paolo raised his clenched fist in a salute. "The Revolution!" he said fervently.

Borovik's eyes sparked. "The Revolution!" he said, and clapped Paolo on the shoulder. The Italian grabbed his bags and went quickly up the stairs.

Borovik looked at his men. "You are all clear on your assignments for tomorrow?" he asked.

They nodded.

"Good," he said. "Jean-Paul, come with me, will you?" Borovik, followed by St. Andre, went upstairs to the little room that overlooked the back garden. Borovik turned to the young man.

"Jean-Paul," he said. "I want to say this. Today, you acted like a professional. Keep up the good work. Tomorrow will be tougher, but I know you can do it. Now, what I talked about before. Can we trust your men to follow orders?"

"I am sure of it," said Jean-Paul.

Borovik mused. "I trust your judgment," he said. "We will use them. They will be assigned to you, temporarily. I will need one driver, and two very good sharpshooters, eh? They must be here by ten o'clock tomorrow. *Not before.* They must remain at your house on the island until nine-thirty. Then they must leave quickly, and they must not be followed. This is most important. Understood?"

Jean-Paul nodded, his teeth clenched.

"Good," said Borovik. "Now, listen to me carefully. There have been too many little things going wrong with this operation. You must promise me – you must not contact anyone in your Organization. The times are too perilous. Our operation tomorrow must not be compromised. Swear to me you will contact no one."

"I swear it!" said Jean-Paul, savagely.

"Good," Borovik said. "Downstairs, and join the others. Now."

St. Andre left the room. On the way down the stairs, he suddenly felt shaky. He couldn't let the others see him like that. He would not allow it. He pulled himself together and continued down.

Half an hour later, the Argentinian arrived. He let himself in and went straight to Borovik's room.

"What happened?" said Borovik.

"I waited as long as possible," said Rafa. "They would have found it."

"Okay," said Borovik. "Changes in personnel. Vasyli is dead. Everyone moves up a notch. New man. This St. Andre."

"Trust him?" asked the Argentinian.

"One false move," said Borovik, "Mahmoud shoots to kill."

Chapter 35

Top Circles

The conference room was filled with powerful men, all top aides to the Premier of Quebec Province. Their power could be seen in the way they talked; in the way they looked at each other.

At eleven in the evening, they were still discussing plans for the coming day. A debate raged between two of them, and the others looked on, silently analyzing the ideas that flew about the room.

“I don’t care what you say he thinks,” said the outspoken one seated in an easy chair in the corner. “We should call the whole thing off and the economic conference as well. Why give them any excuse?” It was his last try.

“Why not close down the entire city; the entire province?” said the second man sarcastically. He paced back and forth along the length of the room. “The Old Man wants them out. He’s mad as hell. He told me he wants them all out, together, in a bunch, where the cops can round them up.”

“What good will that do? Did he say that? Did he actually say that?”

“He’s just damned mad,” the pacing man hedged. “He said he gave them every chance in the world to get behind him. Says the ones who are left are just malcontents. He wants them out so he can expose their structure, haul them in for sedition. He’s talking War Powers Act.”

"Suppose they get out of hand? Look, some of those lunatics are capable of...of...why, hell, they just blew up a goddamned ship. What's next? They could decide to rip this city apart."

"Differentiate," said his antagonist. "Terrorists blew up the ship. The radicals are supporting that action, not creating that..."

"I can see them all now, sitting around in their stinking little cells trying to think of ways to outdo each other. We ought to use the War Powers Act to keep people off the streets, not get them into confrontations, for God's sake. Where is the logic in that? It exacerbates the situation instead of ameliorating it."

"There's plenty of coverage. The cops and the military are stirred up like hornets. They want *at* these radicals. It's a chance to smash them."

"That's not political reasoning. It is anti-human. It's unreasoning. I can't accept that."

"Just the opposite, I say. It's pro-human. It's pro-Quebec. Look, how do you think this looks to the Confederation? We look like a bunch of bomb-chuckers who can't take care of our criminal element. Now get them out, get them into the streets where we can get at them, beat heads, round them up, throw them in the can for a while, destroy their power. Then we look like reasonable law and order people. Then we can deal from a stronger position. Then we can, in the future, act with more autonomy. And what we want will come even faster to us. Don't you see?"

The one with the objections sat and looked down at the glass of scotch in his hand. He swirled the ice cubes around a bit. After a while, he pursed his lips and said, "It's workable."

The room was silent, waiting for him to finish.

"Objections withdrawn," he said.

The meeting was over.

The word was sent out: tomorrow's celebration would proceed as planned. The government of Quebec would never knuckle under to the whims of a few madmen. The state would not fall a victim to anarchists.

When one has power, one has the future in his grasp. When one has the future in his grasp, the world speeds up. With their decision, the oligarchy of Quebec turned the world's speed up another notch that night.

Chapter 36
Closed Doors

At midnight, Le Claire found himself being led down a dark, narrow street in the French Quarter to a short flight of unlit cellar steps.

"In there?" asked the detective as a Mountie held a creaky door open for him. "Where the hell is he, in a coal bin?"

The Mountie snickered.

"I don't believe this," Le Claire said.

He entered a dark hallway lit by a single bare yellow bulb. It was enough to make anyone without business in the place turn around and go back. At the end of the hallway, they reached a locked door. The Mountie knocked on it. One, two, three, a pause. One, two, three, a pause. One.

The door opened. Another Mountie stood in the doorway, behind him a mass of pipes and a huge boiler. Le Claire marched into the room. Beyond the boiler was a third door. It opened and Bannerman came out..

"This time there *was* a password," Le Claire said.

Bannerman smiled. "Like it?" he asked, looking about.

"This beats all," Le Claire said. "How did you find it?"

"It's abandoned," Bannerman replied. "Just right for our purposes."

"It's disgusting," Le Claire said, wiping dust and cobwebs off his coat.

"What did you expect me to do?" Bannerman said. "Bring him up to your office? Or up to the Chateau, perhaps?"

"You have a point," said Le Claire. "Now, do you have anything else?"

"Nothing much. I've got his records. He's been in and out of your jails twice. For minor infractions. Threatened him, but he just laughed. Tried to make a deal, but he's not buying. Tough customer."

"Do you have other options?" Le Claire asked.

"Two," Bannerman said, "but I don't want to use them."

"Don't tell me," said Le Claire.

"No," said Bannerman. "You tell me. What about that fellow your boys found in the warehouse? Villemaire, was it? What about him?"

"Agh! A complete waste of time. Angry and scared, and he told us everything he knew. Even about your friend Chicoine in there. He knew maybe ten percent of the operation, but nothing of the terror. Cartier was a cagey old fox, I'll say that. Didn't let anyone know anything. No, not worth your time. Say," said Le Claire, "why don't you pick up that fellow down in Montreal? The well-dressed one with the attaché case who contacted this one."

"Hefelfinger led a raid on his hotel room two hours ago," Bannerman said. "He was just getting ready to leave for points unknown. Hefelfinger popped him into a car and headed here with him."

"Then we'll know something definite at last!" said Le Claire, excited.

"He's dead," Bannerman said. "A hollow tooth. Poison. They're playing for high stakes."

"Then he was one." Le Claire let his breath out slowly.

"Yes," said Bannerman, with a trace of satisfaction. "Hefelfinger says he can't wait to show me that attaché case. A whole electronics set-up. Push a button from miles away and boom! I would have used the serum on him just like that!" He snapped his fingers. "This one, I don't know if it's worth it." He paused. "Then what do we do with him? Turn him loose? Let him go yammering all over town about the CIA? Not while I'm here. Can you put him anywhere? Keep him fifty years, anyway?"

Le Claire smiled grimly, and felt himself turning grey. "Any place I put him, he'd be out again too soon. He didn't actually do anything, remember?"

"I can't use the serum, then," said Bannerman. "If you can't keep him, I'll have to kill him. His actions don't warrant death. All he did was pass on a code. I'm sure he didn't know the meaning of it." He paused. "Le Claire, where is that other one? The warehouse one? Can you get a hold of him on short notice?"

"Sure," said Le Claire. "Do you want him? I'll send him right over."

"I think maybe I can use him, if he's still talking," Bannerman said.

"I'll get him right to you, if you think he'll do any good. I can't think what. Oh, one other thing. Do you still need my boys out at the St. Andre place? I could use them here in town."

Bannerman mulled this over. "No," he said, "I don't suppose so. So long as we have someone there to watch. Sackman's back here, but I have two of my guys still there. I know how you feel. Hate to leave anyone out there. Seems like a waste." He paused. "Think they're done with the place?"

"Who can say?" Le Claire said. "It's an attractive site."

"Okay. Take yours back. My guys will cover for now," Bannerman said. "Maybe we can pull shifts later?"

"Good," said le Claire. "Anything else?"

Bannerman shook his head. "Nothing right now," he said.

"Okay, I'll be at my office," said Le Claire. "I'm spending the night there, in case you need anything."

"Thanks, Claude," said the American. "Maybe I'll call, if I find out more."

"You should get some rest yourself," Le Claire said. "Big day tomorrow." He paused. "Say, do you know what that ship was carrying?"

Bannerman shook his head.

"Rice!" said Le Claire. "Tons and tons of rice. It's swelling up like a bloated horse, right there in the middle of the channel. They say it'll push the sides out of that ship so far…well, it will take some time to get it out of there, I'll tell you. What a mess!"

"Sure," Bannerman replied. "Typical. If it can get worse, it will. I'm just glad we stopped that tanker from going on down to Montreal. Can you imagine what an explosion like that would do to the Seaway?"

Le Claire shuddered. "I hate to think," he said. "Well, have a nice night. I'll send Villemaire over with a couple of my men, if that's all right with you."

"Could you please take him to the corner of Garneau and St. Flavien? My men will take him from there."

Le Claire laughed. "Of course, Harvey. Anything you say."

"I need some coffee," said Bannerman, and disappeared through the far door.

Le Claire didn't reach his office until one o'clock. He flipped on the light switch in the outer office and heard a muffled groan from the corner of the room. Startled, he looked sharply over the cluttered desk, and there was Sandy, rising groggily from a cot she had set up an hour before.

"Sandy!" he said, delighted.

"I set up a cot for you in your office," she said.

Le Claire laughed and went over to her. She had taken off her dress, and lay wrapped in a blue blanket on the bare cot. She was using a book as a pillow. Jagged lines on her shoulders showed where the hard canvas and wood had jabbed into her as she lay still.

Le Claire knelt by her and began to massage her shoulder. "Above and beyond the call of duty," he said.

"Don't touch, you old goat," Sandy said, pulling away.

"Sandy!" Le Claire said, "You disappoint me!"

"Letch," she said. She sat up, and the blanket dropped from her shoulders. Her perfume filled the small, warm office. "Besides, you've got work to do. The tape's set up and…"

"Later," said Le Claire. He put his arms around her and drew her down to kneel on the floor. "Isn't the carpet softer?" he asked, unhooking her bra.

Sandy sighed as the bra came off. "I just wish we had a bed," she said. "Is that too much to ask? I just want a bed. I feel like an animal here. Home…in bed."

Le Claire didn't answer. He looked at her, and kissed her, and guided her down to the carpet.

"You're not supposed to do this to your sergeant!" said Sandy, pouting. "I want to go home. Ouch!" she suddenly shouted.

"What's wrong!" said Le Claire, startled.

"Rug's prickly," muttered Sandy. "…want sheets…silk… satins…a mattress, for God's sake…" she said, pounding the rug gently with her fist.

"I wish you liked fishing," said Le Claire. "Then we could do it in the woods, by a stream, on the rocks…"

"You are a fuckin' idiot," she said. "Want warm…peace…bed… home…" She snuggled up to him, drawing him to her.

"No time, Sandy," said Le Claire quietly. "There's no time for home. This is home…"

"Damn," said Sandy. "Lousy home. Come here, you old goat…"

Chapter 37

The Latest News

By 2:00 AM, the news media had more news than they knew what to do with. CBC had received the following press release from the FLQ:

"The Neanderthal bandits who have taken it upon themselves to direct violent changes in the structure of Quebec society, and who no doubt will attempt to blame the FLQ for their nefarious and counter-Revolutionary acts, are hereby warned that the cadres of the FLQ Revolutionary Council are ever-vigilant, and will not stand still for such bloodsucking parasites as may be hidden and lurking in the swamps of depraved counter-Revolutionary activity. Vive Quebec! Vive Quebec Libre!"

"What does that mean?" asked the young reporter who retrieved the message from the designated telephone booth on the corner of Rue Buade and Rue du Fort.

"It means they didn't do it, and they wish they had," said the city news editor.

La Presse, the major morning newspaper, had a message delivered through its front door. The message was attached to a brick:

"People, Comrades, and Workers of the glorious City and Province of Quebec! Let it be known with rejoicing that the Organization of Quebec Workers and Peasants is entirely, gloriously responsible for the destruction of the capitalist tool *Donvegan Castle* earlier this evening. Do not be misled by the swine of the FLQ and other revanchist malingerers who will undoubtedly claim credit for this heroic act of Revolutionary fervor. Under the blood-stained banner and cross of the OQWP, onward to glory! Cast off the imperialist chains! Victory is ours if we but unite under the true direction of the Socialist masters and steer clear of the toadying petty dictators who would be your new kings. Victory to the masses!"

That was from the remnants of Cartier's Organization, delivered on his previous orders. It was considered as a definite, legitimate claim to the act, mainly because of the brick.

WQEP, the major independent French-speaking radio station, received the following report, over the telephone:

"Citizens – do not be misled by recent activities, heroic as they may seem. They are counter-revolutionary in nature, and are led by madmen bound on visiting intrigue and death on our fair nation for their own malicious and negative intentions. Do not follow these fools, these madmen. Rather, rid our glorious socialist-oriented populace of their cancerous presence!"

The caller indicated that he was speaking on behalf of the 'Activist Cadres of the True Workers' Movement.'

The call was from Charles de la Montagne, a fact well known to Richard Vallieres, the station manager, who taped and transcribed the message.

It was a busy night for La Presse.

The final major claim was also the most spectacular in its delivery. Accompanied by two small bombs and bursts of machine-gun fire out of the night, it was directed at the loading platform of the newspaper. When the smoke had cleared, the following message was found in an unsealed envelope:

"Socialist-minded Comrades and Workers of Quebec! Do not be misled by spurious claims, even by certain splinter factions who claim they speak for the FLQ. They do not! There is only one voice of the FLQ, and it says: Yes! All glorious credit for the revolutionary act in celebration of our nation devolves upon us, the true followers of socialist philosophy! Hurrah for Quebec! Hurrah for the true followers of the FLQ! Death to our enemies, capitalist and anarchist both! Long live the Revolution! Long live Quebec! Join with us tomorrow in supporting the great demonstration in favor of our nationhood! Vive Quebec! Vive Quebec Libre!"

That was from Sparrow, who was beginning to feel much better, although he was still confined to his hospital bed. It was meant to confuse the situation, and it worked.

There were over a hundred other messages, both telephoned and written, but none bore the stamp of legitimacy that seemed to accompany these four.

SATURDAY, JUNE 26th

"There are a lot of bleeding hearts around who just don't like to see people with helmets and guns. All I can say is go and bleed…It is more important to keep law and order in society than to be worried about weak-kneed people…Society must take every means at its disposal to defend itself against the emergence of a parallel power which defies the elected power."

Pierre Eliot Trudeau, Prime Minister of Canada

Chapter 38

The March of the Red Brigades

Saturday dawned brilliantly. There were hundreds of spectators lining the Dufferin Terrace when Kearney started out for his rendezvous with Genevieve. He picked up pieces of conversations. There were two American teenagers hanging on the railing, looking out at the blown ship in the river, commenting as he passed.

"Biggest fuckin' bowl of cereal in the whole fuckin' world, man."

"No shit. Cereal shot from guns, man."

They cackled and sucked on their thin cigarettes. Kearney felt like joining them. From the look of things, it was going to be a tough day.

Under the leafy trees by the stone wall at the top of Cote de la Montagne, he found Genevieve waiting for him. She smiled and kissed him and they began walking along the ramparts, stopping every once in a while to look out through the dark-leafed branches at the river. It was one of those sparkling northern mornings that combines the lushness of mid-summer with the sharp air that comes with autumn. It was a spectacular day.

"And will you be leaving soon?" Genevieve asked as they walked along.

Kearney didn't answer. She stopped and looked up at him.

"I don't know," he said finally. "I don't want to. I want to stay here. But this is a mess, isn't it?"

"Where will you go?" she asked.

"Out to Ontario, maybe beyond. To the prairies," he said. "Maybe north on the prairies. I've always wanted to do that."

"May I come with you?" she asked quietly. "Just for a while? A week, ten days, how long will you be?"

He put his hands in the rear pockets of his jeans, sighed, and looked down at her. "Would you want to?" he asked.

"There is nothing for me here," she said, and she stood and waited.

Kearney looked out at the river and said, like he was thinking out loud, "I was going to go south from there, swing around on a curve back toward New York."

"I would not mind that either," Genevieve said. "I would like to see New York again. I was so little when I was there." She stood under the trees, looking down at the ground…

"Yes," he said.

She raised her eyes.

"Yes," he said again. His eyes were laughing.

"Really!" she yelled, and jumped into his arms. They stood there laughing in the summer sun.

"Oh, Jack," she said. "Let's go somewhere we can be alone. Let's go celebrate. To hell with the stupid parade."

"Hey, no fair," he said. "I like parades. Parades are good places to celebrate things. I want to go to the parade."

"Parades are stupid!" she insisted.

"If we go to the parade, I will treat you to lunch. At a fancy American hotel."

"Bah! Garbage on your American hotels! And then we can be alone?"

"Yes."

"I don't know what good it will do, being alone with a ten-year-old who must have his parades."

"If you're an eight-year-old, it can be fun."

"Pervert! Very well. Off to the parade. I'll buy you a balloon."

"Did you ever do it with a balloon?" he asked.

"Animal!" she said, and broke up laughing.

They went fast, almost running, joining a large, excited crowd that was pouring down the Cote de la Canotière to the Lower Town. The parade was forming in the large open areas around the railroad yards. It would come down Rue St. Paul, then through Cote Dinan and Cote Samson, around the edge of the old walls to the Parliament Building, where a reviewing stand had been set up.

Kearney and Genevieve stood on the windy corner of Samson and Lacroix and watched the marchers go by. First came a contingent of the 22nd Regiment with their band, who were heartily booed by Genevieve. Then came the Grand Marshall of the parade, along with a host of waving, smiling officials and dignitaries, who also came in for their share of good-natured abuse from the girl. Then there were bands and parish societies, flags and giant papier-mâché clowns and garish floats fitted out with flashing lights and flowers, and little girls in traditional dress, and Boy Scout troops, and nurses from the hospitals, and fiddlers from the countryside – all of Quebec seemed to be at this brilliant, sunny noontime display. Parish after parish paraded down the street.

Then, from far away, sounds swelled in the air from a different kind of celebrating contingent. Down the street they came, and now the spectators could see the red and black flags of revolution that mingled with the white and blue of the fleur-de-lis of Quebec.

Then they were passing, and there seemed to be thousands of them: radicals of all different stripes, united for once in an attempt to show their power. They came with their flags and banners held high, and as they marched they raised their fists in salute and chanted. "Quebecois! Quebecois! Quebecois! Quebecois!" The sound echoed and bounced off the dirty old walls of Lower Town and thundered into the senses, by sheer power transforming the meaning of the day. Along the route, some people were silent with pride, and some were silent with fear.

It was a thrilling and terrifying spectacle.

"Quebecois! Quebecois! Quebecois!" Some marched in strict military formation, and some wore quasi-military outfits. Others danced along in mobs, and as individuals, to the beat of whatever anarchic sounds ran through their heads. They laughed and they clapped and they frightened in their wildness. And the anarchists and the disciplined formations were equally frightening.

Genevieve was carried away by the whole experience, and laughed happily as she pointed. "Oh, look! There's Marcel. And there's Eva and Marc. And there's Francois. Hey, Francois!"

"Come on," said Kearney, "Let's join them!"

"Really?" said Genevieve, laughing. "You really want to?"

But Kearney had already grabbed her hand and dragged her into the parade. She laughed as she walked beside him. There he was, his hand making a raised fist, his voice thundering out "Quebecois! Quebecois! Quebecois!" as if he had been born in the city. She laughed and steered him over to Marc and Eva and Francois.

"Hey, where's Angelique and Rene?" he shouted over the noise.

"They were afraid," Genevieve shouted back, "after the Justice Ministry and all. They don't want to be spotted." She shrugged.

"Smart," said Kearney.

They joined hands with their friends and all of them marched along together. Every once in a while, as he shouted and thundered away, Kearney would smile at the girl who marched by his side, and her eyes would twinkle, and all she could do was laugh. The day was bright, and it was good to be young and strong and happy.

The march wound around the base of the old walls, on into the early afternoon sunlight. Finally it turned southwest. The land leveled out. They were out from under the frowning gray granite of the cliffs, and they marched across the wide Rue Dauphin toward Parliament Hill.

To the left of the marchers were the old walls, seeming lower now, viewed on a level. On the right was the brass-embossed bulk of the Quebec Commodore. A rage grew in some hearts, and fists were raised against this symbol of the foreign economic domination of French Quebec.

Beyond the Commodore was the Parliament Building. "Look at it!" cried some unknown marcher. "Hand in hand with the American pigs!"

A roar came from the radical march, and out of it, once again, redoubled, swelling, as though the sound could change the fact, came the thunderous chant, "Quebecois! Quebecois! Quebecois!"

Now they were passing the reviewing stand, and some anonymous voice rang out through a bullhorn over the massed ranks. "Let's take it away from them! Give the government back to the people! Take the Parliament!"

Immediately, one of the large para-military contingents wheeled in formation to the right and charged the reviewing stand. Screaming and yelling radicals came running from all directions to join the charge.

Within seconds they were in the seats. Boards and chairs went flying through the air. The screams of politicians' wives mingled with the shouts and hoots of the demonstrators as they went storming up the stairs. They gave no quarter. Dignitaries who attempted to fight back were picked up and thrown bodily from the platform. But the radicals' first aim was the destruction of the reviewing stand, and that was where most of their energy went.

It didn't make any difference to the police what the berserkers' objectives were. This was the moment they had been expecting, and they slammed into the radical ranks with everything they had.

A platoon of Mounted Police came first, the scarlet-coated riders charging their mounts down Rue Dauphin into the leftists. As the horses slowed, the officers lay about them with their nightsticks, left and right, using the sticks like swords.

Knives and hatpins were drawn from hiding places, and soon horses were rearing and kicking and screaming in pain and fright. Two officers fell from their saddles. Others were dragged down by the incensed mob.

Phalanxes of riot police, armed with shields and sticks, smashed their way into the crowd. Enraged marchers, in turn, charged the police formations..

Disciplined fighting formations broke into individual slugging matches. Bodies began to drop, and were dragged this way and that by opposing forces.

Caught between the reviewing stand and the charge of the Mounties, Kearney tried his best to fend off the swarming bands of fighters. It was difficult. Genevieve was no help. She kept attracting attention, screaming into a nearby mobile TV crew's microphone. "Will you shut up!" he yelled to her, as a wave of police toppled the TV crew to the ground and swept over them. He grabbed a cop in the melee and threw him into his buddies. But it was getting to be too much. He was too successful. The cops could sense that he was a trained fighter. He seemed to be a leader, and they wanted him. They started to fight their way toward him.

"Come on, dammit!" Kearney yelled to Genevieve. They held hands and ran, making their way through the breaking crowd.

All this time, cadres of the Organization had been gathering together, forming a thin line, guiding the fight in one general direction. Now they were ready. All together, they sent up a cry and it spread through the chaotic ranks of radicals all around them.

"To the Commodore! Take the Commodore! Take the Commodore! Show the Americans we are a nation! Down with imperialism! Down with its lackeys!"

A thousand voices yelled, and a thousand bodies flew across the lawns of Parliament House. Across the wide St. Cyrille Est, with its stringy gardens and bourgeois attempts at landscaping, pounded a thousand committed hearts.

"Vive Quebec!" they shouted as they poured into the courtyard of the Quebec Commodore Hotel. "Vive Quebec Libre!"

The attackers left a thousand others behind in a frenzied battle with the police.

Far away and high above, there was the lightning-like rattle of machine-gun fire.

Chapter 39

La Caravelle

Signor Paolo di Gordini had specifically requested, several weeks before, a room on the tenth floor of Hotel La Caravelle, with a view facing south and overlooking the old walled city of Quebec. The North American representative of Ferrara Leathers, he was delighted with his accommodations.

And after spending the night in the arms of a woman he met outside the doors of the hotel on Boulevard Laurier, a woman who hadn't been afraid to try anything for a price, he awoke refreshed, had two breakfasts delivered to the room and another delightful romp with the squealing, laughing blonde. He then thanked her, giving her a tip in the form of a pair of exquisite leather gloves, and showed her the door.

Then he went about his business, opening one of his suitcases and removing the necessary tools for the job.

When the telephone rang a little after eleven, he was delighted to hear that the two Canadian businessmen with whom he was scheduled to meet had arrived. He instructed the desk clerk to send them directly to his room.

He opened the door to their knock with a broad smile on his affable face.

"Ah, gentlemen!" he said. "So glad you could make it. Come in! Come in! What a wonderful view of your city I have been enjoying!"

And when the door closed, he said, "I understand you know about guns."

The two men nodded.

"Look out this window," said Paolo. "What do you see?"

The two men looked. One of them shrugged and said, "Nice view."

"Ah!" Paolo said. "It's probably too big for you to see, eh? Look. Straight down, almost. The flat roof, a block away."

The larger French-Canadian smiled. "You mean the low one with the helicopter on it?"

"That's the one," said Paolo. "The Quebec Provincial Government Headquarters Building, I think you call it. It seems to sit right under this monstrosity of a capitalist hotel, does it not? Right under its thumb."

"You see now why we hate the British," said the Quebecois.

The Quebec Government Building, seen from Boulevard Laurier, gave the appearance of a medieval fortress done up in modern lines. From ground level it looked impregnable, but from the air it was as vulnerable as a cheesecake.

The helicopter was at the disposal of the Premier, who liked to supervise things personally. Yesterday evening he had spent a great deal of time hovering over the river. Today, supposedly, the Premier was scheduled to be in Montreal for the parade there, but Paolo was quite sure he hadn't gone. The helicopter was still here.

"Well," said Paolo. "Perhaps today some politicians will find out just how heavy the British hand can be, right? Let's get to work."

He took up a glass cutter and drew a circle on the sealed inner pane of glass on one of the two windows. Then he took a plunger from the suitcase, pressed it firmly against the circle, created a vacuum, and pulled. The glass popped and came away easily.

He repeated this procedure on the inner pane of the second window, then returned to the first. He enlarged the hole and proceeded to cut another one in the outer pane. But this glass was heavy-duty, thick, resilient. It wouldn't snap.

Paolo returned to the suitcase, took out a high-intensity torch, and proceeded to melt the glass. It melted quickly enough, and soon he had created a firing port. He went to work on the second window, with the Organization gunmen an attentive audience. He made quick work of it. Street noise and unfiltered air made their unaccustomed way into the room.

"Now," Paolo said. "All we have to do is to turn on the radio and wait. The demonstration should begin around 1 P.M. It should draw the fox from his lair just about then."

"And what if your tools hadn't opened the windows?" asked the tall one. "What then?"

"I had a more rugged tool to use if necessary," Paolo said, grinning. He went to the other suitcase, opened it, and removed two bricks. "A bit disruptive," he said, "but effective."

They enjoyed a laugh together.

"I thought you might be interested in these, also," he said, drawing two machine guns out of the suitcase.

From below, the tinny sounds of a marching brass band rose on the air. The head of the parade was passing the reviewing stand.

In Provincial Headquarters, the police captain acting as liaison poked his head into the situation room. The Premier and his advisors were seated casually about the room, the Premier drawing on his customary cigarette.

"Radicals approaching rue Dauphin," said the captain. "They're shouting slogans, and they're raucous, but nothing unusual." He popped out again.

"I guess this is the target," said one of the aides. "Nothing at all happening in Montreal yet. Odd."

"I just hope they have the Seaway covered," said the Premier, exhaling. "Every damn inch of it."

Five minutes later the captain barged in again, excited, the color up in his face.

"All hell's broken loose!" he shouted. "They're going for the reviewing stand, the Commodore, the parliament. It's a free-for-all!"

"Let's have a look," the wiry Premier said, stubbing out his cigarette. He led them out through a corridor at a quickening pace – three aides, the pilot, and the police captain.

"Steady," said Paolo, "Steady." They could hear the sound of the street battle far below. "The sound of my weapon will be your signal to fire, Comrade Norman. Continue to fire then until your clip is exhausted. I will replace it for you." He addressed the other gunman. "Comrade Robert, I will hand my gun over to you. Finish the clip. I will replace it. When you have finished the second clip, leave this place. The emergency stairs are down the corridor to the left. Go together or separately, but it's every man for himself. Understood?"

A door opened onto the Provincial Headquarters rooftop. A group of six men, widely spaced, started across to the helicopter.

"There they are, comrades," Paolo said. "Fire!" He automatically squeezed the trigger and sprayed the group twice. Short bursts. He saw two men fall, one bend and clutch his leg. The others hadn't even reacted yet. Paolo jumped back, gave the machine-gun to Robert, clapped him on the shoulder, and raced to the second window with a replacement clip for Norman.

The Premier hit the cement and scrambled across, finally ending in a tumble to the wall. "The north wall!" he shouted. "Get to the north wall!" Machine-gun bullets whined across the roof, ricocheting off the cement and the rotor blades of the helicopter. The Premier found himself in the dubious shelter of the low north wall in the company of the police captain.

"Where's your radio?" he demanded. The captain looked at him blankly. "Your radio! Where is it?" the Premier snapped.

"Out there," said the captain, and gestured toward the center of the roof. Bullets kicked up cement chips around the black box.

There was a sudden lull in the firing. One of the aides jumped up, ran with a limp to the door, and disappeared inside.

"I hope he keeps his head," said the Premier. "Are you okay?"

"Yes, sir," the captain said. "But sir? Look, sir, at your leg. Better let me have a look at that."

The Premier glanced down and saw blood trickling midway down his left thigh from a wound somewhere beneath the tattered remnants of his pants leg. "Well, I'll be damned," he said. "Didn't even feel it. Got a cigarette?"

Paolo fitted a clip into Norman's gun, then jumped across to Robert's position and jammed a new clip into that one. Paolo's eyes darted from one man to the other. "Fire!" he shouted. "Fire!" The two machine-guns barked simultaneously.

Paolo backed to the door. "That's the way, lads!" he shouted. "Keep it up!"

He opened the door, darted into the corridor, closed the door behind him. He ran down the corridor to the emergency exit. Before the gunmen knew he was gone, he was down three flights. He burst into the seventh floor corridor and yelled to a startled chambermaid and two tourists, "Men with guns! One floor above, firing at everything! Run! Run!" then he was back into the emergency stairwell again, slamming the door behind him.

Chapter 40

Je Me Souviens

Up on the second floor of the Commodore Hotel, divided into a ballroom and a number of conference rooms named after Quebec suburbs, Sir Harold Holsworthy, M.B.E., was about to address two hundred assembled Canadian economists in the large room labeled *Sillery.*

Back in the last row, near the doors, Harvey Bannerman slid into a seat next to Claude Le Claire.

"Well," said Le Claire. "This is a surprise. Finally accepted my theory, I see."

"I came in for some peace and quiet," said Bannerman. "The streets are full of radicals. There's a battle brewing up by Parliament, and bunches of them seem to be heading this way."

"So, come in out of the rain," Le Claire said, chortling. "I'm glad I'm not with the municipal police today," he snickered. "They've got their hands full with this one."

"How many men do you have here?" Bannerman asked.

There was a short round of applause as the master of ceremonies walked onto the stage. He acknowledged the greeting and, motioning for quiet, began to speak.

"I have five minding the back doors, one with the manager, two in front, and three in the hallway…"

"Saw 'em," Bannerman said.

"Plus myself," said the detective. A disturbed economist, two rows ahead, turned and frowned at them. "What about you?" whispered Le Claire.

Bannerman leaned toward him. "I have two small teams, three men each, plus a couple of Mounties on loan from Sparrow."

"Guarding our prisoners?" Le Claire asked.

"Beside them," said Bannerman. "Tough nuts, those two. Still haven't finished with them. Damned tiring. Sewer rats."

"Wore you out, eh? Use anything on them?"

"No," Bannerman whispered. "I'll admit this to you. I hate that stuff."

The economist, red in the face, turned again and looked at them angrily. He put his finger to his lip. "Shhhh!" he hissed loudly.

"Sorry," said Bannerman, smiling apologetically.

"…and so, to show us something of what the future might hold for us," the MC was saying, "it is my distinct pleasure to introduce to you our highly esteemed scientific friend, Sir Harold Holsworthy…"

There was a round of enthusiastic applause, and Sir Harold walked across the stage to the lectern.

"He's a good man," whispered Le Claire. "Understands the situation."

"Shhhh!" said Bannerman.

Caught up in the rush of radicals and panicked people trying to escape the sudden battle, Kearney and Genevieve ran with the herd toward the Commodore. To their right they could see a column of riot police running parallel with them. The run turned into a race, as the Organization cadres cheered the rioters on, trying to get them to the hotel ahead of the cops. It was a draw, the police stringing a line of men across the front door area as the rioters arrived simultaneously.

"Vive Québec! Vive Québec Libre! Vive Quebec!" chanted the radicals, surging forward. The police, outnumbered, stood their ground and held their truncheons across their chests. They expected the demonstrators to stand and chant.

But these were no ordinary demonstrators in the front ranks of this crowd. These were the street-fighting vanguard of the Organization rank-and-file, come with specific orders to trash the hotel. They waded into the police line, took their lumps, and gave more back to the startled cops.

The Quebec police were well-trained in mob control, but too late they realized that this was no mob. It was a phalanx of trained fighters. The police line wavered, faltered, fell back. Before their captain could react, their center was broken and they were simply pushed aside. An army of enraged young Quebecois swept through the main doors of the hotel and, screaming like Indians, began to ransack the hotel lobby.

The police captain called for reinforcements, gathered up his men, and charged inside.

At the height of the battle, two large nondescript cars pulled up to the service area of the Commodore with portable flashers stuck to their roofs and sirens screaming. Six men in khaki uniforms jumped out. Le Claire's three men stationed at the service door tensed.

Borovik held up a police shield. "Special Action Team," he shouted. "Reinforcements for the front."

In the same moment, a machine-gun stuttered and Le Claire's men fell. Borovik, Abdul, Jean-Paul, Dietrich, and the Argentinian dashed through the door. Jaime followed them, finishing off the detectives with single shots from a pistol. Mahmoud stayed by the cars, covering the street.

"With due regard for my host," Sir Harold began his lecture in the conference room two floor above. "The future is now. I have not labeled this talk, but I hope to consider five categories as I meander about. I will be talking about space as industry, advances in applied science brought about by the space industry, energy from space, raw materials from space and production from space factories, and finally, spin-offs from existing space programs. I tell you this so that you will be able to see where we are as I drone on, and decide whether you want to stick with it further, or stick...well, never mind."

There was a murmur of laughter.

"Now the space industry, regardless of the fate of Skylab, which is a purely political problem, is a main factor of consideration in..." Holsworthy stopped short, and looked puzzled. The sound of muffled shots came from the corridor outside. The doors flew open and four terrorists ran down the center aisle. They screamed like banshees and fired bursts from their machine-guns into the ceiling and walls. They swarmed onto the stage and grabbed Holsworthy from behind the lectern. Then they surged back down the aisle, forcing Holsworthy into a stiff-legged run between Jean-Paul and Dietrich. Borovik, Jaime, and the Argentinian were already outside the meeting room. A machine-gun sounded as they cleared the corridor.

Abdul brought up the rear. As he went by, Bannerman shouted "Now!" and simultaneously, he and Le Claire drew their automatics, dropped to the floor behind the slim protection of the wooden seats, and fired. They caught Abdul just as he was turning to fling a last satanic spread of bullets through the room.

The man crashed heavily to the floor.

Even before the terrorist lay still, Bannerman grabbed the machine-gun and rolled out the door, followed immediately by Le Claire, just in time to see the terrorists slam through the emergency exit doors, and hear the shriek of an hysterical crowd.

Amid the carnage and shambles and screams of terror and rage that were the Commodore lobby, Kearney knew this melee for what it was – a diversion, an immense diversion, for what purpose he did not know. But he suspected. And he knew that sticking around the hotel was not going to do any good at all. He ran across the lobby filled with swarms of fighters and berserkers, dragging Genevieve with him. He pushed through the exit door into the stairwell and sprinted up the stairs to the second floor.

But others were coming up after them. The door slammed open and a horde of hotel patrons and radicals alike, all fleeing from the now-reinforced police, crammed into the small stairwell and pushed and shoved their way upstairs.

"Come on," Kearney said, pulling on Genevieve's hand. "One more." And he started for the third floor. Breathless, the two of them sprinted up another flight.

As they arrived at the landing, they heard a door below them slam open, then the immediate chatter of machine-gun fire as Borovik cleared a path for himself through the throng coming up the stairs. The crowd screamed in terror as they fought and clawed to get out of the line of fire.

"Up!" Borovik ordered his men, and started to race up the stairs. "Follow!"

Kearney and Genevieve pushed through the third-floor door and it crashed shut behind them. Kearney crushed the girl into the corner between the door and the wall, and jumped in front of her just as the door burst open once again.

Borovik, the Argentinian, and Jaime ran full-tilt down the hall and made a left into the elevator corridor. Two more followed, tugging Holsworthy along. None of them looked back, not yet realizing that Abdul was no longer with them.

An icy fear touched Genevieve's heart like a steel blade. As she watched the terrorists turn into the hidden corridor, she saw the face of her brother.

The door flew open once more and Bannerman and Le Claire appeared. Bannerman saw his quarry just as they turned the corner. He let loose a burst of machine gun fire after them.

Something activated Bannerman's sixth sense and he spun around, leveling the gun at Kearney's waist. Genevieve screamed. Bannerman's jaw dropped, and for a split second he seemed ready to speak to Kearney, but then he spun again, ready to pound down the hallway after the terrorists. But Le Claire clapped his shoulder hard and motioned him off to the left. Bannerman followed his direction instantly, taking up a position that gave him cover while allowing him to monitor the farther hallway. That way was clear, and Le Claire knew that Borovik, Holsworthy and the others were still in the connecting corridor.

Like many of the contemporary high-rise hotels, the upper floors of the Quebec Commodore were built in the shape of an H. Each floor had two main corridors with a third transverse corridor where the elevators were located. Le Claire had positioned Bannerman at one end of the farther of the main corridors, while Le Claire had taken a vantage point at the end of the nearer hallway. They had Borovik trapped in the transverse, but they couldn't get at him.

Borovik was working on his own quandary. Quickly he dismissed the idea of using the elevators. He had no wish to open the doors to a hail of bullets. There was also the possibility that police might turn the power off while he was in there. The damned things took too long, anyway. No, he would stick as much as possible to the original plan.

Holsworthy was happy with that decision.

"Dietrich!" Borovik snapped, and made a throwing motion with his arm.

Dietrich lobbed a grenade down Bannerman's corridor. But he extended his arm a little too far and Bannerman, quick as a cat, ripped a snap shot at him and jumped back behind the protecting wall a second before the grenade went off.

Dietrich yelped, holding his arm with its jagged flesh oozing, the dark blood welling up slowly around torn sinews.

Behind the screen of the grenade, Borovik moved his small force into the hallway and began a retreat to the far end of the building. When Bannerman jumped back into position, the only clear shot he had was of Harold Holsworthy. The terrorists were in a straight line on the far side of him, Jaime walking backwards with a gun to the scientist's head, and moving fast to the far exit door.

Le Claire was on his walkie-talkie. "All units. All units. Observe and report. Do not close in. They have kidnapped a hostage. Hostage important. Do not jeopardize. Cover northeast exit."

Bannerman came running back to Kearny and Genevieve at their door. "Come on, Jack!" he said. "I need you." Then he and Le Claire were through the door and gone.

Genevieve looked at Kearney. "Who was that man?" she asked slowly. "How did he know your name?"

Bannerman's voice echoed from the stairwell. "Where the goddam hell are you, Kearney? Get down here!"

"Come on," said Kearney. "I'll explain later."

"No!" Genevieve yelled.

"Come on!" he ordered.

She held on to the door frame with one hand and clawed at him with the other. "Goddamn you!" she screamed. "Goddamn you, you spy!"

He pinned one arm and pried the other off the frame. She tried to bite him as he ran down the stairs, carrying her under his arm.

Kearney waded his way through the wounded and hysterical people on the stairs and followed Bannerman and Le Claire down past the lobby level to the service entrance one flight below. He got there just in time to see Le Claire fling open the outside door for Bannerman. Bannerman started outside and jumped back immediately as a hail of machine-gun bullets thudded and whined into the building.

"Close the door!" shouted Bannerman, and Le Claire slammed it shut. "Your men are dead." he said evenly.

"My God, all three of them?" said le Claire, turning pale. "Three of them... ! I hope the rest..."

"What are you doing with that?" Bannerman shot the question at Kearney, who had his hands full with Genevieve.

"Her brother is with them. She might be valuable."

Genevieve twisted and clawed, trying to bite the hand he held over her mouth.

"Oh, hell," Bannerman said, "More trouble than she's worth."

"All units," said Le Claire into his walkie-talkie. "Stand clear. Stay out of the way. See which way they go if you can, but stay out of the way!" Switching frequencies, he said, "Muni. Muni. This is Le Claire of Justice. Give me a helicopter. Give me a helicopter."

"She's valuable," Kearney insisted.

"Helicopter over Parliament Hill. I'll patch you in, sir," came the gravelly static over the transmitter.

"Suit yourself," said Bannerman in disgust. "Just don't get her near me." He started up the stairs. "Let's go."

"Watch for men in khaki uniforms in vicinity of Commodore Hotel," Le Claire spoke into the walkie-talkie. "Don't get too close. Heavily armed. Follow and report. Don't lose them!"

Le Claire went pelting up the stairs after the American, leaving Kearney to follow after them as best he could.

"Bannerman," shouted Le Claire. "My car. In the parking lot. Wait!"

Kearney went up the stairs slowly. He had the still struggling Genevieve in an armlock. The stairs were slippery with the blood of the moaning wounded.

Bannerman and Le Claire stopped for an instant in the doorway to the lobby. "Jesus Christ!" said Bannerman in disbelief.

The lobby was a shambles. The elegant restaurant on its raised platform was a forest of overturned tables and smashed chairs. Draperies and sconces had been ripped from the walls. Potted plants, swung and released as gigantic missiles, littered the floor.

Le Claire pinned his badge to his coat pocket.

The three men, Kearney still dealing with Genevieve, picked their way quickly through the aftermath of organized riot. Rows of demonstrators were lying face down, their hands cuffed behind their backs. Police milled about. Patrons and tourists stood to the side in various states of shock. The wail of approaching police and ambulance sirens came from outside.

Le Claire's black sedan was parked in a far corner of the lot, away from the unorganized mayhem of relief attempts just beginning. Bannerman and Le Claire jumped into the front seat. Kearney loaded Genevieve into the back seat and slid in beside her.

Once in the car, Genevieve relaxed. She sat like a baby, breathing heavily, taking everything in. She didn't speak, and nobody spoke to her.

Le Claire pulled out of the parking space and was on the radio immediately, calling his office.

"Sandy, patch through to RCMP."

"Right, boss."

Static and a click.

"RCMP."

"Le Claire of Justice here. I need assistance. Clear the matter with Captain Sparrow, if necessary. Heavily-armed terrorists. We are tracking. Will require assist when game goes to ground. Over."

"Will assist, Justice. Contact when ready. Over and out."

Bannerman was holding his own conversation over his transmitter. "Boys, get ready to jump. Don't know where he's going, but we've got him tagged."

Le Claire again. "Muni helicopter, Le Claire of Justice here. Where are the terrorists?"

"Heading east," came the crackling reply. "Easy tracking. Two vehicles. Autos. They're using flashers. Assume sirens also. Crossing St. Charles, onto Capucins. Heading 138. Over."

Hitting the gas and the siren, Le Claire went roaring down the hill toward the eastern approaches to the city. A minute later, the radio crackled.

"Quarry on 138, Montmorency area."

"Where do you suppose he's going?" Le Claire asked.

"Somewhere he can hole up, someplace he can defend easily," Bannerman replied. "Where he can play for time."

"You don't suppose he's heading for her place, do you?" Le Claire said, jerking his thumb in Genevieve's direction.

"Why not? It's a good place. He knows the place," said Bannerman.

"But he must suspect we have it covered," argued Le Claire.

"So what?" countered Bannerman. "What does he care? He has Holsworthy. He knows we won't touch him."

The radio crackled again. "Subjects heading across bridge to Ile d'Orléans. Over."

"There's your answer," said Bannerman.

Le Claire smiled. "But doesn't he have an interesting mind, Harvey!" he said.

In the front seat of the lead car, Borovik sat with the heat sensor recorder in his lap. He adjusted it and exclaimed, "This is not bad at all! I detect only two of them. One in the woods outside; one, unfortunately, somewhere inside the house. We will have to deal with him. Comrade Jean-Paul, you know the house best, of course. When we arrive, you and Comrade Rafa will flush him out. Try to take him alive, but don't put yourselves in any danger. If he resists, kill him. Got that?"

"Yes, sir," said Jean-Paul, smartly.

"I wish to know what your plans are," said Holsworthy, who was seated in the back seat, guarded by the silent Argentinian.

Borovik turned and leered at him. "Oh, do you?" he said, and laughed.

"You don't frighten me, you know," Holsworthy said. "You wouldn't have gone to all the trouble of capturing me if you were simply going to kill me. And what I have, you can't get. You'd have to deliver me to some place, I'd say."

"You talk too much, I'd say," retorted Borovik.

"And I shall continue to," Holsworthy said, "and you will listen…"

Borovik lashed out with his meaty hand and slapped Holsworthy across the face. He grabbed the scientist by his tie and hauled him toward the front seat. "I need your brain, Doctor," Borovik said, "Not your miserable body. Not much of it, anyway. Remember that, and shut up."

The Russian pushed him against the back seat and turned away. He spoke into a two-way radio hook-up. "Car two. Mahmoud? Listen. When we get to the house, there's an agent hidden in the woods on the western side. You and Jaime get him if you can, but if he's too...look, just don't put yourselves in jeopardy. I need you. Dietrich will come with me. Now when the car stops, explode out of it!"

Holsworthy, shaken, sat silently in the back seat, under the watchful, glittering gaze of the Argentinian. He worked his jaw and felt the blood trickle out of his mouth.

"That goes for you two, also," Borovik ordered. "Get into that house and secure it. Immediately!"

The two cars pulled up the driveway at speed, and came to a screeching halt. The men jumped out, Mahmoud and Jaime fading into the bushes, Jean-Paul and Rafa smashing through the front door of Jean-Paul's house. Borovik took a position against the side of the house, with Holsworthy held in front of him. Borovik had his left arm around Holsworthy's neck, and with his right he had an automatic jammed into the scientist's ribs. Dietrich took a defensive position by one of the pillars on the portico.

Bannerman's man had been reconnoitering the second floor of the house when his walkie-talkie began to squawk with a warning from his partner outside. He ran down the stairs and through the house toward an open rear window just as Jean-Paul and Rafa crashed in through the front door. They picked up the sound of his footsteps and raced after him.

When they got to the window, he was already half-way across the lawn to the shelter of the trees. He was standing there, not running, pointing his pistol at something in the bushes.

Rafa snapped his machine-gun into position and fired. But simultaneously, the CIA agent fired, just before he fell.

The Argentinian had him finished off even before his body hit the ground, but the damage had been done. Mahmoud came running across the lawn and jumped through the window. "Jamie's dead," he reported, winded. "They got him right through the throat. No question."

"We can't afford…damn!…Well, secure the house," said Borovik. "We'll be out of here soon enough." He had entered with Holsworthy and Dietrich immediately after Jean-Paul and Rafa, and made his headquarters in the large main room. Dietrich covered the front, Mahmoud the rear, and Rafa and Jean-Paul prowled along the sides of the house and gave aid wherever it seemed likely to be needed. The position was extremely vulnerable, but Borovik, holding the ace that was Harold Holsworthy, was betting that no attack would be mounted.

Le Claire's car swerved into the grounds of the retreat house that stood to the west of the St. Andre mansion. Sackman pulled in directly after him, followed immediately by Hefelfinger and his two men. These agents left their cars and faded into the trees. Another car containing two of Le Claire's Justice men arrived, and they followed the Americans into the bush.

Bannerman turned and grimly handed Kearney his automatic. "Stay right behind us," he said, "and keep a good tight grip on your girlfriend there. She just might be helpful after all."

Bannerman and Le Claire went into the trees and disappeared. Kearney opened the car door and held out his hand to Genevieve. The shaken girl accepted it as she left the black sedan, and once out, she leaned against the side of the cruiser and hid her face in her hands.

"If you want to do anything for your brother, you'd better pull yourself together," Kearney said.

"You have used me enough," she said with dignity. "You will use me no more."

"If you do not help him, they will kill him."

"You're so sure of that, aren't you, spy? What makes you so certain? Do you read their minds, perhaps?"

"They will kill him just as they killed *my* brother," he said.

"Your brother?" She was puzzled. "What brother? They killed your brother?"

"Do you remember the night I recorded your songs?" he asked. "The night we went down to the Guitar?"

She nodded, still confused.

"Do you remember that dark street, where Rene pointed to where the blood had been spilled on the road?" His voice turned low and savage. "Where he laughed about it? About my brother's blood?"

Genevieve turned pale. Her breath came in quick, shallow gasps. "Oh, my God," she said, looking into his eyes. "Oh, what a horrible world this is!"

"They will do the same to Jean-Paul," Kearney whispered. "As soon as they get what they want from him. You must help. When they attack…"

"They will never attack!" Genevieve said. "While they have the scientist, your friends will not attack. You heard them say that."

"Yes, they will," Kearney said. "If they cannot rescue the scientist, if negotiations don't work, they will not let them take him. He knows too much. They will attack."

"And Jean-Paul will die," she said.

"Will you help?"

"What can I do?" she asked.

"When they attack, we must be inside that house. We must be in a position to cover Jean-Paul, to help him. Can you get in without being seen?"

The Canadienne shuddered and was still for a moment. Then she said, "Come with me. I know every inch around this house. We will go in through the cellar. Follow me."

Le Claire and Bannerman had penetrated as far as possible. They were at the edge of the bushes surrounding the house. They could see it across the lawn through the few remaining branches. Le Claire bent down for a better look, and out of the corner of his eye saw the glint of metal or plastic on the ground, flashing in a beam of the afternoon sun. He bent further to examine his discovery.

"Bannerman!" he whispered, picking up the small globule of wired plastic. "Look at this!"

Bannerman turned. "Heat sensors!" he exclaimed. "He's got heat sensors, the savvy son-of-a-bitch. No wonder he came back here. He knew there were only two men here. And now he knows we're here. And exactly where we are. Shit!"

He paused.

"Sackman, Hefelfinger," he called, beckoning. His two lieutenants came up. "Get all of our men around to the other side of the house. Go wide-spaced. Make it seem like as many men as possible. Le Claire, you and I and Kearney can spread…" He looked around. "Where's Kearney?" he said, and then the rage grew in him. "Where the fuck is that kid, goddam it? Where is he?"

No one had seen Kearney, or the girl.

"You see him, you bring him here," said Bannerman, red in the face, small flecks of foam clinging to his lips. "You bring him, here, understand? Get moving. We'll fill up this side as the Canadians come in."

The CIA men melted into the brush. Le Claire was listening carefully. "Listen," he said to Bannerman. "Reinforcements."

"That stupid sonofabitch," said Bannerman.

"Quiet," Le Claire said. "A helicopter."

The police helicopter swung in from the river in a wide arc. It came across the lawn, flying low, dropping rapidly. The pilot obviously intended to land as close to the house as possible.

"What the hell are they doing?" said Bannerman, startled. "They'll come right down into Borovik's lap."

Le Claire looked and rubbed his eyes and shouted over the 'copter's noise, "That is not one of our helicopters! It is painted to look like one, but it is not! We have none like that!

"Well, it sure isn't one of mine!" Bannerman shouted. He leveled the machine-gun and fired.

"What are you doing?" shouted Le Claire.

"Shooting the fucker down!" said Bannerman.

Bannerman was an excellent shot. The dead pilot's hands came off the controls, and the 'copter veered wildly, like an injured bug. The great rotors turned vertical and dug into the lawn. The pod smashed into the ground and the gas tank exploded.

"What the hell!" Borovik swore from inside the house. "What are they…damn! Whoever took that shot is good. Quick as a cat! Secure the house!" he screamed at his men. "They might try a rush now! Damn!"

The Argentinian sensed he should check out the cellar. Padding silently down the stairs, he was waiting there to meet Genevieve and

Kearney when they came through the tiny basement window. He disarmed Kearney and smiled softly. “Up,” he said.

On the main floor, Rafa motioned them into the main room.

“Well, well, well, what is this?” said Borovik, turning to observe them with narrowed eyes.

Jean-Paul, standing beside him, was startled. “Genevieve!” he stammered.

“Oh, you know this girl?” asked Borovik.

Jean-Paul turned white. “She is my sister,” he said, “but I do not know this other one.”

“Well then,” said Borovik, addressing Kearney, “and who are you? A Mountie, perhaps? No, no horse. CIA? Some form of shit, at any rate. What are you doing here?”

Kearney was silent.

“Well, it makes no difference,” Borovik said. “You will soon find, my friend, that interlopers do not always hang around to pick up the pieces. Sometimes scavengers themselves are disemboweled.” The Russian laughed. “So,” he said, with an air of finality. “Two more hostages. We can blow their brains out, to show our adversaries we mean business. That’s what we’ll use them for! Good!”

“My sister is not a hostage!” Jean-Paul blurted out in alarm. “She is a good socialist! She must have been subverted, coerced, by this, this…”

“Are you telling me who is who around here?” Borovik yelled. “I don’t care if she is the Virgin Mother of Lenin the Second! Your own situation is none too stable either, my young friend. Watch yourself. Back to your post!”

Jean-Paul gulped, glanced furtively at Genevieve, and resumed his watch at the eastern wall of the house.

There was a shout from outside.

“Borovik!” came the voice. “Borovik! We want to parley!” A pause. “Do you hear? We want to parley!”

Borovik frowned, considered. He went to the front window. “What is your authority?” he bellowed.

“The authority of the Province of Quebec,” Le Claire shouted back.

The Argentinian came to Borovik's side.

"Will the Province be bound by your negotiations?" yelled Borovik.

"It will consider my recommendations," shouted Le Claire, "and regard them with favor."

Borovik and the Argentinian exchanged glances. "They hold many cards," said the Argentinian, gesturing toward the approaches to the house held by their adversaries.

"We can still get out of this in good order," said Borovik with confidence.

"How?" Rafa asked.

"Let us see what we can get out of them, eh?" He paused, and looked into Rafael's eyes. "It has been a long fight, my friend."

The Argentinian studied him. "A valiant struggle, Vladimir. A glorious struggle. And we shall win it in the end."

"It has been worthwhile," said Borovik.

"Yes."

They grasped hands and smiled at each other.

"All right!" Borovik shouted through the window. "Come forward!"

Le Claire and Bannerman stepped out of the bushes.

"Dietrich," said Borovik, stepping to the center of the room. "Let them in. Remain by the door." Dietrich nodded. Close to shock, his eyes were beginning to go vacant.

"Holsworthy, get up," Borovik commanded. "Here, stand by me. You two," he said to Genevieve and Kearney. "Over there, opposite."

He motioned to the Argentinian and Mahmoud, and they took up positions forming a third side to the square, facing the front door. "Cover them," he said, pointing to Genevieve and Kearney.

When the Canadians came to the door, Borovik wanted them faced with his best troops. The wiry Argentinian and the massive Mahmoud made an impressive appearance, with machine-guns and grenades slung haphazardly across their bodies.

"You," Borovik said to Jean-Paul. "Up here, next to the professor. Anything goes wrong, kill your sister's boyfriend first." Jean-Paul marched up and flanked Holsworthy, wedging the scientist between himself and Borovik.

The Russian took out his revolver.

The shadows of two men approached the door.

"Open the door, Dietrich," said Borovik.

Bannerman couldn't believe his eyes. Not only Borovik, but the apparition that had no name, who was known throughout the world only as the Argentinian, the ghostly figure who had done twice as much as Che Guevara had ever dreamed of doing. The shadow of these two men fell across the entire western hemisphere; their influence was felt from the lowliest peasant huts to the highest circles of power in twenty lands.

It was like finding a giant night-flying moth, long thought to be extinct, in a cave filled with the scent of long-ago death.

And here they were, thought Bannerman. Both of them, and almost in his hands. He could feel it – it was the thrill of power, the surge that came when you knew the game was won.

Bannerman and Le Claire stepped forward, forming the fourth side of the square. Bannerman looked across at the Argentinian. "Christ," he thought. "He looks like Christ."

The Argentinian gazed at Bannerman. The pupils of his eyes were deep black, laughing, playful. A wry smile was on his lips.

"He's a good man," thought Bannerman. "He really believes in what he's doing. Damn."

There was respect for Bannerman in the Argentinian's eyes, also. The two men looked at each other, saluting each other with the silent, subtle respect great warriors reserved for others of their kind.

"Hello, Bannerman," said Borovik nonchalantly. "Nice to see you again. Your boys with you?"

"Could be," said Bannerman.

"Could be, my ass," said Borovik. "A bit different this time, eh? The situation, I mean."

"Hefelfinger is outside," Bannerman said. "He wants to pull your skin off with his pliers and hear you shriek."

"Always was a nasty streak to him," rumbled Borovik.

"Well, considering how you treated him…"

"Deserved it!" shot Borovik. "Let's get down to business."

"Spoken like a true capitalist," Bannerman laughed.

"I'll kill this silly bastard right now, and you too!" cursed the Russian, pointing his pistol at Holsworthy. "Mind what you say!"

"Sorry," Bannerman said, backing off. "Monsieur Le Claire is the man you want to speak to anyway."

"Monsieur." Borovik nodded to the detective, recognizing his position.

"Comrade," said Le Claire, bowing slightly, as per protocol.

"First," Borovik said, "I want a 707. I don't care where you get it. I want it within the hour. Second, I want safe conduct to the airport for myself, my men, my hostages. I want the plane filled with fuel, a pilot, a co-pilot, and a relief pilot. I want safe conduct to Cuba."

"Why don't you just go straight to Moscow?" said Bannerman. "It's closer."

"Now how would that look?" said Borovik.

"Monsieur," said Le Claire quietly. "I will report your demands to my superiors. But consider, sir. Consider your position. You have few men. Your situation is precarious. Would you consider giving up something for your freedom?"

Borovik looked at him as if he were insane.

"Would you give up your hostages? That is what my superiors would ask," Le Clair continued. "I know this. It is what I would ask."

"You mean these two?" said Borovik, pointing his pistol at Genevieve and Kearney.

Dietrich finally collapsed from lack of blood. He crashed to the floor.

"I mean the three of them," said Le Claire.

"Soon you will be outnumbered by your captives, if your soldiers keep keeling over," Bannerman observed.

"You must be joking," Borovik said to Le Claire, and to Bannerman he added, "There are plenty of men to replace that one."

"Sure," Bannerman said. "That's why he's resting comfortably in the infirmary instead of fainting out here."

"I will show you what I intend to do," said Borovik. "Here is a message of my intent for you to take back to your superiors. I do not believe they wish to jeopardize Dr. Holsworthy's life in this fashion."

"Please," said Holsworthy. "I don't feel well." He took a handkerchief from the breast pocket of his suit jacket and dabbed at his forehead.

"Comrade Jean-Paul," Borovik said. "Shoot the male hostage across from you."

Jean-Paul looked Kearney in the eye and leveled his machine-gun.

"Please," said Holsworthy. He fumbled with his handkerchief, tried to cram it back into his pocket. His hand was shaking and he jostled Jean-Paul, clung to him.

Across the room, Mahmoud screamed and clutched at his eyes.

Holsworthy held the pen in his hand and waved it just the slightest bit. The laser beam swept across Rafael's face. The Argentinian dropped to the ground and rolled.

Jean-Paul, startled at Mahmoud's scream, looked at him. The jelly of the man's eyes had turned to liquid. The Arab's eyes were running down his face.

Kearney dropped to the floor, jackknifed and reached for his boot, came up with his Mannlicher .25, and pointed it at Borovik.

"No!" yelled Bannerman.

Kearney squeezed the trigger, aiming between the Russian's eyes. Borovik looked surprised when the small bullet struck. It glanced off his skull and ran around under the skin, leaving a mole's track, to bore in just behind his left ear, where it entered his brain.

Mahmoud was kneeling in the middle of the room, screaming. The blind Argentinian ripped a grenade from its mooring, tried to pull the pin.

Bannerman jumped for Dietrich's machine-gun and let loose a volley at the Argentinian. It blew him into the wall.

Jean-Paul was about to clobber Holsworthy, who was still grappling with him, when Kearney's second shot caught him in the arm.

Genevieve screamed and jumped on Kearney. He knocked her to the floor.

Borovik's left arm shot up to his head. His right arm jerked. His pistol went off wildly, catching Le Claire across the back, ripping the muscles out of his left shoulder. The detective spun and fell.

"Uhhh!" Borovik grunted. His eyes cast wildly about, uncomprehending. His rational brain had ceased to function, the brilliant campaigner rendered an animal by the searing power of a tiny piece of lead. "Uhhhh!" he bellowed, and charged out the door, waving his pistol in the air.

"Don't shoot, goddammit, don't shoot!" yelled Bannerman, pounding his fist on the floor. "Don't shoot!"

"Uh," said Borovik, the blood streaming down his face in rivers. "Uh, uh, uh…" He ran down the driveway, grunting like a wounded bear. He stared wildly behind him, and groaned in panic and agony. He squealed, feeling the life spurting out of the small hole in his head. He gasped, and found no air. He ran to the road, through the gates, across the asphalt. He saw the green trees ahead of him. He took one last rattling gasp, and staggered across the road to the trees. Blood came up in his throat and splattered against his lips, down his chin. He tasted his own blood, and he gagged. He reached for a branch, and felt the softness of a green leaf.

The Russian's big body lay half in and half out of the gutter. A Mountie came up to it and stared at it. A car filled with tourists drove by. They slowed, almost stopped.

The Mountie waved them on. "Accident," he said to the driver, "Hit and run."

The tourists shook their heads sadly. After they had driven on, the Mountie took his handkerchief and laid it across the bloody face.

"I'm going to have your ass for this," Bannerman yelled at Kearney. "Of all the damn dumb stupid tricks…"

"What the hell are you talking about?" Kearney yelled back. "He was going to have me shot. He told this jerk to shoot me!" He pointed to Jean-Paul, who was on the floor, moaning and holding his arm.

"You weren't even supposed to be here!" Bannerman exploded. "Do you know how valuable he was? Don't you realize what we could have picked out of his brain?"

"Gentlemen, gentlemen," broke in Holsworthy, who was kneeling over Jean-Paul, examining his wound, "We could do with a little less bickering. There is plenty of work for us to do here."

"Damn!" said Bannerman, bending to inspect Le Claire's wound.

"He's the one who started it," Kearney said to Bannerman, gesturing toward Holsworthy. "Why don't you say something to him?"

"I did not start anything, young man," said the scientist. "I was minding my own business. Your friend Borovik started it, and took the consequences."

There was something in the clinical way Holsworthy spoke that made them listen, and think, and dwell on horror. Agents began to pour into the house. Kearney decided to get the hell out of there. He felt sick as he helped Bannerman prop Le Claire up on the sofa. The detective spoke almost jovially even as his shoulder leaked blood.

"Harold," he said, "You told me that that pen was just a toy."

"Well," said Holsworthy, "It has controls for variations of duration and intensity. I readjusted the thing. Made it more effective. A little too effective, actually. Didn't need to do that." He indicated Mahmoud, who knelt shuddering, his hands covering his face. "But then, dammit, he didn't have to come looking for me, did he now?"

Genevieve was kneeling and watching Holsworthy work on Jean-Paul. Kearney took her by the arm and began to lead her outside. She offered no resistance.

"Where the hell are you going?" Bannerman asked.

"Look at her," said Kearney, softly. "I'm taking her out of this goddamned mess."

"Don't disappear again," Bannerman grumbled as Kearney went out the door.

Kearney led the girl through the trees to the retreat house grounds. He put her in Le Claire's car, found Le Claire's keys still in the ignition, and started the engine. He drove slowly back toward the city. Once off the island, on the other side of the bridge, Genevieve spoke.

"You knew about my brother," she said. "How did you know he was with them?"

"I saw him in the hall. At the hotel," Kearney said.

"But how did you know it was Jean-Paul?" she asked.

"I saw him before. One night, he came looking for you in Rue Trésor. Marc pointed him out to me."

"Did you know about him before that?" she asked.

Kearney took a deep breath. "Yes," he said.

"Jack," said Genevieve, "Did you know about me before, also?"

Kearney was silent.

"Did you?" she asked again.

He didn't answer. He looked straight ahead, keeping his eyes on the road.

Genevieve didn't ask him again. There was no need to ask him again.

He stopped the car in front of Rene's and Angelique's, and walked up the old stone steps with her once more. They came to the landing where long ago – not three days before, but yet somehow long, long ago – she had whispered into the night that she loved him. They went inside.

Rene and Angelique sat listening to garbled radio reports of the aftermath of the rioting and attempted assassination and kidnapping.

"Take her," he said. "And treat her as well as you know how." He bent and kissed Genevieve on the forehead. "I'm leaving," he said. He went to the door. "And stay out of politics," he said to no one in particular. "It stinks."

The door closed behind him, and Rene and Angelique took Genevieve, sat her on the low, makeshift couch, and held her. They were silent, all of them, and the cold clouds of a new Canadian storm came silently over the old gray granite walls of the City on the Rock.

Kearney dumped Le Claire's car, went to his hotel, picked up his few belongings, and paid his bill. He picked up the Mustang around the corner and drove through the streets of a city turned suddenly cold and foreign. Strange, he thought, how lonely, how forlorn those streets were. He had never noticed that before.

Picking up speed, he drove down Boulevard Laurier, past the university and the modern shopping centers and plastic motels, onto the approach ramp to the Pierre Laporte Bridge. Then he was over the bridge and away, heading west on Autoroute 20. He headed west like Americans always headed west, looking for some elusive beautiful thing that was always somewhere else. Faster and faster he drove. Twenty miles down the road, he glanced at his speedometer. He was doing 98 MPH. Startled, he slowed and pulled over onto the gravelly break-down lane.

His hands were shaking when he got out of the car. He fumbled at a pack of cigarettes, taking a long, long time to light one. He finally got it lit, but when he took a drag, it had a strange, disgusting taste to it. He looked at it, puffed once or twice at it, and finally just cupped it in his shaking hand.

He looked around. Hundreds of cars were passing him every minute under the grey, overcast sky. Thousands of people were bound east and west, all of them encased in their little metal capsules that protected them from life. He wondered how many of them were running from something. He wondered how many knew they were running from something.

"And when I get there," he said out loud to the passing cars, "Wherever the hell that is...what the hell am I going to do there?"

If you get there, he thought. If Bannerman doesn't decide to have you picked up. And what are you going to do, anyway? Go back and find a place in the Firm? No way, buddy. What for? So I can hurt more people the way I hurt…

And his mind went to Genevieve, and he knew the real reason he was running. He was ashamed. He had done his best to use her, to destroy her, merely to make her a part of his scheme for vengeance. Coldly, cynically, he had gone about destroying her happiness. He had met a young girl full of happiness and song, and left her life and her mind and her future shattered.

And that was what mattered in this whole mess. His brother was dead. He couldn't help his brother, no matter what he did now. The killing of a terrorist leader meant nothing; there would always be other terrorist leaders. Borovik had said it: "There are plenty of men to replace that one."

And he hadn't even shot the right man; hadn't even come close to finding him. And that man was only acting on orders himself. Orders from some leader. Not the leader he shot. Some other damned leader entirely. A leader whose name he didn't know, probably would never know. Goddam! It went around in circles.

And the only thing that came clear was – there was a girl he should have helped, and instead he had tried to destroy her. Oh, maybe not directly, but that was the result of it; the result of his actions.

He got back in the Mustang and drove back onto the highway. He pounded down the road heading west until he came to a turnabout. The sign said "For Official Use Only".

"Screw you, too," Kearney said to the sign, giving it the finger. He sent the Mustang scrambling and spitting into a sliding U-turn. He was going back to Quebec. He was going back to Genevieve.

Chapter 41

Soldiers Three

Some days later, Sparrow hovered over a chess board set up on a rolling table beside Le Claire's bed. Le Claire's hospital room was just down the hall from his own, and he could manage now to get around a bit.

Le Claire was propped up at a 45-degree angle, placidly watching Sparrow set the knights and bishops, kings and queens and rooks and pawns onto the board.

Bannerman was pacing across the room at the foot of the bed.

"It must be your training programs, Harvey," Sparrow said. "Ineffective weeding out, I should say."

Bannerman stopped short, seemed about to speak, and thought the better of it. He continued his pacing.

"I thought the young man did rather well for himself," said Le Claire. "Certainly handles a gun well, and knows how to infiltrate."

"Bullshit!" said Bannerman. He stopped pacing and went to the window. "He certainly knows how to screw things up."

"Don't be so harsh on him, Harvey," said Le Claire. "You and I might be dead by now if it weren't for him."

"If he hadn't been there," Bannerman said, turning to look at the two of them, "Borovik wouldn't have had any hostages. If he hadn't had any hostages, he wouldn't have tried to prove how bloodthirsty he could be. And if he hadn't started that nonsense, ordering that fool Jean-Paul to shoot Kearney, who shouldn't have been there in the first place, Borovik would have been alive and well and with my interrogators today."

"*My* interrogators, Harvey," Le Claire corrected him.

"Very well, Claude," Bannerman conceded the point. "Your interrogators. Today. Mine tomorrow."

"Besides," Sparrow said. "Borovik was asking for it. He should have known better than to try to act towards Canada as if it were some kind of banana republic."

"But I suppose we must admit it," said Le Claire. "The lad did go beyond bounds. He shouldn't have shot Borovik."

"Isn't cricket," said Sparrow, absentmindedly. "Poor training."

"Indeed," said Le Claire. "I should say we are in for some hot times for a while, eh?"

"Damned fool broke every rule in the book," Bannerman groused. "There'll be KGB around every corner now, waiting for me. And you. Have to wear a tank to go out at night."

"Yes, that will be a bit awkward," said Sparrow.

"It'll be like the Mafia around here," grumbled Bannerman. "They'll try to hit everyone." He paused. "Damn fool kid opened up a whole new ball of wax."

"He put them on notice, Harvey," Sparrow said. "He told them, whether or not he knew he did, he told them that they had come too far, that we were hitting back at last. There's a bright side to this, after all. Look, they didn't get Holsworthy, did they?"

"Why the devil would they want him anyway?" asked Bannerman. "Here I spent a week thinking Claude was off his rocker. What am I missing?"

Le Claire and Sparrow chuckled.

"Should we tell him?" Sparrow said.

"But Henry, it's classified!" replied Le Claire. "Besides, shouldn't he know about it already? I mean, a representative of the greatest secret service in the world, eh?"

The two Canadians laughed.

"Say, Claude, you promised me a file on your scientist. I haven't seen it yet. Where is it?" Bannerman asked.

"Oh, my friend!" Le Claire exclaimed. "Pardon me, please! But I have been busy of late. You know, operations, stitches, infections. But I will get it to you."

"When?" Bannerman asked.

"When and only if you stop pacing," Le Claire said. "You Americans! You don't know how to relax."

"I'm relaxed," said Bannerman, standing stiffly, without moving.

"Do you recall that space systems development company in southern Quebec, right down by your border?" Sparrow asked. "The one with the 180-foot space cannon that could fire projectiles from here to Canberra?"

"Yes," Bannerman said. "Good solid reputation for delivery, bad political image."

"That's the one," continued Sparrow. "Well, they were having a bit of trouble with it," he said. "So they asked our friend Harold to come take a look at the poor thing. He did. He has quite a knack for things like that, you know. He made some recommendations. Last month, he came back for his second visit, and they had a trial shot. It doesn't shoot to Australia anymore. It just goes up and up, and around and around. In orbit. And it carries all sorts of interesting paraphernalia. And that's what Harold Holsworthy…excuse me, I meant to say *Sir* Harold Holsworthy…was doing here, and it might give you an idea or two about why the Russians would like to chat with him at some length."

"Just one trip, and he corrected its malfunction…" Bannerman mused.

"That's right," said Sparrow. "Just one trip. Harold is like that. Has an innate knowledge about things like that. Has all sorts of information stored away. A lot about your spy satellites, for instance."

"He's valuable, isn't he?" said Bannerman.

"Oh, extremely," Sparrow said. "To us. To you, to the Russians, the Chinese. To the world generally. To everyone, possibly, except your Pentagon, and your Congress. They don't want too much to do with him. Doesn't waste enough money, you see."

Bannerman didn't say anything further. He knew they were right.

A man like Holsworthy would play the devil with a fat bureaucracy like the Pentagon.

"At the risk of bringing down your wrath, Harvey," Le Claire asked. "Where is your young protégé? I suspect Sir Harold would like to thank him, even if you wouldn't. And so would I. I think he did us a service."

"Oh, he's somewhere in town, trying to get on with that girlfriend of his – St. Andre's sister, you know. You should hear him on the phone. It's depressing. Disgusting, actually. They're in love, and she won't talk to him. You know, the usual."

"He's given her some shocks, Harvey," Le Claire said. "And so has life. Not been too kind to her lately, I'm afraid. Nor him, come to think of it. But you know, I have something for him, something he might be very interested in. Perhaps you could take him a message. Actually, it's for you, too, I suppose."

"I'll tell him," said Bannerman. "And I'll tell him to come see you, too."

"Why, thank you, Harvey," said Le Claire. "I would appreciate that. Well, here it is: I know who killed his brother."

"My, my," said Bannerman. "That *is* news, Claude. Who did it? How did you find out? Tell me."

"Excited again, eh?" said Le Claire. "Well, I'll tell you anyway. It wasn't any superior sleuthing on my part. The type of person that is called an informer told me. Simply told me. De la Montagne told me, in a conversation I never held with him. Taped. And like a damned fool, I never gave myself enough time to listen to the tape. Would have saved a bit of trouble."

"Well, well," Bannerman said. "So you know who the assassin is. Someone we know?"

"Someone we have," Le Claire said. "You have him, but I want him back. I can put together a case on him. It's Villemaire, and we've had him all the time, courtesy of my friend Charles. Thank God we didn't let him go. You haven't let him go, have you?"

Bannerman laughed. "No, I still have him, but I don't think I'll pass on your message to Kearney until you have Monsieur Villemaire safely back in your care. I don't want the responsibility for what happens when Kearney finds out who it is. He'll try to kill him."

"Oh, I doubt that, Harvey," said Sparrow. "I'll bet young Mr. Kearney has had enough of killing for a while. I hope so, anyway. He'd be really insane, crazy insane, if he's still out for blood after all this."

"Well, I suppose you're right, Henry," Bannerman replied, "but still, I'm not going to take any chances. Borovik misread him, and look what happened to Borovik." Bannerman paused. "Oh, by the way, gentlemen, I believe I owe you both some thanks. That last piece of information makes it slightly like Christmas around here. So, a small token of my own…"

"You've found out where Borovik's helicopter was going!" interrupted Sparrow.

"Oh, nothing of that sort," said Bannerman. "Just something for good times." He drew three large cigars out of his coat pocket. "Cordilleras Rojas," he said with a broad grin.

"Havanas!"

SUNDAY, JULY 4, 1971

"Vive, Quebec! Vive Quebec libre!"

Chapter 42

Angelique

On the following Sunday, mid-afternoon, at the ebb of the tourist tide, departures of the past week gone, arrivals for the week ahead not yet arrived, Jack Kearney sat half dozing on a bench in the center of the Parc Jardin des Gouverneurs. The park was at the height of its summer heat, which is to say, not very hot at all. A light breeze blew off the river and the leaves of the trees in the park sang a gentle, peaceful song.

Kearney was tired and perplexed and beset by any number of problems. Chief among them was how to get Genevieve to love him again the way she had in the sporadic hours they had spent during the week before all hell had broken loose and he had been exposed by circumstances and that bastard Bannerman as a CIA operative, unwilling as he had been to assume that role. He was not paying attention to anything, really, except feeling sorry for himself, and so he heard no sound until a woman's whispered voice came from behind him.

"It would be well for you to be more alert, Monsieur. There are many in this town who would wish to kill you, given the opportunity."

Kearney turned and saw Angelique hovering over him with a quiet smile, a few strands of her honey-colored hair wisped by the gentle breeze.

"Including you, given the right moment?" he asked, his voice flat and sarcastic.

"That moment has passed, Jack," she said. "Now I simply feel sorrow for you, and for Genevieve, and for my people."

"Good of you," said Kearney. "What do you want?"

"To share your bench for a while? To talk? May I sit with you?"

Kearney considered. "Sure," he said. "Why not?"

"Merci, Monsieur Jack," she said, and moved in her graceful way around the end of the bench. She sat down comfortably, half turned toward him. Kearney automatically adjusted his position to accommodate her, and silently waited for her to speak.

"What are you thinking right now, Jack?" Angelique said playfully. Kearney didn't say what was on the top of his mind right now, which had a lot to do with Angelique's sense of herself, her ability, at first glance, to look casual, until you looked again and realized she was anything but casual. She was Quebecoise, all right, and dressed with a particular élan. Her shoes might be casual loafers, but they fit just right and there wasn't a scuff on them. New, probably, but maybe not. Her white tee-shirt and butterscotch slacks were summer light, and as light in color as they were, he was sure that when she got up from the bench they would be as spotless as when she first sat down. Her shoulder-length hair, although originally displaced by the breeze, had gotten itself back in place somehow, and was perfect.

Yes, Kearney was thinking, absolutely beautiful; perfect. They knew how to dress, how to present themselves. They had presence. Haut-couture in slacks and a tee-shirt and loafers. Sophisticated. And gold earrings. Amazing. And who knew what kind of dainty lingerie dwelt… and with that, his mind turned to Genevieve, and he asked, "How did you find me?"

"Easily," said Angelique. "I called that hotel you took Genevieve to before we realized you were a spy." She nodded toward the row of hotels fronting the park. "They verified you were still in residence."

"Oh, just like that," Kearney said.

"Well, that was the outcome. No need to tell the details. We too can spy, eh, Yankee?" She laughed at her use of the English Canadian expression. Kearney had no idea why she was laughing, and he sat with a puzzled look on his face.

"And of course I knew where it was, where you had taken her, and I did not approve," Angelique said, her anger beginning to grow. "And when we were taken by the Sureté, and released quickly on orders of the Justice Minister, and you put up that absurd yelling and gesturing and then they took you and separated you…after that, I knew you were bad. For Genevieve. For us. For our Movement. For my country, Quebec."

She stilled a tear. Whether of sadness or rage, Kearney could not tell.

"And then, Mon Dieu! Sir! How did you dare to involve her in such danger!"

"Now wait, Angelique! You could just as well say that she involved me at that point. She agreed to let me drive her to her house, and all of a sudden I got jumped by…"

"Don't try your excuses…your sophistry!... on me, sir! You knew what danger you were in from the beginning. You had dossiers on her and her brother. And Rene. And me. And God knows how many others. I know this because Genevieve told us. You refused to answer her when she asked if you knew about her as well as her brother. Twice! Twice you refused!"

"I did not refuse…" he began, but Angelique cut him off, her hand knifing through the air.

"We all know what silence means in that instact…instance! Ah! You make me so mad that I can not keep my English straight."

She crossed her arms and they sat there silently, she in a rage, he at a loss. Finally, he let out his breath and said quietly, "So then there is this other question: why did you come to find me? And why did you come alone? I just hope you don't have a knife hidden anywhere on you." He smiled.

"Of course I don't have a knife hid…" She stopped in mid-word, realizing his joke, and she began to laugh a choked-up, frustrated sort of laugh.

"I'm sorry," he said. "For everything. All I want to do is talk with Genevieve and help her. You know that. I call your loft every day, trying to reach her. I want to take her with me, out west, maybe. Out of this city, anyway. Somewhere she will be safe from her brother and his thugs. Somewhere she can heal."

Angelique looked at him sorrowfully. "Genevieve can never truly heal. I believe that, Jack. But you know, there are two things which save you. One, the reason I came to you today. Her father has arrived from England. He is in Montreal, and he is heading here. He has spoken with Genevieve. Quite harshly. On the phone. He wants her to go to the doctor. To the hospital. I know what he wants. He wants her in the psychiatric ward. Genevieve is hurt and confused, Jack, but she is not a mental patient. And if he gets his hands on her, he will destroy her, just like he destroyed her brother, and, I am sure, her mother before her. She must be hidden from him. And from others, also, I think. It is said that some of the terrorists have survived and are still at large. You would know better about that than I, am I right?"

Kearney began to grin. "Somehow, I doubt that," he said. "Come on, let's go for a walk."

"Wait," she said, and placed her hand on his shoulder, holding him there. "I said two reasons, no?"

"Yes, you did," he said, and he sat back.

"That was not all Genevieve told us, Jack," said Angelique. "She told us about your brother. What brought you here. Why you are in our city. I am so sorry, Jack." Kearney said nothing. His face turned to stone. Sighing, Angelique went on. "Both of us. Rene as well as I. Rene possibly deeper. He remembers that night in rue Sainte-Famille, where his excitement overruled his judgment, and he capered about, laughing about the dead American diplomat. How hard that must have been, for you to say nothing. To be in grieving, and to say nothing." She ended in a voice just above a whisper. "Oh, Jack, we are so sorry for you."

Kearney remained silent, and watched the artist. "Thank you," he said, finally. "You know, Angelique, I really like you, and Rene, too. For the things you did for Genevieve, of course – that was always my first thought. But also for your fierce patriotism. For your nation; for Quebec. And for your ability to stand up and fight for what you believe in. But first, for the way you protected Genevieve. I remember what you said: 'Don't hurt her, Jack.' I remember you saying that. And you know, I love her. I really, really love her."

He sat with his hands in his jeans pockets. Angelique sat quietly beside him. Minutes passed. Then he said, "So, you seem to be saying that I should protect her. But isn't that up to her? What do I do? Show up at your door and say, 'Let's go'"?

"Coming down to that," Angelique said. "Yes, that is what you do. And she will go with you, I am sure. Beyond that, we will have to see what happens. But it is not a lark, Jack. She will have to be prepared, to be steadied, to confront the fact of what her father will propose..."

"Have to be fast, if he's in town."

"Yes. And you will have to be gentle with her, and expect nothing of her until she offers it. It is a rescue mission I am proposing, not a fling. So, it is more than not hurting her, Jack. It is more of, of, respecting her, and her wishes, and her hurt."

"How long do you think we have?" asked Kearney.

"Not a day," Angelique said. "This evening, it would be better for her to be gone from our garret. We do not know the capabilities of her father, but we know they are vast."

"Not to my place, either. If he has the reach you say he does, he probably knows about it already." Kearney made an instant decision. "I'll get a new one."

"I know a nice small hotel," Angelique said. "Inexpensive, not cheap, you understand the difference?" She looked back over her shoulder at Kearney's hotel.

He caught her looking, and laughed. "What? You don't think my old place was worthy of my girlfriend? She thought it was okay."

Angelique said nothing, but shot him a look of wry disdain.

"No," he said. "Point taken. But you said 'small.' Small may be beautiful, but it won't work in this case. Big will work here. Bigger the better. More people, more crowds, easier to hide in a crowd. Don't forget your ideology: if you are a fish trying to hide, swim in an ocean of fish. Chairman Mao, I believe."

"So, rich American, what do you propose? The trashed Commodore? The Caravelle, with your guys swarming all over it looking for the remains of snipers?"

Kearney looked up at the towers of Le Chateau Frontenac, sighed, and grinned. "How about this one?" he said.

"What! The main symbol of our oppression! She would never agree..."

"Why not, Angelique? It's perfect. It is a castle fit for a princess. A castle fit for my princess, safe from her enemies, who would never dream of looking for her here. And it would only be for a night or two. I think she could stand it for a couple of nights, anyway. Just until I have the time to get new passports for us. What do you think? Come on, let's walk."

They got up and began to walk toward the river. "I think you have gone soft in the heart, Jack," she said. "You Americans are supposed to be the hard ones. We French are supposed to be the romantics."

"So," Kearney said, "you will be my contact. And unless you tell them where she is located because you have been tortured by the Sureté – and I don't believe they do that here in Canada yet – she should be safe." He looked down into her eyes and held them. "Think about it. Really. What better place?"

"No!" said Angelique. "Listen to me. You think about…" She stopped and breathed deep. "They will track you down."

"What? An ex-CIA operative with no aliases? With no resources? Who ever heard of such a thing?" He laughed, tilting his head up and gazing once again at the hotel.

Angelique looked at him, a smile appearing on her lips. "Imaginneur du Disneyland!" she said, and laughed.

"Are you calling me immature?" he snorted, pretending to be offended.

"Maybe. More like, simply an idiot."

Angelique stopped at the top of the flight of stone stairs leading from the park to the Dufferin Terrace. "And so," she said, her eyes beginning to twinkle, "I am supposed to engage in a conspiracy with the despised American?"

"Mais oui, Madamoiselle."

"Oh, my! He speaks French! Our culture must be having some effect on him…oh, Jack. This is silly. Why do I talk of conspiracy? Why not just plan what we are to do?"

"That's a good idea," said Kearney. "Let's do that. Let's say I get out of my place and make a reservation at the Chateau, and you get Genevieve and get her to me at some place so we can show up at the hotel like a regular couple. Oh, and don't forget, she'll need some luggage."

"We will need some time. We will have to find her some new clothes, if she is to appear as one of your princesses, as you say, or a rich Am…er…whatever. And you will need at least a sports coat and slacks. Do you travel with them?"

"I can find the coat. I have the slacks. And if you're taking her shopping, I had better make arrangements for a late arrival at the hotel."

"Certainly. Of course."

They walked down the granite stairs to the wide Dufferin Terrace, and along it, crossing in front of the massive brickwork of the hotel.

"Where should we meet? I don't suppose you want me showing up at your place," Kearney said.

"True," said Angélique. "Mon Dieu! I almost forgot. It is Sunday. No stores but restaurants will be open. Ah! She can have some of my clothes. I am larger, but I have some things that will do. Tomorrow, or whenever you leave town, you can take her shopping on the way out."

"Oh, no, I can't. I won't," said Kearney emphatically. "You do that."

"Very well, I shall. And I will be very pleased to do that. And you will pay from your CIA budget."

"The way you Canadiennes dress, the CIA doesn't have enough in their budget. Besides, I don't belong to that firm any longer, remember?"

"So." said Angelique, ignoring him. "Where to meet tonight. I know. A restaurant, for dinner. Why not? A nice little restaurant, not expensive, if you don't eat too much. 'The Sign of the Dove,' it is called in Anglais, on rue Ursuline. Shall we say Seven PM? I will make the reservation. And I make a concession. I will pay for Rene and myself, and you will pay for Genevieve."

"This is getting expensive," said Kearney. "I will have to get an advance on my severance pay."

"Do so," said Angelique. "That will give you something to do while I get the bride's…oops! Ooh la la! What have I said! I have let the bag from th…no, that's not right."

"The cat out of the bag, is the correct order. But don't get any ideas. You're all on the outs with the Church and the civil authorities. Who is left to marry us?"

"And we should have a nice long dinner, so tell the hotel perhaps 10 or 10:30? So I have time to say good-bye to my sweet little sister. You be sure to treat her well, Mister Jack, or you will hear about it from me!" Angelique's eyes began to glisten with tears. "Well," she said, "Do we have agreement? On duties? On time?" Angelique paused for the slightest of seconds. "Ah, Jack," she said, sighing lightly. "Take care, Jack," she said. And then she reached up and kissed him on both cheeks, and then, on his mouth, grinning. "For good measure!" she said. "See you at seven."

"And as you say," said Kearney, "Au revoir."

"No, no, no," Angelique said, "You do not know very well yet our language. Au revoir is for…for…perhaps, forever. The better term, for now, is 'Adieu.' "

"Oh, okay," Kearney laughed. "See you later. And I will try to learn your language. I am sure Genevieve will see to that."

Angelique grinned. "See you later, Jack, as you say."

She left him, moving quickly down the Dufferin Terrace, until she was only a small dot in the distance.

Kearney walked slowly to the railing of the Terrace. He looked out over the broad St. Lawrence, following its flow downstream, down past the Ile d'Orléans, down, eventually, to the sea. He turned then, heading through the park toward his old hotel. Suddenly, the refrain of an old Quebec song came to him: ":…for the sun, the sun it will shine, over flowers and fields in the morning, and the beauty of light in that dawning, will banish the darkness of night…"

Yes, he figured, smiling softly. Yes, it will.

AUTHOR'S NOTES
PART I – HISTORICAL REVIEW

It was called Canada's Quiet Revolution. Actually, it was anything but quiet, and it lasted twenty years at least, from 1960 through 1980. In the United States, it was granted minimal space in the daily news, except, of course, when a mailbox or a government building or a hotel was bombed. Or when a Labor Minister of Quebec Province was assassinated, or a British Trade Minister was kidnapped and his kidnappers, who belonged to the Front de Liberation du Quebec, the FLQ, demanded and received a plane with enough fuel to get them to Cuba. Or when General Charles de Gaulle, President of France, stood on the balcony of Montreal's City Hall in July of 1967 and, at the culmination of his speech, shouted "Vive Quebec! Vive Le Quebec Libre!", which was, of course, the slogan of the Séparatistes of the FLQ, who wanted to separate Quebec from Canada, and which earned the General the displeasure of Canadian Prime Minister Lester Pearson, who kicked him out of the country, diplomatically, of course. Or, when Ren é Levesque, the leader of the Parti Quebecois (PQ), succeeded, in 1977, in having a law passed which made French the official dominant language of Quebec, which of course it had been, unofficially, since 1608, if not before. That law was the direct cause of over 100,000 English-speaking Montrealers, perhaps fearing the collapse of civilization as they knew it, to flee to Toronto and other places of safety. They took their businesses with them, leaving a void in commerce, which the French Canadians filled up, with happy results for everyone of both French and British extraction. And civilization, far from collapsing, became enriched with the long-repressed spirit of the Quebecois. The end of the revolution could be said to have occurred in 1980, when Rene Leveque called for a referendum seeking the separation of Quebec from Canada and the formation of an independent nation. Its failure, by a margin of 60% to 40%, left the stalwarts of the PQ in tears at a rally in Montreal, at which they sang Gens du Pays, written by Gilles Vigneault, which became the anthem of the revolution. And that was that, except, of course, that the history and the fortunes and the rights of the French-speaking people of Quebec in subsequent years changed dramatically for the better.

Song of Quebec is a novel of those times, and its title reflects the fact that the revolution, like so many other revolutions, was driven by song: song which remembered the past; song which called to the future; song which gathered the spirits of the people and sent them marching to reclaim their ancient regime and their pride; and love songs – to the nation of Quebec, to the revolution, and to each other – which, of course, are the best and purist songs of all. But the Song of Quebec is not any one song. The Song of Quebec is the revolution itself. It is the story of the French-speaking people of Quebec – the Quebecois – who, after two hundred years of servitude – perceived and real – began to discover their birthright, slowly at first, and then with increasing momentum, until it at last exploded with the force of a flower in spring.

PART II – ON THE QUOTATIONS

First, let it be stated that this novel is a work of fiction. Although the Quebec revolution was a real historical occurrence, and many of the place names referenced in this story reflect the geography of Quebec City and other locations in the Province of Quebec, the story, all names, characters, and incidents portrayed in this production are fictitious. No identification with actual persons (living or deceased), places, buildings, and products is intended or should be inferred.

Second, I cite a quotation at the beginning of each day of the action of the novel. It should be noted that these quotes are not connected to those dates, which extend from Sunday, June 6th to Sunday, July 4th, 1971, but are used to suggest the prevalent mood in Quebec during that time period. The actual dates of the quotes are as follows:

Charles de Gaulle: "Vive Quebec! Vive Le Quebec Libre!" July 24th, 1967, during a speech to a Quebecois crowd from the balcony of Montreal City Hall.

Pierre Elliot Trudeau, Premier of Canada: "I am speaking to you at a moment of grave crisis…ff" is from a long speech during which he, as Premier of Canada, invoked the War Powers Act on October 16th,

1970. This was the only time the act has been used throughout Canadian history, and it was in response to the action of separate cells of the FLQ in their kidnappings of James Cross, British Trade Minister, and Pierre Laporte, Quebec Minister of Labor. It should be noted that the FLQ also intended to kidnap an Israeli diplomat as well as the American consul assigned to the Montreal consulate, and that the Russian government was suspected of influencing the FLQ at the time.

The second quote from Trudeau: the "bleeding hearts" quote, is from an interview with Tim Ralfe of the CBC, on October 13th, 1970. It is archived in the online Canadian Encyclopedia. When Ralfe subsequently asked Trudeau just how far he intended to take the crackdown on the FLQ, Trudeau answered, "Just watch me!"

The quote from Pierre Vallieres: "And it is by force that we, too…ff" is from his book "Negres blancs d'Amerique", published in 1968.

The quote from Rene Levesque, Premier of Quebec Province: "There are some guys behind me who…ff" is from his Memoirs, published in 1987.

'Gens du pays' © 1976 was written by Gilles Vigneault when a friend asked him to write a birthday song comparable to 'Happy Birthday To You' in French. Well, Vigneault's song did much more than that. It touched the hearts of the Quebecois and was adopted by the Parti Quebecois as its anthem. It is still played today. Except for 'Gens du pays', 'l'Hymne du Printemps' © 1959 by Felix Leclerc and 'File la Laine' © 1957 by Robert Marcy, all other songs, parts of other songs and poems, and quotes can all be blamed on this author.

ACKNOWLEDGEMENTS

Joan Bowker - we met at a party in New York City, in an apartment on the 14th floor of a building on 14th Street, on the 14th of February, 1973. We are still together - a testament to her love, forbearance and wisdom. **Pat Goudey O'Brien** - editor extraordinaire! Whose invaluable guidance delivered the manuscript from the nefarious depredations of the pluperfect tense of the verb 'had', among all sorts of other great advice. **Cindy Ellen Hill, Esq.** - not only a great intellectual rights attorney and essayist, but a terrific fiddler, guitarist, banjo picker, bodhran thumper, and singer for the Irish Folk group o'hAnleigh. **Jodi Picoult** - an inspiration to lesser-known authors; always willing to listen. **Betsy Lawrence,** who proofed, and proofed, and proofed, and proofed! **Shelly Curran** - who typed the original manuscript. Thank you, Shelly! **Elizabeth Naven, Professor of French Emerita, University of Vermont** - and my neighbor, who helped me to understand the French language a lot better. She did many of the translations in the book, hard to do, since the English is spoken by French speakers not entirely comfortable in English. Their mistakes are the mistakes of the characters, not of the translator!

Gary Dulabaum - a singer-songwriting musician from South Burlington, Vermont, now residing in Palm Springs, California, who was terrifically helpful and always full of good advice, who told me about **Lisa Ornstein**, formerly of the Canadian folk group La Bottine Souriante, who was a magnificent fount of knowledge regarding Canadian folk music. I sent her my CD of Quebecois folk songs originally recorded on tape in 1964 and she not only identified them, she told me where to find them - on YouTube, of course! I had been stuck in 1964 reel-to-reel technology.

Special thanks to **Alan Sackman** and **James Hefelfinger**, my old landlords in New York City where I wrote the original version of 'Song Of Quebec.' They are still in business, although with a greatly expanded operation. I thought their names were great names for CIA operatives, so, in the spring of 2018, I called them and asked if I could use their names in the final version, and they said 'Yes'! **Butch Hendricks, USN, SEAL, Ret.**, lived downstairs from us in the Sackman/Hefelfinger building on East 89th Street. He was intrigued by my need for underwater demolition information, and gave me a great bunch of really grand ideas.

My colleagues of **The League of Vermont Writers, The Poetry Society of Vermont, The Burlington Writers Workshops,** and especially **John Coyne** and **Marian Haley Bell** of **Peace Corps Writers** – my literary support teams! **Eric George**, songwriter and musician from Burlington, VT – who worked on the playlist with me.

Chris Velan, music publisher from Charlotte, VT, who directed me to **Patrick Curley, Esq.** of Montreal, PQ, who directed me to **Simon Henri** of the Society for Reproduction Rights of Authors, Composers, and Publishers of Canada (SODRAC) in Montreal, PQ, who got me in touch with the correct resources for copyright permission rights.

The Poets/Musicians/Singers and their representatives, all of whom were extraordinarily helpful, once I figured out where they were and how to contact them! **Gilles Vigneault**, writer of 'Gens du pays'(considered by many the national anthem of Quebec Province), represented by **David Murphy** et. cie, of Magog, Eastern Townships, Quebec, especially **Melanie Fuller, Valerie Gauthier,** and **Kathleen Morin** (the et.cie of D.M.)

Madeleine Depuis of Espace Felix Leclerc, Ile d'Orleans, Quebec Province, who directed me to the representatives of Felix Leclerc, located in Paris. **Felix Leclerc**, writer of L'Hymne du printemps', represented by **Editions Raoul Breton**, Paris, France. Special thanks to **Pacome Descamps** of ERB. **Robert Marcy**, writer of 'File la laine', represented by **Alfred Music**, Hollywood, California. Special thanks to **Gabe Morgan** of Alfred Music.

My techies :

Geoff Brumbaugh of **Common Ground Audio,** Montpelier, Vermont re-recorded my original reel-to-reel tapes onto compact disc form, thus making possible all these other contacts.

Dakota Deady – who did the 'gofundme' video and the original graphics for the novel – a trustworthy guide through the unknown territory of internet funding and technology.

John Arnst – who re-set and trouble-shot (shooted?) our computer system during our move from Underhill to South Burlington, and who delivered invaluable assistance.

Adam Zuchowski of Williston, VT – who set up the phonic playlist for presentations.

My merry band of supporters, steadfast over the years: Anonymous, Marian Haley Beil, Margie Bekoff, Nancy and Ron Berry, Karen Blanchard, Richard and Mary Bowker, Deb and Greg Chrisman, Tom and Maureen Crossett, Nancy Desany, Karl Drobnic, Bill and Bev Frank, Roger and 'Trotl' Frey, Ed Gallagher, Sam Greer, Negesse and Juanita Gutema, Nancy Horn, Tim Jerman, Mary Myers, Miguelina Leon, Elaine Ludwig, Jim Poitras, Willa Seybolt, Don and Jackie Schlenger, Robert (The Mighty Bowk) Bowker and Lesley Stillwell, Charlie Sutton, and Ted and Marie Tedford. Thank you all for your patience!

And lastly, the late **Sir Arthur C. Clarke**. The character of Sir Harold 'Hal' Holsworthy is based on Clarke. Everything that Holsworthy tells Le Claire during their meetings in the Chateau Frontenac actually occurred during a cab ride in Manhattan, I being the cab driver/emerging novelist, Clarke being driven by me to a session at Caedmon Records to record the last four chapters of *2001-A Space Odyssey*. On the way (this was in 1974), we dropped off a compact disc to his publisher—it was the first novel ever delivered to a publisher using the medium of a Floppy Disc. Oh, and the scene where Holsworthy shows Le Claire how to point the laser pen—that was an incident which occurred originally on the roof of the Hotel Chelsea on West 23rd Street in NYC, except that it wasn't Holsworthy and Le Claire. It was Clarke and Asimov. How do I know? Clarke told me. He also told me something else which I will never forget. When I tried to present him with a copy of a book I had recently had published, he looked at me, snorted, and said, "I most certainly will ***not*** accept your book as a gift. I will **buy** it from you. We writers must stick together!"

Thank you, all!

More books by Dan Close

Glory of the Kings, (2014): Detailed historical novel, dealing with Imperial Ethiopia during the years 1895-1896 and the first Italo-Ethiopian War, it won the Peace Corps Writers Maria Thomas Award for Best Fiction work of 2014.

A Year on the Bus, (2010): Fun and poignant depiction of events and a sense of community on the school bus. Although the identities of the students involved were disguised to protect the innocent (and the guilty), the events that took place are real. If the actions and attitudes of the students are any indication, the future of the nation is in good hands.

What the Abenakis Say About Dogs, (2008): A collection of poetry and prose included in the official collection of the Lake Champlain Quadricentennial Commission. Endorsed by Jodi Picoult and Donna Moody, Repatriations Chief of the Western Abanaki, the work brought the author into a close relationship with some of the First Nation people in VT.

Stories From the Arusi Hills, (1973): Tales of Ethiopia, based on stories from Ethiopian students. Collected, translated, and edited by Dan Close. This book has been accepted as a part of the Peace Corps Permanent Collection of the Library of Congress, Washington, D.C.

CPSIA information can be obtained
at www.ICGtesting.com
Printed in the USA
BVHW070715171221
623984BV00001B/4